Lora Leigh's novels are "electrically charged [and] erotic."
—*Joyfully Reviewed*

Jaci Burton's novels are "flaming hot . . . sweet and spicy."
—*Romance Junkies*

Praise for Lora Leigh and her novels

"Leigh draws readers into her stories and takes them on a sensual roller coaster."
—*Love Romances & More*

"Blistering sexuality and eroticism . . . Bursting with passion and drama . . . Enthralls and excites from beginning to end."
—*Romance Reviews Today*

"A scorcher with sex scenes that blister the pages."
—*A Romance Review*

"A perfect blend of sexual tension and suspense."
—*Sensual Romance Reviews*

"Hot sex, snappy dialogue, and kick-butt action add up to outstanding entertainment."
—*RT Book Reviews* (Top Pick)

"Wow . . . The lovemaking is scorching."
—*Just Erotic Romance Reviews*

Praise for Jaci Burton and her novels

"Burton delivers it all in this hot story—strong characters, an exhilarating plot, and scorching sex—and it all moves at a breakneck pace. Forget about a cool glass of water, break out the ice!"
—*RT Book Reviews*

continued . . .

NAUTI AND Wild

LORA LEIGH
and
JACI BURTON

BERKLEY BOOKS, NEW YORK

THE BERKLEY PUBLISHING GROUP
Published by the Penguin Group
Penguin Group (USA) Inc.
375 Hudson Street, New York, New York 10014, USA

Penguin Group (Canada), 90 Eglinton Avenue East, Suite 700, Toronto, Ontario M4P 2Y3, Canada
(a division of Pearson Penguin Canada Inc.) • Penguin Books Ltd., 80 Strand, London WC2R 0RL,
England • Penguin Group Ireland, 25 St. Stephen's Green, Dublin 2, Ireland (a division of Penguin
Books Ltd.) • Penguin Group (Australia), 250 Camberwell Road, Camberwell, Victoria 3124, Australia
(a division of Pearson Australia Group Pty. Ltd.) • Penguin Books India Pvt. Ltd., 11 Community
Centre, Panchsheel Park, New Delhi—110 017, India • Penguin Group (NZ), 67 Apollo Drive,
Rosedale, Auckland 0632, New Zealand (a division of Pearson New Zealand Ltd.) • Penguin Books
(South Africa) (Pty.) Ltd., 24 Sturdee Avenue, Rosebank, Johannesburg 2196, South Africa

Penguin Books Ltd., Registered Offices: 80 Strand, London WC2R 0RL, England

This is a work of fiction. Names, characters, places, and incidents either are the product of the authors'
imagination or are used fictitiously, and any resemblance to actual persons, living or dead, business
establishments, events, or locales is entirely coincidental. The publisher does not have any control over
and does not assume any responsibility for author or third-party websites or their content.

NAUTI AND WILD

A Berkley Book / published by arrangement with the authors

PUBLISHING HISTORY
Berkley Sensation trade paperback edition / August 2010
Berkley mass-market edition / September 2012

ISBN: 978-0-425-25444-8

BERKLEY®
Berkley Books are published by The Berkley Publishing Group,
a division of Penguin Group (USA) Inc.,
375 Hudson Street, New York, New York 10014.
BERKLEY® is a registered trademark of Penguin Group (USA) Inc.
The "B" design is a trademark of Penguin Group (USA) Inc.

PRINTED IN THE UNITED STATES OF AMERICA

10 9 8 7 6 5 4 3 2 1

ALWAYS LEARNING   **PEARSON**

CONTENTS

NAUTI KISSES

LORA LEIGH

This last Nauti book is dedicated to the fans and readers of the Nauti series who asked for just one more.

The finale in the series, for all of you.

Prologue

There were times in a man's life that remained indelibly imprinted on his brain for one reason or another. Events that threw open the window to a dark, shadowed corner of his soul and revealed truths he'd search for within himself all his life.

That day had come for John Calvin Walker Jr.

He'd awakened that morning with the knowledge that life no longer held challenge. He had a job that he was too successful at in his father's law firm. His fiancée was the perfect socialite, an exquisite hostess, and also considered one of Boston's most beautiful and successful female lawyers. She was about as emotional, compassionate, and passionate as a lump of clay, though.

According to his fiancée, he needed to find a hobby to replace his overly sexed inclinations. This coming from the woman who had spent the better part of the first month they were together exhausting him in his bed.

The passion had waned, slowly at first, until now, six months later, she thought he needed a hobby instead.

His life had gone to hell. Or perhaps, he was only now realizing that his life could be so much more. What, he hadn't decided yet. How to deal with the complications, he hadn't decided yet. One thing was certain, the restlessness inside him was growing to the point that it was becoming an ache.

As he sat across from her at her favorite Italian restaurant and pretended to listen to her quiet rant where one of his charity projects was concerned, he realized something was changing within him.

Accepting it was another matter. Dealing with it would be harder. As she talked, he flicked his waiter a look. He was a good man, John thought, he'd waited on John enough to know what that look meant. Within minutes there was a glass of whisky sitting unobtrusively at his elbow despite Marlena's disapproving look.

She didn't like the whisky he drank. She didn't like the friends he associated with, and he was beginning to wonder if she liked anything about him other than the Walker name and the fortune his father had built over three decades. That fortune, added to the centuries old Evanworth inheritance from his mother, Brianna's, side of the family, made John an impressive catch, and he knew it.

It had nothing to do with him, personally, and John was beginning to suspect that where Marlena was concerned, it was the fortune rather than the man that appealed to her.

"I believe we should be going now," Marlena announced as he finished a second whisky.

She glanced around the restaurant, directing her attention to a table of giggling young women celebrating a recent engagement of one of their friends.

Marlena looked at them as though something didn't quite smell right. "We're going to have to find another restaurant, darling. This one is beginning to accept a less than desirable crowd."

John looked around. "It looks like the normal one to me." He shrugged.

The young women at the nearby table were regulars, just not together in a group often.

He swore he saw the same faces every night they ate there.

"As though you pay any attention." Her delicate nose lifted disdainfully. The narrow lines of it were sharp, too sharp, almost giving her the appearance of a rodent.

John narrowed his eyes. He'd been out of town for a few weeks; had she had a nose job in that time? He couldn't remember it being that narrow before.

Nodding to the waiter, he indicated that they were finished, knowing his card on file would be charged an exorbitant amount within minutes.

As they moved through the luxurious lobby, his hand settled at his fiancée's back. A second later his jaw clenched and his hand fell away as he felt her stiffen.

As passionate as ice. Hell. And maybe that second whisky hadn't been a good idea, because his temper was beginning to brew.

"Oh dear, don't look, darling, but that hussy Sierra is here." There was an edge of anger in her tone. "And isn't that your friend Gerard?"

John felt his jaw tighten at the sight of Sierra Lucas, slender, almost fey in appearance, with her long, thick curls cascading down her back.

The white silk dress she wore showed her curvy figure to advantage. Her full, pert breasts were obviously unbound and as tempting as hell. As he watched, tiny nipples hardened noticeably at the same rate his cock thickened. Damn, he'd known her all her life. This reaction to her was becoming irritating.

He really should have foregone that second whisky.

"John." Gerard's smile was as cool as always as his gaze flicked to Marlena. "I haven't seen you in a while. Is this your lovely fiancée I hear so much about?"

John stepped forward. In the three months he and Marlena had been engaged, he had yet to introduce her to the friend that would serve as his best man.

And then Sierra opened her mouth. "You should know, Gerard, since she's the same woman I saw leaving your brownstone every morning for the past two weeks."

It was then John saw the raging hurt and anger in Sierra's slate gray eyes as she glared at Marlena and Gerard while stepping back slowly.

John's eyes narrowed, his gut tightening in suspicion. "What did you just say, Sierra?"

The one thing that hit him faster than even the words was the fact that neither Marlena nor Gerard was denying it. Guilt flickered in both their eyes instead.

"My God, that little tramp has nerve," Marlena finally muttered. "Where is her keeper?"

Gerard was watching John, though. It was a damned good thing, John thought, because he wasn't certain himself of his reaction. Was that an edge of relief mixed with the sudden anger that his best friend and his fiancée had been lying to him? Lying. Cheating him as though he were too damned stupid to eventually catch on to it?

"Why were you at Gerard's house?" he asked. "You told me you didn't know him."

"Really, John, these things aren't discussed in public." Her cold blue eyes narrowed on him. "Your roots are showing, dearest. A marriage such as ours doesn't necessitate such answers."

A marriage such as theirs? Where the hell had that come from and what made her think their marriage would be any different than any other couple's?

"The hell it doesn't." He was aware of the looks nearby diners were giving them. The subtle hunger as they smelled the juicy gossip getting ready to roll. "If you're fucking my best friend, then it's as good a time as any to discuss it."

Marlena's eyes widened.

"Hell, John," Gerard muttered, looking around in embarrassment. "Business arrangements don't include jealousy."

"Business arrangements?" Fury was beginning to envelop him.

"Well, surely you didn't think it was a love match,"

Marlena drawled. "Your money, my family. That does not a passionate affair make."

Her family? Her father didn't have shit compared to his in financial success. Did she honestly believe the Genoa name held an advantage to him?

"John." And there was Sierra, sliding in close, her tiny hand settling on his arm. "This is the wrong place to fight. You don't want witnesses when you kill them, right?"

He almost laughed. Hell, he was almost amused as he stared down at her somber little face. "I have a good lawyer," he promised her in a loud whisper. "And diminished capacity goes a long way."

Lifting his gaze, he watched as Marlena and Gerard both stepped back. "What's wrong, Gerry, buddy? You don't have as much money as I do?"

Gerard winced; they both knew he didn't.

"Fuck both of you," he growled. "You can mail the ring back, keep it, or flush it, who the fuck cares. Now I know why I hesitated to give you the heirloom Mother has. You don't fucking deserve it."

Marlena gasped in outrage, and her lips parted to deliver what he was certain would be a scathing retort when he turned his back on her and walked away.

"Go home, Sierra. You did your good deed for the day," he snarled down at her as he hailed a cab then jerked the door open as one pulled in beside him.

"John." Her hand was on his arm again. Her nipples were pressing tight and hard against her dress. Hell, there were days he wished she wasn't his father's goddaughter. It made it damned hard to give her the fucking he'd wanted to give her since he'd learned just how easily she could be had.

"I'll deal with you later, you little troublemaker," he snapped as she jerked her hand back. "Until then, stay the hell out of my way."

"You had a right to know, and she had no right to an opportunity to lie to you." She bit her lip, anger and conviction shining in her eyes, along with her tears.

"I'm not so easy to lie to," he informed her sharply. "Fuck

it, Sierra. Go play with your little artist boyfriends and leave me the hell alone."

Sliding into the cab, he slammed the door, the sight of her pale, serious little face in his periphery as the cab pulled away. Giving the driver the address to his penthouse, John sat back in the seat and closed his eyes briefly.

Hell. He should have known she was cheating on him. He should have known the entire relationship was nothing more than a sham. In the year and a half they'd been together, not once had he felt what he knew he should have felt from Marlena. There had been no depth, no passion. He'd convinced himself that would change once they married. He should have known when his mother gave the news of his engagement such a cool reception that something was wrong.

When he walked into his penthouse half an hour later, he went directly to the bar. He'd been doing that more and more lately, he thought. Heading straight to the bar the minute he walked in the door.

He'd been doing it for the past three months.

What had ever convinced him that marrying Marlena was a good idea?

Oh yeah. She was cool. Calm. She demanded very little from him and gave even less.

He went for the whisky.

Sometimes, a man just needed a little false courage to make the decisions he had known for years were coming.

That was why he had asked Marlena to marry him. One last-ditch effort to conform to the life he had been born into, the society that was part of his birthright.

His mother's family had been an integral part of Boston society for more than two hundred years. His last name might be Walker, but it was his mother's Boston Brahmin side that had assured him carte blanche in the world he lived in.

It was a world he was leaving.

He accepted what he had sensed for a while now. He may have been born into this world, but it was one he found himself unable to accept now.

It was time to go.

Whisky burned its way to his stomach as he inhaled through the slow, blooming heat.

Hell, he had no right to come down on Sierra as he had. She was damned protective, and it wasn't as though he hadn't watched out for her in similar ways when he caught her lovers cheating on her in the past.

He'd always watched out for her, especially when she was involved with people he didn't particularly approve of.

He downed another shot of the expensive liquor.

It was his own damned fault.

He'd had enough reservations about asking Marlena to marry him that he hadn't asked his mother for the heirloom engagement ring to give her. He should have known when he hadn't given her that damned ring that something was wrong.

A marriage of convenience. His money for her name. As though his family needed her fucking name. His mother's patrician line opened doors for him that the so-called revered Genoa name would never open.

As he tossed back another shot, a key scraped in the door and it opened slowly.

Son of a bitch, she just didn't give up, did she?

Marlena stepped into the foyer, her nose lifted with haughty arrogance.

She had definitely had a nose job and he hadn't even cared enough to notice before.

"We need to discuss this." Hip cocked, that nose tilted, model thin and superior.

"When did you get the nose job?" He narrowed his eyes.

Surprise shifted in her pale blue eyes. "Months ago."

He shrugged. "We don't have shit to talk about. Get your things and get out or I can have them delivered to you tomorrow."

"Really, John, you act as though you had no clue as to what was going on." She sniffed coolly. "You should have known. As perverted as you are, do you really believe any decent woman of class is going to want anything more than the bankroll backing you?"

He let his gaze drift slowly down and back up her reed-thin body. "You made a lousy whore then."

Her lips thinned as she pulled the engagement ring from her finger and laid it calmly on the antique table next to her. "Very well, then, if that's how you feel. Once you sober up, you'll call."

"Don't bet your nose on it," he grunted. "Get the hell out of here, Marlena, before I say something I'll regret."

"No doubt you will." She sighed. "Really, John, you should do something about those nasty roots showing. Just because you come from hick stock doesn't mean you have to live down to the name."

"Beats living down to yours," he informed her caustically. "Have fun with Gerard. Maybe he'll like the ice-queen act."

Her lips curled. "He didn't have the ice queen, darling. I was there for fun. You were the responsibility."

"Lucky him," he drawled. "Now go ruin his perfect little life instead."

Her tinkling laughter grated on his nerves as she turned and walked out the way she'd come. Damn. As relieved as he was that the engagement was over, the taste of betrayal was still thick in his mouth. His best fucking friend and fiancée. How classic was that? The cliché was enough to drag a mocking snort from him.

He stared at the whisky then poured another drink.

He'd no more than shot that one back when, son of a bitch, the door opened again. He was seriously going to have to collect the keys he had given out to the penthouse. This was getting out of control.

The place was fucking Grand Central Station tonight, and he'd just about had his fill of it.

And there she was.

Imp.

The little demon sprite.

The torment of his life.

Too fucking young, but getting a head start on experience. She'd been running with a promiscuous set of friends for years. Friends that had no problem bragging about the privileges she allowed.

He didn't blame her for them. Hell, she was a beautiful woman. She was almost family. That was the problem. She was "almost" family. That tormented him, because he was damned for wanting exactly what she had gifted those other men with. He wanted that and more. So much more that he kept as far away from her as possible.

He didn't hold it against her. Hell, he'd done worse in his sexual past, but it burned in his gut like a sore because he wasn't one of the lucky ones. How fucking brutal was that?

"Go home, Sierra." He was too drunk for this. He'd had his life nicely planned out, and as much as he felt relief that the engagement was over, still, it had been his plan, and she'd fucked it up. And he was just drunk enough that his logic capabilities weren't at their strongest.

"I don't want you to hate me." She was braver than Marlena. She actually stepped into the main room and faced him boldly.

With her hard nipples.

With her lush lips and hungry slate gray eyes.

"Why the hell did you have to make it your business?" He growled.

The same reason he would have made it his business, of course. It was happening, it was wrong, and they were friends. Close. They hungered for each other, and they both fought it.

"Because I care about you," she whispered. "You're my friend, John. When Gerard asked me to the restaurant, I knew what he was doing because your mother had told me you and Marlena were supposed to be there tonight. They were going to stand and lie to your face. They were rubbing your nose in it, and I hated that."

Her hands were clasped tightly together, sincerity and that damned hunger flickering in her eyes.

"Bullshit," he snapped. "You're not my fucking friend, Sierra. Friends gloat later, they don't give a fuck if you make a mistake while you're making it."

He should know. Other than possibly Sierra, it was the only type of friend he'd ever had.

Her lips thinned. He liked the lush look better.

"Then marry her already," she charged back in anger. "If you're so pissed at me, get down on your knees and beg her back. I'm sure she'll be more than happy to watch you beg."

"Fuck you, Sierra!" And only God knew how bad he wanted to fuck her.

His cock was pounding, hard and desperate. She always affected him like this, and now the alcohol was only intensifying it. He never drank around Sierra for a reason. It totally screwed with his self-control.

"Why did you even fucking care?" He couldn't get it out of his mind. No one else would have told him, and he knew Gerard. Gerard hadn't hidden it from anyone but John. And of all his so-called "friends," only Sierra had dared to reveal the truth in a manner neither Marlena nor Gerard could deny it.

"Because I care about you, dummy," she burst out in exasperation. "Do I have to beat that into your head?"

It was more. He'd seen it in her eyes at the restaurant and he saw it now.

He saw something he didn't want to see. It went beyond a sensual awareness or hunger for him. It went beyond what he had wanted to see in the past.

"You're jealous," he accused her softly, the truth slapping him in the face. "You think you're in love with me? Have you lost your mind, Sierra?"

Incredulity echoed in his voice even as it pulsed through his mind. He hadn't seen it before. Why hadn't he seen that emotion in her eyes before?

"I did that a long time ago." Her voice was husky now, her eyes glittering with dampness. With tears. Fuck, she was not going to cry on him.

"Don't you dare cry." He moved to her, jerking her against him.

Big mistake, but there she was, against him. So fucking young and too damned tiny. And he was hungry for her. That hunger had pulsed inside him for too long, burned in his gut and tormented him. He didn't want this, not with Sierra. With the only person in his life that he had counted on as a friend.

"I didn't want this with you," he snarled down at her. She was too soft for what he wanted and he knew it. Too vulnerable, even if she was experienced enough for it. But he was drunk. He was hard for her. And he'd fought it for too damned long.

"Why?" The vulnerability in that single word struck at his heart. As though he had just broken all her dreams, all her hopes. "Why not me, John?"

"Because damn you, I didn't want to hurt you."

He didn't give her a chance to retort. His head lowered, his lips taking hers quickly, parting the lush curves as he slid one hand into the riotous curls that surrounded her face and gripped the soft strands to hold her to him.

The silken curls wrapped around his fingers as though hugging him to her. Like living strands of heat, they caressed his flesh, stroked it.

The taste of her, the adrenaline and hunger coursing through his veins, only made him drunker. Drunk on her. He'd known touching her would be hazardous, and how right he had been.

Growling at the surge of lust tearing through him, he dropped the empty glass to the floor and gripped the slender strap of her dress to drag it over her arm. It would only go so far. He couldn't find the zipper. It wasn't at her back. He didn't want to look for it.

The sound of the material rending didn't faze him; what it did do was give him entrance to the bodice of her dress and the swollen curves of her breasts, the tight, hard nipples topping them.

"John?" Pleasure and confusion filled her voice now. "Oh, God, John, what are you doing?"

What the hell did she think he was doing? Giving them both what they were hungering for.

His lips slid down her neck, moving for those tight little

berries. The feel of them against his tongue sent a groan tearing from his chest.

Sucking one into his mouth, he laved it with his tongue and loved it with his mouth as he lowered his hand again, this time to his trousers.

If he didn't release his cock, he was going to go insane. It pressed against the zipper of his pants, demanding to be set free. Like a ravenous beast, it throbbed and pulsed at the confinement, silently demanding attention.

Demanding her mouth, her fingers, the lush, hot folds of her wet pussy. He groaned at the thought of fucking her. Of pumping inside her, deep, hard, feeling the snug tissue rippling over his dick.

As he released her nipple, his lips pulled back.

His hand tightened in her hair as his gaze centered on her lips and he pressed her downward.

God, he wanted her mouth on his dick. Her tongue licking over the bulbous crest, her lips covering it, her mouth sucking him inside.

He wanted it with a hunger he had never wanted anything with before. He'd lost all reason, all logic. Objectivity was simply a thing of the past. Nothing existed now but getting his cock in her mouth.

Sierra lost her breath at the silent demand in his face, his gaze, as he tugged her lower. She knew what he wanted. With one hand he gripped her fingers and dragged them to the heavy length of his cock as it speared from the opening of his trousers. Long, thick, the heavy crest dark and flushed. It throbbed, glistened with dampness, and caused her mouth to water at the thought of the taste of him. Her fingers wouldn't wrap around the width of the pulsing flesh, like silk over iron, it heated her palm and made her ache for the feel of it.

She could feel her pussy growing wetter, hotter. The ache between her thighs, her hardened clit, pulsed with the need for touch in ways it had never done before.

"I've dreamed of you sucking my dick," he groaned as

she went slowly to her knees in front of him. "Nights of it, Sierra. So many nights spent sweating at the thought of having you."

He had no idea what he was doing to her—he couldn't. He had no clue she had never done this before; all he had were the rumors he believed of her wild ways. Rumors she knew he believed because he teased her over it. Always gently, always with affection but always with a glimmer of some darker emotion in his eyes.

He believed them though. How surprised would he be when he learned she was a virgin?

Kneeling in front of him, her fingers caressing his hard flesh, she swallowed tightly, fighting to keep her mind clear enough to please him. She wanted to go hungry on him though. She wanted to lose the overwhelming need to simply devour him.

"Give it to me, Sierra," he demanded, his violet-blue eyes darker, glittering with intoxicated lust.

His lips were fuller, his face flushed beneath his darkened flesh, his eyes glittering. She had never seen such need, such arousal in a man before. It should frighten her, but this was John. This was the man she had ached for since she'd been old enough to realize what aching was.

She was shaking at the sight of the thick, demanding crest, her chest tightening with excitement and fear. She'd never, ever touched a man like this before. Could she actually do it?

Leaning forward, she touched the tip with her tongue, licking over the dampness that collected on the wide head. The salty, stormy taste of him exploded against her tongue, and she swore she was becoming as drunk as he was.

Her fingers caressed the thick shaft, and she rubbed her tongue over the head as she fought past her fear and inexperience. She wanted to memorize this moment in time. Every taste, every feeling, every sensation.

"Damn you, Sierra, suck me. Let me fuck your mouth before I die for it."

Her lips parted for him, a moan slipping from her throat as he filled her mouth, sliding slowly inside to burn against her tongue.

She moaned again. Her lips tightening as she began sucking the iron-hard flesh, excitement and hunger rising inside her until she didn't know herself any longer.

That hunger was loose now. She had no way to control it, no way to hold back the needs suddenly filling her, flooding her entire body.

She wanted this. She wanted him, until she felt as though she were dying for it.

"Ah, yes," he groaned, pleasure filling his voice, his hands sliding into her hair as his hips began to move. "So fucking hot. I knew your mouth would be sweet and hot. Those pretty lips feel like silk."

His fingers tightened in her hair as his cock began to shuttle back and forth between her lips, deep into her mouth, nearly to her throat, as she struggled to accept the heavy length.

"Relax, Sierra," he grated, his voice harsh with lust. "Breathe easy, sweetheart. Take me deeper. Let me have you."

She'd read about it. She'd even watched it. She could do this. This one time, with this man that she loved above all others. Breathing in through her nose, she struggled to take the wide crest to her throat, sucking on it, her tongue rubbing against the underside as he groaned in approval.

"Hell, yes." She could hear the pleasure in his voice as the strokes in her mouth lightened, became shallower. "Look at me, Sierra."

She struggled to stare up at him, her eyes tearing as his erection passed slowly through her lips this time. Pleasure pulsed through her veins, flooded her body. She was the woman she had always wanted to be. She was his woman. For this moment, this hunger, she was his woman.

"So fucking pretty," he groaned. "I've dreamed of this, baby. Dreamed of fucking you. Watching your mouth take me. Feeling that wicked little tongue rubbing my cock."

And she was rubbing against it, licking it. He tasted of

midnight and man, and the effect on her senses was devastating.

As his gaze locked with hers, he reached down, gripped her hand as it clenched against his hard thigh, and moved her fingers to the taut sac between his thighs.

"Touch me there," he demanded, his voice rough with hunger. "Let me feel your soft fingers, Sierra. Give me what I need."

Her fingers trembled as she cupped the weight of his testicles before caressing them tentatively. She couldn't believe this was happening. Finally, after so many years. But she knew it couldn't last. She knew when morning came, whatever lapse he was having in self-control would be quickly repaired. John was nothing if not controlled. He had a plan for his life, and she had always sensed it. A plan that had never included her. Come morning, he would remember that plan. But Sierra would always have tonight.

She couldn't help herself. She was desperate for him. So desperate that she wanted to create as many memories as possible.

Stroking the tight flesh she cupped, Sierra sucked at his erection, pulled back, and let her lips trail down the hard shaft as her tongue flickered against it. She moved lower, staring up at him, watching his violet-blue eyes darken further as her tongue began to lash lightly at his balls.

A harsh, tortured groan tore from his lips as he gripped her hair, lifted her head, and pushed his cock between her lips once more. Fucking her mouth harder, his strokes short and tight, he looked like a conqueror above her.

"I'm going to come," he groaned. "Ah, hell, baby, give me your sweet mouth. Take my dick, Sierra. Suck it, baby. Sweet and deep . . ." He fucked deeper, shuddered.

The feel of his cock throbbing, flexing, warned her. At first, the warning wasn't clear, until his fingers tightened in her hair, then the heat and stormy taste of his semen erupting in the back of her mouth sent her senses clawing for each sensation.

The jetting spurts were hot against her tongue. His voice

was harsh, low, as he growled her name when she swallowed the lush taste of him.

She wanted to relish it, to relive each second in time as it happened, but John was moving. Pulling back from her, he lifted her, pushed her against the couch, and went to his knees between her thighs.

Before she could react or even think to stop him, her dress was at her hips and his hands had torn her panties from her body. He didn't hesitate once her flesh was revealed. His lips went straight to the sensitive, violently responsive flesh between her thighs.

Then he kissed her there. An intimate, hot kiss against the folds of her pussy, his tongue lashing at her clit, the wet velvet feel of him firing every nerve ending in her body. Lush, vibrant pinpoints of incredible sensation raked along her flesh, arching her body and drawing a strangled cry from her throat.

She'd never thought she could have this.

She'd never believed John would ever touch her like this.

It was nothing like she had ever imagined it would be. She'd fantasized, she'd dreamed of this with John, but she had never in her wildest imagination known how good it would be. That it would rain sensation over every part of her body. She felt flush from her toes to the top of her head. She felt as though a fire was being stoked in her very womb.

Pleasure seared every nerve ending he touched. Riotous frissons of heat tore through her body. His lips and tongue caressed, licked, kissed. His tongue rubbed around her clit, stroking and caressing with silken hunger as it destroyed her balance and left her spiraling out of control.

She had to hold on to him. Sinking her fingers into his hair as he pushed her thighs farther apart, Sierra wanted to scream out his name. There was no breath to cry out, let alone to scream. There was barely enough oxygen to sustain her as pleasure rushed through her system like a fiery windstorm.

His tongue was wicked, destructive. His fingers pulled the folds of flesh apart as his tongue licked and stroked, blazing a path of ecstasy through her system as she strained to get closer.

His tongue flickered over her opening, a rumbling growl vibrating against her flesh as she cried out in pleasure.

"No. Don't stop." She gripped his hair as his head lifted, only to release him as he forced himself back.

"Is this what you want, Sierra?" His hand gripped his cock, tucking it against the swollen, wet folds of flesh as he stared back at her.

"Please." She was shaking, the need was so great now.

"Please what, sugar? Please fuck you like the beautiful little troublemaker you are?" His words slurred just slightly, whether from the drink or the lust she wasn't certain.

"Why, baby?" he whispered as he pressed closer. "Why are you even here?" There was a tortured, hollowed sound to his voice.

Sierra shook her head. "I love you, John. I've always loved you."

His hips bucked, driving him inside her, the sharp burst of heat, pleasure, pain washing through her at his entrance drawing a cry from her lips as he settled against her.

His head fell to her shoulder.

At first, Sierra wasn't certain why. He hadn't penetrated her fully, just enough to draw that sharp cry, to tear aside the veil of virginity she had possessed. Now, he was silent.

Because he had passed out.

Sierra blinked up at the ceiling, fighting to just breathe through the incredible emotional burst of pain that flooded her.

He had passed out. As though this moment in time meant so little, that he didn't even struggle to stay sober enough to keep awake.

Tears spilled from her eyes as she stared up at the ceiling, a sob tearing from her chest.

"Shhh, baby," he mumbled against her neck. "S'kay."

He settled closer, his hips shifting, dragging his cock from her a second before the lightest snore fell from his lips.

Silent sobs shook her body as she managed to wiggle

from beneath him, then she struggled to get him on the couch. Pulling his handkerchief from his jacket, she quickly cleaned the smear of blood from him, then cleaned herself before dropping the square of linen on the floor next to the couch, wondering if he would even connect the smears of blood to this night.

She had dreamed of this night. Dreamed of him finally wanting her, and perhaps it served her right that it had ended as it had.

Kneeling next to the couch, she brushed his hair back from his forehead, the light brown strands thick, not overly long, but framing his face devilishly.

He was her personal heartbreak. For as long as she could remember, the love she had felt for him had driven her to impossible lengths to gain his attention. It had driven her here, to a night she knew would haunt her forever.

"I'd rather have you hate me than have you marry that bitch," she whispered painfully as she wiped at her tears.

And he probably would hate her when he awoke. When reality surfaced and he realized the lengths she had gone to in ensuring his engagement was broken.

She wondered, though, if he would remember her arrival here, or the brief time he had touched her as a woman, rather than the troublemaker he had always called her.

Forcing herself to her feet, she left the penthouse, locked the door on the way out, and told herself this was over.

No more.

Loving John Walker was a dead-end street, and Sierra needed more than brick walls to bang her head against.

It was time to go on without those girlhood dreams.

It was time to go on without her heart.

One

John C. Walker Jr., son of the formidable John Calvin Walker, had finally come home. He could feel the knowledge sinking inside him, filling all but one part of his soul and reaffirming a decision that had been made on a rainy Boston night a year before.

Standing on the upper deck of the *Nauti Dreams* as it coasted slowly down Lake Cumberland, he drew in a deep, relaxing breath and felt something slowly relax inside him further. Some inner tension, a deep-seated longing that had finally come to rest.

His father had left Kentucky years before, long before John had been born, and wiped the dust of the Kentucky mountains off his feet. Unfortunately, as his father liked to claim, some of it had managed to adhere to his children.

One of his daughters, as well as his only son, had retreated back to Kentucky.

The mountains rose around him like comforting arms, nestling him within a strong, nurturing embrace. A whisper of a breeze rustled through the trees and over his sweat-dampened shoulders, while the strong heated rays of the sun further bronzed his once pale flesh.

He felt stronger here, more in charge. He felt as though, for the first time in thirty-two years, he was finally himself.

The sun had bleached his thick, light brown hair almost blond, darkened his flesh, and put small lines at the corners of his eyes. The hard, physical labor of helping his sister and her husband build their home, and rebuild the bar that had been burned down by an arsonist the year before, had honed his muscles and sculpted his body.

He'd been in good shape before, but now, he felt at his peak. He felt invigorated and alive.

The houseboat he'd bought from the Mackay Marina was perfect. A floating home that suited the need to push away conformity and embrace that vein of gypsy wildness his father had always scowled over. It gave him peace. Or at least a large measure of the peace he had been searching for.

For the first time in his life, John Walker was close to finding satisfaction. If there was one little niggling worry that continued to prod at him, then he fought to ignore it. Nothing was perfect. No life was completely serene, but he was as close as he had ever been to it.

If dreams haunted him of one woman, a night he wasn't so certain of, and a pleasure so perfect it couldn't be real, then he tried to push it behind him.

Other than that night, that woman, he'd finally found a place he belonged.

Now, he understood why his sister had fought her family's insistence that she return to Boston when the people of this county had turned on her for a brief time. Why the gypsy in her had rebelled and returned to where the mountains nurtured that spark of rebel fire inside her.

He understood things now that he had never grasped before, and the regrets that had once filled his life began to fade away.

All but one.

Shaking his head, he refused to allow himself to touch that thought again. He was beneath the sun, the water lapping at the boat as it coasted gently along the channel. Above, an eagle soared and called out to its mate while a coyote watched him suspiciously from the far bank.

Deer grazed in a small clearing close to the water across from the coyote, as though taunting it with its inability to reach them in time for a meal. It reminded him of the woman he refused to think of, and the months he had spent attempting to chase her down.

The sounds of nature enclosed him. The traffic, squawking, blaring horns, and raised voices of the city were blocked by distance and by his own determination to put it behind him.

He'd found friends here in the past year. He'd found purpose. And he'd finally figured out the sister he'd never understood before.

Rolling his head, he let the breeze caress his neck as his eyes narrowed, his hands confident on the wheel of the large craft as he maneuvered it along the lake.

He wasn't John Calvin Walker Sr.'s son here. Here, he was that damned Walker boy, and that suited him fine. He had family here that understood the mountains, brewed their own liquor, and laughed when he choked on it.

Mountain parties, barbeques, and pig roasts. And he was loving every minute of it.

Hell, he was more than loving it, he was reveling in it.

He worked when he wanted to, took the legal cases that interested him, and the rest of the time he worked with a nonprofit group that built homes for the poor and looked after the elderly. And he let the mountains embrace him.

The only thing he couldn't run away from, though, was the damned cell phone he couldn't seem to throw away, no matter how many times he tried.

The bastard insisted on getting excellent reception, even here, deep within the forested land rising around him. Proof of it was the insistent beeping at his hip.

Glaring at the water stretching out before him, he pulled the phone from his pocket, scowled at the number on the display, and against his better judgment, accepted the call.

"No, I'm not bored yet," he told his father as he brought the phone to his ear.

A second of silence greeted him.

"Of course you're not," his father's cultured voice drawled sarcastically. "There's rarely time to be bored when you're pretending to be the luckless playboy of Lake Cumberland. The novelty hasn't quite had a chance to wear off, has it?"

"Not yet," John agreed happily. "Do you know what I'm doing right now?"

"Do I want to know?" his father asked warily.

"I'm maneuvering my houseboat down the lake. I'm sweating like a pig and grinning from ear to ear. When was the last time you did that, Pop?"

"You don't want to know," John Sr. growled warningly. "When are you returning home?"

"I told you, I *am* home," he retorted. "If you called to argue with me again, then you're wasting your time and I have better things to do."

He could almost see his father, an older version of himself, his lips thinning, his eyes narrowing in irritation at his son's refusal to return home.

This was home to John, and he couldn't see that changing anytime soon.

"You sound like your sister." Anger throbbed in his father's voice. "You'd think after what she went through in that damned county, she would have left before that sheriff managed to tie her to him. What are you doing, John? Why are you doing it? How many times do I have to tell you what's coming? Those people will turn on you as fast as they accepted you."

John shook his head. The hell his parents had faced here had been the fault of the individuals who had kept a hold on the county, not the people itself. The few had ruined much for the many, for too many years.

They were gone now, but John understood his father's hatred for them, and his distrust of the county. He understood it, but he refused to return to what his life had been before.

Here, he had a sense of purpose. There, he'd had nothing but his family. A damned good family, he admitted, but there had been nothing to anchor him, nothing to ease that restless hunger that tormented him.

"How's Mom?" he asked, rather than arguing again. He always tried to stem the flood of anger that rose between them each time they talked.

His father sighed heavily. "She misses her children. This wasn't what she wanted, John. She raised her children with love and now you're all deserting her."

In other words, his mother was doing what she always did, refusing to step into the middle of the arguments that waged between John Sr. and his children.

Not that the older Walker didn't love his children. He did. Too much sometimes. He could never understand that he couldn't shelter them from life, no matter how hard he tried. That he couldn't force them to live the life he'd attempted to create for them.

It was the same fight they'd had when John had joined the Marines just out of high school. The argument they had when John had gone into criminal law rather than corporate law as his father had done.

The argument they had had when John had told his father he was asking Marlena Genoa to marry him.

"Tell her I love her," John said.

"Sure you do," his father grunted. "That's why you're cruising down a damned lake rather than having dinner with her today."

It was Sunday. Every Sunday it was dinner at home, no matter what, that was, as long as the particular child was in town.

"I'm sure Candace and her children are keeping her busy."

Candace Salyers was his sister, the oldest of the Walker siblings. Married, with three beautiful kids and a doting husband, Candace had a life she thrived on. She swore she couldn't exist outside of Boston, and abhorred anything even remotely "country."

Silence filled the line again, this time longer.

"Fine, if you insist on bumming in Kentucky a little longer, then you can do me a favor," his father finally growled, his tone darker now, assuring John that whatever was coming was serious.

He waited, knowing it would take a moment for his father to perfect his pitch.

"It's Sierra, John. She's in trouble."

John froze.

He didn't want to hear her name, he didn't want to talk about her, hell, he refused to think about her. She had made the decision to run from him, not the other way around.

"Last week, someone broke into the house and attacked her. She was hurt, John. Hurt bad enough that for a few days we wondered if she was going to come out of it."

Shock resounded through him. John stood perfectly still, fighting to take in the information, to control the rage tearing through him, threatening to release itself with such a wave of violence that for the first time in his life, John frightened himself.

"What did they do to her?" Fury pulsed through him now.

His father breathed out roughly as John waited. And waited. It seemed to take forever for his father to speak.

"She was nearly raped. Bruised severely and strangled. She would have been killed, but her new roommate arrived and scared him off. The girl was terrified. After the guy escaped through the bedroom window, she was certain Sierra was dead."

Every muscle in John's body tightened. Rage began to burn in his gut as he imagined the petite, fragile young woman being strangled, attacked.

A wave of possessiveness tore through him, a distant thought that someone had dared to hurt what belonged to him tearing through him.

"You didn't call me," he snarled. "Why?"

For a moment, his father was silent before he answered heavily.

"Because I knew something bad had gone on between you two before you left. I didn't know if you wanted to be involved, John. I wanted to wait. But I need to get her out of town until I figure out why she was attacked. It doesn't make sense. Hell, Sierra's temperamental, but she doesn't poke her nose in dangerous stuff. And it's rare for a damned decorator to make the kind of enemies that attempt to kill you in the middle of the night. I have a bad feeling about this, John. I want her safe while my investigators check it out."

Someone had tried to harm Sierra. It was almost too much for John to attempt to take in. He couldn't believe anyone would dare touch her. It was common knowledge that she was all but family to the Walker and Evanworth families. And John Walker Sr. had established that he took care of his own decades before.

John himself had always been incredibly protective of her as well. And Sierra simply didn't get into that type of trouble. She was nosy as hell, but only where her friends were concerned. She didn't tolerate bullshit well, and liars even less, but still, that didn't necessarily place her in harm's way. "Serial attack?" he asked, wondering if perhaps Boston had acquired yet another serial rapist.

"Not that my investigators have dug up." His father shot that idea out of the water. "Don't worry, I'll find the bastard, John. But she needs to get out of Boston. Like I said, my gut is rolling on this one. I don't think it's over and I don't think she's safe."

Which meant she wasn't. His father's gut was notoriously right when it came to warning the man that something was wrong. It was a warning his son knew to heed. If he said Sierra was in trouble, then there wasn't a doubt in John's mind that Sierra was in serious trouble. Sultry, innocent, determined. She had seen to the breakup of his engagement when she'd caught his fiancée cheating. She had looked out for him, and despite her refusal to speak to him after that night, he would make damned certain he protected her now.

"What does she think about this? She's not exactly speaking to me at the moment." Not that he cared what she thought. If he had to go to Boston and force her into his protection, then that was exactly what he would do.

"You're the only choice," John Sr. barked. "Dammit, John, she cried for you in the hospital. She was beaten, bloody, bruised to hell and back, and out of her mind with fear. When I got there, she was begging for you. They called me because they couldn't find you."

His teeth clenched, his fingers wrapped so tight around the controls of the houseboat that he wondered he hadn't broken the column. Pure, almost mindless fury surged through his brain at the knowledge that he hadn't been there for her.

"I'm not asking what went on with you, Marlena, and Sierra." His father sighed. "I never asked. I figured if you wanted to talk, you'd come to me or your mother. But whatever happened, whatever Sierra did, she did because she felt it was right."

She had done it because she had believed herself to be in love with him. John knew the reasons why. He didn't fault her for it now, but he had faulted her for it then.

"Does she know you're asking me?" he repeated roughly.

"Not yet." His father's tone was filled with sudden weariness. "She's terrified, John. She won't leave the house, and your mother and I have to head to Europe next week. Sierra won't let me hire a bodyguard, and she's threatening to run. She's my goddaughter. I can't let anything happen to her."

John stared around him, his jaw clenching at the thought that Sierra was threatening to run rather than coming to him. Damn her. She'd refused to see him after that night, wouldn't talk to him. She'd gone so far as to leave town for months. He'd taken the message and left her alone, hoping time would heal whatever he may have said to her.

That night was a little sketchy. He'd been pissed, he remembered that clearly. Just as he remembered kissing her. After that, things were a little hazy and mixed with fantasy more than reality.

"Do I need to drive in to pick her up?" he finally asked. And he would. There wasn't a chance in hell he was going to allow her to face more danger without him at her side.

"As much as I want to see you, I advise against that," his father stated. "I'll have her brought to you. Candace and her husband and kids are taking the family jet to the West Coast tomorrow. An unscheduled stop will be made at the Hickley landing strip. It's private and Raymond Hickley will make damned sure no one knows they landed there. I'll call you back with the details."

John rubbed at the bridge of his nose as he grimaced. "Yeah, I'll be waiting."

Waiting wasn't what he did best. His preference would be to go after her, but he understood that having her slipped aboard the family jet and deposited secretly in Kentucky would be far better.

"John, your leaving destroyed her," his father suddenly stated. "She cried for weeks. Whatever you did to her before you left, don't do again. Please. I hate seeing your mother cry, and she made her cry."

Then Sierra shouldn't have run. And that was exactly what she had done. She wouldn't answer his calls, she wouldn't answer the door when he went to her apartment, and she was never where she was supposed to be.

She had run from him until he had stopped chasing her and chased what little chance he had of peace instead.

John shook his head. "Later, Dad."

Disconnecting the call, he carefully maneuvered the huge houseboat around and back toward the marina. If he knew his father, it would only be a matter of hours before he called back, before he had the details worked out and Sierra prepared to leave.

If Candace was leaving early, as she normally did when she and her husband flew to California to spend time with his family, then he would be at the Hickley Dairy Farm before the sun rose, hours before his day normally began.

This was exactly what he didn't need. Peace had been a

long time coming, the serenity he'd found here was hard won, and now, that last niggling barrier to complete contentment was rearing its innocent, gorgeous head. And it had the potential of destroying his peace, just as the potential of completing it existed.

Sierra.

Two

Sierra was silent as the jet landed, her heart racing, a sense of panic nearly overwhelming her at the realization that a year of running was over.

"I want to go home," she whispered.

She'd made a mistake. It was the worst mistake she could have made.

Lifting her head, she stared back at Candace. She saw John's eyes in the other woman's gaze. That beautiful violet-blue, though the features were softer, feminine, and gentle with compassion.

"Do you want to die, Sierra?" It wasn't the first time Candace had asked her that question.

It wasn't the first time Sierra had mentioned going home.

"The pilot is preparing to land," Thomas, Candace's husband, said softly.

He'd opened his home to her, just as Candace's father had. They had taken her in, watched over her, and provided the medical care she had needed.

Thomas was one of the senior attorneys at Walker, Delmar, and Farley Legal Associates. He was quiet, calm, a bastion of strength.

"Hickley radioed," the pilot announced. "We have five minutes on the ground. Contact is waiting to accept delivery."

She was the delivery.

Sierra wanted to cover her face and hide. She wanted to find a way to simply disappear and forget that any of this was happening. To convince herself that the last year was nothing more than a nightmare.

How had she let her life come to this?

By running from John. By being a coward. That was how it had come to this. There was a part of her that wondered if she hadn't run, if she had faced John, if she would have even been in her apartment at the time? She'd moved from the more secure building the Walkers owned interest in months before to the apartment closer to her office.

She'd taken the apartment she had because it was in the same building as John's penthouse suite. To be closer to him. What a mistake that had been.

She felt the jet dip, a smooth stroke of metal through air as it began to descend.

"He's angry at me," she whispered as she stared back at Candace. "He hates me, Candace. After what I did, I don't blame him."

She'd destroyed his engagement. He'd been furious over that, despite the circumstances. Only in hindsight had she realized how she must have humiliated him. In public. She should have found another way. She shouldn't have allowed her anger to rule her.

"Sweetie, John doesn't hate you," the other woman promised. "He could never hate you. He may be angry, but he gets over the anger if you face him. You should have faced him rather than running."

She didn't need anyone to tell her that now. She had actually known it at the time, but she had been too hurt, too raw, to do anything else.

He'd passed out on her even as he took her virginity. In all the messages he'd left on her cell phone not once, not even once had he mentioned what they had shared. As though he didn't remember it, hadn't seen the handkerchief she had used to clean them both.

No, each message had contained references to Marlena, Gerard, and the fact that Sierra wasn't answering her calls. Not a single message had been tender. Not once had he implied that he wanted to speak to her over anything other than the breakup of his engagement.

And nothing had changed. The thought of facing John now terrified her, just as it had the year before.

"We're landing, Sierra." Thomas's broad hand covered hers where it lay on the armrest of the leather seat. "Remember. Don't back down. Stare him in the eye and stand strong."

"He's not an animal, Thomas." Candace's amused chiding brought a smile to her husband's face.

"Sweetheart, all men are animals. Feed us, pet us, and use a firm hand, and we'll worship at your feet."

Thomas worshipped at his wife's feet, but it was clear Candace cherished him just as deeply.

"Don't put up with his temper, Sierra," Candace advised her softly. "And remember, at the very heart of it all, John would never harm you. You are truly important to him, or he wouldn't have spent so many months chasing after you." A twinkle in her eye indicated that perhaps he had chased after her for reasons other than the ones he had.

They simply didn't know the truth.

But it didn't matter. John Walker Sr. had made it clear that the only way to protect her was to send her here, where no one would suspect he would send her.

His hatred of Kentucky was well known. His hatred of its people went even deeper.

The wheels of the plane touched down, the slight jolt doing nothing to cover the little whimper that fell from her lips.

She wanted to cry, but did she have any tears left? She'd shed them all when John had left Boston. When she had realized that what she had done had forced him from his home, and took him from her forever.

As the plane rolled to a stop, Thomas rose and unclipped her seat belt and helped her from her seat.

The copilot opened the door and lowered the steps while Candace and Thomas flanked her.

Lights blazed up at her from a vehicle as a dark, shadowed shape materialized. There was no mistaking that form. Strong, bold, and broad. He was the living personification of every dream and fantasy she had ever harbored.

"Come on, brat." Thomas lifted her in his arms rather than allowing her to walk down the steps.

He'd done that two other times. He'd carried her from the hospital, and he'd carried her into John Sr.'s home hours afterward.

Like her father had always carried her.

And then he was moving down the steps, growing steadily closer to the silent form standing below.

Sierra thought he would set her on her feet once he reached the bottom. She hoped he would. She was certain he would. But men were conspiring against her in this lifetime.

Instead, he handed her to the tall, coldly silent male waiting for them.

"Take care of our girl, John," Thomas ordered lightly. "And remember, she bruises damned easy."

Sierra winced, but she didn't speak. She didn't stare up at the man that fate had conspired to throw her back with. She stared straight ahead, all too aware of the bruises that still covered parts of her body, and the knowledge that she rather doubted John Walker Jr. would really give a damn.

She'd had a chance to think about it. He wasn't stupid. He hadn't been stupid a year ago. He had known what Marlena was and he had asked her to marry him anyway. She should have thought of that before she had furiously decided to reveal their duplicity.

She had struck at his pride by throwing it in both of their faces. He had wanted that marriage of convenience or he wouldn't have put that ring on the other woman's finger.

Still refusing to speak to him, Sierra remained stiff in his arms as he turned to the vehicle and moved to the passenger side. Thomas opened the door and a few seconds later John was setting her carefully on the luxurious leather seat of the SUV.

Stepping back, he closed the door and turned to his brother-in-law. And God, she wished she could hear that conversation.

"I just have a few minutes," Thomas told him. "She's still showing a lot of bruising. Her throat, breasts, and thighs. Candace says it still looks like hell. She had pain pills in her luggage but she won't take them until she goes to bed, and she wakes up often screaming with nightmares. She screams for you, you know?"

John only barely managed to control his flinch. He hadn't been there for her, when he should have been. The regret of that would likely haunt the rest of his life.

"Did he send the doctor's report?" John asked, knowing how thorough his father normally was.

"Everything is in the leather briefcase. The pilot is unloading her luggage now." He nodded to the plane. "X-rays, everything is there. Your father wants you to take her to Dr. Landry in Somerset and tell him the situation. He can be convinced not to contact the doctors in Boston and he'll take care of her."

John nodded. "I know him."

Landry was old, but he was a damned good doctor. He was also part of a very small network of undercover Homeland agents positioned in the area and under the guidance of a special undercover agent who was supposed to be retired from the Office of Homeland Security.

"Good. Time for me to go." Thomas nodded to the pilot waving him back. "Take good care of her. She's fragile, John, no matter how tough she acts." He clapped John on the shoulder before loping back to the plane and disappearing inside.

John, joined by the owner of the airstrip, ran to the bags and hauled them back to the Denali quickly as the Learjet began to taxi to its takeoff point.

The lights flared back on, and within less than a minute the small jet was airborne once again.

"Let's load 'em up," John called to the owner of the Dairy Farm whose private strip was often used for covert landings.

Raymond Hickley was one of those former friends John Walker Sr. rarely spoke of. Men who had helped him when he was younger, and were still there for him now that his children were in the county.

At fifty-five, still fit, and as redneck as they came, Raymond was proud to say he'd served his country without ever stepping off his farm.

John pulled open the back of the Denali and stored the luggage. He loaded the leather briefcase last, setting it to the side to ensure the X-rays it contained didn't become bent.

"Dawg called while you were talking to your friend," Raymond told him quietly after they loaded the luggage and the door was firmly closed. "He and his cousins and uncle will be at the houseboat this afternoon. He said don't make them come looking for you. You should have known Dawg would glimpse that Lear landing and know whose it was. He's smart like that." The other man grinned at the warning he was relaying.

John grimaced. Just what he needed, a plague of Mackays descending on them.

At least they were waiting until afternoon. Enough time for him to get Sierra settled in and hopefully to catch a few hours' sleep.

Opening the driver's side door, he stepped into the vehicle, started it, then turned and stared at the too quiet young woman beside him.

"Well, lollipop." He grinned at the nickname that suddenly snapped into his mind. The perverted reasoning behind it had his dick becoming instantly hard. "Looks like your running days are over, doesn't it?"

He glanced at her, relaxing now, a sense of sudden balance invading that. That last measure of restlessness was easing now. He had Sierra back. Come what may, for the moment, she was his.

Her lips thinned. "It's nice to see you again, too, John."

She stared straight ahead, like the perfect little manne-
quin despite the edge of nerves in her voice. She better be
nervous, because he was damned upset that she had run as
she had. If she had stayed, if she had faced him, she would
have been here with him rather than in an apartment without
protection when a rapist came looking for her.

She likely wouldn't admit it. Yet.

"I bet it is." He grinned.

This might end up being fun. Hell, yes, he was going to
make damned certain it was going to be fun. She had a whole
lot of time to make up to him, he decided. A whole lot of
pleasure to fit into a very short amount of time if he knew his
father. And if there was one person he knew well, it was
John Sr.

Maneuvering the Denali to the now empty airstrip, he hit
the gas and raced down the clearing to the farm road at the
end of the strip.

"Don't worry, you're going to have lots of fun," he promised her. "I intend to make certain of it."

He could have sworn resignation pulled at her expression
before it cleared once again.

She was quiet again. Too damned quiet. This wasn't the
Sierra he knew. She wasn't quiet. She was either laughing or
she was raging. There was rarely an in-between. Happy or
angry, that was his Sierra. But this Sierra was a stranger. A
woman who wasn't even bothering to pretend to be the little
troublemaker he had known all her life.

That was okay, though. Give him just another hour or so,
and he was confident that the Sierra he knew would once
again appear. He was going to make sure of it. If he knew
how to do anything, then he knew how to piss his Sierra off.

John's father had told her that John was now living on a
houseboat, but Sierra hadn't exactly known what to expect
when they pulled into the small Mackay Marina.

The houseboats there ranged in sizes, colors, and names,

spreading out to the larger, almost home-sized crafts at the end of the docks.

"I can walk," she informed him as he opened the passenger side and reached in for her. "There's nothing wrong with my legs or my ability to move."

It hurt though. Walking for more than short distances could leave her breathless with the pain that shot through her bruised ribs.

"Nothing but the bruises that went bone deep, you mean?" he grunted as he lifted her in his arms anyway. "Don't argue with me, lollipop. The walk to the *Nauti Dreams* is a long one and you're not used to the shifting of the floating docks yet."

He picked her up out of the seat, turned, bumped his shoulder into the door to close it, then hit the remote lock.

He did it all so seamlessly, with such male grace and effortless ease that Sierra nearly sighed in envy. No man should be able to move so smoothly. She was already at such a disadvantage with him, he didn't have to make things worse.

"The bruises are getting better," she muttered defensively, even though she knew they were still extreme.

"I'm sure they are." The comment didn't do much to stem the rising nervousness building inside her.

There were times over the years that she had sworn she knew John better than she should, and she knew he was angry right now. She could see it in the hard set of his jaw when she glanced up at his face, the glitter in his violet-blue eyes.

Those eyes should give him a feminine appearance, but they did more to maximize his masculinity instead.

God, he'd changed so much. He wasn't just darker, his hair lighter. His muscles were harder, his chest broader. She was beginning to wonder if he was even the same man she had known in Boston.

"Here we are." He stepped confidently from the floating walkway to the deck of a two-story houseboat whose side was emblazoned with the words NAUTI WET DREAMS. The play on words would have had her eyes rolling if she weren't so damned tired.

The sliding glass door swung open easily and John

stepped inside to the dim, cool recess of the craft. Moving several steps to a large sectional couch, he set her down easily before staring down at her for long moments.

"Stay put," he told her, his voice rougher than she remembered. "I'll bring your luggage in then we'll see about getting you some breakfast."

"I don't need breakfast." She needed to sleep. Between preparing to leave, the stress, and the early morning flight, she was exhausted.

"You'll eat it anyway," he informed her, arrogance fairly oozing from his pores. "I'll be right back."

He would be right back, which meant she had very little time to shore up her defenses, and to hopefully find a way to keep her heart from being broken. Again.

Three

John didn't walk back to the Denali, he stomped. His heavy work boots pounded against the floating docks as he made his way back to dry land and the marina parking lot.

Her throat was still bruised. He could see the marks against her pale flesh.

His fists clenched at his sides as he fought to breathe through the agonizing fury. It tore at his insides with a force that made him want to howl. Son of a bitch. He'd kill the bastard responsible if he ever had the chance.

She was tiny, so fucking petite. He could span her waist with his hands and likely have room left over. Large, marbled gray eyes stared back at the world with an innocence that made him wonder, considering the crowd she used to run with when she was younger and the rumors he heard, if his fantasy dreams of that night with her might be more reality than wishful dreaming. That long swath of blue-black ringlets that fell from her head only made her look more endearing, more fragile. So fragile he couldn't believe the bastard that bruised her hadn't managed to break her.

Sierra wasn't a woman who could be handled with anything less than gentleness. A hard wind bruised her tender white skin, everyone who knew her knew that. She often joked that she couldn't walk through a room without marring her skin.

And it always hurt. She would pout if she bumped against something, rub the offended flesh, and glare at it as though the weakness irritated her.

She was strong-willed as hell though, so he'd always thought it evened out. She would stand up to anyone, nose to nose, and had on occasion out argued even John's father. That wasn't easy to do.

John couldn't handle the emotions rising inside him at the moment, the thought of the attempt that had been made to hurt her. To destroy her. The pure anger. The need to go to his knees before her and kiss every inch of bruised flesh, to beg for her forgiveness for not being there to protect her. The need to demand explanations, to beg that she stay, to simply hold her, was tearing him apart.

He'd never had so many emotions surging through him. For a man that prided himself on his control, he was growing close to losing it. Because despite the bruises, he wanted her. He wanted to touch her, kiss her from head to toe, show her all the gentleness he could find within himself, and he wanted to fuck her until they were both screaming from the pleasure.

She was too damned young, he kept telling himself. Her gentle twenty-four was a far cry from his thirty-two. But she was his.

The thought implanted itself in his brain and he refused to let it go. Sierra was his.

"Hey, John." The sound of Rowdy Mackay's voice calling out had him pausing, his jaw clenching before he turned back to the other man before stepping from the dock to the parking lot.

Rowdy loped from the entrance of the marina to the parking area, his eyes hidden behind dark sunglasses but John knew the other man was likely processing every telltale emotion John couldn't keep from his face.

"Hey, man, you were out early this morning," Rowdy stated as he pulled up to him.

"I was," John agreed as he continued to the SUV.

"Dawg said he saw your rig out at Hickley's, meeting an unscheduled landing. You have problems?"

There it was. The Mackays weren't just notoriously nosy, but also notoriously protective of their friends. And they considered John and his sister Rogue friends.

It wouldn't do any good to keep the truth from the other man; John knew him. Dawg was likely already running the Lear's call numbers, ownership, and flight plan.

Stepping to the SUV, he leaned against it wearily and gave the other man the information he knew Rowdy would come up with eventually.

Besides, letting the Mackay cousins in on the truth would provide Sierra with an added layer of protection.

As he explained the situation, Rowdy drew the sunglasses from his eyes, his gaze narrowing, lips thinning as tiny sparks of anger filled his sea green eyes.

The information would hit too close to home for Rowdy. His wife had suffered at the hands of a stalker, a man they had trusted. One who had nearly raped Kelly while Rowdy was in the Marines.

John knew the other man still blamed himself for being away, for not protecting her.

Just as John blamed himself now because he hadn't been there to protect Sierra.

What the fuck was happening to the world, he wondered. A woman wasn't safe, no matter where she went, no matter what she did. There were simply too many men determined to prey upon them.

"How close did the bastard come to raping her?" Rowdy's voice edged with latent violence.

"Her roommate frightened him off before he actually raped her. Her thighs, breasts, and neck are bruised extensively. I can see her neck . . ." He turned away, his jaw tightening as the guilt threatened to eat him alive. "Hell, Rowdy, I shouldn't have left. God, her neck . . ." He swallowed tightly. "That bastard nearly killed her."

"Hindsight, bro." Rowdy sighed. "That guilt will always follow you. You have to find a way to cover it, to bury it, or you'll never live with it. And make damned sure it never happens again."

Livid pain gleamed in Rowdy's deep green eyes as John turned back to him.

"Kelly doesn't sleep well if I'm not there with her, at least in the house at night," he stated, his voice rough. "I never forget how close I came to losing her, and I never forget how important she and our child are to me."

"Dad did his best to ensure no one knows where she is," he informed the other man. "We're hoping that gives him the time to figure out who attacked her. But like Dad, I have this feeling . . ."

And it was in his gut. The first time he had ever had the feeling his father described. The sensation of a phantom blade across his gut.

John stared out over the marina, his gaze moving instinctively to the houseboat where Sierra was awaiting him.

"She's still in danger, then." Rowdy nodded. "You have it bad, man, if you can sense that. The only woman that ever triggered that response in me was Kelly. She keeps me breathing. Be damned careful, because if she leaves you, I don't imagine breathing would be easy."

No, it wouldn't be. He didn't have to wait to know that. He could already sense it. He'd already experienced the feeling a year before when he'd left town, walked out of her life. Now that he was back, he realized exactly how hard breathing had been without her.

He'd always known, in part, how important she was to him, but until that hazy night a year before, until she ran from him, he hadn't realized how deep that importance ran.

"Let's get this luggage to the *Dreams*," the other man finally stated. "I'd say you can expect the family to descend on her soon, so save time somewhere, somehow while you're convincing her to stay." The snicker in Rowdy's voice assured John that the fact that John was dying to touch her wasn't lost on him.

Sierra hadn't packed much. There were two suitcases, the briefcase, and a small box that he knew held all the family pictures she owned.

Sierra didn't own much; since her father's bankruptcy and death, there hadn't been much for her to own. Getting back on her feet had been hard, and Sierra was a saver rather than a spender.

The small amount of furniture she owned was in storage, overseen by John's father. The rest of her belongings had been packed and sent to her, as though John Sr. knew his son wasn't going to allow her to leave easily.

And he wouldn't.

Stepping back into the living area of the houseboat, he quirked his lips at the sight of her sleeping, stretched out on the couch. The second Rowdy stepped inside, she was awake.

Just that quickly she sat up, eyes wide, a hint of fear and pain glowing in the marbled gray depths until she caught sight of John once again.

"Sierra Lucas, Rowdy Mackay," he introduced the two of them as he carried his half of the luggage to the steps leading to the master suite on the upper level.

"Ma'am." Rowdy nodded as he passed her. "Just excuse me, John decided he needed a pack mule this morning."

Laughter echoed in the other man's voice as he followed John and they moved upstairs with the luggage.

Rowdy sat the luggage by the bed and turned to John. In the other man's eyes Rowdy saw all the demons that had haunted him when he realized Kelly had been hurt while he was away from her.

He saw the torment and knew the agony his friend was feeling.

"Damn, she's fucking tiny," Rowdy hissed, anger flaring inside him. "She's even smaller than Kelly, John. How the hell did she survive an attacker?"

"Sheer stubbornness." John sighed as he shook his head and placed the items he carried on the floor. "Hell, Rowdy, I haven't slept since Dad told me about it. The nightmares will haunt me."

And they would, Rowdy knew that. There was no way for a man to ever go back once he realized he'd left his woman unprotected, and she had been harmed.

John had marked that woman for his own before he left Boston. A man who had left something important behind just had an air of loss around him. It was an air John no longer possessed. What he possessed instead was the pain of knowledge, the awareness that he hadn't kept her from harm.

"You sleep better when she's with you." He slept better now that Kelly was in his arms than he had his entire life. "But I saw her eyes, bro. She doesn't seem as smitten quite yet."

John would have his work cut out for him. Rowdy had seen the look she gave John. She was angry. There was a glitter of stubbornness, of pure feminine determination to make this as hard as possible on the other man.

Whatever had happened before John moved to Lake Cumberland, it had to do with this woman. And she wasn't in the least happy with him over it.

Once he couldn't see the bruises on the girl's throat, then Rowdy was certain he would find John's predicament amusing.

"I'll get out of here and let you take care of this then." Rowdy nodded. "I'll let the others know what's going on and we'll see what we can do to catch the bastard if he's stupid enough to try to follow her."

God help any man that tried to hurt Sierra Lucas where John Walker or one of the Mackays could get hold of him. Nothing but death awaited such stupidity.

As they returned downstairs, Sierra was still sitting on the couch, but watching the stairs warily.

"Later, Rowdy." John all but ordered him off the houseboat. He couldn't bear seeing that fear in her eyes for so much as a second longer.

"Catch you later, John, and remember what I told you."

Rowdy paused at the glass sliding door. "The family will be around soon. Babies and all." With that, he slid open the door, stepped outside, and headed back to the marina.

"What was that all about?" she asked as he moved into the kitchen.

"That means to expect the Mackay horde to descend upon us at any time," he grunted. "Rowdy's parents, cousins, their wives and babies. It's worse than Thanksgiving dinner at the grandparents' house." And she knew exactly what those were like, since she had attended enough of them.

"You didn't make friends that easily in Boston," she said softly. "I guess I thought you were playing hermit here in Kentucky as well."

"Only when they let me." John watched her intently, debating on breakfast or hauling her straight to bed. She looked exhausted. "What time did you get up this morning for the flight?"

She shrugged. "I didn't sleep well, so I was up in plenty of time."

Meaning nightmares had kept her awake.

John's jaw clenched. Breakfast, then bed.

"Why did you agree to this, John?" she finally asked as he pulled eggs from the fridge. "I'm not your responsibility, you know."

Not his responsibility? Fuck that. She belonged to him, she just didn't know it yet. That made her fully his responsibility whether she wanted to admit it or not.

"We'll discuss that later, Sierra."

"I don't want to discuss it later. I want to discuss it now." She rose to her feet and he noticed the small wince she almost hid.

His lips quirked. He could hear the nervousness in her voice, but he could also detect the knowledge in it. She knew exactly what he wanted from her.

"Lollipop, now isn't the time."

"And why are you calling me that horrendous name?" Exasperation filled her voice.

This time, he couldn't stop the grin that curled at his lips.

"Lollipop? Because you're so damned sweet to lick and suck on. And I think I developed an addiction that night, lollipop. I want more. A whole lot more."

The statement stopped Sierra in her tracks as she began to stalk across the room to him. She swore every erogenous zone in her body jumped into hyperdrive, and every spark of anger he could have possibly ignited flared inside her as well.

He spoke as though he remembered it. As though it possibly meant something to him? She doubted very seriously he had a clue.

"How would you know? You passed out."

"Right between the sweetest thighs I think I've ever had surrounding my face." He grinned rakishly. "I remember that part, baby, just before passing out. Licking the sweetest, hottest little pussy I think I've ever had my mouth on."

So that was the last thing he remembered? Asshole. He didn't even remember kneeling between her thighs, taking her, then passing out.

"So you think I'm just going to be your little plaything while I'm here?"

The idea actually had its merits. Of a limited variety anyway. She could feel her breasts swelling, her thighs tightening, her pussy flushing and dampening.

Her clit was so sensitive now she wondered if she could come as she stepped closer to the kitchen.

Being John's plaything would introduce her to a world of supreme pleasure. Unfortunately, it would also include a world of heartache unlike anything she wanted to deal with.

Her heart had already been broken, and she preferred that the parts still intact stayed that way.

"I could handle that," he agreed as though the thought had never occurred to him.

"Oh, I bet you could." Her arms crossed her breasts despite the tenderness there. "Too bad it's not going to happen."

And to that, he laughed. The rich, dark male sound ricocheted up her spine and sent shivers of anticipated pleasure racing through her body. She knew that sound. Sexy, filled with intent. But she had never heard it turned on her before now.

"Sweet Sierra." He sighed as though with relish. "You think you can sleep in my bed night after night, put up with me holding you, touching you, and still deny me?"

"I'm not sleeping in your bed." The very thought of it was more dangerous than she wanted to contemplate.

"Sorry, but that's exactly where you're sleeping." A pan slid on the stove, and as though they were discussing nothing more than the weather, he began making breakfast. Enough breakfast to feed an army.

Sierra could only stare back at him in shock. Unfortunately, she knew John too well, and she knew that tone of voice. Finding an argument against him wasn't going to be easy.

"You think only weeks after that attack that I want any man in my bed?" The words popped out of her mouth before she could stop them.

For a second, she could feel the fear tearing through her, but only for a second, quite simply because she knew John was the last man in the world that would ever harm her.

It wouldn't matter how angry he was with her, it wouldn't matter what she had done. He would never harm her.

"No, I don't think you want any man at all," he agreed much too easily. "But I'm not just any man, lollipop, I'm the man you actually want."

The sheer audacity, the supreme confidence in his voice had her lips parting in momentary, complete surprise. The problem with that surprise was the fact that he was right. Of all the men in the world, John was the one she would never stop wanting, the one she would never stop aching for. The one she would never fear would hurt her physically.

She watched silently as he scrambled eggs and made toast, trying to come up with an effective argument. One that would ensure he would stay out of the bed with her, one that would aid her in keeping secret the sheer depth of hunger that arose in her where he was concerned.

God help her if he actually touched her while he was

sober. If he didn't pass out and forget all the important parts. She didn't know if she could bear allowing him to possess her, to know what he was taking from her, only to send her on her way when this was finished.

"You overrate yourself." And that had to be the lousiest comeback that she could have let slip past her lips.

It was met with a small, confident grin. "We'll find out later," he promised her. "Once I have you in my bed and I see how deep those bruises are, how much loving you can take. But be prepared, Sierra, you're sharing my bed, and I'll touch you when I want to, when I need to. You might have run before, but I think we both know your running days are over here."

Her running days were over?

Did he even have a clue how hard it was to stay away from him? How she had cried each time she had ignored his messages, how she had grieved when he had left Boston.

Damn him. He had broken her heart that night and had no idea what he had done to her. Just as he had no idea that he had taken her innocence a second before he passed out on top of her.

The bastard!

But she couldn't deny him, either.

She knew damned good and well that she wouldn't make it an hour in the bed with him without giving in to the needs he aroused in her.

Oh, a perverse, angry part of her wanted to. She wanted to throw his offer back in his face and show him exactly how easily she could refuse him. The problem was, as angry as he made her, as much as he hurt her, she didn't want to refuse him. Her body didn't want to refuse him.

She remembered the pleasure just as vividly as she remembered the heartache, and she wanted more. More pleasure. More touch. More of those lethal kisses, and that would require more of the pain as well.

Could she hold on to what was left of her heart and still give in to him?

There wasn't a chance. He would destroy her and she was going to let him do it.

"You didn't do enough to me while you were in Boston, did you, John?" she asked him softly. "You didn't hurt me enough, right?"

"What did I do to you, Sierra?" Confusion crossed his face, filled his eyes. "I kissed you, I touched you. We nearly had sex and then you ran off. You didn't give me much of a chance after that to do anything."

"And I don't intend to give you a chance to do anything now," she warned him, despite the fact that she could barely breathe for the erotic implications running through her mind. "I can sleep just fine on the couch."

Damn him. Every nerve ending in her body was rioting at the thought of him touching her, finally finishing what he had begun that night a year ago.

But she had learned something that night, something about herself at least. She had learned that she wanted more from John than his kisses, his touches. Once, she had thought it would be enough, if that was all she could have. It wouldn't be, though. He would rip her heart from her chest, leaving her lost and alone. As lost and alone as she had been when she learned he had left Boston.

No, she wanted John's heart.

"Couch won't do, baby." He was shaking his head as he fixed breakfast, his broad back to her.

John had been lean, metro muscular rather than bulky. He had been strong before, but as she watched him move, watched the muscles in his back and shoulders shift, she realized his body had changed more than she had once suspected.

Those muscles were now tight, hard, powerful. She wondered what it would feel like if she ran her hands over them, dug her nails into them.

"You're making my dick hard staring at me like that," he stated without turning around.

Sierra almost lost her breath at the husky, controlled lust in his voice.

"What makes you think you're worth looking at, dummy?" she snapped out angrily.

He chuckled and the sound went straight to her thighs, tightened them, then zipped to her womb with a blast of heat. Damn him, she could feel her juices flooding her pussy, her inner muscles tightening, clenching in hunger.

"I can feel you looking at me. I've always been able to feel you looking at me." By the sound of his voice, it wasn't an admission he particularly liked.

"It's called killing looks," she informed him as she moved to the bar to watch him more closely. "Most of the time I slap you upside the head with something."

He flashed her a grin. A charming, rakish grin that had the butterflies in her stomach doing cartwheels in arousal.

"That doesn't explain why it's always felt like a very inti- mate stroke, now does it, darlin'? Personally, I think you've wanted to be in my bed for years."

He knew she had.

John turned back to the stove for the simple reason that if he kept looking at her, breakfast would burn and his dick would likely rip right through his jeans.

He should have realized years ago what was going on with her, but he hadn't. Just as he should have realized what was going on with him.

Half the time he'd either been angry with her, or per- plexed by the fact that she affected him. He'd done every- thing to excuse his arousal around her, from the very convincing lie that she was simply a pretty woman and he was too damned sexual, as most of his lovers accused him of being.

The fact of the matter was, he'd wanted her. She'd been a part of his life since she was little, so admitting it hadn't been easy. Until the night his pretty little Sierra had rescued him from a life in a frozen marriage with Marlena, he hadn't wanted to face exactly what she had been doing to him since she hit the tender age of eighteen.

"Personally, I think bumming around in the mountains has rotted what little brains you had left in your head," she snapped back.

He didn't have to look at her to realize her gray eyes were lit with equal parts anger and arousal. Hell, he could hear it in her voice, he could feel it flaming in the air around them.

He glanced back at her anyway, and hell, he should have kept his eyes on the food. His gaze was drawn instantly to the small imprint of her nipples beneath her blouse.

She wasn't wearing a bra.

He'd realized that earlier, and it made sense that she wasn't. If the bruises were as bad as he'd learned, and he had no doubt they were, then a bra would have been extremely painful.

Without a bra, he could see his effect on her, though, and the thought of getting her nipples in his mouth again had his cock throbbing in response.

He could feel the sweat beading on his forehead as he jerked his gaze back to the bacon frying and almost cursed before flipping it quickly.

Yep, she was going to make him burn her breakfast, and he didn't want to do that. She needed a good meal and plenty of sleep.

"Don't you have drugs to take before you eat?" he asked, changing the subject quickly.

"I don't like taking them." There was a mutinous tone to her voice. "They make me dopey."

"They make you heal, now take them." He wasn't arguing with her where her health was concerned. "Dad has a doctor lined up for you, he's a good man. He'll be here tomorrow afternoon. You can discuss the prescription with him. Until then, take the medicine."

He laid the bacon out on a plate, slid the skillet back, and turned to look at her.

Her arms were crossed over her breasts, her eyes narrowed.

"You can't make me," she informed him, her chin tilted stubbornly.

John sighed at that. "Do you really want this fight, Sierra? Over something as important as your health? Take the pills, or I won't let up. I'll harass. I'll bitch. I'll call Rowdy, and his dad and stepmother will come to the boat, and trust me, Ray can be a bigger mother hen than Dad is. If that doesn't work, then I'll call Rowdy's cousins and wives in. They'll bring the babies, and won't let you hold them. They'll frown, they'll advise . . ."

"Stop already!" Her hands went in the air as she turned, stalked to her purse, and pulled out the bottle as he grabbed water from the fridge and set it on the bar for her after opening it.

She was too sore to stomp back, but she tried. She did take her medication, though, glaring at him every second. He could see so much in her expressive face, emotions and needs that infuriated and drew him. Infuriated him because he should have seen them all along.

"I'll make you pay for this," she warned him furiously. "See if I don't."

"As long as you're healthy enough to attempt it." He shrugged with a grin. "Then you have my permission to try."

"Try to knock some sense in your head," she muttered as she sat down gingerly on one of the bar stools. "You're a pain in the ass, John."

"Not yet," he promised, and the thought of that sweet ass nearly took his breath away. "But I will be. I promise, lollipop. I will be."

Four

Breakfast was eaten in a strained silence. Sierra could almost feel the clock ticking, the knowledge that once the meal was finished, she wouldn't be able to fight his insistence that she go to bed.

She was so tired, and the medication only made the weariness sink deeper inside her.

The doctor had warned her that she needed to sleep as often as possible, to rest and recuperate. Whoever had attacked her, for whatever reason, had been strong. Strong enough that the blows to her thighs as she fought him had gone incredibly deep, not to mention the hold that had left the prints of his fingers in her flesh.

Her breasts were still so tender she couldn't bear a bra, and her ribs ached. She hadn't simply been groped roughly, she'd been struck, gloved fists striking her body as she fought and screamed.

Forcing the memory back wasn't easy. The pain medication made it harder to do. It was one of the reasons she hated taking it.

"Come on, you're falling asleep where you're sitting," John announced as he rose from his chair and collected her dishes. "You need to rest."

It was the middle of the morning and she would probably end up sleeping the day away. She hated doing that. The sun was bright, it was warm and clear, and the breeze off the water was invigorating. She would have loved to be able to lie out on the upper deck and soak up the healing rays of the sun.

"Come on, darlin'." Sierra's chest clenched at the gentle sound of his voice as he moved to her chair as though he were going to carry her again.

"I wish everyone would just stop trying to tote me around like a damned newborn." Rising from the chair gingerly, she took a deep breath and would have glared at him if her eyes didn't feel so heavy. "I'm sore, not broken."

She hated feeling helpless, and she couldn't afford to be in his arms again. Being in his arms meant feeling the strength of them, the warmth of them, and remembering too clearly what she had almost had.

"You worry me with your stubbornness, Sierra," he growled, but he didn't try to pick her up. Instead he stayed close until she moved for the couch. "Try to lie down on that couch, and I'm going to carry you straight up those stairs anyway. I told you. You're sleeping with me."

He hadn't had a nickel's worth of sleep since his father had called the day before. He'd lain awake most of the night imagining the horror she must have felt the night she was attacked. It had kept him from sleeping, kept him from enjoying the peace of the summer night.

He wanted her in his arms. Hell, he'd nearly driven to Boston and simply picked her up rather than waiting for his sister to deliver her.

"I'm calling your father," she muttered, but she turned and headed for the stairs. "I'm going to tell him you've turned into a bully."

"He'll understand completely," he assured her, his lips almost twitching at the little feminine snort of displeasure that she gave him.

She made it up the stairs, but by time she walked into the luxurious bedroom, it was obvious she was more exhausted than before.

"Strip." He could see her intent to lie down in that bed fully clothed.

Moving to the larger-than-king-sized bed, he pulled back the comforter and sheets then turned and looked at her once again.

She was staring at him with wounded gray eyes.

"Why, John?" She sighed. "What does it matter?"

"Because some bastard dared to abuse what I consider mine," he snarled, surprising himself with the vehemence in his tone. "I want to see what he did, Sierra. I want to know so that when I get my hands on him, I'll know exactly what I owe him."

Sierra stared back at him, some hidden, previously unknown part of her soul beginning to relax. She had known John would never hurt her. He would never let anyone else hurt her, but now it seemed something deeper inside her recognized that as well.

Licking her lips, she gripped the hem of her T-shirt and tried not to wince as she drew it over her head. She wore no bra, nothing to hide the bruises that still marked her flesh.

Her flesh marked easily; it always had. And bruises remained for what seemed like forever on her skin. Two weeks, and the black and blue marks still looked almost fresh.

She ignored John, refusing to look into his face as she toed her sneakers from her feet and then slid her jeans from her hips and down her legs.

She wore panties, but the soft, pale cream silk was little protection.

"Someone's going to die."

The sound of his voice had her gaze jerking to his face. Violet-blue eyes were raging with fury, his expression dark, forbidding, as Sierra felt tears come to her eyes.

"I fought," she whispered, suddenly shaking, her voice trembling. "You always told me to fight, John. I fought . . ." She'd fought as hard as she could. She'd screamed, she'd ignored the pain. All she could think was that a stranger was trying to steal from her one of the most vital choices she could make.

"My God! Baby." A few steps and he was in front of her, lifting her into his arms despite the fact that she had asked him not to carry her.

He had lifted her, only to lay her carefully on the bed before sitting beside her, his hands gently lifting her arms until they were stretched above her head.

John could feel a burning agony tearing through him. He should have never left Boston. Not so soon. He should have forced her to see him, found a way past her stubbornness. He should have been there to protect her.

With the backs of his fingers, he stroked down the underside of her arms and the purple marks that led to her full, hard-tipped breasts. Harsh finger marks marred her flesh, but her nipples, so sweet and tight and hard, were the same tender pink, unbruised and tempting as hell.

Below her breasts were fainter bruises, where she'd been struck, though the blows hadn't connected as hard as he knew they were meant to. He could tell by the placement that the son of a bitch had been trying to damage her ribs.

Lower, along her rounded thighs, was heavier bruising. Finger marks, thumb imprints.

He parted her thighs gently, trying to ignore the dampness he could see against the silk of her panties. Trying real fucking hard to ignore the fact that there were no curls beneath the silk.

He hadn't remembered that for some reason. He'd had his mouth on her pussy, licking it like a starving man devouring a treat, but he hadn't remembered that there had been no curls there.

Drawing in a hard, deep breath, he slid his fingers beneath the band of her panties before he lifted his eyes to hers. "Let me take them off, Sierra."

Her hips rose. Hazy sensuality filled her gaze now, flushed her face. Pert lips parted, a lazy pink tongue licked over them with a slow, damp stroke as he drew the silk from her body.

"God, I've dreamed about this for a fucking year," he whispered.

For far longer than a year. He'd dreamed before and refused to allow himself to acknowledge those dreams.

"John, touch me." The plea went straight to his cock.

Why the hell did he keep hearing innocence in her voice, seeing it in her eyes? When he stared into the slate gray depths, he saw a woman who had no idea the pleasure her body could experience, the heights arousal could take her.

His gaze went down her body once again, a groan tearing from his throat at the sight of the honeyed glaze glistening on the folds of her pussy. Her clit, a sweet pink little pearl, peeked from between those folds, tempting his lips, his tongue.

"You don't know what you do to a man," he growled as he moved closer, leaning over her until his lips could brush against hers. "You make me hungry, lollipop."

A slow smile curled the lips beneath his. "Your lollipop?"

Hell! He wasn't going to survive this. The low, sleepy sensuality in her face and voice was more than he could bear.

"My lollipop." And he'd be damned if he let another man have a taste of it now.

His lips lowered against hers more firmly, his tongue licking at the seam of her lips until they parted for him, until her tongue came out to meet his and a low, feminine groan met his kiss.

God, he remembered her kiss. Of all the things he remembered from that alcohol-hazed memory of nearly having it, it was the taste of her kiss. Like the sweetest innocence.

How the hell did she manage it? She'd dated more men than he could name over the years. There was no way that innocence was as pure as it seemed.

He'd be damned if he cared, though. Hell, he wasn't exactly a virgin himself and he didn't expect to ever encounter one. He didn't give a damn. From here on out, she would belong solely to him, though; he'd ensure it.

Threading his fingers into the thick, blue-black curls that framed her face, John held her in place and deepened the kiss. His tongue sank into her mouth, touched hers, and felt her lips close on it with a sensual grip. She suckled at his tongue with lazy enjoyment, causing his dick to clench and tighten at the memory of her lips sucking him there as well.

Damn, she was making him hot. He should have turned the AC up before bringing her to the bedroom.

The sweet brush of her nipples seared through the material of his T-shirt as she arched against him. Full, swollen breasts were cushioned against his chest, and the heat of them rushed through his body like a narcotic.

He couldn't think of anything better than releasing his dick and sinking balls deep inside the tight, slick depths of her pussy.

For just a second, for one flash of imagery, he could have sworn he'd done so before. Felt her, so fucking tight he thought he'd die from it. Then it was gone, remnants of dreams he'd had over the years. Fantasies he hadn't been able to help.

Tearing his lips from hers, John set about giving her pleasure. Simply pleasure. No pressure. This time wasn't for him, it was for his Sierra.

She'd been hurt, bruised, almost broken. He wanted to wipe that memory from her mind. Wipe it and replace it with sweet pleasure, with satisfaction. He wanted her to know gentleness, to know the heated arousal, the warmth of sexual fulfillment.

She was exhausted, worn, but he knew she didn't sleep well. That was something he intended to help her with this morning.

Sierra barely restrained the cry that would have torn from her lips as John's lips moved down her throat to the rise of her breasts. Her entire body was sensitized, but strangely, she couldn't feel the pain.

There was no pain.

There was only John's touch, the feel of his lips and tongue stroking their way to a nipple as it rose hard and tight for his lips.

"Don't tease me, John," she moaned, arching closer to his lips, desperate to feel them enclosing her nipple.

"You've teased me," he whispered, pure sex filling his voice. "For a year, Sierra, the thought of your touch has teased me to near insanity."

His head lowered, the feel of his tongue licking around the sensitive, hard tip of one nipple stole her breath. The damp warmth stroked sensations through the flesh that sent her senses spinning.

Slow, deliberate licks, each one avoiding the nipple, stroking around it, teasing her so unbearably that her hands slid into his hair to hold him to her.

Which was more destructive? she wondered. Those lazy licks, or if he actually took her nipple into his mouth?

She had no idea of the answer to that question, but she wanted to know it.

Before she could voice the demand, the plea, his lips covered the tender peak, sucking it inside his mouth as the nerve endings began to riot chaotically.

Sierra could feel her nipples becoming impossibly harder. The tender tip he held between his lips throbbed and ached, ecstasy spiking through it and slicing to her womb as he sucked it harder.

Rubbing his tongue against it, a murmured growl of approval rumbled in his chest as she arched, trying to get closer, fighting to press deeper into his mouth.

The feel of his shoulders, the muscles shifting and bunching beneath her hands, had her nails digging into the flesh as his tongue licked over her nipple again.

The suction of his mouth combined with the lash of his tongue against the nerve-ridden tip had a cry tearing from her lips. He sucked her harder now, deeper, his tongue whipping over the sensitive tip with such destructive pleasure that she felt her senses rushing out of control.

Her hips arched, her thighs opening wider as she pressed the wet, aching heat of the enflamed folds against the hard strength of his thigh and rode it in pleasure.

He had to know how desperate she was for his touch now. How desperate she had always been. There was no disguising it at this point. No matter how much she wished she could fight against it, it was still overwhelming.

"John," she panted his name as his hand slid from her waist to her bare thigh. "What are you trying to do to me?"

She was so wet she could feel her juices collecting thick and heavy on the bare folds of her pussy as he moved back, holding her still with one hand as the other caressed and stroked. His fingers stroked along her thigh, growing closer as his lips moved to her other nipple, enclosing it in the heat of his mouth as she arched and allowed her thighs to fall wider apart. She needed his fingers closer to her aching flesh, to the pulsing heat of her clit.

As his lips drew on her nipple, his fingers found the delicate knot of tissue, surrounded it, and oh so delicately began to milk the little kernel.

Sierra's eyes widened. Her thighs tightened until she could feel the muscles straining, trembling. She could feel the orgasm rising inside her. She could feel it pulsing, pounding through her senses, riding a wave filled with heat and desperation.

What the hell was he doing to her?

She strained, trying to lift closer as he milked her clit with slow, firm strokes. Strokes that edged pleasure-pain, that had her body straining in pleasure.

"John . . ." she panted his name, her head thrashing in desperation.

Sierra could feel her juices easing from the flesh between her thighs, a thick, heavy dew, coating the intimate folds, preparing her flesh for a penetration she felt as though she were dying for.

Lifting his head slowly, John stared back at Sierra's dazed features. He licked one nipple, then the other, feeling her shudder in response as he continued the delicate plumping of her swollen clit.

She was so fucking close to orgasm. So close he could nearly taste it spilling to his lips.

"I remember tasting you that night, Sierra," he groaned as

he began kissing his way down her torso, loving the sweet-salty taste of the perspiration lying on her skin. "The feel of my tongue inside your pussy, feeling how snug and hot you are. I swear, the taste of you haunts me."

She jerked in his grip, hips arching, nails pricking his shoulders as his lips neared the silken, flushed, glazed mound of her pussy.

Damn. He was going to enjoy this. He was going to make sure she enjoyed it.

This was his sweet. His treat.

His tongue slipped inside the narrow slit, and in one long, slow lick he swore he became drunk on her. The taste of her exploded against his tongue like spicy honey, like addictive, sensual nectar.

Sierra felt a rage of heat rush through her pussy. His tongue licked, lapped slow and easy, circling her clit gently, too gently. She strained against him, needing a firmer touch, more heat to trigger the explosion she was reaching so desperately for.

Knees rising, heels digging into the mattress, she ground the intimate folds against his lips, her fingers twining into his hair, and she fought to breathe. Heat rushed around her, perspiration dampened her flesh, making her body almost as slick as the folds John caressed so intimately.

His tongue was wicked, destructive. Licking around her clit one last time, he moved lower, his fingers parting her bare folds and moving ever closer to the aching center of her pussy.

"Yes," she whispered. "Oh, God, John, please . . ."

Her head thrashed against the mattress and still he gave her no mercy. He licked against the entrance, increasing the dampness moving from her vagina to his eager tongue.

Her hips moved, rotating against his lips as she gasped, reaching, fighting for that explosion of pleasure that she knew he could give her.

It had been so long.

So many dark, lonely months with nothing but the memory of his touch, nothing but the memory of his pleasure.

Sierra could feel desperation rising inside her. Pleasure burned through her body, tore through her senses.

"Damn you, let me come already!" The cry was ragged, pleading, demanding.

John tensed between her thighs, his hand clamping on her upper legs, drawing them farther apart a second before his tongue plunged into the liquid hot, clenching depths of her pussy.

Almost. Almost.

Sensation washed over her like a tidal wave. Sierra held her breath, fighting to ride that sensual edge as his tongue began to move inside her. Thrusting, plunging, fucking into the slickened depths as Sierra began to writhe beneath him. She couldn't lie still. She had to orgasm. If she didn't, she wouldn't, couldn't, survive it.

Crying out his name, she felt his tongue ease from her, his lips moving, covering her clit and sucking it into his mouth again. He drew on it, his tongue lashed around it, until the explosion that rocked her drew a strangled, ecstatic scream from her lips.

Her fingers tightened in his hair. Her thighs locked around his head, and as he sucked her deeper, two fingers pressed inside the spasming depths of her pussy and threw her higher.

She felt him fucking her with his fingers, plunging them inside her, pleasure and pain rushing through her, drawing muted screams of pleasure, tightened her body, lashing her senses with pure, absolute rapture until she swore she exploded into fragments.

She was pulsing, flames slowly easing, throbbing through her body as she felt his lips and tongue easing, stroking now rather than ravishing. Caressing rather than devouring until Sierra felt her senses slowly darkening.

Exhaustion raced through her with almost the same force as her orgasm. Before she knew it, it overwhelmed her, sucked her in a deep, dreamless void and forced her to sleep, to rest, to finally escape the loss that had been haunting her. The loss of the man who now held her once again.

Five

Sierra drifted awake slowly that evening, a sense of lazy contentment radiating through her at the feel of warmth along her back and the hard, male arm lying across her hips.

She was on her side, her back tucked against his chest, the heavy width of his cock rising thick and heavy along the seam of her buttocks.

Full consciousness hadn't taken hold yet, and she knew it. The feeling of adventurous sensuality was like a glow, bright and hot, heating her womb and sensitizing her flesh.

She was hungry for him. She hadn't had enough. She had years and years of need to make up for, and very little time to do it in. She expected John's father to call at any time to inform them that he knew who had attacked her and that he was in custody.

She was lying in his arms on borrowed time.

She should make the most of that time. She could be angry with him later. She could remember later all the reasons why she wasn't supposed to be in his arms. But for this moment, she could be the woman she always wanted to be with him. A woman who knew what she wanted. The woman that could take him, love him, bind herself to his heart.

It made sense.

Stretching, she rubbed against the hard length tucked against her buttocks, her breath catching as his fingers flattened against her abdomen and moved slowly to a full, sensitive breast.

His fingers cupped, his thumb stroked against her nipple, and when she laid her head back against his shoulder, turning her face up to him, his lips covered hers.

The lazy hunger built, moving through her like the low flames of a fire rapidly heating out of control.

The embers were blazing, the flames licking over her flesh, turning her into the sensualist she had always known she would be in his arms.

"I won't be easy," he groaned as he nipped at her lips. "Do you hear me, Sierra? This stops right now, or taking you won't be done as gently as this first time should be."

"Hmm, it's not the first time anyway," she reminded him sleepily as she shifted against him, her thighs parting as she felt his cock nudge against her.

"The first time with me," he growled.

"You don't remember so well," she whispered before her back arched and another cry left her lips.

The wide crest was parting her, stretching the entrance, pressing inside to complete the destructive possession he had begun a year before.

He wouldn't stop this time, she assured herself as she felt him lift her leg and ease it back, over his. It opened her farther, allowing the hard flesh of his erection to penetrate deeper.

Holding on to his wrist, Sierra felt the low burn become a hard, controlled flame. Her hips shifted as she pressed back, her breathing rough, uneven as she felt him beginning to move inside her.

The entrance was a slow, rocking glide that penetrated her farther with each inward thrust of his hips. Each retreat had her crying out into the hungry kisses he took from her lips.

Tongues twined, fervent tastes became raging hunger as each second, each slow thrust buried him deeper, stretched her farther.

Her fingers dug into his wrist as the fiery agony-ecstasy of the penetration razed through her senses like wildfire now.

"Damn, you're fucking tight." Tearing his lips from hers, he moved his hand from her breast to the hard kernel of her clit.

There, his fingers circled, stroked, and built the flames raging beneath her flesh.

"John." She stretched against him, opening herself farther and taking more. More until she could feel her pussy burning with the invasion as her clit began to pound in an agonizing need for release.

Pushing back against him again, she felt the heavy thrust against her, inside her, and froze in shock. He was buried inside her now, fully, his balls pressing against her as she felt his cock throbbing inside her.

The fingers of one hand clenched into the sheets beneath them. She didn't know whether to back farther against him, stroking him deeper inside her, or to thrust her clit closer against his fingers.

"Sierra, I can't do it this easy," he groaned.

"This is easy?" she panted. There was nothing easy about this. She was so full, stretched to the point that the burning of her flesh blended with the pleasure, creating a conflagration of sensations that threatened to drive her insane.

"Ah, hell." He pulled back, thrust.

Sierra jerked and arched, her body suddenly so hungry for the pleasure-pain of that hard penetration that she was shaking in reaction.

He moved, pushing her farther to her stomach as he came over her, arms braced at her shoulders, his knees bracketing her hips as he began to move. It was then she knew what he meant by easy. By being unable to be easy.

She felt his sweat drip to her shoulder and looked up at him, seeing the wild violet-blue eyes, the narrowed gaze, the lust that burned in his face.

And he was moving.

Sierra began to shudder as sensation after sensation began to rage through her body. She was dying beneath him now.

"More." She couldn't hold back the plea, the demand for more.

Her hips lifted closer, her knees digging into the mattress as she fought for the more that she needed, hungered for.

"John, so good," she moaned, feeling drunk on the sensations racing through her body, just under her flesh, tearing through her womb.

Behind her, his lips settled to her shoulder, taking sharp little kisses as his hips lunged inside her, thrusting hard and deep, filling her until she felt ready to burst from the pleasure.

Every inch of her body was primed for orgasm now. The stroke of his cock inside her, rasping against tender, untouched nerve endings and sensitized tissue, was too much.

She felt as though she were dying of pleasure beneath him.

"Better than the dreams," he groaned. "Fucking you is so damned good, Sierra. So fucking good."

The thrusts became harder, filling her as she felt the muscles he was invading clench tighter on his cock until they were both groaning, breathing harsh, desperate as she felt her orgasm rising, burning closer, tightening through her until the explosion ripped through her body and her senses.

Shaking beneath him, Sierra fought to hold on to him as he thrust inside her, pushing deep and hard until he jerked free and she felt his release burn against her rear as he gave a hard, heavy groan of pleasure.

She hadn't even thought of birth control. She hadn't considered the fact that he hadn't donned a condom and she wasn't on anything herself. There was no need to be. John hadn't been in Boston; there hadn't been a chance of him touching her.

"Sierra." He whispered her name against her shoulder as he kissed it gently, giving one last shudder above her as the spurts of semen against her flesh eased. "Sweet God, baby. You've killed me."

He collapsed behind her, pulling her close against him as he fought to catch his breath.

"Hmmm," she murmured. She didn't have the breath nor the intelligence to form a response at the moment.

All she could do was feel. Feel the warmth that suffused her, the satiation that filled her.

"Did I hurt you?" There was an edge of concern in his voice now.

Sierra managed to shake her head. "Killed me."

"Killed you, huh?" Amused now.

She imagined his expressions with each tonal change. She knew him, she realized. Knew that with his amusement, his gaze would sparkle with laughter; with his anger, it would gleam with fire. Concern was a furrow above his brows; sympathy was somberness that gave his expression a look of heavy emotion.

Did he know her so well? she wondered.

Of course he didn't.

"You're thinking too hard, Sierra," he drawled lazily. "I can feel your mind working, going over things, dissecting them. Let it just flow, baby." Another kiss to her shoulder and she was frowning at the wall across the room.

"Is that your new philosophy, John?" she asked warily. "Worry about it tomorrow?"

He chuckled at that. "Not hardly. But there's no sense in thinking something to the ground that hasn't firmly established itself yet, either. Just be easy, lollipop. Things will work themselves out how they should, no matter how you worry over them."

"Hell of a way to live." She sighed, moving away from him despite the obvious reluctance as he allowed her to leave his arms.

"A better way to live."

She looked back at him, seeing his obvious unconcern over his nakedness as he watched her from the bed. For her part, she jerked the sheet that had fallen to the floor and wrapped it around her naked body.

She felt more in control, less vulnerable with at least partial covering.

"How can it be a better way to live, John?" she asked. "Perhaps I need to figure out how to defend myself against you. You're going to destroy me before this is over."

He frowned back at her. "Because we had sex? Has your heart been broken every time you've gone to bed with a man?"

"Pretty much," she snapped back, her lips thinning. After all, she hadn't had a lover before John.

He shook his head. "Bobby Worthington was pretty heartbroken himself, if I remember. Said you walked right out of his bed and never looked back."

Bobby Worthington, she almost laughed at the thought, but the seriousness in his expression forestalled the amusement. She'd be damned. He believed the gossip and rumors? All along, he had believed it every time one of those bastards had sworn she had slept with him.

"Tell me, John, would you ever admit that a woman simply walked away from you?" she questioned him caustically. "Think about it. Bobby had more ego than good sense, and evidently it's simply a male trait, because you don't appear to be any smarter at the moment."

She shook her head as he frowned back at her, his gaze narrowed as though he were deciding whether or not to believe her.

"I need a shower." She wasn't defending herself against this, and she sure as hell wasn't going to cry again. What she would do was exactly what he said she shouldn't. Figure out how to keep her heart from being broken.

He rose lazily from the bed. "Shower's through there." He pointed to a door off the side. "I'll lay your bags on the bed, you can unpack into the extra dresser." He pointed to a low set of drawers built into the wall of the bedroom. "I'll order dinner in. Tonight, we have some things to figure out, plans to make, then we'll go from there."

"I can't imagine what kind of plans you might need to make." She shrugged as she headed to the shower. "Your

father will have this figured out soon, then I'll be going
home. No big deal."

No big deal?

John watched as she moved into the shower, the door
snapping closed behind her.

She was angry.

The look on her face when he'd mentioned Bobby. There
had been such an edge of disillusionment there, as though
she couldn't believe he'd mentioned that.

What the hell was going on with her?

She'd been as tight as a virgin, but he knew for damned
sure that she was no virgin. So close to it that she may as well
have been, a part of him argued.

And what had she said? That he hadn't remembered that
night correctly.

The hell he hadn't. He'd passed out right between her
thighs, the taste of her sweet pussy still on his lips. There
was no way he would have forgotten taking her.

Hell, Sierra had always confused him, though. She never
came right out and said anything. She kept things to herself,
whether pleasure or pain, and rarely shared them. Getting
information out of her was often like pulling teeth.

There was information that was going to have to come,
though. There had to be a reason why she was attacked. His
father had ruled out a serial rapist, there were no attacks that
matched the MO, and there was no reason to believe it was
anything other than personal.

Who would want to hurt her?

That was what John intended to find out, and then he intended to do something about it.

Six

etting her to talk that night didn't work out as John
had hoped. Once they had dinner, Sierra drifted off to
sleep on the couch while John called his father and
discussed the investigation into the attack.

There was no new information.

John paced the upper deck of the *Nauti Wet Dreams*, frustration eating at him as he tried to piece together the information he did have. Which wasn't much.

The assailant had obviously been male. The roommate who had burst into the bedroom that night hadn't seen hair color or eye color, but judged his approximate height to be around six feet. It could have been anyone.

As John stood at the railing, a beer in hand, the sound of slow, even footsteps making their way down the dock drew his attention.

Watching, he almost groaned in irritation. Most people groaned in irritation when Timothy Cranston made his appearance, though.

The rabid little Leprechaun, the Mackay cousins called

him. A former Homeland Security special agent who had retired to Somerset after the completion of an investigation that revealed a domestic terrorist organization in the area.

He paused at the front of the boat.

"I'm up here, Cranston," John called out, the night and the water carrying his voice clearly to the other man.

"Ahh, the elusive John Walker Junior." The amusement in the other man's tone was just the wrong side of grating.

He moved across the deck to the spiral staircase that led to the sundeck of the houseboat.

"Too bad I'm not a little better at the elusive part," John grunted. "What the hell do you want?"

Cranston stepped onto the deck, a quiet grin on his face as John leaned against the rail and glared back at him.

"The Walkers have quite a history in this area," Timothy mused as he walked across the deck to the portable fridge and removed a beer.

John watched as he uncapped it and took a long drink, wondering what the ex–special agent was doing here.

"Calculating" and "manipulating" were two of the kinder terms used to refer to Cranston.

Turning back to him, Cranston moved closer, opting to sit in one of the deck chairs across from where John stood.

"I won't ask again," John stated with far more patience than he felt.

Cranston only chuckled. "The Mackay boys use that same tone with me, John. It doesn't help them any more than it's going to help you."

No doubt. The little fucker was going to get himself killed one of these days. From what John understood, he was far too prone to fuck with too many people's lives.

"You have a problem," Cranston finally stated.

"And you're one of them," John pointed out.

To which Cranston's low laugh filtered through the night.

"This could be true," the other man agreed, nodding. "But honestly, JW, I could easily become your best friend."

"Not if you keep calling me JW."

He might just have to kill the little bastard himself if he kept that up.

"That's what most people in these parts call you, you know," Timothy informed him. "Especially those who knew your father."

John restrained a sigh. Too many people in this area remembered his father before he moved to Boston. Or perhaps escaped to Boston would be a better way of describing it.

"Cut the shit, Cranston." John shook his head wearily. "Why are you here?"

"Because someone was in town today asking some very pointed questions about John Walker Junior. Someone obviously not from the area."

John froze. No one but his parents and sisters knew where he was, and there was no reason for anyone he knew to have followed him to Somerset, Kentucky.

"Who was he?"

"She." Cranston grinned. "The intrepid investigator claimed to be your fiancée."

John stared back at him in silent shock.

"I don't have a fiancée," he answered the other man.

Cranston tipped the beer back, finished it, then set the bottle on the floor of the deck.

"She didn't seem much like a lady," Cranston remarked. "Strange, I can't imagine you hooking up with such a woman, even for a short time."

John remained silent, refusing to answer the subtle question.

Cranston stared back, just as silent.

John couldn't imagine Marlena in Somerset, Kentucky, for any reason. There had to be a mistake. But Cranston wasn't a man that made mistakes.

"Strange, in the year you've been here, no one has questioned your arrival, nor followed you. It struck me as rather funny that this woman arrived only hours after you met your sister's plane on Hickley's private airstrip and collected a passenger."

John crossed his arms over his chest and restrained the heavy curse hovering on his lips. Hell, he didn't need this.

"What business is it of yours if someone claiming to be my fiancée is in town?" John tilted his head and stared back at the other man.

"Well, normally, I really wouldn't care," Cranston assured him. "But the last name *Genoa* tipped me off. Were you aware your ex-fiancée and her family were suspected of being involved with one of the largest crime families in the nation?"

Fuck!

John rubbed at the bridge of his nose and couldn't imagine why he wasn't surprised.

"No, Cranston, I had no idea."

Cranston nodded in reply. "I had your family investigated rather heavily once I met your sister." He grinned at some memory. "She's a hell of a woman, but I had a job to do at the time. Of course, this was before your engagement. The thing I learned was that the Walker family was incredibly loyal, not to mention patriotic. When I learned you were engaged to the Genoa woman, I was rather surprised."

"It didn't last too long," John pointed out mockingly.

"Because Sierra saved your sorry ass," Cranston grunted. "There were agents with the Office of Homeland Security at the restaurant that night who had Ms. Genoa under surveillance. The reports were fairly precise. Once I checked further into it, I learned that Ms. Lucas had been instrumental not just in breaking up your engagement but also in stopping a much-needed infusion of financial prosperity into the Genoa family, which would have boosted them back into the good graces of their extended family. Walker capital would have been used to launder some rather dirty money."

John could only shake his head. "Cranston, what makes you think that even criminals can't marry for love?"

"Of course they can." Cranston stared back at him as though surprised. "They just don't normally survive it. Which works out for all us hardworking law enforcement officials."

"I should have taken my uncle up on his offer to move to California," John breathed out roughly, though he knew he could have never done so. Hell, he loved Somerset, especially on the days he didn't have to deal with Cranston.

He was learning things tonight he didn't really want to know. Things he really didn't give a damn about.

"Marlena is no longer a part of my life, Cranston," John pointed out.

"That explains why she was in town then, correct?" Cranston's smile was benign, almost innocent.

No, that didn't explain anything.

"She did leave this afternoon," Timothy went on to say. "But not before, as I understand it, she made a trip here, to the marina."

Thank God, Sierra had slept the afternoon away, and John was certain there was no way Marlena could have gotten the information that Sierra was there. No one knew she was there but the Mackays, and they wouldn't tell anyone, he was certain of that.

"What's going on, John?" Cranston asked then, his tone completely serious. "There's reports from Boston that Ms. Lucas was attacked after you left town, nearly raped, beaten. She disappeared after being taken in by your family, and now a member of the Genoa family is here, looking for you. After a year? Tell me, boy, do you believe in coincidence of that sort?"

Hell no, he didn't, but it couldn't be anything else, could it?

"You think Marlena was behind Sierra's attack?"

"Personally, I wouldn't put it past her to have made the attack," Cranston grunted. "But Ms. Lucas seems certain her attacker was male. My point is, your ex-fiancée is here, after a year, within hours of Ms. Lucas's arrival. With her connections, finding your friend wouldn't have been hard, John. Find you, they find Sierra. A ten-year-old could have figured that one out."

"And why the hell does this even concern you?" John asked even as he let the information turn over in his mind and considered the possibilities. "Why are you involved in this, Cranston?"

The other man breathed out heavily. "It's damned hard to

retire, John. I see things. That was always my strength in
Homeland Security. I could take coincidences and pin them
together, and I could see the links when there didn't appear
to be any." He stared back at John soberly. "My gut's rioting
here. It has been ever since I recognized Marlena Genoa
walking into the Mackay Café in town and learned who she
was asking for. Her arrival here isn't a good thing."

And John couldn't defend her. He couldn't protest. He
couldn't defend her and try to claim Marlena wasn't capable
of being involved in something as sinister as the attack on
Sierra. He knew Marlena's vindictiveness. If he added that to
her possible criminal connections . . .

"Why come here herself if she has all these connections?"
John asked Cranston, frowning as he tried to make the pieces
of the puzzle fit in his mind.

"As I said, her family has lost financially, which lowered
their cache within the family. Her marriage to you would
have fixed that by providing a way to either launder money,
or to embezzle funds to finance smaller investments for the
family. Either way, her family could have moved back into
the working stream. She's doing her own dirty work because
she has no choice. If she's like other members of her family,
then she's after revenge now. The other girl is winning."

John snorted at that. "This isn't fucking high school,
Cranston."

"No, it's real life, and where the hell do you think games
like this begin, if not in school? These women learn from
preschool how to manipulate and play payback. Don't imagine life doesn't often imitate those school yard games."

Making it fit in his head wasn't so easy, though. Marlena
wasn't above social revenge, but staging an attack against
Sierra?

"So you're saying Marlena arranged the attack to get back
at Sierra for informing me of her affair with Gerard? Why
wait for a year after I break off the engagement then?"

"I'm saying my gut is burning," Timothy growled. "I see
her, hear her questioning people about you and any guests
you might have living with you, and things start adding up in

my head. And I'm a nosy bastard, John. Nosy and damned particular about things like this. Somerset is my home now, and I look after what's mine. That means you and that innocent little girl you now have sleeping in your boat. From what I've learned, she's a damned fine woman. Women are to be protected, JW, and that's our job. That's a job I take damned seriously."

He'd heard Cranston had taken Pulaski County as his own, and he was driving both Sheriff Mayes as well as Somerset's chief of police, Alex Jansen, crazy with his interference. Crazy, because he was invariably right. And invariably, Cranston's issues always revolved around women.

John pushed his fingers through his hair wearily. "If this is what is actually going on, then what's the threat level I'm looking at?"

Cranston tapped his fingers against the arm of his chair. "The Genoa family is cash poor, but there are still a few favors they can draw on. Not many, mind you, and contract killings cost money. I'd say if she doesn't try to do something herself, then the person working with her will owe her a personal favor of sorts. My advice is to keep Ms. Lucas out of sight, and if you come in contact with Ms. Genoa, see how hard you can piss her off. Women are women, my friend, and many of them will always give themselves away in anger."

John shook his head. Marlena was cool; hell, she was cold as ice. Getting her to crack wouldn't be that easy.

"There's no chance she'll simply give up," John mused aloud.

"Not a Genoa," Timothy grunted. "She's here to do the footwork, then whoever's helping her will strike. We need to find out who's helping her, why, and put a stop to it."

"And we do this how?" John asked curiously.

"I've always found a Glock works really well." He sounded way too serious, and John found the idea much too appealing.

"I like the idea, but I think if we both want to stay out of prison, we come up with another idea."

Timothy chuckled as he rose from his seat. "I knew I'd like you, JW."

"Keep calling me JW and I'll kill you for sure," John warned him.

Timothy only gave another short laugh. "Since we can't kill them, we're going to have to prove conspiracy and intent. That will be harder. We have help, though. The Mackay boys are looking for a little excitement. Marriage suits them, but I think they miss the adrenaline a little bit, too. I have a former agent or two in the area. We'll work on them. Sit tight a day or so and I'll see what I can come up with."

John's brows rose. Strangely, he couldn't remember asking Cranston to handle this for him. But he knew the things he had heard about the former special agent. He'd let the little Leprechaun do his thing for the time being. John had a woman to protect. His woman, and learning about Sierra was more important than hunting up Marlena.

"How do you intend to handle it, Cranston?" Curiosity was getting the best of him.

"By doing what I do best." Cranston's smile was innocent, amused, and frankly terrifying. "By doing what I do best."

By manipulating anyone and everyone involved or who could be involved, John thought. That was what Cranston did best. That was a damned scary proposition if even half of what John had heard about him was correct.

"Cranston, you're retired, and you're still trying to protect the world?" John would have been amused if he wasn't fully aware of exactly how dedicated Timothy Cranston had always been to justice.

The former agent paused and stared out into the darkened lake for long moments before speaking. "I had a daughter once." He spoke low, his voice filled with a haunted, aching loss. "I had a wife, and you know, they loved me." He turned back to John. "I'm rumpled, a smart-ass, and when I met my wife, God knew I was fast on my way to becoming an alcoholic, but she saved me. And my daughter made me realize the reason for my existence. When she was born, my wife made me swear that no matter what happened, I'd never let myself sink again." He shook his head as he took a deep breath. "Monsters took my ladies from me, John. Men who had no respect for the law or even humanity. I swore to my beautiful wife I'd never get drunk again, but I didn't swear I wouldn't wipe as many of the monsters as possible out of existence. That's what I live for. That's all I live for. Because if I kill myself, then I don't have a chance of meeting my ladies in heaven, now do I?"

With that, Cranston turned and moved to the stairs.

"That's why you're here," John said before he left. "That's why you stay in Somerset, because the Mackays are family now, aren't they?"

He shook his head. "No. I'm here because a Mackay married an agent that so reminded me of my daughter that I couldn't help but love her as one. I stay here because there's work to be done here, and because the Mackays allow me to be a part of their lives. Without them, I don't know if I could keep that promise to my wife once the Department cut me loose. That's why I'm here."

For a man as rumpled, lazy, and clumsy looking as Timothy Cranston, he moved with a silence John could only envy as he left the houseboat, and left John with more to ponder than what he felt he actually needed.

He wondered if the Mackays were aware of the reason why Timothy Cranston had settled in Somerset. They were tolerant of him for the most part; they liked the rabid, calculating little bastard, there was no doubt. But John had a feeling they had no idea the true reason why the other man was still here, poking his nose in their lives and calling himself "Unca Timmy" to their children as he slid their parents mocking looks.

And now it seemed Cranston wanted to adopt him and Sierra as well.

Shaking his head with a rueful laugh, John turned to make his way back to the interior of the houseboat when a movement on the bank caught his eye. It was subtle, a gleam of metal where there shouldn't be. A small dot of light, almost like that of a pair of night-vision binoculars. It was just there for a second, though, and then it was gone.

A trick of the light? He'd seen it before over the past months and that was the explanation he had given himself. What if it was something more?

Moving to the steps, John descended them quickly until he was once again in the living area of the houseboat.

Sierra was still sleeping peacefully in the bed, her thick, heavy lashes cushioned against her upper cheek, the long, thick strands of black curls falling around her face and shoulders. She looked like an angel. So damned innocent, and so sexy at the same time.

The oversized T-shirt and shorts she wore gave her a girlish appearance, and that innocence. He grimaced, a flash of something flitting through his mind as he frowned. Rising between her thighs, fitting himself to her?

He shook his head. The fantasy of that first night, the night he had nearly had her, still tormented him. There was no figuring it out quite yet, though.

Locking the doors and pulling the drapes, he moved to the back of the houseboat and the small office he used the guest bedroom for. There, he edged the side of the curtain aside and watched the bank closely.

Shadows shifted and moved as his gaze narrowed. That tingle at the back of his neck that he'd acquired as a Marine kicked in.

There was definitely someone there, definitely a threat. And it had been there far longer than Sierra's arrival. Only tonight had that knowledge that it could become a threat begun to tingle at his nape.

Because Sierra was there.

He pulled his cell phone from his hip and hit speed dial.

"Dawg." Dawg Mackay answered on the first ring.

"I have eyes on me," he said quietly.

"Where?" Dawg was instantly alert.

"At the rear, at the nine o' clock position. Meet me there in the morning."

"Fuck morning," Dawg growled. "I'll call the others, we'll be there within minutes."

"And they'll be gone," John guessed. "I have a situation here, Dawg. Just catching whoever or whatever watches won't fix it. But we can use them."

There was a long moment of silence. "I'll call Cranston."

"Cranston just left but call him. Slip in tomorrow morning separately. Let's do it all at once, or Sierra will never be safe."

And nothing mattered but her safety.

Seven

Sierra awoke to strong arms holding her, the warmth of John behind her, his head resting against the top of hers, his legs entwined with hers.

It was definitely unusual. She had never slept with a man before John, and she was almost frightened at how easy it was becoming to get used to it.

Not once had she awakened wondering who was behind her, or terrified that the nightmares were returning. Not once had she felt uncomfortable, or that she shouldn't be here. Unfortunately, a part of her felt as though she were at home.

She turned slowly, trying not to awaken him, but wanting to see his face.

The laugh lines at the sides of his eyes hadn't been there before he left Boston. Come to think of it, it had been years since she had truly seen John happy, until now. He laughed now. Amusement and fun gleamed in his eyes as it had so long ago. Before he had gone to the Marines. Before he had returned from blood and death.

As she had noticed before, he was stronger, tighter, broader. He was, on the outside, the man she had always known existed on the inside.

Lifting her hand, using only the tips of her fingers, she slowly pushed back a long, thick strand of hair that had fallen over his face.

He looked more arrogant than ever before, she thought in amusement, and John Walker Jr. had arrogance in abundance before he ever left Boston. He was more relaxed here, though, less austere and critical. He was the man who had stolen her heart years ago as a young girl.

As she watched him, the hunger for him rose. It was a natural extension of any thought of John. That need that filtered through her body, heated her flesh, and left her aching for him. She felt it in her breasts, in her erect nipples. That sensitivity that only arose whenever John was present, whenever she thought of him.

The heat that built there worked its way lower as well. It heated her clit, burned in her pussy, and clenched in her womb. From there, she felt the sensitivity working beneath her flesh, filling her with a hunger for him that she knew would never be completely sated.

She trailed her fingers from his hair to a broad, muscled shoulder. Lightly. She kept her touch light, wanting to feel the subtle heat and texture of his flesh rather than the well-honed iron beneath.

She had always loved his body, but she loved it even more now. It was a rich, golden bronze. It was heated, pulsing, and hard like living iron.

As her fingers roamed over his shoulder, his lashes drifted open. Sleepy violet eyes stared back at her for a second before he turned slowly to his back.

An invitation. An invitation to touch as she pleasured, to pleasure as she wanted. He was giving her carte blanche to his body and her senses exploded with chaotic hunger at the realization.

Moving over him, she couldn't help but ache for his kiss

now. A kiss she could measure, control, relish. Her lips lowered to his, brushed against them, and her entire body clenched in need as they responded beneath her.

The kiss flamed, but rather than blazing out of control, it only began to burn brighter, hotter, while maintaining the need for a slow, easy caress.

Lips stroked, tongues licked, tasted, and built the desire rising between them.

Touching him was like being in the center of a firestorm, protected, yet awash with the heat. It was like drawing in that heat, filling her soul with it.

The taste of him infused her senses, his kisses growing hungrier as she felt the need rioting inside her.

Dragging her lips back from his, Sierra drew them down the rough flesh of his neck as her hands stroked his hard abs. She nipped and licked, tasted and enjoyed him as she had never enjoyed anything in her life.

She felt as though she were becoming drunk on him. Each taste of him was more intoxicating than the last. When his hands threaded into her hair, his body arching against her, the knowledge she was bringing him pleasure amped up her own arousal.

Her nails scraped along his thighs, feeling them tighten beneath her touch as her lips trailed down his abs. She knew where she was going, she knew what she wanted.

His control was shot. John could feel the last threads of restraint beginning to slip through his fingertips despite the battle to hold on to it.

He'd seen Sierra's face, her expression as she began kissing her way down his body. She wasn't just pleasuring him, hell, she was finding pleasure in each touch she was giving him. He'd never seen that expression on a woman's face before. He'd never known of a time that a woman had actually known pleasure just from touching him.

The only way to hold on to that control was simply to watch her, even though he knew that was the fastest way to lose his control.

Swollen lips sipped from the flesh of his abdomen as her

nails pricked at his thighs. A delicate pink tongue lapped at the flesh just a breath above the rigid head of his cock as it rose from between his thighs.

Damn, he wanted her. Needed her. But even more, he wanted to watch her face, watch her pleasure.

As her adventurous little tongue licked over the wide, throbbing crest and stole his breath, he watched her eyes darken, her face flushing further. Electric pleasure zipped through his body, sizzling up his spine as his hands tightened in her hair.

Hell, this was torture. It was the worst torture he had ever allowed himself to endure.

Her hot little tongue lapped at the head of his dick before her lips parted and drew it, but only momentarily, into the heated depths of her mouth.

As she released him, a tight grimace pulled at his lips as his fingers tightened further in her hair.

"You're killing me," he groaned.

A low, light moan vibrated against his shaft as she licked her way lower, then back to the tight head.

When her lips drew him inside her mouth once again, he swore he nearly lost his mind. She sucked him deep instantly, as though the need for his taste overwhelmed her.

Her fingers cupped his balls timidly, but that hesitancy was sexier than the touch of the most experienced woman who had ever been there. The pleasure of it, the sensations, the sight of her face, her lips surrounding his cock, was exquisite. Hell, the pleasure went so far beyond just the physical sensation of it that he wondered if he could ever make sense of it.

"Damn, Sierra, you're making me crazy." His fingers tightened in her hair once again, holding her in place for just a second as his hips arched slowly.

Then she smacked him.

John jerked back, blinked at the sting in his abs, and her little hand still pressed to it as her head jerked up.

"This is my treat." The look in her eyes was determined, fierce, and hungry.

John stared back at her, his eyes narrowing.

"I woke up first," she informed him. "I started this. So leave me alone to have my fun."

Carefully, he laid his hands on the bed, palms down to allow his fingers to curl into the sheets when the pressure became too great.

Sierra proceeded to make him insane.

Her lips and tongue moved over the head of his cock like a hungry sensualist, taking him as he fought to keep his hips from arching, tried to keep from thrusting deeper.

Ah, hell. She was going to destroy him.

Her fingers played with his balls, weighed them, stroked them as her lips and tongue wreaked havoc on his dick, and there was nothing he could do to ease the torture, the pressure. She refused to let him.

This was her turn, but his turn would come. As he watched her, watched the dampness of her mouth as it lifted from his dick, watched her lips redden, her eyes glaze with hunger, he promised himself he would drive her just as crazy, very soon. In ways she couldn't imagine.

Slowly, with exquisite relish, her lips lifted from his straining cock as she stared back at him with drowsy eyes.

"I've dreamed of this," she whispered as she moved back up his body. "Dreamed of every second of this."

"Payback's hell," he groaned.

She smiled a sexy siren's smile as long black curls cascaded around her body. Easing up his body like a sleek little cat, satin skin brushing against him, the heat of her pussy glancing his hard shaft until she was straddling him, she blew his mind with her sensuality.

"In your arms, payback would be paradise," she assured him, hips shifting, the heat of her pussy nudging at the wide head of his cock.

"Ah, hell." He was going to lose himself in this, he could feel it. Hell, no other woman had ever taken him like this, had ever loved him like this.

Pleasure tore through his body as she shifted again, the blazing heat of her intimate flesh beginning to enfold his erection, tender muscles working over the head as she moved, taking him by slow increments.

A firestorm of sensations overtook his body. His balls were tortured with the effort to hold back, his cock straining.

"Where's the condoms?" she whispered as she eased up again. "Oh, God, John, I don't know if I can pull off you in time."

Her body was shuddering as his hands moved, trembling for the drawer of the nightstand. He'd found one earlier. A single fucking rubber, and he knew damned good and well one would never be enough.

Tearing the package open as she lifted, he rolled the latex quickly down his cock, then gripped her hips and waited. It was like waiting for death and birth, and his patience was wearing thin.

But hers was as well.

She eased down.

She fucking destroyed him.

His dick jerked, throbbed, sweat popped out on his brow, and a thousand fingers of sensation began to race over his flesh.

He couldn't handle it.

Bucking beneath her, he drove in deeper, expecting that very feminine smack once again. Instead, she cried out in pleasure, the sound wrapping around him and driving him harder.

Tightening his hands on her hips, he fucked her deeper, feeling her press down on him hard and fast as he surged upward. She kept up with him. Thrust for thrust, her pussy milking his cock as he stretched the inner walls until they created a snug, intimate little embrace around the desperately hard shaft.

He wanted to fuck her forever, but first he had to hold on long enough to simply feel her coming around him. He couldn't forever, despite the agony at the thought of losing the pleasure enveloping him now.

What she did to him should be illegal.

Rising, she sat astride him, that small sexy little curl of

her lips going straight to his balls. He swore he wouldn't last another thirty seconds.

Then she moved.

"Fuck, Sierra," he groaned, his neck arching as she began to ride him with a smooth thrusting motion of her hips that he knew neither of them would survive for long.

His hands slid to her buttocks, gripping the rounded globes and guiding her motions, entranced by the fact that she wasn't adept at this, simply adventurous. And that was all the more arousing.

They moved against each other, their thrust and parry escalating in seconds. Watching her face, he knew the moment her release began. The way her eyes dazed at the same time her thrusts became jerky. The way her pussy began to ripple and tighten, the smooth, heated flow of additional juices, and then the ragged, tormented cry that tore from her lips.

She was there, coming around him, falling against his chest as he continued to thrust inside her, to take her, to fuck her past the last ecstatic shudder before he gave in to his own release.

A release that felt as though it was pouring from his soul. Arching hard and deep and inside her, he heard her name slip past his lips, felt his body shake, tremble, and then the harsh, electrifying pulses of sensation as they began to tear rapidly through his body.

And just as he feared.

He lost himself in her.

Eight

She was tearing him apart. John watched as Sierra dressed an hour later, her gray eyes pensive, too somber as she stared in the mirror over the dresser and carefully smoothed moisturizer over her face.

There was that edge of fear in her eyes that he hated seeing, the same edge he saw in her gaze as he carefully tracked the healing bruises against her flesh before allowing her to leave the bed.

Long, black curls rippled down her back, the thick strands gleaming like silk against her pale skin. He wanted to get her on the upper deck, naked, slicked with sunscreen, and basking beneath the summer sun.

The sun was a healing balm; it would heat her pretty flesh, darken it, and give her a look even more exotic than what she had now. First, he would have to move the houseboat for the day, though. He had one of the far docks, one of the most private, but it wasn't private enough to keep preying eyes from watching her naked body.

He hadn't told her they were being watched. It wasn't something he was looking forward to telling her. She'd come here for safety, and the thought that the danger she had faced in Boston had followed her here made him homicidal.

"We're having company soon," he told her as she drew a pair of light cotton pants over her legs.

She paused as she picked up a dark blue T-shirt.

"What kind of company?" she asked carefully.

"This morning, some friends of mine and their children," he told her. "Rowdy's cousins, wives, and infants. Rogue's not back from her honeymoon yet so just the Mackays. It's like a madhouse when they all get together, so be prepared. Their wives are hellions, their children are adorable little angels, and they'll pump you for information, brag on their husbands, and decide who and where to begin matchmaking. So don't let them know we're sleeping together. It'll give them something to wonder about." He grinned with a wink in her direction. There was no way to hide the fact that he was sleeping with her. He'd kissed her lovely neck just a little too hard earlier, leaving the faintest red mark that he considered a stamp of supreme ownership.

Sierra rolled her eyes. "Dummy. As if they'll believe that one."

At least she was calling him "dummy" again. The playful little insult had always assured him that he was in her good graces and once again the love of her life.

He'd missed that, he realized. As he realized only just now how the playful little name had always made him feel. Sierra didn't call anyone else "dummy." As completely immature as it sounded, even to himself, John had to admit it gave him a bit of hope.

Hell, he had no intention of letting her leave him. She was his. He just had to convince her of that, and of the fact that it didn't matter to him how many men she had been with before him.

He almost frowned at that thought as some part of his mind flashed back to that drunken night and the too hazy memory of pressing inside her.

Wishful thinking? He was starting to wonder about that.

"So how long are your friends staying?" she asked, drawing him out of his musings.

"An hour or so." Pushing his fingers through his damp hair to tidy it, he watched as she drew a wide-toothed comb through hers. "The doctor will be here to check you out later this afternoon. While he's here, explain the problem with the medication. He should give you something that doesn't make you so drowsy."

Sierra faced him as she arched her brow mockingly. "When did you get so bossy, John? You're starting to sound like my father."

He didn't like that. Sierra almost grinned at the dark look he flashed her.

"Don't get sassy, lollipop, or I might have to retaliate by talking to the doctor myself."

"Go ahead." Shrugging in unconcern, Sierra laid the comb on the dresser and faced him fully. "If you're going to treat me like a child, then you may as well do it fully. Since when did you begin believing that I couldn't take care of the simplest things by myself?"

Was that surprise in his deep, brilliant violet-blue gaze?

"I thought no such thing, Sierra." His voice was quiet, sincere, sending a flare of remorse racing through her. "I was concerned. No more. But if you don't take care of it, then you'll be proving your own point. Won't you?"

Damn him. The remorse chilled quickly enough in the face of his arrogance.

"Okay, lollipop, you have about ten minutes to finish dressing and bring your perky little ass downstairs if you want to meet the babies. Trust me, they're well worth being on time for."

With that, he left the bedroom and moved quickly down the stairs, leaving Sierra to stare after him in confusion. He was too playful, she decided. John had always had a nice sense of humor, but she swore the man he was now was joking more often than he was serious.

This playfulness was going to drive her insane, though,

because she had no idea how to handle it, or how to handle him.

She finished dressing quickly, as he advised, wondering at the Mackay family that John seemed to have made friends with so quickly.

He hadn't been a man that made friends easily before. She had seen when she met Rowdy that John was close to these people, though.

His sister Candace said that John had found his roots. That he had finally found a place where he felt he belonged. Sierra wanted to see that place. She wanted to meet those people.

Moving down the staircase moments later, she could hear the murmur of conversation, the sweet, melodic gurgle of infants. Not just one, she saw as she stepped into the kitchen area and looked into the living space, but four. Four approximately twelve-month-old toddlers with thick, thick black hair and varying shades of devilish green eyes. And all four turned to stare at her, just as their protective mothers and fathers did.

What a very interesting group. The women were so diverse at first glance, ranging in height, hair color, as well as expression. Of the four men, only one didn't have black hair, but he looked just as hard, just as arrogant, as the other three.

"Sierra." John's voice held an odd tone, one she had never heard when he spoke her name before. "Come, meet my friends."

The introductions were made easily as John placed his hand firmly at her lower back and led her into the thick of the group to the empty recliner that faced the sectional couch where Chaya, Kelly, and Christa Mackay sat with Janey Jansen. Janey was a Mackay before she married Somerset's chief of police, Alex Jansen, the man who stood beside his wife's seat, his gray eyes watching Sierra curiously as the Mackay cousins watched her with varying degrees of curiosity and, strangely, acceptance.

It was the tiniest of the four babes who drew her attention, though. Barely walking, her spring green dress flaring around her fragile body, she toddled over and offered Sierra a bite of a baby biscuit that she held in her hand.

The biscuit was well gnawed, gooey at the tip, and the smile the little girl aimed up at her stole her heart.

"Do you have goodies, sweetheart?" Sierra whispered as she leaned close, her arms crossed on her knees as the little girl chortled up at her. "I bet it tastes very good."

It was offered again, this time more solemnly.

With a grin, Sierra leaned close, pretended to take a bite, then grabbed a quick little kiss from a chubby cheek.

And the child was well satisfied. She laughed, held on to Sierra's knee, and turned back to her mother as though she had just undertaken a miraculous feat and jabbered a string of unintelligible words with lots of "ma-ma" mixed in.

"And that little charmer is Janey and Alex's, Erin Jansen. She's the baby of the family. Behind her is Natches and Chaya's daughter, Bliss." Bliss looked back at her solemnly, as though she were considering every nuance of the moment before she went back to the toy she was playing with. "In the yellow dress is Dawg and Christa's little tomboy, Laken." The baby playing with the little toy truck. Sierra couldn't help but grin. "And the lazy one over there sleeping is Rowdy and Kelly's, Annette." Rosy cheeks, black hair, and a perfect little baby face, Annette was snoozing through all the commotion from a padded spot at her mother's feet. "And here's Faisal and Timothy Cranston. Faisal is Natches and Chaya's adopted son, and Timothy is the pest no one can seem to get rid of."

Sierra smiled back at the young man of Middle Eastern heritage, who looked perhaps twenty-three or -four years old, but it was Timothy Cranston that held her gaze the longest.

He looked rumpled, his thinning hair mussed, his brown eyes somber and intense yet shaded with a hint of mockery. He was older, she guessed late forties, and the lines at his mouth, forehead, and lips bespoke a man who had known far too much grief.

"Mr. Cranston, it's nice to meet you." He reminded her of her father.

Timothy's head tipped to the side as a small smile played about his lips. Stepping carefully over babies, diaper bags, and toys, he offered his hand.

The handshake was gentle, his gaze respectful.

"John's mentioned you a time or two," he stated. "He didn't tell us how pretty you are."

Erin jabbered again in excitement before Sierra could reply, her arms reaching up as her animated little face creased into one huge smile.

"And there's my girl." Cranston's voice softened, became filled with emotion as he picked the little girl up off her feet and cuddled her against his chest. "Unca Timmy missed you, sweetie."

Unca Timmy?

Sierra looked around and saw the looks the others were giving him.

"You'd have to know Cranston to understand." John chuckled. "You'll figure it out."

She rather doubted it, but she let the memories soak in rather than fighting them. The women were a friendly bunch, talking easily about far more than babies. The conversations shifted until she found herself locked in a lively political debate as she noticed John and the others slipping out to the deck then up the outside staircase.

"Ignore them," Kelly, her blue eyes shimmering with laughter, advised her. "They always escape when we all get together."

"Unless there's food involved." Chaya rolled her expressive, dark gray eyes as Christa laughed over the comment.

"John says he's known you most of your life," Chaya commented. "He's told us your favorite food, favorite drink, favorite movie, and how you came by those bruises. Tell me, Ms. Lucas, are you using our John for safety then running out on him, or do you have something more permanent in mind?"

Sierra blinked back at her. The woman looked like an interrogator now rather than a mother, a friend, or a wife.

"Perhaps that's a question you should ask John," she stated as she stared back at the other woman directly. "Funny, the only proposal I've ever heard come from his lips was for another woman."

"And I understand you took care of that one right quickly," Chaya pointed out as the other women looked on in amusement.

"She was cheating on him." Sierra narrowed her eyes at the other woman. "Do you have a problem with me, Mrs. Mackay?"

"Only if you intend on breaking John's heart," Chaya informed her.

"Then, we may all have a problem with that," Kelly chimed in.

"And if he breaks mine instead?" she asked. "Excuse me, ladies, but I truly don't think you have anything to worry about where John's concerned. He's a really big boy, and trust me, he takes care of himself very well."

She wondered at these new friends of John's even as she wondered if anyone had cared when he had broken her heart.

"We would care if your heart was broken as well, Sierra," Christa stated then, drawing Sierra's attention. "We know John, though. We know how he's spoken of you over the past year, and we know you're important to him. Forgive us for being protective."

Sierra stared back at her and for a moment wished she had friends such as these four women. Women who might have understood, who might have supported her those months when losing John had hurt so much.

"I have no designs on your friend," she told them all clearly. "He's the one that left Boston, not me. Now, I think it might be a rather good idea if we change the subject."

John eased away from the open doorway and glanced back at the men who had followed him down from the top deck, intending to move to the office by the quickest route of straight through the room.

Instead, he turned, moved quickly to the side of the houseboat, and made his way to the back.

Son of a bitch, he'd heard the pain in her voice and he hated it, just as he was certain the others had heard as well. He was coming to the conclusion that something more than he remembered had definitely happened that night in Boston when she had come to his apartment.

He knew Sierra. He knew her like he had never known another woman, and he knew a simple case of him passing out on her wouldn't have produced this result.

"Boy, you have something to fix with that girl," Timothy muttered as John pushed open the glass sliding doors off the back deck.

"Let it go, Cranston," he ordered.

"We're going to back him this time, John," Dawg stated, his deep voice quiet, intense. "That girl sounded as lost as a whipped puppy, and you know that's not going over real well."

The four men behind him were protective, especially of women. As John understood it, they always had been, even during their wild, often lascivious pasts.

"Let's concentrate on finding out who the hell is trying to kill her, then I can concentrate on making damned sure I don't lose her," he growled as he turned back to the other six. "Can you give me that much?"

They stared back at him with varying degrees of suspicion.

"We'll give you that time, JW," Cranston drawled. "And if she runs back to Boston in tears, then we'll see just how hard we can kick your damned ass."

John didn't doubt that in the least.

"Here's what we have," Dawg stepped in. "There were definitely prints on the shoreline, though someone tried to brush them out. By the position our watcher was sitting in, they were watching your boat, and they were there for a while. One set of prints, definitely male, I'd say about a size ten, maybe eleven, it was hard to be sure with the deliberate attempt to erase them."

"Ms. Genoa is still in town as well," Timothy informed him. "She was going into the Mackay Café for lunch as I headed here."

"She's been there every day for the past four days," Faisal broke in, his tone hushed. "She asks questions about John Walker and if he has a lover, who his friends are, though many simply shrug, and others tell her to ask him herself." Faisal was likely one of those "others" if his mocking smile was anything to go by.

"No one knows you have anyone on the boat with you, that I can tell," Rowdy told him. "There's no gossip about it at the marina. Most people here really don't give a damn, but I doubt they'd lie if asked, if they have seen her."

John shook his head. "She's been inside so far. The doctor should be here later this afternoon to check her out, then maybe it would be a good idea to pull out for a while."

"Not yet." Natches shook his head then. "Dawg and Christa are keeping Bliss for me tonight, Chaya and I are going to do a little midnight hunting. Just keep her inside, keep the curtains pulled, and we'll do the rest."

"I hate this." He pushed his fingers restlessly through his hair. "I want to catch the bastard myself, but damn if I want to leave her alone long enough to do it."

He would trust the other men to look after her at any time, but he knew Sierra would start asking questions if they did. And he didn't want the fight that would come with it. He had a very bad feeling she would head straight back to Boston if she knew the trouble had followed her.

"Let us take care of this, John," Natches stated, his voice hard. "If things start to look dangerous, we'll reassess then. Right now, we're just watching. Agreed?"

At any other time, John would have never trusted that statement from a wild-assed Mackay, but he knew since they'd found the women who held their hearts, each of them was more careful.

He nodded slowly.

"And while we're all watching your back, why not see what you can do to hold on to that girl," Dawg ordered him in a slow, lazy drawl. "She suits you, John. She suits you real good."

And she did. That was something John knew all too well. Sierra suited him far too much.

Nine

She had always suited him.

John watched Sierra with the wives and children of the friends who were more like brothers to him. He'd always fought that knowledge, and now, he simply couldn't understand why. He'd wasted so many years of his life running from the one woman he knew now was meant to be his world, and he didn't even know why.

A bachelor's self-preservation perhaps. It was damned hard to acknowledge that a woman can strip your soul down to its base level, but she could rebuild it as well.

As the boat emptied of the chaotic Mackay clan and friends, John acknowledged the things he hadn't wanted to face before the night Sierra had forced the breakup of his engagement to Marlena.

He almost grinned at the thought. She had no idea that she'd done him a great favor that night, and it had taken him a while to realize it, too, he admitted.

It hadn't been the loss of Marlena that had affected him so severely, though. It had been the realization that Sierra would risk their friendship, risk everything basically, to save him from a marriage doomed to failure.

He had known that night. That unacknowledged part of himself he had hidden from for so long had known that not just his bachelor days were over, but his heart was caught. And it was caught by a tiny bit of a woman who had been a part of his life for as long as she had been alive.

Securing the houseboat, doors locked, drapes drawn closed, he made his way to the bedroom, where Sierra had already retired.

Stepping into the large, open room, he was caught by the quiet pain in her face as she sat in the recliner next to the wide, securely draped windows, and stared at the dark material.

"If I weren't here, you'd have the curtains back and the windows open," she said softly. "The breeze from the lake would drift inside and you'd be at peace."

"I'm at peace now, Sierra. It's not open windows or a breeze that brings that peace, baby. It's what's inside a man or a woman's soul."

And how the hell had he ever realized that?

"You'll never move back to Boston, will you?" she whispered, her gray eyes lifting, her somber expression filled with a particular sadness. "When this is finished, you'll stay here. This is your home now."

"It's my home now," he agreed as he moved across the room and took a seat in the chair that sat facing her. "But I'll visit."

Her lips tightened as a small, almost hidden flinch crossed her expression.

"I never truly thought you'd stay away forever," she said. "I thought you'd come back. That one day, someone would tell me you had moved back into your penthouse, that you were back in the office. That you were home." She rubbed at the fingernails of one hand with the pads of the fingers of the other. "That's not going to happen, is it?"

He shook his head slowly. "I'd never be happy there again, Sierra," he told her. "I was never happy there before, I just didn't know it. You were never happy there, either."

She looked up at him in surprise. "It's home, John. I was raised there."

"Were you happy there, Sierra?" He leaned closer. "Do you have friends there?" He placed his fingers over her lips as she started to protest. "Who did you go to when I left? Who did you go to, Sierra, when I passed out on you just after penetrating you?"

She paled.

John had suspected, but he hadn't wanted to admit he'd been such a complete fucking fool.

He cupped her face gently. "I was completely drunk."

She swallowed tightly and the distress in her pretty eyes tore at his heart.

Pushing the wild blue-back ringlets back from her face, John saw the indecision, the fears.

"What did I do to you that night, Sierra?" he asked gently. "Did I hurt you?"

"Physically?" Her lips thinned. "No, John, you didn't hurt me."

But he didn't remember, and she wondered if he would even believe she had been a virgin.

She didn't want to talk to him right now. There was too much inside her, too many emotions she didn't want to deal with tonight.

"Why are you keeping all the curtains closed?" She changed the subject, stared around the room then back at John as she fought the questions in his eyes.

"Perhaps I'd prefer no one sees or hears the pleasure I give you." His lips curled in amusement.

Shaking her head, she stared around again. "We don't have sex twenty-four-seven, John."

She wanted the truth. She sensed it, she could feel it, just as she sensed the fact that he had disappeared with his friends that afternoon for a reason.

He watched her thoughtfully for several long moments as Sierra wondered if he would continue to try to lie to her.

"I think the boat is being watched. I want to keep you

hidden for a few more days until we figure out exactly who is watching and why."

The knowledge, though she expected it, was still a shock to her. She stared back at him, fighting the sense of impending panic trying to rise inside her.

Someone was watching the boat, and had been only since her arrival.

"It wasn't just a random crime, was it?"

The attack had been planned. That meant someone specifically wanted to hurt her.

"This is my fault, Sierra," he said quietly. "I'm sorry."

"Your fault." She shook her head in confusion. "How can this be your fault?"

"I think you were targeted because of me. Someone wanted to get back at me."

She blinked at him. Get back at him?

"Who would want to get back at you?" She shook her head in confusion. "And why use me? John, do you realize how little sense that makes?"

She couldn't imagine any reason why anyone would think she could be used to strike back at John.

For a moment, she watched the banked fury in John's gaze and realized he wasn't joking. He meant what he was saying.

"John, that's insane." She shook her head at the thought of it. "There's no reason anyone would believe I could be used against you."

"Except Marlena."

Marlena? "But a man attacked me."

"A man I suspect she hired or was associated with," he stated. "Your attack has been investigated by a former agent of the Department of Homeland Security as well as Father. What was learned is that Marlena is connected to an organized crime family, Sierra. A very distant relation, but one all the same. Her marriage to me would have allowed her the chance to move up in that family. A renowned attorney, the Walker money, the backing of a highly respectable law firm. She was banking on that marriage for more than one reason."

There had always been rumors that the Genoa family was related to organized crime, but it had never been proven.

"Her father never seemed like a criminal," she whispered.

John's lips twisted with an edge of rueful amusement. "James Genoa is as honest as the day can be long, Sierra. That doesn't mean the rest of the family is, and it doesn't mean that Marlena isn't determined to recover the status she had before her father's losses several years before."

What the hell was going on?

Rising to her feet, Sierra paced across the room, staring at the draped windows, feeling closed in, feeling that same anger rising inside her as she realized that, once again, Marlena was winning. She had won the first time when she managed to get John's ring on her finger, the second time when John had taken Sierra and hadn't even remembered it.

She was winning now. She was winning because Sierra wouldn't have the chance to gain his heart. By the time this was over, he would be eager to rid himself of the trouble she brought to his life.

"Wonderful." Mockery filled her, surprising even herself with the depth of it. "Just what the hell I needed—Marlena Genoa screwing up my damned summer." She almost laughed. She would have laughed, but not even mockery could fire enough amusement for that. "You know, John, for as long as I've known her, she's been a pain in my ass!"

John stared back at Sierra in surprise. This wasn't exactly the response he'd expected. And he'd be damned if he'd ever seen Sierra quite this angry. Or this strong.

There was no fear, there were no tears.

"I thought it was a random crime." She threw her hands up as she turned back to him. "I couldn't imagine what I had done, or why it was happening to me. I couldn't figure it out. I couldn't figure out how I had been careless enough to allow myself to be targeted, you know?"

He tilted his head and stared back at her curiously.

"Random crime doesn't exactly happen that way, Sierra," he pointed out, trying to hide his amusement.

Here was his Sierra. Angry, yes, but that fire, that flame of stubborn determination, was back in her eyes. And there was something more.

Her hands were propped on her shapely hips. "To me, it would," she snapped back at him. "I'm careful. I rarely talk to strangers. I stick to what's safe. Haven't I always stuck to what was safe? Admit it."

"Oh, I admit that." He nodded. And it was the truth. Sierra was perhaps one of the most cautious people he knew, outside of her questionable choices in sex partners. As she said, she rarely took chances.

"She was cheating on you. She was marrying you for your money and whatever the hell she needed to get into some stupid crime family, and she was using your so-called best friend to screw you over, and she thinks I should pay for this?"

His brows lifted. "You always were one to catch on rather fast," he pointed out, holding back a chuckle.

Her eyes narrowed on him.

"How many men do you think I've been with, John?" she asked then.

The question surprised him.

"What does it matter?" It wasn't something he wanted to think about. He didn't give a damn how many men she had been with, and he didn't want to know.

"I deserve an answer to that question."

"At least three," he snapped back. "You weren't exactly trying to hide it when you were with Bobby Worthington. Jack Marsden, Martin Kincade. And if there were more, I don't want to know about it."

Sierra glared back at him. "Wrong."

"What the hell do you mean, wrong?" Damn her, she made him crazy. She could make him see red faster than any other woman in his life.

"Figure it out, dummy," she snapped back at him. "Because I'm not explaining it."

She wasn't explaining anything to anyone anymore. Bobby had started out as a friend until he told everyone he had slept with her. The other two had been close, she admitted. There had been a chance of a relationship with them, until for one reason or another, seeing John again had interfered in it. Reminded her of what she wanted, who she wanted, and she had broken it off.

Now she was paying for what she hadn't done.

Well, she wasn't paying for it, except for the fact that John would never believe she had been a virgin that night.

Damn Marlena Genoa. She had managed to completely fuck Sierra's life up and she hadn't even really tried until now.

John's arms crossed over his broad chest.

"You know, Sierra, I remember why you make me crazy," he growled. "You have to be one of the most stubborn women I've ever met."

"I'm not one of anything," she informed him heatedly. "Trust me, John, I am the most stubborn woman you'll ever meet, you've just never pissed me off enough to prove it until now."

"Hell, Sierra." He couldn't blame her. His own decisions had slashed back on her with a vengeance. "I can't even blame you for being pissed."

"And of course, you think it's because that cow Marlena might have hired someone to attack me." The complete disgust in her voice surprised him. "John, sometimes you're such a man that it's completely infuriating."

"What the fuck!" He couldn't hold back an incredulous laugh at this point. "What the hell else could you be pissed over? Sierra, dammit, if I'd had any idea you'd be hurt . . ."

Her hand slashed up, the flat of her palm held out to him so decisively that he simply shut up. Hell, his mother used that signal for complete silence. It was almost impossible to disobey.

"This has nothing to do with the attack and everything to do with something you wouldn't know if it slapped you right upside the face," she informed him, the haughtiness in her voice having what he imagined was the completely opposite effect of what she was going for.

Because he wasn't in the least chided. Hell, now his dick was straight up, as hard as iron, and throbbing with a force he'd never experienced before.

The need to possess her, to have her, to stoke that wild, brilliant light in those dark gray eyes was suddenly almost impossible to resist.

This effect she had on him was only growing stronger with no peak in sight. Each day, each hour, each moment he was with her, he only wanted her more.

"I'd know a lot of things without being slapped upside the face with it, lollipop."

Sierra caught the rakish sound of his voice, the carnal glimmer of hunger in those wild violet-blue eyes, and felt the defiance brewing inside her rising.

It had something to do with his complete arrogance. Never had John shown this side of himself so clearly. It was normally subtle, normally less blatant. Normally less challenging.

Now, it seemed to fill the entire room, making it hard to breathe, hard to think of anything but the man, the hunger, and the need to claim him.

She was sure he thought *he* was claiming *her*. There was a male superiority about him that had the potential to set her teeth on edge.

"And what do you think you know?" she snapped back. "Trust me, John, when it comes to me, there's so little you know that it's not even funny."

"I know you love me. I know you've loved me most of your life and you'll always love me. That I know for a fact."

Sierra froze. She could feel something crashing inside her, cracking through her heart. He knew that, and yet, he'd left her?

"How long have you known?" Her breath stilled in her chest. There didn't seem to be enough oxygen left in the room to fill her lungs.

"Hell." He breathed out roughly as he stared back at her, his fingers plowing through the overly long strands of his hair. "This isn't where I meant this to go, Sierra. This is my fucking fault, and I'm sorry as hell."

She shook her head. "I don't want your apology. You didn't tell Marlena to make that decision and you didn't ask her to screw around on you. I want to know how long you've known that I'm in love with you."

She had loved him all her life; that was no less than the truth. He was her first love, and no matter how this worked out, no doubt John would be her only love. He would be an incredibly hard act to follow for any man.

His gaze seemed to sharpen before he shook his head again. "I knew the first night you were here and you gave yourself to me, despite the bruises, despite being attacked. I know you, Sierra, you wouldn't have done that without a trust that goes with love."

"According to you, I'll fuck anything in pants anyway," she burst out. "How did that tell you any damned thing?"

Fury flashed through John. Stalking to her, he caught her upper arms, jerked her to him, and glared into the challenge of her furious gray eyes.

"I've never said that," he gritted out between teeth clenched in fury. "I never suggested anything so vile of you, Sierra."

"You may as well," she cried back. "You believed every man who ever claimed to have been in my bed. As far as I'm concerned, you may as well call me a whore outright."

"Sierra, you all but lived with those three men." He was going to pull his own hair out as soon as he fucked the defiance out of her tempting little body. "And what the hell does it matter if you did? Do you think I hold it against you?"

She tried to jerk out of his grip. Not fucking happening. He'd be damned if he was going to let her roll right over him this time. Her temper had always infuriated him even as it fascinated him, but this time, she wasn't even coming close to winning this argument.

"Do I think you what?" She was incensed and completely gorgeous. "You really think I'd give a damn if you did?

No, jackass, my problem is the fact that I didn't sleep with them."

The words were out of her mouth before Sierra could stop them or call them back, causing her to follow up with a quick, "I had better taste in men."

His brows lifted. That look on his face was completely irritating.

"Baby, I really don't care who you slept with before me." Pulling her closer, he glared down at her in determination. "Who you sleep with now is all that matters to me."

How the hell had she managed to turn this around? Where had it gone so impossibly crazy?

Sierra, John admitted. She made him crazy. So crazy that rather than arguing with her further, he decided that the best way to convince her exactly how possessive he could be was to show her.

His lips covered hers as his head bent, his arms surrounding her and pulling her closer against his harder, broader form. God, she felt like living silk and satin against him. Like the most perfect bit of passion he had ever had in his arms.

Sweetly curved lips parted beneath his, a temptress's tongue licked at his, drawing him inside the heat of her mouth, daring him to possess her.

She made him feel alive. Even more than the mountains around him, she filled him with that extra something his soul hungered for. That sense of peace he had never truly known until he had her in his arms.

Just as he had never known the true measure of his own sexual and emotional hunger for her until now. She was a perfect fit for his life, against his body, in his bed.

She wasn't timid. He would run right over a timid woman. She was fiery, passionate, and she was his. She could say what she wanted, she could think what she wanted, she belonged to him, and John intended to claim each and every ounce of the hunger he could feel inside her.

"Feel this," he snarled as his head lifted. "What I've fought as long as you've been an adult, Sierra. Feel what I fought without knowing what the hunger inside my own fucking soul actually was. Do you think I'd ever, for so much as a second, question anything or any man that came before me?"

Her fingers clenched in his hair as some ragged emotion tore through her gaze. "Feel me, John, and see if I give a damn."

She jerked his head down, her tongue licked over his lips, and the challenge coupled with the lust, the emotion, and the pure fiery heat consumed him.

It consumed them both.

She definitely gave a damn.

Anger, hurt, and determination rose inside her like a chaotic storm she had no chance of holding back.

A part of her wondered if she could blame him for his perceptions, while another part yelled, "Hell, yes," she could blame him. He had taken her virginity. He had been the first and he had been too damned drunk to remember it.

He remembered everything but that, and perhaps that was what pissed her off. That anger only seemed to feed the hunger, though. There was something about being touched by John that was unlike any other sensation she knew, any sensation she had ever imagined before him.

She'd experimented before, but no kiss had ever been like this. Long and devouring, lips and tongues meeting, mating, starving for more touch, for more taste.

She should have more pride, she told herself.

Another part argued, what did pride have to do with this pleasure?

Arching into his arms, her arms twined around his neck,

her fingers pushing into his hair to hold on tight as he swept her from her feet and moved quickly to the bed with her.

Her back met the mattress as he came over her, his fingers hooking in the band of her light pants and pulling them from her hips, pushing them down her legs as she pushed her sandals from her feet.

Her own hands were busy. Pushing his T-shirt to his shoulders, he jerked back from their kiss long enough to strip it and her own shirt from their bodies before he was kissing her once again.

His kisses were wild.

She loved them.

Running her hands along his upper back, the feel of his muscles flexing beneath her palms sent a shaft of pure heat racing to her womb, to her pussy.

Her thighs tightened on the heavy leg insinuated between hers, her hips lifting, falling, pressing into the hard muscle as it caressed the flaming bud of her clit through the silk of her panties.

"You always make me feel as though I'm burning alive." She couldn't hold the words back as his lips parted from hers, moving along her jawline with stinging little kisses as she writhed in pleasure, rubbing her nipples against his harder chest.

"God, Sierra." He paused above her, his gaze locking with hers. "You're like a flame yourself. So fucking hot and sweet."

Her neck arched for his lips before her head turned, her lips moving to his shoulder, nipping at the hard flesh as she fought to taste just as much of him as he touched of her.

She could feel the complete hunger brewing inside him, feel the tension tightening his muscles as it burned through her.

Before she could do more than gasp, he was rising, coming to his knees as he straddled her waist, his cock sliding between her breasts as he pushed them together to create a snug enclosure for the raging, burning flesh.

Sierra's head lowered. Tucking her chin against her chest,

she covered the very tip with her lips, licking at it with her tongue.

She hadn't expected this. She knew he was wild sexually; if he had heard lies about her, then she had heard nothing less than blow-by-blow dissections of his sexual exploits from the lovers he had left behind. As though they thought by telling her, they could somehow make themselves feel better that they had lost him.

"Damn, your pretty lips." He pressed her breasts closer together, slid the head of his cock deeper between her lips, and groaned as she sucked it firmly.

The taste of him was like cinnamon and a mountain breeze. The slight salty male taste of pre-come met her lips. The essence of him exploded against her tongue, filled her senses, and amped the raging hunger higher than before.

"How fucking pretty," he groaned. "Do you know what it does to me, Sierra, to see those pretty lips wrapped around my dick?"

She knew what the feel of it was doing to her. Sensuality, sexuality steamed around her, through her, until she felt as though she were burning alive.

His hips moved, the feel of his cock tunneling between her breasts, the head fucking into her mouth, and she could feel her juices flowing freely between her thighs.

The turn-on value was out the roof. Sierra's stomach clenched tight as her tongue stroked over the tip of his cock, her lips parting over the wide head. She was starving for the taste of him, dying for the touch of him.

"Sierra, sweet baby." He pulled back before she could stop him, her back rising from the bed as she fought to taste him once again.

Moving down her body again, his lips went to her nipples, sucking them into his mouth, tonguing them, drawing at the tight, hardened buds and exciting the already sensitive nerve endings.

She needed this. She needed him.

His lips moved lower, calloused palms pushing her thighs apart as his tongue swiped through the narrow slit of her pussy. Electricity sizzled through her body. Pleasure raced through every nerve ending until she arched against his mouth, fighting for more sensation, for more touch.

"I want your tongue," she moaned. "Inside me, John. I want your tongue inside me."

She wanted it all. She wanted every touch.

"John!" She cried out his name, her fists clenching in the sheets beneath her body as his tongue drove inside her.

Once buried in the sensitive channel of her pussy, he licked, slowly. His tongue flickered against tissue so sensitive it was nearly painful as she arched her hips, trying to drive his tongue deeper.

The licking strokes against the tender walls had her hips writhing against him. Each devastating thrust burned brighter inside her, pushing her higher.

John pushed her legs back, spreading them farther, lifting her pussy higher to allow his tongue to fuck inside her deeper, harder.

Sierra could feel her orgasm rising, brewing in her womb, tightening through her body. She was dying. She needed more—deeper, tighter. Her pussy tightened around his tongue reflexively as the strokes became harder.

"Don't stop!" she cried out in protest as his head suddenly rose.

He knelt between her thighs, draped her legs over the tops of his, gripped his cock, and pressed it against the clenching opening of her pussy.

John stared down at the darkening of Sierra's gray eyes, the innocent pleasure, the flush and uninhibited response, and for a second, the briefest moment, he remembered that night. Kneeling between her thighs, and then it was gone.

It was washed away by the heat of her juices touching the head of his cock, her pussy milking at it, attempting to draw it inside.

John pressed closer, his teeth clenching as his gaze lowered to where he was taking her, slowly. He wanted to take her slowly, wanted to feel every nuance of the pleasure racing through his body.

John felt the fist-tight heat enveloping him, felt her muscles caressing each particle of flesh as he pressed inside her.

Her hips arched to him, taking each inch with hungry desperation as her cries echoed around him.

He remembered this.

John shook his head, sweat dampening his body now as memory and reality began to converge.

His hips jerked, driving his cock deeper as pleasure locked around the hardened shaft. It felt as though a million pinpoints of electric sensation were attacking the portion of his cock buried inside her.

His hand clenched on her hips as he fought to take her slow, easy.

"Never needed like I need you," she cried beneath him. "John, never known anything like this."

A growl tore from his lips. "Sweet baby. I didn't know pleasure like this existed. Sweetest, tightest little pussy."

He slammed in deeper, almost burying himself to the hilt as he fought to breathe, fought to keep his come from spilling inside her.

He had condoms now. He'd made certain to have Dawg bring a box. But he'd already taken her bare, he already knew the pleasure of having her naked, and being sheathed. And sweet heaven, this was so much better.

Pulling back, he thrust deep and hard inside her once again, burying in deep and hard and snarling with the extremity of the pleasure.

"Sierra, fuck," he groaned. He couldn't do this. Reaching across the bed, he snagged one of the condoms from the bedside table and fought to pull back.

It took all he could do to pull back, to release her.

"John." Her hand touched his. "It's not the same."

Innocence. Pure sweet love and innocence filled her face as she stared back at him, her breathless words striking his soul with the force of a fist.

"I won't let you go, Sierra," he snarled possessively. "Do you understand me? If you become pregnant, I will never let you go."

"Do you want to let me go, John?"

"Hell no."

One hard stroke and he was buried inside her once again. Deep. He could feel her womb pressing against the tip of his cock. Delicate, tight flesh milked at his dick, stroked it, sucked at it.

John knew he couldn't hold back. He was dying to thrust into her with all the speed and strength he possessed. The hunger raging so deep, so hot inside overwhelmed him.

Sierra threw her head back against the pillow as he began moving inside her, thrusting into her pussy, separating the tender muscles with hard strokes of pleasure-pain and sizzling heat.

Her hips lifted, her heels digging into the mattress as she moved into each thrust, feeling him fuck her with the same desperation she could feel tearing through herself.

Each pounding thrust threw her higher, raced through her, until her orgasm slammed through her system with such force that she was trying to scream his name as it ruptured inside her.

At the same time, she felt his release overtake him as well. Each hard spurt of his semen inside her burned, fiery blasts that extended her release, threw her higher, exploding through her body with a force that had stars exploding before her eyes.

Shudders wracked her body as he came over her, pulling her tight against him as his hips continued to rotate, thrust, sink his cock inside her, his semen spurting inside her until finally they both collapsed against the bed in exhaustion.

He held her.

Sierra was aware of the fact that John wasn't letting her go. His body covered hers, sheltered her.

His cock was still buried inside her, the feel of him still trying to catch his breath matched her own.

There was something . . . Sierra let her fingers curl at the nape of his neck, stroking his hair. There was something different this time, as though emotions held in check by both of them were slipping free without their volition.

"I fought this," he whispered at her ear. "I fought it, because I looked at you, Sierra, and saw all the ways I could never make you happy then. All the ways I'd end up destroying us both because you were so sweet, your emotions so tender. And I felt so hard inside."

Her eyes closed as hope and need began to build inside her.

"I made excuses." He kissed the shell of her ear. "I tried to tell myself we were friends. That you were as close as a sister, but all the while, I knew better."

Her breathing hitched at the admission.

"I hated who I was, and every time I saw you, heard your laughter, saw your smile, glimpsed that core of pure sweet love inside you, you shamed me."

His head rose then.

Sierra promised herself she wasn't going to cry. She wouldn't cry.

"I left Boston to give you time," he finally admitted, those violet-blue eyes nearly glowing in his sun-darkened face. "I would have been back. I was afraid of what had happened that night, that perhaps I had hurt you, said something cruel out of my own stupidity. But I would have never let you go completely. Do you understand me? I would have been back soon. And I would have caught up with you."

"I wouldn't have run again," she admitted, fighting those tears. "I missed you, John. I missed you until a part of my soul was withering away without you."

"And there was no peace inside mine," he confessed. "Because you weren't here, baby. You weren't in my arms."

"How fucking sickeningly sweet. I'm going to puke."

John froze at the sound of the feminine voice behind them. He felt Sierra still, felt the fear that suddenly transformed the relaxed, sated curves of her body.

Moving quickly, he jerked around, keeping Sierra close behind him as he faced Marlena and the weapon she held in her hand, aimed directly at his head.

Marlena smiled. "How careless, John. Just because you lock the doors and set an alarm doesn't mean it can't be broken. When you have the right friends, you can acquire the most amazing little toys to access damned near anything you want."

Meaning those friends had given her the state-of-the-art electronics it would have required to get past his locks and security.

That gave him a chance, because it also meant the Mackays had been sent a silent alarm warning them of the break-in. He just had to hold out until they arrived.

"You figured it out, didn't you, John?" Marlena sneered, her once pretty features twisted with such vile jealousy and greed that for a moment John wondered how he had ever believed the woman attractive. "That's okay. You're the only one. You and Miss Goody Two-shoes behind you. Bitch."

"Marlena, you're making a very big mistake," he warned her.

"No, darling, you made the mistake the night you fucked that little whore in Boston." She smiled with icy intent. "Because I simply can't let that little slut win. I won't let her get away with all the plans she destroyed. Which means now, both of you simply must die."

Eleven

Sierra stared back at the impeccably dressed Marlena Genoa and wondered exactly how such insanity could have been missed. Was it detectable in the genetic strand perhaps? Scientists should create a test for it to ensure that such children are carefully overseen and raised to control their own reckless impulses.

Then again, insanity born of greed, a lust for power, and overconfidence likely wasn't truly part of the human genome. Too bad, because the world would have benefited had Marlena's madness been detected.

Sierra stared over John's shoulder with the faintest feeling of morbid curiosity, wondering what Marlena was actually going to do with that gun in her hand.

"Have you lost your mind, Marlena?" John's tone seemed entirely too controlled for the situation. Yet Sierra knew this tone of voice. It had a hard, icy edge that concealed pure fury. He was in control. He was planning. And God help the person he was planning against.

Unfortunately that person seemed to have the upper hand

for the moment. The gun she was holding trumped any amount of unarmed fury that John might possess.

Fortunately for them both, Sierra was rather confident of the fact that John was saner, and therefore, possibly had a much better chance of coming out of this. She just hoped he could pull both of them out of it alive.

"Really, John, did you truly believe I'd give up so easily?" Marlena propped a slender, graceful hand on a silk-clad hip, her nails tapping against the material of her white slacks as her gaze narrowed on him. "You know, I really thought you'd come to your senses, return home, and realize what an incredibly stupid mistake you had made. The advantages of marrying me were by far better than becoming some Kentucky hick bumming on a lake with his little whore. And a virgin to boot?" She laughed as Sierra flinched. "I returned to the penthouse, bitch, and found the bloodstained handkerchief." She glanced at John again. "You never even knew, did you?"

"I've always known." The answer shocked Sierra. Was he saying that only to throw Marlena off, or did he truly remember?

Marlena shook her head. "What a mistake."

John's shoulders were tense beneath Sierra's hands. Whatever he was planning, he would move quickly, she thought. She dug her nails into his flesh. If he moved, Marlena would shoot. Sierra could see it in her eyes.

"And what mistake would that be?" The deceptive laziness in his tone was actually frightening.

"Leaving me, of course, especially for that little twit you've been screwing nonstop for the past few days. Are you two related to rabbits, by chance?" There was genuine confusion in her voice. "Really, John, it's disgusting how often the two of you have been fucking. It's rather nasty, if you ask me."

The disgust in her voice, in her expression, proved she actually believed her opinion. The woman couldn't have a truly sensual bone in her body. Making love with John was like flying.

"I don't remember asking her," Sierra pointed out, unable

to keep her mouth shut at this point. "And since when does she find sex disgusting?"

Wow. This woman had been in John's bed and she hadn't even enjoyed sex? She and John were going to have to discuss this later.

Marlena narrowed her gaze as her lips curled into a sneer. "Still such a stupid little virgin. Sex for its own sake is a waste of time and energy," she snapped. "The two of you have been wasting both, no doubt." The gun lifted. "But since you have so little time left, what does it really matter?"

Sierra didn't think John's shoulders could tense further, but they did just that. They felt like iron or steel as she clenched her fingers around him.

"What do you think that gun is going to accomplish, Marlena?" John asked then. "Killing us? It will get you nothing but a fucking prison sentence. If you live long enough, that is."

Deadly, uncompromising, it was a warning Sierra would have definitely heeded if she were in the other girl's shoes.

Marlena's answer was another classic sneer.

"I would have never been forced into this decision if you had just returned to Boston and resumed the engagement as you were supposed to do. You could have fucked your little bunny all you wanted to then and I would have been all for it. All I needed was your ring and your influence, darling."

"As long as you and your little crime family had their greedy fingers in my bank account, you mean?" John growled.

Surprise glittered in Marlena's eyes. "You think it was your money I wanted?" A light laugh left her lips. "Darling, it wasn't that. It was your prestige, your law firm, it was your sterling reputation and your ability to save the worst of the criminals from their own crimes. My family needed your legal abilities, not your money."

John stared back at his ex-fiancée in shock. He couldn't believe the words coming out of her mouth.

"What the hell makes you or your family think I would have ever defended them? What the hell makes you think you're going to fix the problem by threatening us?"

"I'm not simply going to threaten you, I'm going to kill you, John," Marlena promised him. "I made a lot of promises to my family, and there are very few ways to make up for the fact that I couldn't deliver. Killing you is one of them."

John stared back at her silently for long moments. "You're telling me they demanded you kill me?"

She rolled her eyes. "I'm telling you I broke a promise and now I have to prove my loyalty to them in another way. This is the only way I have of doing so. There are very few entrances into this world, John. And if getting what I want means I have to bloody my hands a bit, then so be it."

"And that's all life means to you?" he asked her, suddenly realizing that her apparent lack of emotion truly went clear to the soul.

The realization didn't surprise him, though he imagined it should have. After all, he had been engaged to her and hadn't known the true measure of the woman she was.

Marlena shook her head at his question. "I didn't say I would enjoy killing you, John." She glanced back at Sierra. "Though I believe I will truly enjoy killing your little sex bunny. I think I want to hurt her first though. Hurt her in ways she can't even imagine for daring to attempt to take what was mine."

The hell she would.

As though Marlena weren't holding a gun, John reached over, snagged his pants from the floor, and, making certain he was between Marlena's gun and Sierra, pulled them on and zipped up.

"Do you think you can keep sheltering her, John?" Marlena asked curiously. "Once I put a hole in your heart, I will have a clear shot to your little whore."

Marlena peeked around John's shoulder and smiled back at Sierra.

Sierra hadn't moved. She sat with the sheet pulled to her breasts, simply watching Marlena. There was a strange glint to her gaze, a darkening of those marbled gray eyes that warned John she was up to something.

He just prayed it was something that wouldn't get her killed.

Turning his gaze back to Marlena, he stared at the gun once again. She was too far away for him to jump her. He wouldn't have a chance of getting to her before she fired.

"John, I know you so well," Marlena murmured. "Well enough that we're going to take your little houseboat from the docks and go down the lake a bit. I'd hate to have anyone see me leaving once I've completed this little task."

He shook his head. "I'm not going to cooperate with this, Marlena. You're not going to kill anyone."

Her smile was condescending. "Don't test me, John. I know your guilt complex. I was going to be nice and kill you first, but if you keep pushing, then I'll kill your little whore first and make you watch."

John's jaw clenched. He was growing sick of hearing Sierra referred to as a whore.

Marlena laughed. "I can see how irritated you're becoming, lover."

John shook his head again. "Not irritated, Marlena, confused perhaps. What makes you think I'm going to allow you to do any of this?"

He was perhaps two feet closer. Not nearly enough.

From his periphery he glimpsed Sierra moving. She pulled his robe from the headboard, slid to the edge of the mattress, and began putting it on slowly, drawing Marlena's gaze.

Marlena laughed. A light, amused sound. "Do you truly think I'm here alone, John?"

Fuck. He had hoped she was there alone. He had prayed she was.

As Sierra tied the belt of the robe around her waist, another figure moved up the stairs. John wasn't surprised. He'd be damned if anything could surprise him at this point.

Gerard. He wanted to disbelieve the fact that his former friend was actually there, but he couldn't quite do it.

"You're taking too long," Gerard snapped at Marlena.

"I've untied the boat and we're ready to move out. Bring them downstairs."

John stared at the other man, gauging the icy, merciless intent in his face, and John knew there was the possibility he and Sierra were really fucked now.

"Why, Gerard?" That part made very little sense.

Gerard glanced back at him coolly. "Who do you think chose you for Marlena to go after? Who do you think is her backer in the organization, John? Her reputation wasn't the only one damaged here. The only way to fix this is to get rid of you." He glanced at Sierra. "And your troublemaking little bitch."

Where Marlena had appeared almost playful, Gerard was deadly serious.

"See, none of this makes sense," John pointed out. "You should have been smart enough to know that even if I had married her, I would have never let her use me."

"You would have once she had a child," Gerard informed him. "As you said, I know you, John. And I know your weaknesses."

Yes, he did. John would have protected his child, but never by allowing himself to be manipulated. He would have found a way to resolve any threat. But how the hell was he supposed to resolve this one?

"Let's go." Gerard stepped back and motioned to the stairs. "The security on the controls requires a passcode that my electronics hasn't cracked yet and I'm growing impatient. You're going to input the code or Sierra's going to die right in front of your eyes." He smiled. "And I know about the fake codes on these boats, John. Push those numbers in, and you'll regret it."

But Gerard didn't know about Natches Mackay and his little paranoias. Paranoias that had caused the other man to tinker a bit with the security he'd had installed.

Waiting for Sierra, John kept her close to his side as they moved to the stairs, his hand at her waist tightening, warning her to caution.

Moving to the living area, John walked across the floor to the console that sat off the sitting area with its old-fashioned ship wheel, controls, and monitors.

He placed Sierra in front of him and started praying.

Turning the key, the monitor flashed the demand for the passcode and John punched in the code that would immediately alert the Mackay family that the need for help was now dire. But if they hadn't arrived yet, there was a chance they were too far away to arrive at all.

It also slowed down the motor, which chugged sluggishly.

"What's the problem?" Gerard's voice vibrated with anger now. "Don't play games with me, John."

"It's not a game, Gerard," John snapped back. "You should have done your homework. I haven't had this boat out of the marina but twice this summer for a reason."

That reason being that he'd been helping the Mackays on various projects, but no one should know that. And if he knew Gerard, the man hadn't done his homework. That was normal for him, come to think of it.

Turning the motor over again, he played it out as long as possible, pushing buttons, staring at the monitors in confusion. It wasn't going to last much longer. Where the hell was the cavalry when he needed them?

In front of him, Sierra's hand covered his as he laid it comfortingly against her hip and moved it lower with a subtle nudge. Then lower.

John barely held back his response to the feel of the gun in the pocket. He hadn't forgotten about it, it was simply that he normally kept the weapon on the bottom shelf of the bed table.

He hadn't been able to get to it himself because Marlena had been watching so closely. But John had been shielding Sierra as she moved from the bed and evidently she had managed to slip it from the shelf.

His resourceful little Sierra.

He fiddled with the key, tapped a monitor, pushed his hand into the pocket of Sierra's robe, and gripped the gun.

He would only have a second.

He had to find a way to take out Gerard, and hopefully to disarm Marlena in no more than a second or two.

That first moment of surprise would be the only chance he had.

"I'm going to need to check the electronics." He sighed, glancing back to Gerard.

"And that would be where?" Gerard asked icily.

"Below the controls." John nodded to the small door at the bottom of the console.

"Move back." Gerard waved the gun at him.

John and Sierra did as he said as Marlena moved closer, her weapon pointing toward them, her gaze hardening.

"Please don't try anything, John," she warned him quietly.

Gerard knelt, worked the panel loose, and John moved.

As he did, mayhem suddenly exploded through the boat.

The long, wide window at the side of the console shattered as a hard male form launched itself into the room. The front door burst in and John jumped for Gerard.

He had almost moved too late. Gerard was coming up with the weapon when John jerked hold of him and slammed his head into the console as the gun went off.

John felt the bullet tear along his bicep, the fiery blaze of pain shocking him for a moment, giving Gerard the opening he needed to come back.

Another gun fired.

Gerard stared at John in shock, in surprise, as a bloom of red began to stain across the perfectly pressed white silk shirt he wore.

In the distance, he heard Marlena screaming in denial as Dawg Mackay quickly restrained her. She was fighting him tooth and nail, screeching when Sierra walked up to her and smacked her full handed across the face with enough force to immediately shut her up.

Gerard fell to the floor of the boat, his gaze sightless. Marlena shut up, thankfully, and Sierra turned back to John.

"It's over now," she said softly, those gray eyes so filled with pain that his heart broke for her.

Twelve

Sierra felt John lift her in his arms and move to the couch where he sat down with her, holding her close against him, breathing deep and hard as Dawg Mackay pushed a restrained Marlena into a chair on the other side of the room.

"How fucking romantic," she snarled. "You're so weak, Sierra. So stupid. Do you truly believe fucking him is going to hold him to you?"

She didn't. She had always known better. It wasn't fucking him that would hold him to her.

"Loving him will be enough."

Marlena laughed at that.

"Shut the fuck up, Marlena." John's voice held a vein of weariness. "Your little games are over, and I've simply had enough of your mouth for the moment."

"You stupid country hick," she cried out. "You could have had everything with me."

"He could have had nothing." Sierra pulled herself from John's grip, stood, and glared at the other woman in rising fury. "You've destroyed Gerard, yourself, and now you actually believe you would have done anything but destroy John?"

"You moralistic little bitch," Marlena screamed as the Mackays and Timothy Cranston stared at her in loathing and pity. "You're as ignorant as he is. He fucked you and passed out, he didn't even remember he'd had you." She laughed as Sierra flinched. "You're such a stupid little whore."

"I remembered."

Sierra whirled around, staring back at him in surprise as his arms came around her.

There were too many witnesses, she thought. He was lying to help her save face, nothing more.

"I remembered," he swore, staring down at her as she fought to believe him. "I was drunk as hell, baby, it just took time, but nothing that important, nothing that special to me could have been forgotten for long."

His fingers touched the single tear that fell from her eye as those behind her were forgotten. Nothing existed but John. Nothing existed but the fact that he was holding her, that he was there, that he loved her. And that he remembered.

"You'll regret it." Marlena suddenly laughed behind her. "Love wears off, trust me, I know." The bitterness in her voice was self-explanatory.

Turning back to her, Sierra stared at Marlena with true pity. Nothing could have hurt worse in Sierra's life than losing John forever, but never would she have destroyed herself to get back at him.

"True love doesn't wear off," she told Marlena. "It doesn't strike back, and it keeps the heart warm, even when it wants to forget, when it wants to stop hurting. You never loved anyone but yourself."

The sound of sirens outside, the rush of officers nearing the boat drew her attention. It was over. The danger was gone. If John asked her to leave, if he decided their time ended with the summer, then she would face it with no regrets.

It would break her heart. It would destroy her. But the love she felt for him would never allow her to harm him or to strike back at him.

Marlena stilled as the officers came through the shattered door. Her gaze flashed with fear before she turned to John with a twisted smile.

"I'll never see prison," she whispered.

"I'm afraid you will," he promised her.

She shook her head. "They won't let me live long enough."

John watched, almost smiling as Timothy Cranston stepped forward. Calculated interest filled his expression. "We could discuss that, Ms. Genoa," he stated with such false innocence that the men in the room couldn't help but chuckle. "We can discuss that in depth."

ONE MONTH LATER

Sierra watched, a small smile on her face as the Walker clan, including John's sister Rogue and her husband, Sheriff Zeke Mayes, filled the huge backyard of Dawg Mackay's two-story ranch house. The Walkers weren't the only ones there. The entire Mackay clan, including Faisal, Natches's adopted son, the four precocious toddlers, and Timothy Cranston's lady friend, as well as a young woman he called his adopted daughter, mingled around the tables of food and the pool, and lounged in the comfortable patio furniture set out.

It was a true barbeque. This was no catered affair. Sierra had been at the house for the past two days. Sierra, Rogue, Kelly, Christa, Janey, and Chaya had helped the men prepare for what they called a family reunion.

She'd never been to a family reunion, and she had to admit, she was rather enjoying this one.

John Calvin Walker Sr., "Calvin" to everyone here but his wife, watched the children, his two grandchildren as well as the Mackays' toddlers with a small smile as he sipped the clear, homemade liquor Dawg had supplied him with.

Sierra had never seen him in jeans until today. Even Brianna Walker wore jeans, a smile, and a ponytail. She looked as though she had come from the same mountains her husband had been born in.

"It's about time you managed to snag John's heart." Rogue moved up to her, brushing back her long red-gold hair, her gaze affectionate and filled with warmth as she gave Sierra a quick hug. "I swear, I thought my big brother was a goner when he gave Marlena that ring."

"John was too smart for her." A satisfied smile curled Sierra's lips.

She'd learned to live for the moment. She didn't ask for promises, she never hinted for any from John. It was enough to have each day as it came. To store each memory, each touch, each kiss, just in case he asked her to leave.

"He was indeed," Rogue agreed. "You love him terribly, don't you, Sierra?"

She and Rogue had always been friends. No one could have missed her more than Sierra had when she had left Boston so long ago.

"With all my heart," Sierra agreed.

"He loves you," Rogue told her then.

Sierra nodded. He told her often that he loved her. He held her, even when she had nightmares, drew her into every facet of his life, and gave her a sense of contentment that she had never known.

But he asked for nothing. No commitment, no nothing. And the time was coming that she had to make a decision. She had a career to return to, a job; she couldn't live off John, and she wouldn't live off him. But she couldn't make the final move without an invitation, without some sort of commitment from him.

"It's so great to see you together." Rogue hugged her again. "And I'm so looking forward to having you here. You can help decorate the new house."

Sierra kept her answer vague and once again pushed back the unsettling thought that perhaps John didn't want her to stay. Maybe he hadn't asked for a commitment because he didn't want one.

"Ah, I see my honey calling me." Rogue moved away, drawing Sierra's gaze to Zeke Mayes as he motioned to his wife.

John was moving across the lawn as the music blaring from the speakers at the side of the house quieted and everyone turned to her.

"Hey, lollipop," John whispered in her ear as he kissed her cheek. "Ready to have some fun?"

"With you?" She laughed back. "You're always fun, dummy."

"I'm about to become more fun."

He knelt in front of her as he caught her left hand.

Sierra stood in shock, her heart suddenly hammering against her chest, throbbing in her throat as she stared down at him.

"You enrich me, Sierra Lucas," he suddenly announced. "You break the rules, you made my heart full, and you bring me a peace I only dreamed of having."

Oh, God.

She couldn't cry.

She stared down at him, barely daring to breathe as he held her hand in his and lifted his free hand.

"Sierra Lucas, I've requested the approval of your godfather for your hand in marriage. And I now ask you, the other half of me, the one woman that completes me." A ring slid onto her finger. "Will you marry me?"

She stared at the ring in awe. A single diamond surrounded by deep, violet-blue sapphires. It was the heirloom engagement ring John Walker had purchased when he made his first million. A legacy for his wife to pass on to their son's wife.

The antique ring had been fashioned in the sixteen hundreds, the burnished gold rich with age and priceless sentiment, and it now sat on her finger.

"Don't leave me cold, Sierra," John whispered as he stared up at her. "Don't let me ever have to exist without you again."

She could feel the eyes watching them, and she didn't care.

She could feel the men's amusement, the women's interest, and none of it mattered.

"I love you," he stated. "With my heart, my soul. Forever."

Her lips trembled as a tear fell from her eye.

"Yes."

He didn't give her time to say anything more.

He was on his feet, she was in his arms, and he was twirling her around as the sunlight glinted blue off the diamond and struck fire to the sapphires as she curled her arms around his neck and buried her head against his shoulders.

And the tears fell then.

Happy tears. Tears of joy, of love, of all the hopes and all the dreams she had ever harbored inside her.

They all existed here, in this man's arms, in the fiery love he gave and the sense of belonging.

She was adrift no more.

"I love you." Her arms tightened around his neck. "So much, John. I love you so much."

He sat her gently on her feet, framed her face with his hands, and let his lips touch hers. "Until the day after forever, Sierra. I'll love you until the day after forever."

And that was all that mattered.

Her lips parted beneath his as his tongue licked against them and he gave her another of those naughty kisses she loved so much. Deep, powerful, filled with love, arousal, heat, and a promise.

A promise to love her until the day after forever.

RIDING THE EDGE

JACI BURTON

To the wonderful Lora Leigh.
I'm honored to be your friend.

One

Rick Benetti had been fucked, and not in the fun way. No potential to shoot the bad guys, no uncovering a drug smuggling ring or going after gunrunners—he'd gotten the babysitting job instead. God forbid he should get a kick-ass assignment like the other Wild Riders.

One would think working undercover for the government would give him a hot job like the other guys. Like Mac had done when he'd had to carry around a live virus from Chicago to Dallas to make sure it didn't fall into the wrong hands. Or when Diaz and Jessie had gone undercover to join a bike gang that was selling guns to survivalists. Or Spence, who'd had a prime job working with Agent Shadoe Grayson in a strip club in New Orleans in order to bring in a rogue federal agent who was working with the Colombians to smuggle drugs.

Now those were the juicy cases.

Him? He had to go find and babysit some Nevada senator's daughter who thought it might be fun to join a biker gang.

Like that was a national security threat?

Fuck. More likely some bored college student thumbing her nose at Daddy's authority by joining up with the Hellraisers biker gang. Though Rick had to admit, the Hellraisers weren't exactly the soft and cuddly type of bikers. He should know—he used to be one of them.

And the last thing he wanted to do after being out of the club for ten years was get back in it. Which was what General Grange Lee, head of the Wild Riders, told him he'd have to do.

His criminal past behind him, Rick had lived a clean life for the past ten years. Not by choice, initially. At seventeen he'd been bad and about to get worse. Until one bust and the chance of a lifetime had changed his life. General Grange Lee had come into his life and offered him the opportunity to go to work for the United States government. Facing the alternative of prison, Rick had taken General Lee up on his offer.

Now he was heading back into his old life again, insinuating himself into the gang that had caused him so much trouble. And the leader of that gang in Las Vegas? His cousin Bo.

Yeah, that made sense. Bo had always been a badass. Kind of like himself—a badass with delusions of grandeur. General Lee had kicked that out of Rick. Made him a team player. Bo, though, that was another matter. Bo hadn't had the benefit of General Lee's firm but fair guidance.

Maybe the Hellraisers had cleaned up their act in the ten years Rick had been out of the picture. But from the intelligence he'd gotten from General Lee at Wild Riders headquarters, it didn't look that way. Which was why he'd been given this assignment. First, because he used to be part of this gang and he could get in easier. Second, because Ava Vargas's involvement with the Hellraisers could be a potential embarrassment for Senator Hector Vargas, not to mention a national security risk, especially since Senator Vargas was currently working on significant national antidrug legislation.

Rick supposed having one's daughter involved in a suspected drug-running biker gang would be a PR nightmare for a senator about to write a major antidrug law.

Still, Rick would rather be going undercover anywhere else but back with his old gang, even if he did see the logic of why he'd been given this particular assignment.

Didn't mean he had to like it.

He'd fired up his Harley and ridden from Dallas to Las Vegas. Bike week in Vegas was about to roll out, so the Hellraisers should be on the Strip. Now he just had to find them and get himself back in the old gang again.

Rick rode the Strip, ignoring the colorful neon flashing lights of all the casinos, his focus on the bikes and riders that had poured into town for the big blast that would last a week.

Some were single riders, or a group of friends. Others were part of clubs, their jackets and vests labeled with their gang names. It didn't take long for Rick to find the Hellraisers. They were a large group and their leather vests bore the flame insignias and their club name across the back. He goosed the throttle and increased his speed to catch up, riding past the gang until he spotted his cousin at the lead, then turned his bike around. Bo had pulled up at a local hangout for bikers—a bar. Rick rode in and parked next to Bo.

Bo gave him a cursory glance of contempt, a "don't fuck with me" kind of attitude. Rick smirked, realizing Bo hadn't even looked at him, just given him a quick once-over and labeled him an outsider.

"Still an asshole as always, aren't you, Bo?" Rick said as he got off his Harley.

Bo's head shot up, then recognition dawned. His face split in a wide grin. "Rick? Son of a bitch. It is you." He grabbed Rick in a bear hug. "How long has it been?"

Rick hugged him back, then separated. "Ten years, man."

They headed inside the bar and ordered two beers. Rick noticed only some of the Hellraisers had come in with Bo. The others stayed outside. Watchers, no doubt, keeping an eye out for rival gangs the Hellraisers might have a beef with. The last thing the Hellraisers would want is to be cornered inside the bar. The ones outside would give a heads-up if Bo and others needed to make a quick exit.

Bo took a long pull from his bottle of beer, then settled his gaze on Rick. "Last time I saw you, you were getting arrested."

Rick laughed. "Same for you, since we were getting arrested at the same time for the same thing."

Bo shrugged. "I did six months and got three years' probation on that one. But I never saw you again. What the hell happened?"

"You know as well as I do that wasn't my first arrest like it was yours."

Bo grinned. "I was sneakier than you. And a faster runner."

"So you say. I think you threw me under the bus."

Bo laughed. "So, you did time?"

"They sent me down for three years."

Bo winced. "Ouch. That's rough."

"Yeah. After that I took to the road. Prison was damned confining. I needed some space."

"So where've you been?"

"Chicago, mainly. But mostly I just ride all over. Settling in one place too long usually means problems for me."

"Why are you back?"

"Figured I'd been gone long enough. I wanted to come home for a while."

"Missing family?"

Rick snorted and took a drink of beer. "I think we both know better than that. We don't have family. Except each other."

Bo tipped the top of his beer to Rick's. "Amen to that. Useless fucking families is what we had. But we did have each other. Hey. I'm sorry I didn't know about you doing time. You know how it is."

"I know." When you got arrested you were on your own. If you disappeared, the gang figured you were either in jail or dead. No one bothered to check up on you. You were family as long as you were in the gang. If you left, you were history. End of story.

"So are you back for good?"

"Maybe."

"Interested in rejoining the club?"

"Maybe."

Bo nodded. "So that means yes."

Rick smiled over the rim of the beer bottle. "Maybe."

Bo laughed. "You're such a dick. I'll have my people check you out. Make sure you've been where you say you've been. Not that I don't trust you . . ."

"But nobody gets into the Hellraisers—or back in—without being investigated. I know." And that's why Grange had set up a phony background for him, including a drug bust in Chicago and the prison record he'd just told Bo about. If there was one thing the Hellraisers loved, it was a badass with a reputation. And Rick wanted to make sure he had the rep to ease back in. Which was probably why Senator Vargas was pissing himself over his daughter's involvement with the gang. Not exactly a club filled with choirboys. If Rick had a daughter riding with the Hellraisers, he wouldn't be too happy about it, either. Not that he was ever going to get married and have a kid. But if he did, he sure as hell wouldn't allow her to run with a group like this.

"In the meantime, you can ride with us. Background check should only take a day or so. If you want back in, that is."

"I might. What are the Hellraisers into these days?"

"Mostly trouble."

Rick laughed. "Just my kind of action." He figured it would be easy to get back in the gang again, especially with Bo at the helm. Now he'd just have to find Ava Vargas and get close enough to her to figure out her angle.

Ava Vargas stared at herself in the mirror of her bedroom.

"I don't think leather is a good look for me." She turned this way and that, unused to seeing herself decked head to toe in leather jacket, chaps, and boots.

"Are you kidding? You're hot." Lacey came into the bedroom and studied Ava, then shook her head. "I'd kill for boobs like yours."

"These things are what I'm afraid of. Does this top really have to be so . . . tight?" She plucked at the clingy spandex that seemed to want to mold to her breasts and outline them like the neon signs on the Vegas Strip. Her breasts were large enough. She didn't need to advertise their existence.

"All the girls wear their tops like that. Trust me, you'll fit right in."

That's what Ava was going for, wasn't it? To fit into this biker gang that her best friend Lacey had immersed herself in for the past year. The one that had ripped Lacey away from school, that had changed her best friend's life, her personality, everything.

A year ago, Lacey had been a graduate student. She and Ava had done everything together. But then Lacey had met a biker and had all but disappeared from Ava's life. Lacey had quit school and become a biker babe, spending all her time riding with her boyfriend. Even worse than that, she'd become a slacker, and that wasn't Lacey at all.

And Ava would know, because she and Lacey had been friends since kindergarten. They knew everything about each other. They'd been in each other's classes all through school, and roommates in college. After they'd gotten their undergraduate degrees, they'd shared an apartment while they'd studied for their master's degrees. And that's when Ava had lost Lacey to the biker world.

Ava had completed her master's this year. Lacey indicated zero interest in going back to school, saying she was "over it."

There was something just not right about that. Was this biker gang some kind of cult? And had Lacey drank the Kool-Aid? With Lacey so out of touch and unwilling to communicate about this new lifestyle other than waxing poetic about the new guy in her life and singing the praises of life riding on the back of a Harley, Ava figured the only way to find out what was going on in Lacey's life was to join it.

So she'd started hanging out at the biker joints over the past couple months—especially since it was the only way she could spend time with Lacey. She'd meet her at bars and

clubs that catered to the bikers. She didn't see anything unusual going on there, other than beer, pool, smoking, and just
general mayhem. Still, Ava wasn't convinced. Because the
Lacey she saw there was so . . . different from the one she'd
always known.

She had to make sure Lacey was safe, that the decisions
she was making were from her own free will. And right now,
Ava just wasn't certain that was the case. She was a little
suspicious of Lacey's boyfriend, because as soon as Lacey
had started up with this gang, she had packed up and moved
out of their apartment, telling Ava that life in the biker gang
was nomadic and it didn't seem fair to stay in the apartment
with Ava. She'd suggested Ava find another roommate. Cold,
harsh . . . cutting ties just like that.

And that wasn't like Lacey at all. Lacey was warm,
family-oriented, and friendly. They'd been thick as thieves
since childhood.

Ava didn't want another roommate. She didn't need one,
could certainly afford the place on her own.

She wanted her old friend back. Or at least she needed to
know that Lacey was okay, that the decisions she made were
her own. Because whenever she saw Lacey—infrequently as
that was—there was just something not quite right about her
friend. Something in her eyes . . .

Which was why she stood in front of the mirror decked
out in a skintight top, body-hugging jeans, and leather.

"I'll fit right in, huh?"

Lacey giggled and threw herself on Ava's bed. "Well, at
least physically. It's a unique lifestyle, Ava. It might take
some getting used to. It's not all five-star hotels and room
service."

Ava glared at Lacey in the mirror. "I'm hardly spoiled,
Lace."

Lacey rolled her eyes. "Please. Senator's daughter. Only
the finest schools. And the idea of sawdust and peanuts on
the floor, not to mention spilled beer, probably makes you
want to faint. Look at this place. No knickknacks or art on

the walls." Lacey ran her finger over the bare tabletop next to the bed. "Not even a speck of dust. You have no clutter. You're a clean freak."

Ava lifted her chin. "I am not. I just like . . . order in my life."

Lacey laughed. "That's exactly what I'm talking about. A biker lifestyle is anything but orderly. Are you sure this is what you want?"

Lacey used to like things orderly and neat, too. Ava went and sat next to Lacey on the bed, surprised that the leather she wore was soft enough to give when she sat. "Yes. It's what I want. I'll give it a try, anyway. I think it'll be fun."

Lacey grabbed her hands. "Oh, I'm so glad you're going to be riding with us. I've missed you so much."

"I've missed you, too. We don't see each other enough."

"I was afraid we'd drift apart. But you've been busy with school, and that's just not my life anymore."

Ava wanted to ask her why it wasn't, but Lacey had made it clear she didn't want to talk about school anymore, so she let it pass. "Where's your boyfriend?"

Lacey grinned. "He's on the Strip now. Probably getting drunk with all his friends."

She said it with such pride. Ava resisted wrinkling her nose. "Uh, great."

Lacey looked at her watch. "We should get going. We're meeting them at eight."

"Okay." Despite only being here for Lacey, Ava ran into the bathroom to take one last look. She had no idea if she looked appropriate or like a fish out of water. She supposed she'd have to take Lacey's word for it.

Finally she'd get a chance to see Lacey's world. Spend more time with Lacey's boyfriend.

Then she'd find out if she had anything to worry about.

Riding again with Bo and the Hellraisers was a lot like old times, and then again not. Last time Rick had ridden with Bo and the gang, they'd been kids and low on the totem pole.

Ten years later and Bo was in the upper echelons of the organization, riding lead in this particular group.

That said a lot about what Bo had been doing for the past ten years. And that meant whatever the Hellraisers had been doing, Bo was really good at it. They rode the Strip for a while, and Rick realized it really had been ten years since he'd been there. A lot had changed. Growth had exploded the Strip. There were more casinos, hotels, and a lot more to do than just gambling now. He gawked while he rode, barely noticing the throng of Hellraisers adding to their numbers until the congested group pulled to a stop in the older part of town. Bike upon bike pulled into the parking area. It looked like a freakin' parade. There must have been a hundred Hellraisers by the time the last one parked.

"Damn. The Hellraisers have expanded."

Bo nodded as they walked from the parking area to the street. "Membership grows by about ten to fifteen every year. We've gotten really popular."

"Yeah? What do you attribute that to?"

Bo grinned. "We get laid a lot. Guys notice all the chicks that have joined the club."

Rick laughed. "I guess I came back at just the right time."

Bo slung his arm around Rick's shoulder. "Yeah, you did."

They got to the corner and a flash shot by Rick. A skinny female leaped onto Bo, wrapped her legs around him, and planted one hot, tongue-involved kiss on his lips. Bo grabbed the woman by the ass and held on to her, returning the kiss.

When he broke the kiss, the woman squealed, "I missed you today, baby!"

"Missed you, too," Bo said, letting the woman slide to the ground. He wound an arm around her waist. "Lacey, this is my cousin, Rick Benetti. Rick, my girlfriend, Lacey."

So Bo had a girlfriend, huh? Interesting. And a pretty one at that. Not at all like the skanky girls he used to hang out with. This one had straight brown hair, a nice body, and pretty blue eyes.

"Your cousin? Wow. I didn't know you had a cousin." Lacey held out her hand. "Nice to meet you, Rick."

Rick shook her hand. "Nice to meet you, too, Lacey. And I've been out of town the past few years, so that's why you didn't know about me."

"Really. Are you joining the Hellraisers for bike week?"

"I am."

"Have a girl with you?"

"No. I ride solo."

She grinned. "That's perfect. My best friend is here and she doesn't have anyone to ride with."

"Uh, I don't think—"

The woman had been standing behind Bo. With all of Lacey's flash and exuberance, he hadn't even seen her. He did now as Lacey pulled her in front.

Wow. To Rick, one woman was just as good as another.

This one was different. She was stunning, with rich black hair, silvery gray eyes, and a lush body that rocked his dick into shocked awareness.

And she looked damned familiar.

"Rick, this is my very best friend, Ava."

This was Ava Vargas? It had to be. She looked a lot like the picture he'd been given, only the picture must have been a few years old. This Ava was a hell of a lot sexier now that she was gift wrapped in leather.

And she'd just been dropped right into his lap.

Two

Ava sized up the biker she'd just been introduced to. Tall, damn fine-looking, with dark hair, dark eyes, in need of a shave, and looking all too dangerous. Classic biker look in jeans, chaps, and leather jacket.

Wow. Just . . . wow.

"Hey, Ava." Rick held out his hand.

Polite, too. She hadn't expected that. She slid her hand in his and felt the sizzle of . . . something electric and very warm.

"Nice to meet you, Rick."

"This is just perfect, isn't it?" Lacey said, bouncing on the balls of her feet. "I was hoping you would find someone to ride with. With Bo's cousin here, you have a seat now."

"Yes. Perfect." Ava couldn't help staring at Rick. She supposed she had these preconceived notions of bikers. Dirty, scruffy, mean, and scary looking. None of those characteristics fit Rick. Or, for that matter, Lacey's boyfriend, Bo, who was tall, lean, and very attractive. He resembled his cousin in many ways.

"Hi, Bo," she said.

"Howdy, Ava. You look great in leather. Glad you decided to join up with us for bike week."

Bo was friendly, too, had been since she'd first met him at one of the bars. Maybe she'd expected something different.

"Let's take a walk, see what's up around here tonight," Bo said.

He slung his arm around Lacey's shoulder and off they went, leaving Ava alone with Rick. And about a hundred other bikers, who started brushing by them.

Ava had no choice but to slide her gaze over at Rick.

He smirked at her. Could he see right through her as the fraud she was?

"You look lost."

She lifted her head, her pulse skittering just looking at him. "No, really, I'm fine. I'm sorry about Lacey dumping me on you. Really, you're free to go. You don't have to babysit me."

"I'm a lot of things, darlin', but a babysitter isn't one of them. Come on." He grabbed her hand and they started walking. Slow.

"Should we catch up to Bo and Lacey?"

"I'm not attached at the hip to my cousin. I'm fine right where we are."

Ava supposed she was going to have to be, since Lacey didn't seem to be concerned about leaving her with some guy neither of them knew. And she and Rick had fallen farther back in the crowd of Hellraisers, so now they were bringing up the rear. This guy could drag her into an alley and murder her, ravage her. She could disappear. Would anyone even notice? Or care?

Yeah, her imagination was definitely in overdrive, wasn't it?

Nice.

"You're sweating."

She jerked her gaze to him. "What?"

He lifted his arm, showing her where their hands were linked. "Your palm is sweating."

She pulled her hand away and wiped it on her jeans. "Oh. Sorry."

Again, that smile of his. The one that said he knew why.

"Are you nervous? I won't bite, ya know."

And wasn't this just the perfect time for her imagination to conjure him doing just that. Right on the nape of her neck. While they were in bed. Honestly. She didn't have vivid fantasies of men doing wicked things to her. Especially men she'd just met. Men she didn't know at all. That wasn't where her mind went. Usually. But he had that sexy, bad boy look about him that made her shiver all over. And apparently sweat.

"No, I'm not nervous at all."

"You're a terrible liar."

"Spoken by someone who's so good at it?"

He winked. "Yes ma'am."

She laughed, and felt the tension in her body begin to dissolve.

"So how long have you been with the Hellraisers?"

How was she supposed to answer that? She didn't want to appear as if she had no idea what she was doing, even though she had no idea what she was doing. "Not long."

"How long have you been riding?"

She looked down the street to see if she could spot Bo and Lacey. "Oh, not very long."

"Do you like bikes?"

"I find them fascinating. How long have you been riding?"

"Since I got my driver's license at sixteen. Before that, actually. I rode a bike before I drove a car. I've always loved them."

Now she focused on Rick. "Really. Why?"

He shrugged. "I don't know. Motorcycles were just a part of what we did back then."

"We?"

"Bo and me."

"A family thing, huh?"

"Yeah, I guess you could say that."

"So everyone in your family had bikes?"

He let out a soft laugh. "No. Just Bo and me."

"Oh, I see. You two must be close."

"We were. We got separated for a while."

"How so?"

"I was out of town the past ten years."

"Doing what?"

"This and that."

Vague answers. Things he didn't want to say. It made her curious, made her want to know more about him. "You grew up here?"

"Yes."

"So you've just come back home."

"Yeah."

"Welcome home then, Rick."

He smiled. "Thanks."

"I'm sure it's nice to reconnect with your family again."

"I don't have family. There's just Bo."

"I'm sorry."

"Don't be."

She heard the venom in his short, clipped words, wished she could ask more, but there was a finality in his statement that told her he wasn't going to explain further. Any time the topic of family arose, his chin came up and something in his eyes went . . . cold. If there was one thing she'd learned in her studies it was how to read body language.

The Strip was alive tonight, people crowding the sidewalks on both sides, wanting to see and be seen. She'd heard about bike week, but never took part, never cared. It wasn't her lifestyle. She was always in school, always studying, had gone from getting her undergraduate degree to her master's in social work. And next up would be her doctorate.

But through all of it, there had been Lacey. At least until a year ago. And without her support system, her best friend, the last year had been difficult, nearly unbearable.

She hadn't realized how isolated she'd become until Lacey was no longer there.

How pathetic. Where had her life gone?

She knew—she didn't have one. Everything had been about school for so long she couldn't remember when it wasn't. But now that she had her master's, she was taking some time off before she went for her doctorate. What better time to reconnect with her best friend and make sure all was right with her?

"So are you from around here, Ava?"

"Yes, I am. I've been here my whole life."

"What do you do?"

And wasn't that the question of the hour? What did she do, besides spend her life with her nose buried in a textbook or her mind engrossed in a lecture? "I just finished up my master's in social work."

Rick stopped, half turned, stared at her. "Social work?"

"Yes. Why?"

He shook his head and started walking again. She ran to catch up, grabbing his arm to stop him again. "Why did you give me that look?"

"What look?"

"The one that made me feel like a leper."

"Did I? Sorry. I didn't mean to."

"Do you have a problem with social workers?"

His smirk was his answer. He jammed his hands in his pockets and started to walk away.

"Rick. Seriously."

He stopped and turned to her. "Let's just say that social workers haven't always been my allies."

"Why?"

He looked up and down the street. "It's nothing."

"It's something."

He let out a short laugh and his step quickened. "Look, you don't know me. I don't know you. Let's just have some fun, okay?"

She linked her arm in his. "Then get to know me. I want to know more about you."

He looked down where her hand was resting on his arm.

Yes, it was a pretty bold move. She had no right to ask him to trust her. He was right. He didn't know her. And she was just a recent graduate. What could she do to help him? She didn't know his story or what he'd been through.

But she knew pain and resentment when she heard it. She'd been through plenty of cases in the past few years to understand how families fell apart, and how children were often the biggest casualties.

Is that what had happened to Rick? Is that why he'd called Bo his only family?

She suddenly wanted to know a lot more about Rick Benetti, and not just because he was a biker, part of this gang, and a link to some knowledge about Lacey's current lifestyle.

Rick didn't know what to make of Ava. What was her purpose in the Hellraisers? She acted like some shy mouse one minute, then was bold and confident the next.

And he needed to figure her out, find out the extent of her involvement with the Hellraisers—who she knew and what she knew. None of that included her finding out a goddamned thing about him. That wasn't part of his assignment.

She was a social worker. Jesus. From the time he was six years old until the cops arrested him when he was seventeen, he'd seen plenty of social workers. And not a single damn one of them had helped him, had cared enough about him to actually listen to what he was saying. He was just another number, another file to pass from one side of their desk to another, to funnel through the system. They wore this façade of caring on their faces, but their only function was to operate like robots and get as many files off their desks as possible. Not people—not kids who were actual human beings—just files. Case numbers.

Ava was young and fresh and beautiful. In a few years she was going to think differently, would be worn out, wrung dry and numb from a system that would suck the very life out of her. He'd bet that right now she thought she was going to single-handedly save the world.

She could keep thinking that. But it was way too damn late to save him.

He quickened his pace, forcing her to keep up. They finally caught up with Bo and Lacey at the head of the pack.

"Hey, there you are," Bo said. "Thought maybe you two had hit it off and found some dark alley to get it on."

"Well, the night's still young." Rick put his arm around Ava. Ava gave a nervous smile. Rick grinned. For some reason he liked making her uncomfortable. Maybe it would take her mind off wanting to delve too deeply into his past. Maybe it would send her running home to her daddy. He liked that idea even better. It would shorten his assignment so he could get onto a real case.

"Not much action going on here. I thought we'd take a desert ride tonight. Maybe have a bonfire over at Joey's place."

Rick nodded at Bo. "Sounds good." He turned to Ava. "Ready to ride?"

"Uh, sure."

They circled around the block and made their way back to their bikes. Rick pulled a helmet out of his saddlebag for Ava and handed it to her. He put his helmet on, climbed on his Harley, and waited for her.

She stood next to the bike and stared at it, helmet in hand.

"Is there a problem?"

"Uh, no." She fiddled with the straps of the helmet.

"Ava."

"Yeah?"

"Have you ever ridden before?"

"Sure. Lots of times."

"Remember when I told you earlier that you were a terrible liar?"

"Yes."

"You're still a terrible liar."

She cocked her head to the side. "How did you know?"

"You don't know how to put a helmet on." He got off the bike and put the helmet on her head and helped her fasten the strap so it was tight, but not too tight. Then he opened up the saddlebags and pulled out an extra pair of gloves and some goggles. "Here, you'll need these, too."

"Thanks." She put on the goggles and the gloves.

He grabbed the zipper of her leather jacket and started to pull it up, pausing when his knuckles brushed against her breasts. She inhaled with a sharp gasp.

"A little tight here."

"Um. Yes."

She seemed to try to make herself smaller, as if pushing her shoulders forward could make her breasts smaller.

"Honey, you can't downsize them. They are what they are." He pulled the jacket edges closer, then finished zipping her up. "They're really nice, by the way."

She seemed to relax then, because she laughed. "Thanks. They get in the way a lot."

"Yeah, but I'll bet they're a lot of fun to play with."

She seemed to consider saying something, but instead she closed her mouth and her lips curled upward in a knowing smile.

It made his dick twitch.

"Ready?"

"Yes."

He got on the bike and she climbed on behind him.

"Lean the same way I lean. Press your thighs against mine. It'll help with your balance. And hold on to me if you feel unsteady." He had a back pad for the rider, but a new rider sometimes felt a little wobbly until they got their bearings. He started up the bike and let it warm up while he waited for everyone else, giving the throttle a boost. Ava leaned closer and slid her hands in the pockets of his jacket.

Okay, he had to admit he liked that, enjoyed the feel of her body pressed against his back. He very rarely had someone on the back of his bike. He'd grown so used to his solitary lifestyle that it was unusual to have a rider behind him. And hell, who wouldn't like those great tits of hers pillowed against his back?

Sometimes he had shitty assignments. He'd thought this was one of them.

Then again, riding with a hot woman against you could be a definite perk, so maybe it wouldn't be all bad.

Three

Ava had done a really bad job trying to portray herself as a seasoned bike rider. At least to Rick, who hadn't fallen for it. She thought she could just slip right in and act like she belonged there, like she fit in.

Apparently not.

Then again, what was she trying to prove? She supposed she wanted to look like she belonged. No point in that. She was totally out of her element here and everyone knew it. She might as well just hang on and enjoy the newness of the experience and let a seasoned veteran like Rick teach her the ropes.

Like riding in darkness into the desert, where the roads curved and the biting wind stung her cheeks and made her wish she'd applied some lip balm to keep her lips from drying out.

There was a lot she didn't know.

The riding part? She loved it. Hanging on to Rick while the bike hugged the corners of the road was a thrill she hadn't expected. She felt like she was part of the motorcycle itself. It was exhilarating. And the closer she got to Rick, the warmer she felt, which was a nice side benefit. He didn't seem to mind her pressed up against him, either. His body was solid and as she laid her chin on his shoulder, it gave her a great view. He had a good command of the bike, knew what he was doing, which helped her relax. He never once even seemed to notice her weight or the fact he had an extra body on the back. He just focused on the road ahead. The ride was smooth and she wished it was daylight so she could see the desert.

After riding for a while—she'd lost track of time and had no idea how long they'd ridden—they pulled down a stretch of road that led to a large, sprawling homestead. In the darkness she could make out fences and heard the rustle of horses, so maybe a farm or a ranch or something? Dogs barked in the distance, and loose dirt shifted under her feet after they climbed off the bike.

And, oh, she was sore, her muscles tight from being in one position for so long. She resisted the urge to rub her butt.

"How do you feel?"

"Fine." She took off the helmet and handed it to Rick.

"Stiff?"

"A little."

He smiled and ran his fingers through his hair. "You'll get used to it. It's like riding a horse. Your muscles have to adjust."

She hoped they adjusted fast. "Where are we?"

"Joey's house. He's one of the Hellraisers, owns a ranch out here in the desert. The Hellraisers party a lot out here because it's away from the watchful eye of the law."

"Really."

"Yeah. Come on."

Ava wondered what kind of partying went on that the Hellraisers didn't want the police or county sheriff to know about. She caught up with Lacey, who was just ahead of her.

"Have you been here before?"

"At Joey's? Sure. Lots of times."

"What goes on here?"

Lacey squeezed her hand and laughed. "Relax, Ava. We're just here to kick back and have some fun. You'll see."

Lacey moved off with Bo, leaving her—once again—until Rick moved up and swept his arm around her. "I won't leave you alone. Don't worry."

"I'm not worried at all." And she wasn't. Not about herself, anyway. She was more concerned about what Lacey had gotten herself involved in. That's why she was here. Though she had to admit, having Rick's arm around her wasn't bad at all. He was tall, gorgeous, strong, and he smelled damn good. Like leather and soap and the outdoors. And he was fine to look at. Lacey could have stuck her with some ugly guy with a gross shaggy beard and butt crack hanging out of his pants. She counted her lucky stars that she'd managed to get a riding partner that looked like he could be a male model instead of some grizzled, greasy biker type.

They went up to the house. By the time they made it in there, loud music was playing, the lights were blaring, there was a fire in the fireplace, and there was plenty of beer lined up in large metal buckets on the floor in the living room.

The place was very rustic, all wood floors and paneling. Very little décor and Ava could tell immediately that this was a guy's place. It had no feminine touches anywhere. No pictures on the wall and only a mounted deer's head over the fireplace. And it was kind of a mess, though people just shoved things out of the way and no one seemed to care.

Ava shuddered at the clutter, clenched her hands into fists, and forced herself to refrain from jumping in to straighten things up.

She'd grown up in a spotless environment, her mother a politician's wife almost from day one. Ava had never been allowed to leave her toys lying around, and had always been required to pick them up every night before bed. Of course all her toys had been relegated to the playroom, never in any of the common areas of the house.

As she got older, she remembered coming home from college and not being allowed to study at the kitchen table. She'd been sent to her room. After her first semester she'd stopped coming home. It was more comfortable—more homey—at school. Though even then, she kept her room at college immaculate. Habit, she supposed.

The chaos at this house was truly something to behold. Loud and raucous, a hundred bikers crammed into this guy's house, talking over the music, laughing, sitting anywhere and everywhere, from the fireplace to the stairs to the kitchen and even spilling into the front and backyards. And discarded beer cans everywhere.

"Want a beer?" Rick asked.

"Sure. Thanks."

He reached into a round metal bucket and grabbed two cans, popped them open, and handed her one. She took a couple gulps, looked around for a napkin, and of course didn't find one. Not in a guy's house anyway, so she did the next best thing—she wiped her mouth with the back of her hand, glancing around to see if anyone had noticed.

"Manners don't count here. Quit worrying about it."

"Sorry. Old habits die hard."

"You can drool all over yourself in this group and no one will say a word."

She laughed. "I'll keep that in mind."

Instead of staying put in one place—something she'd probably have done—Rick began to wander around. He knew a lot of these people, stopped to say hello, and was nice enough to introduce her to those he talked with. Most of the guys seemed surprised to see him, asked where he'd been, indicated it had been a long time since he'd been around. They all welcomed him back.

Ava wondered where he'd been, too.

"You son of a bitch."

Ava froze at the angry tone of someone behind her. Rick pulled his attention from the person he'd been talking to toward the sound of the voice, then smiled.

"Hey, asshole, what's up?"

She stepped out of the way as the two men shook hands and laughed.

"Goddamn. What did you do, fall into a black hole or somethin'?" the guy asked.

He was big—all over—a giant of a man. Even his hair had as wild a look as his face, tumbling in wild curls halfway down his back.

"Something like that. Great to see you, Joey."

Ah. So this must be the guy who owned the house.

"Joey, this is my friend Ava."

Joey turned to her, eyed her from head to foot, then picked her up and planted a big kiss on her cheek. "How ya doin', sweetheart?"

When he set her down, she exhaled. "Fine. Thank you. It's nice to meet you. Thank you for having us over."

Joey paused, then laughed and turned to Rick. "Polite little thing, ain't she?"

Rick's lips lifted. "Yeah."

"So, you still in the life?"

Rick shrugged. "More or less. What about you?"

"Hellraiser 'til I die. Bo's done a fine job growing the gang. He keeps us busy runnin'—"

Joey seemed to notice Ava standing there. "He keeps us busy running around."

"I can see that. I remember when there were just ten or fifteen of us."

"Now there are over a hundred in this area. He's done good. And I know he'll be happy to have you back."

"Yeah, I figured it was time to come home."

Joey smacked Rick on the back. "About damn time, too."

Joey moved off to see some other people and Rick and Ava finished their beers. Rick reached into the nearest tub for another, opened it, and handed it to her while they wandered around.

"You seem to know a lot of people," she said.

"A few. Some I don't recognize. A lot of these people are new."

"Joey said you'd been gone awhile?"

"Yeah. Traveling."

"That must have been exciting."

He laughed. "It can be."

She suddenly wanted to know more about him. He must lead such an interesting life. "Who do you ride with when you travel? Groups like this one, or smaller?"

"No one. I ride alone."

She couldn't even imagine that. "Really. Don't you get lonely?"

He slanted a glance toward her. "No."

"So you like being alone."

"I guess so. I never really thought about it. I just do what I do."

"I wouldn't enjoy that."

"What? Riding or being alone?"

"The alone part."

"It's not bad. Gives me a lot of time to think."

Now it was her turn to laugh. "I have too much time to think. I wouldn't want all that time alone. I'd drive myself crazy."

He leaned in, slid his finger on the tip of her nose. "It's good to get to know yourself, learn to be comfortable in your own skin."

Rick had a point, and he definitely looked at ease with himself. Still, she wondered how much time he'd actually spent riding alone. What made a person crave that kind of solitude? Most people liked being with other people, not isolating themselves.

He was certainly an interesting person. And she'd always liked to be around interesting people.

Speaking of people . . . where the hell had Lacey gone off to? Ava hadn't seen her since they'd arrived here. Ava searched her out, but the crowd had thickened and she couldn't find her.

"Looking for your friend?" Rick asked.

"Yes."

"I saw Bo take her upstairs. Let's go find them."

Once again, he took her hand and led her up the stairs, though they had to wind their way through a crowd of people using the stairs as a seating area. They didn't seem to mind though, in fact, made room for Rick and Ava to find their footing until they made their way to the second floor.

Ava studied the hallway that branched out in two directions and led to lots of doors—closed doors.

"Uh, maybe we shouldn't be up here."

Rick cocked his head to the side. "Why not?"

"I think people came up here to find some privacy."

He grinned. "I'm sure they did. But you wanted to find your friend, didn't you?"

"Well, yes, but if she and Bo want to be alone . . ."

He shrugged. "It's just sex. They won't mind being disturbed. Let's go."

Just sex? He was joking, right?

Apparently not. He started down a hallway. Ava ran after him and grabbed his arm before he turned a knob. "Are you serious? Stop that."

"What?"

"You can't just barge in on people having sex."

"Why not?"

"First. It's rude. And second . . . oh my God. Do I have to spell it out?"

He leaned against the wall and crossed his arms. "Sure. Go ahead."

"Do you really want to watch people . . . you know."

"Fucking?"

God. The way he said it. She flushed with heat all over. He made it sound dirty. And exciting. And compelling.

"Yes."

"I guess if people don't want to be bothered they'll lock the door. Unless they forget. Most don't really care. Watch."

She took a giant step back as he turned the knob and opened a door that was, as he said, unlocked.

"Anyone in here having sex?"

"Get the fuck out of here!" came a sharp retort from the darkened room.

Rick laughed and closed the door.

"See? They didn't want guests."

She shook her head. "I can't believe you just did that."

He ignored her, took a few steps down the hall, and opened the next door. "What's going on in here?"

There was heavy breathing. Then giggling, followed by a male voice that said, "Fucking. Why, do you wanna watch?"

"Maybe. I'll get back to you."

He closed the door and turned to her. Ava put her hand over her mouth to smother her laugh. "You're something."

He waggled his brows. "You have no idea, honey."

"You don't mean to go into every room and do this."

"Sure I do."

This time she quickened her step and rushed to cover the next door, putting her hand over the knob in the hopes she could spare another couple some embarrassment. "Really. Stop."

Undaunted, he leaned into her, and her breath caught when he placed his hand over hers. She felt swallowed up, cornered, and for some reason didn't mind at all.

He turned the knob and pushed the door open, sending her flying into the room with him.

"Anyone in here?"

No one replied.

"Hey, we're in luck. Looks like we have this one to ourselves."

Before she could say a word, he'd closed the door behind him. Ava heard the click of the lock.

"The smart ones lock the door to prevent assholes like me from coming in."

She was now locked in a dark bedroom with Rick. And yet she wasn't at all afraid. Intrigued, yes. Excited, definitely.

"Are you there?" he asked, his voice lowering.

"Yes."

"Keep talking and I'll find you."

She licked her lips. "What would you like me to talk about?"

He was drawing closer. She moved farther away, though

it wasn't from fear. She bumped into something with her hip. Dresser, maybe.

"I don't know. Tell me what you're thinking."

"I'm thinking I'm locked in a bedroom with someone I don't know very well."

"Do you need to know me well?"

"I don't know. Maybe."

"What do you want to know about me, Ava?"

He was getting closer. She inched farther to the right. "Tell me where you've been for the past ten years."

He went silent. When he spoke again, his breath brushed against her cheek. "I was in prison for a while for theft. Then I just rode freelance here and there, ended up in Chicago."

She found it hard to breathe with him standing so close to her. But at least he'd been honest. "In prison?"

"Yeah."

"For how long?"

"Three years."

"How long ago was that?"

"Seven years ago."

"Not since then?"

"No."

She inhaled, blew it out, then stopped breathing when he wound his arms around her waist. "Does that bother you?"

"Honestly? I don't know." She thought about it. Just because he did time in jail didn't mean he was a bad person now. People made mistakes. Some people learned from them. She'd seen plenty of that.

He laughed, and took a step back. "Go away, Little Red Riding Hood."

"What?"

She heard the creak of the bedsprings.

"You can't handle the Big Bad Wolf."

Affronted, she moved forward, her knee making contact with the mattress. "Now just a minute. I didn't say that."

"You didn't have to say a word. You're a scared little rabbit."

Dammit. "I am not."

"Aren't you?"

He sounded so smug. "No, I'm not. I just don't have indiscriminate sex with strangers."

He laughed, the sound as dark as the room they were in. "Sorry. I left my resume in my other bike."

What an asshole. She should leave, march downstairs and . . .

And what? "Do you often bully women into having sex with you?"

"I've never had to beg a woman to have sex with me, Ava."

She believed that. Women probably fought each other for the right to get in bed with him. And why not? He was gorgeous, oozed sexuality. So what the hell was wrong with her? She wasn't a virgin. God knows the man got her juices flowing.

"If you have to think that hard about it, you should go. I promise not to chase you."

"What if I wanted you to?"

"Wanted me to what? Chase you?"

"Yes."

"I don't chase women. I like them to be willing."

She blew out a breath. He had a point.

"Ava."

"Yes."

"What's wrong with letting go and just enjoying yourself?"

She didn't have an answer to that because she rarely did it. "I don't know."

"Want me to show you what it's like?"

He was challenging her, daring her to let go. Could she? Her life was all planned out, so orderly, so controlled. This moment represented everything that wasn't her. And everything that was Rick. He didn't appear to be a threat to her, at least not that she could discern. Then again, what did she really know about him?

What had she really known about any of the guys she'd had sex with in her lifetime?

Not much other than what they'd told her. She hadn't

known them any better than she knew Rick. And she was way more turned on by him than she'd ever been by them. Just standing in this dark bedroom with him, listening to him talk to her, had her wet, her nipples puckering and begging to be touched, licked, sucked.

The thrill of the forbidden, she supposed. Was that the lure that pulled Lacey in? The bad boy in leather offering the apple in the garden? Tempting, oh so tempting.

Then again, what was so wrong about going a little wild? She was certainly overdue for it.

She sat on the bed. And suddenly, he was right there, his chest against her back.

And when he leaned in and pressed his lips to the side of her neck, she shivered at the contact, tilted her head back, and let him have access. She turned and he pulled her against him, her breasts pillowed against his chest.

She laid her hands on his arms and felt the corded strength of his biceps flexing, and knew she wanted him naked, wanted to explore his body with her hands and her mouth.

She wanted something she'd never had before.

The chance to live a little bit on the edge.

Four

There were a hundred reasons why Rick shouldn't be doing this, but one primary reason—Ava was his assignment, not some hot random babe to have a quick lay with.

Yeah, right.

Tell that to his dick, which rocked against his jeans, hard and eager to get things started. Tell that to his senses as he inhaled her clean, sultry scent while his lips were pressed against the soft column of her throat.

He should have never brought her into this room, never closed and locked the door, never started teasing her with this cat-and-mouse game.

But damn, she was fun to play with. And right now she wasn't saying no. Oh, hell no, she wasn't. Every sound she made, every movement of her body was screaming yes. Oh, hell yes. And she was touching him, grabbing on to him like a lifeline in the dark.

In the back of his mind, this all spelled epic disaster. Unfortunately his libido had taken over and all logic was gone.

He had a sweet-smelling and willing woman in his arms and he intended to take full advantage of that.

He slid his tongue along her throat, felt the wild beat of her pulse in her neck, and he wanted to do anything and everything to drive that pulse up higher. He'd bet Ava could get really out of control, wondered if any man had done that to her before. Because what he'd seen of her so far led him to believe that she was oh so reserved, which made him want to tear away that reserve and find out just how wild she could be.

And maybe he was assuming, but he'd guess that she was just waiting for some guy to strip down the walls around her and release the animal.

He kissed along her neck, then her jaw, heard her inhale, then exhale as he neared her lips.

He cupped her jaw between his fingers and pressed his lips to her mouth. Her lips were soft, trembling, and as he pressed more firmly, she opened for him.

God, she was sweet. She tasted like innocence, something he hadn't tasted much of in his lifetime. She wasn't at all the type of woman he usually went for—he liked the wild, knew-exactly-what-they-wanted type. Ava was like forbidden fruit—which only made him want her more. He supposed he'd never quite gotten over wanting what he shouldn't have, but damned if he was going to care about that right now. He gathered her close and slid his tongue inside to find hers, testing the waters.

She wrapped her tongue around his and whimpered. She was hot, and he was getting hotter, especially when she wriggled her body against his, making his cock jerk against his jeans, reminding him of just how long it had been since he'd taken the time to be with a woman. Work had occupied him for too damn long.

Now it was time to play. And he intended to play all night long with Ava. He swept one hand inside her open jacket, smoothed it along the curve of her hip and over, letting his fingers press in on the upper part of her ass. She moaned into his mouth and moved closer to him, jacking his pulse up yet another notch. He tilted his head so he could deepen the kiss, used his other hand to slide along her back so he could crush her breasts against his chest. Oh, yeah.

He slid her jacket off, letting it drop to the floor. He grasped her wrists, held on to her, pulled her closer, and felt her full breasts bang against his chest. Damn, she had nice breasts. He couldn't wait to touch them, to bare them so he could lick and kiss them. Ava had one incredible body and he wanted to see it all. Maybe he'd turn the lights back on. It was way too dark in here.

None of this was going to happen fast enough—too many clothes between them. It was time to start shedding some leather.

Until someone opened and slammed a door in one of the rooms.

Ava tensed, her whole body going rigid as if she expected someone to bust through the door. Not that they would since he'd locked it. But her response told him a lot of things, the main one that she wasn't relaxed, wasn't ready for this. That was enough. Rick knew right then this wasn't going to happen. He let her slide off his lap and he stood, bending down to retrieve her jacket.

"What are you doing?"

"Let's go see if we can find Bo and Lacey." He found the light, switched it on, and immediately wished he hadn't. Her lips were puffy from his kisses, her hair messed up and out of its ponytail. She looked as wild as he'd imagined she'd been, her eyes a little glassy, her nipples tight points against whatever flimsy bra contained them.

Damn. And his cock was in no mood to be contained.

He cleared his throat and held out her jacket. "Ready to go?"

She lifted her chin, looked hurt. "Yeah, sure." She stood, took the jacket, and put it on, wrapping it around herself like armor.

He hadn't meant to hurt her, but he knew better than to push a woman into something she wasn't ready for, even if she thought she was.

And God knows he shouldn't have been doing this in the

first place. It was probably a good thing something had happened to slap him back into reality.

This was work time, not playtime, and he needed to remember that.

They went back downstairs and found Bo and Lacey in the kitchen. Ava went to Lacey right away, huddled with her to talk. It was like she didn't want anything to do with him.

He'd keep his distance for now. More watching, less touching. Safer that way and it would make him less likely to get too deeply involved in this assignment. Or at least the woman of this assignment.

Ava was mortified, hoped that her mortification didn't show on her face.

She'd all but thrown herself on Rick in the bedroom, which was totally unlike her. She just didn't do things like that. She didn't have sex—or almost have sex—with strange guys. But she would have, if Rick hadn't been the one to put an abrupt halt on things.

So while she'd been busy throwing herself at Rick, he'd obviously been busy wondering how he could politely change his mind and get himself out of the bedroom and away from her. God, how embarrassing.

Lacey, on the other hand, had pink cheeks, mussed up hair, and looked like she might have had really great sex. And judging from the stupid smile on her face, there was no *might* about it.

"You're grinning like an idiot."

Lacey's smile widened. Then she giggled. "Really?"

"Yes."

"Sorry. I can't help myself. I'm in love."

Ava sat at the kitchen island with Lacey and shook her head. "You're really gone over this guy, huh?"

Lacey sighed. "Yeah. I am. He's wonderful, Ava."

Ava swiveled around on the bar stool and caught sight of Bo and Rick drinking beers and engaged in conversation with a couple other guys in the living room. She turned back

to Lacey. "Okay, so tell me what's so wonderful about him."
So wonderful that you quit school and completely changed your life.

"Everything. He's romantic, gorgeous, sexy . . . he really pays attention to me, Ava. It's like I'm the only woman around when I'm with him. I've never met anyone like him before."

"You hadn't really dated a bunch of guys, either."

"I dated enough. All losers more interested in themselves than in me. Believe me, Ava, I know the difference between someone who genuinely cares about me and someone who doesn't."

"Do you?" She hated saying it out loud, but it was important that Lacey knew Ava cared about her, worried about her. "You gave up school to chase this guy around."

Lacey frowned. "I didn't chase him. He came after me. We met at a party and he started calling me and we went out. We just clicked, Ava. There was nothing and no one but the two of us after that."

Didn't she know it. Lacey had all but fallen off the face of the earth after she'd met Bo. "But, Lacey . . . school. It was so important to you. To just walk away from getting your master's when you were so close . . ."

Lacey waved her hand in the air. "I can still get my master's. You make it sound like my whole life is over just because I'm taking some time off."

"Are you though? Just taking some time off? You've changed so much, Lacey."

"Have I? I think I'm still the same. Maybe I'm not the way you want me to be and you don't like that."

"No, that's not it at all."

"Isn't it?" Lacey put her elbows on the countertop and leaned forward. "Look, Ava. I love you. We've been best friends forever—we're so close we're like sisters. But we both have to grow up. I know you like your life orderly, where nothing ever changes. But everything evolves—including relationships and people. Life comes along and we have to roll with it. I had a chance at adventure and I grabbed it. There's nothing wrong with that."

"Of course not." She made Ava sound selfish. Was she? She hadn't thought so. She was just worried about her best friend.

"And I'm thrilled you're here and experiencing my new life with me. Maybe it'll—I don't know—take you out of your regimented lifestyle and teach you how to bend a little."

"Excuse me?"

Lacey laid her hand over Ava's. "You like your life the way it is, the way it's always been, where you follow the same pattern that's been laid out for you your entire life. You're very . . . controlled."

"What? I am not."

Lacey laughed. "Yes, you are. You have to be in charge. That's not a bad thing. It's just the way you are and always have been. You like everything orderly and in a way that you can control it. I used to be the same way. And it worked fine for me for a while, but now it doesn't. After I met Bo I realized how much I was missing—how much *life* I was missing. Now I want something different. I want this life. Maybe later, I don't know. And maybe this will give you a chance to experience something unique and new and who knows what will happen to you because of it. It's a chance to let your hair down a little—get a little messy. Give up a little of your control. You could use it."

Now Ava felt like she was defending her own life and her own choices. "There's nothing wrong with my life. I'm doing exactly what I've always wanted to do."

"Of course you are. School, more school, and becoming a social worker. You have a flowchart with every step—every day, every month, every year—mapped out so you know exactly where you're going. No deviations. I know it's what you've wanted forever. But it's okay to step away from academia now and then and experience a different side of life, Ava. There's a whole real life out here that's not in textbooks."

Ava blew out a breath, tried to hold in her irritation. "Of course there is. I know that."

Lacey smiled. "Good. Then let's just have fun this week."

Lacey made it sound so simple, when Ava knew it wasn't.

Lacey hadn't just decided to go on vacation, or even sabbatical. She'd tossed everything about her life into the trash to do . . . what exactly? Hang with a biker? Did she even have a job?

Lacey had planned on becoming a psychologist. She wanted to help people. Her entire life had been focused on her studies. Her goal was her career, her future. Just like Ava's had always been.

And then just like that she'd tossed it all away. Years of education, the momentum of undergraduate and graduate school. Lacey was going to be so far behind now. Ava just couldn't fathom it. Not the Lacey she knew.

But this Lacey didn't want to talk about school or what she'd given up. This Lacey only wanted to have fun.

It was a lifestyle Ava simply couldn't comprehend. And that's why she was here, to see if she could figure out what the lure was that would account for Lacey tossing aside her education in favor of a romance with a biker.

And maybe, just maybe, convince her best friend to turn the corner and come back home—back to school—where she belonged.

"Hey, baby, how about we ride on outta here?"

Lacey lifted her head and her whole body perked up as Bo entered the kitchen and rounded the island to put his arms around her.

"I'm game. Wherever you want to go."

Bo tilted her back in his arms and planted a long, passionate kiss on her lips. Ava turned away at the intimacy and her gaze landed on Rick, who stood next to her, smiling.

"You ready to ride, Ava?"

"Sure." Not like she had a choice since she couldn't very well call a taxi to this remote location.

They climbed on the bikes and headed back into town. One thing about the desert—no matter what time of year it was, it got cold at night, especially in the fall. Ava had no choice but to snuggle up against Rick's back to keep the chilly wind from penetrating through her jacket. Next time she was definitely dressing warmer.

Though she doubted there'd be a next time, at least not with Rick. Not after tonight.

Once they'd returned to the Strip, they pulled into the hotel parking lot and got off their bikes.

"I need to go get my bag from my car so I can check in," Ava said.

Lacey looked to Bo, who had a tight hold on her hand, obviously eager to drag her up to their room.

"I'll walk to your car with you," Rick said. "You two can go on ahead."

"Great." Lacey waved to Ava. "See you in the morning."

Nothing like getting dumped by your best friend. "'Night."

Ava pushed the elevator button. "My car's on another level. You really don't have to stay with me."

"I'd feel a lot better if you weren't wandering around in a parking garage at two in the morning by yourself. If that's okay."

She managed a smile. "Yes, that's okay. Thank you."

Once on the next level she retrieved her bag from her car and they rode up to the lobby. "Have you already checked in?"

He nodded. "Earlier today."

"Okay. Well, good night then."

She went to the desk and once she'd checked in, headed to the elevators. Rick was standing there. She cocked her head to the side.

"Again, I don't like the idea of you wandering around by yourself. I'll walk you to your room."

Okay, chivalry definitely wasn't dead. At least not in Rick's case. Why did he have to be so freakin' charming? Especially since it was obvious he didn't want her? "Thanks. Again."

They rode the elevator up to her floor. Rick grabbed her bag and took the key from her hand, then led her down the hall to her room. He slid the key card in the lock and opened the door for her. She flipped on the light and turned to face him, but Rick walked inside. Ava shrugged and closed the door, followed him while he flipped on the bathroom light as if he were looking for . . . something.

He pulled the shower curtain aside, then moved out of the bathroom and into the bedroom, checking things out.

Checking for what, she wasn't exactly sure. He finally set her bag on the bed and handed her the key.

"Okay, you're good to go."

"What were you doing?"

"You can never be too careful about hotels. I just wanted to make sure you were safe."

She melted just a little bit. "Thank you, Rick."

He seemed to want to linger, as if there was something he wanted to say. Or do.

She wished.

But then he took a step back. "I'll let you get some sleep."

She walked him to the door and opened it.

"Rick."

He paused, turned around. "Yeah?"

"Where's your room?"

He cocked his head to the left. "Just a few doors down. Room 238. Call me if you need anything."

"Okay. Good night."

He paused, then leaned in and brushed his lips against hers. Soft, easy, and oh she wanted so much more.

"'Night."

She closed the door and locked it, leaned against the wall and sighed.

This night could have been a lot different, if only . . .

If only what? If only she were more like Lacey? More adventurous, less rigid? Wasn't that what Lacey had suggested?

She wasn't that rigid.

She also hadn't been the one who had stopped things in the bedroom at Joey's house. Rick had.

But why?

She unpacked her bag and pondered the situation, thinking back to the two of them kissing, how Rick's mouth had felt on her. She placed her hand on her neck where his mouth had been, shivering at the remembered contact, how it had made her insides dissolve in a puddle of want and need.

A shower would dissolve any remnants of his touch. She slid under the warm spray and closed her eyes, imagining Rick in the shower with her. His hands soaping her body, cupping her aching breasts and torturing her rigid nipples. She lifted her hands and did just that, which only served to fuel the flames even hotter. She let her hand drift down, over her belly and between her legs, cupping her sex. Her gasp made her eyes shoot open.

With a sigh of frustration, she finished her shower and dried off, brushed her teeth and slid naked under the covers, figuring it was late enough she'd fall asleep right away.

No such luck. Not with her body throbbing with the incessant need for an orgasm. An orgasm she was denying herself.

Why, exactly? She'd certainly seen to her own needs before, so why not tonight?

Because you'd had your chance to be with a rockin' hot biker guy, and somehow you blew it.

And that's what bothered her the most. She didn't know what she'd done to turn him off so abruptly. Maybe if she found out the answer, she could go to sleep.

She reached over and flipped on the switch for the lamp on the nightstand, and stared down at the room number she'd hastily scrawled on the pad of paper.

Room 238. Rick's room. She picked up the hotel phone, the dial tone screaming in her ear.

For God's sake, Ava, it's three-thirty in the morning. He's sleeping. What kind of a neurotic idiot are you?

Apparently a Class A Neurotic Idiot. She dialed his room number, her stomach clenching as it began to ring.

"Yeah."

He didn't sound half asleep. "Rick, it's . . . Ava."

"Is something wrong?"

"No. I'm fine. Were you sleeping?"

"No. What's up?"

This had to have been the dumbest idea ever. She fumbled for the right words. There really weren't any, so she might as well just come right out and say it. "Earlier tonight, at Joey's . . ."

"Yeah?"

"When we were upstairs in the bedroom. Alone."

He didn't say anything. Ava inhaled a breath of courage. "When we were kissing, and touching . . . you stopped."

"Yes."

"Why?"

"Because you tensed up when you heard a door close out in the hallway."

She frowned. "I did?"

"Yeah. I just figured you weren't really into what we were doing. Or maybe you weren't . . . ready. I didn't want to push you into anything you didn't really want."

That was why he stopped? Because she tensed up and he didn't want to push her? Wow. Just . . . wow. He really was thoughtful. Or utterly full of shit. She couldn't tell.

"I wasn't tense at all."

"You didn't want to be in that room with me."

"Yes, I did. I was . . . very much into what we were doing."

"Were you."

He was smiling. She could tell. But was he laughing at her?

"Yes."

"How much were you into it?"

Her body flushed with heat. "Uh . . . a lot."

"Tell me, Ava. Did your nipples get hard?"

Oh, God. She did not have phone conversations like this. Ever. But her nipples puckered. Damn him.

"Yes."

"Did your pussy get wet?"

Oh. My. God. She shuddered out a breath. "Yes."

"Are you in bed right now?"

"Yes."

"What are you wearing?"

She looked down at her breasts. The sheet had slipped down to her waist, revealing tight, hard nipples.

"I still have all my clothes on."

He laughed, the rumbling sound touching her nerve endings. "Liar. What are you wearing?"

His demand, spoken softly, made her want to tell him. "Nothing."

"You're naked."

"Yes." She could barely get the word out. It was like she was standing in the same room with him, showing him.

She heard a rustling on the other end, wished she knew what he was doing.

"The thought of you naked makes my dick hard, Ava."

Now it was her turn to rustle. She reached up and slid her thumb over her nipple, then squeezed her eyes shut as the sensation shot between her legs.

"Does knowing that make you wet?"

"Yes."

"Does it make you want to touch your pussy?"

She didn't want to answer, didn't want to have this conversation with him. And she didn't want to hang up.

"Answer me."

"Yes, it does."

He inhaled and blew it out. A sound of frustration, of need. She'd never heard anything more erotic in her entire life.

"Do it. Touch yourself for me."

"Oh, God, Rick. Please."

"Yes. Touch your pussy. You know you want to."

She did want to. She'd wanted to for hours. And somehow, doing it because he'd asked her to was like Rick putting his hand there. She moved her hand under the covers and cupped her sex, couldn't hold back the gasp as sensation shot through her.

"Feel good?"

"Yes." But she needed more. Much more. "Rick."

"Yeah."

"What are you doing?"

"Stroking my dick."

She squeezed her thighs together, images pummeling her. How was he doing it? Was he naked, too, or were his jeans unzipped, just his cock visible? She wished she could be in the room with him, watching him touch himself.

"Do you like knowing I'm stroking myself while I talk to you?"

She swallowed. Her throat had gone dry. "Yes. Oh, yes."

"Rub your pussy for me, Ava."

She rocked her hand against her pussy. Her clit trembled, the tight bud hard and aching for her touch. She split her fingers, capturing her clit between them, feeling it swell and burst with pleasure. It was so, so good. She couldn't hold back her whimper of pleasure.

"I love hearing the sounds you make. Does it feel good?"

"Yes."

"Tell me what you're doing."

"Resting my palm over my pussy. Teasing my clit with my fingers. Rick, I'm shaking all over. I've . . . never done this before."

"Good. Do it for me, then. I like listening to you. I like hearing your deep breathing."

She shuddered out a sigh. This was wicked. She pressed the heel of her palm against her clit, and let her fingers dive down along her pussy lips. She was wet, hot, anticipating being filled. Sadly, all she had were her fingers, but she tucked two inside. And moaned.

"Christ" was Rick's reply. "What are you doing?"

Now she felt the power of what she was doing, and how it affected him. She pulled her fingers out and pushed them in again, her hips rising off the bed to meet them. "Fucking myself with my fingers."

"Shit. Yeah."

Now Rick was the one out of breath and making noises, and she had to admit it drove her crazy. Because she couldn't see, she could only hear. And imagine. It drove her pleasure higher, faster, made her so close to coming she had to back off.

Not yet.

She was panting now, listening to the sounds Rick made, straining to hear everything. She could swear she heard his hand moving along his cock, the rhythmic stroking in tune to his hard, fast breaths in the receiver of the phone. She'd never seen a guy jack off before. Now she wanted to more than anything.

"Ava."

"Yes."

"I want you to come for me."

"Yes." Faster now, she moved her hand, her fingers, digging the heel of her palm against her clit and driving her fingers deeper inside her pussy.

"Tell me what you're doing."

"Spreading my legs. Fucking myself. Making myself come. Oh, God, Rick, I'm coming now."

"Fuck. Yes. Come on." He groaned, loud, a deep, guttural sound and she knew he was coming, too.

Her orgasm splintered her, wild and filled with a crazy madness brought about by this wicked thing they'd done together. She went off like a rocket, bursting all over. She bucked against her hand with the waves of her climax, yelling at Rick through the phone and not caring at all who she woke up. Not when she was coming like this and it was oh so good.

Spent, she dropped her hips to the bed and panted, listened to Rick do the same thing, and closed her eyes, wondering whether she should be laughing or utterly mortified.

"Damn, honey. You are good."

She smiled, too satiated to be mortified at what she had just done. "So are you."

"Now get some sleep. I'll see you in the morning."

Her smile died. She suddenly felt unsure.

"'Night, Ava."

"Good night, Rick."

He clicked off and she hung up the phone, went into the bathroom to clean up. She stared at herself in the mirror and shook her head at the sight she presented. Naked, her nipples puckered, her breasts still flushed with the aftereffects of her orgasm. Her hair was in wild disarray, her eyes had this . . . what? A passionate look, she supposed.

She didn't look at all like herself.

But this week was supposed to be about doing something different.

What she'd just done with Rick had sure as hell been different, hadn't it?

She turned off the bathroom light and climbed back into bed, hoping this time she could sleep without thinking too much.

And hoping she could face Rick tomorrow without dissolving into a puddle of embarrassment.

Five

Rick had only slept a few hours. After he'd hung up the phone with Ava last night, it had taken all his willpower not to throw on his jeans, walk down the hall, bang on her door, and climb into bed with her.

Reserved? He'd thought she was reserved? Cool? Hell, she was an inferno. Banked, maybe, but tapped the right way, Ava was explosive. And he wanted his hands on her in the worst way. So yeah, sleep had been damned hard last night. His dick had been damned hard last night. Phone sex was fun, but nothing like the real thing.

And now that she'd warmed him up, he wanted the real thing.

He had to keep reminding himself that he wasn't on vacation, he wasn't really home. This was an assignment. She was an assignment. And he had to call Grange and give his report. He dialed General Lee's number. True to form, the general answered on the first ring, his tone crisp and formal as always.

"What?"

Rick smiled and shook his head. "Hey, Grange. Did I wake you?"

"You know better than that, boy. What's going on there?"

"I'm in the Hellraisers again."

"Did your cousin buy your background?"

"I think so. They said they were going to check it out, though."

"Good. We gave you a solid history. Should be no problems. Let me know what they say."

"Will do."

"What about Ava Vargas?"

"I made contact with her last night. She actually ended up as my riding buddy while we're here at bike week. Turns out her best friend is Bo's girlfriend."

"Perfect. Have you found out anything yet?"

"Nothing much. She doesn't seem to be a biker. Seems green."

"Which doesn't mean shit. She doesn't have to be an expert to have something going on with the Hellraisers. Appearances can be deceiving. You should know that better than anyone."

"I know."

"Then get close to her and stay that way. There are several Hellraisers who've been busted in the past few months for drug distribution. Senator Vargas is shitting his pants that his daughter might be even remotely involved in this gang. And DEA is getting a hard-on over it, too. If Ms. Vargas is dirty, DEA wants to know about it."

"I'm on it."

"Good. Keep me updated."

Rick hung up, satisfied that he was on the right track, even if he did think the senator was being overly protective of his daughter and the DEA was totally off base. Then again, like Grange said, appearances could be deceiving and Ava might be deeply involved in the Hellraisers up to her soft, kissable neck.

But Rick had spent a lifetime trusting his instincts about people. And his instincts told him Ava was a fish out of water with the Hellraisers. He was going to have to find out just what she was doing there, and why.

And that meant staying close to her, no matter what he had to do to get there.

Hey, some jobs came with bonuses. And if he had to climb in bed with Ava Vargas to do his job—well, there were worse things he'd done in the line of duty.

He checked out the clock on his phone—it was almost seven-thirty. Would she be awake yet, or sleeping in? He went to the hotel phone and dialed her number, though his first thought had been to go straight to her room to see if he could wake her up.

The tightening in his jeans told him that would be a great way to start the day.

She answered on the second ring. "Hello?"

"Did I wake you?"

She let out a soft laugh. "No. I just got dressed. I'm dying for some coffee so I was going to head downstairs."

"I'll go with you. Be there in a sec."

He hung up, surprised to find himself eager to see her.

Which was probably just his dick talking. Anticipation and all. He knew what was going to happen between them. It was just a matter of time, and hopefully some finesse on his part.

She came out of the room just as he approached her door, looking fresh and pink-cheeked and well rested, though as late as they'd finished up last night and as early as it was now, she couldn't have gotten much more sleep than he had.

"Tired?" he asked.

Her cheeks darkened. "A little."

"You could have slept in."

"You would have woke me up with your phone call anyway."

"Good point."

They walked down the hall toward the elevator, awkward silence echoing around them. Rick felt it rise up between them like a thick, invisible cloud, shattering the ease they'd started with.

And he knew why.

So when they got to the elevator, he pulled Ava into his arms and slammed his mouth down on hers, giving her a kiss that told her exactly how it was going to be between them.

And damn, did she taste good in the morning, all soft and pliant and breathless against him. She tasted fresh—like toothpaste, her mouth cool and inviting. She made his dick hard in record time. He broke the kiss—reluctantly—as the elevator doors opened.

Her eyes were wide pools of stormy gray, her lips parted in surprise.

"I had a really good time talking to you on the phone last night."

She swallowed. "So did I."

He wrapped an arm around her and led her onto the elevator, and pushed the button. "So don't go all quiet and embarrassed on me now. I think we're past that."

She tilted her head to look at him, and he couldn't resist taking another taste of her lips. She didn't balk at being kissed in the elevator, and she didn't push away when the doors opened in the lobby. She kissed him back, her hand on his chest, her body resting against his.

When she stepped back, she smiled.

"All right?" he asked.

She nodded. "All right."

He took her hand and they headed into the coffee shop and found a table. The waitress came right over and they both ordered coffee and breakfast. As soon as coffee arrived, Ava wrapped her hands around the cup and lifted it to her lips, closed her eyes, and took a drink.

"Oh, God, that's good."

Rick watched her, admiring her sensual appreciation of even the smallest things. He wondered if she realized what she was doing. "I think you said that last night."

Her eyes shot open and she blushed. "It was good."

"I thought so. Not as good as the real thing, though."

"Maybe we'll get to experience that . . . soon."

Rick took a long swallow of coffee. "Definitely soon."

By the time the waitress brought their breakfast, Bo and Lacey had come into the restaurant. Ava waved and Lacey dragged Bo over.

"Girl, you look as tired as me," Lacey said as she pulled up a chair and turned over her coffee cup for the waitress. Lacey slid her glance from Rick back to Ava. "So, you and Rick hit it off well enough to stay up late last night?"

"We . . . talked for a while before we went to sleep."

"Talked? That's it?"

"That's it," Rick added.

Bo shook his head. "Man, you're gettin' rusty."

Ava hid her smile behind her coffee cup, then quieted while Lacey whispered to her.

Rick was going to do a little listening in on their conversation, but Bo yanked on his jacket.

"Hey, while the ladies are gossiping on the other side of the table, I wanted to let you know that your background checked out."

Rick leaned back in his chair and put on a knowing grin. "Was there any doubt?"

"Not really, but I have to be careful about who I trust with Hellraiser secrets, ya know."

"I understand. So now that you know I'm legit, what kind of secrets are you going to let me in on?"

"Well, none yet," Bo said with a sly smile. "But trust me, there's plenty going on."

Dammit. Rick wanted to know what and he wanted to know it all now. But he had to play it cool or his cousin would be suspicious. "Anything up my alley?"

"Maybe. I saw you did a little time for possession."

"Yeah."

"Joy drugs or business?"

"I don't do drugs, man. I like to keep a clear head. There's more money in selling them. Costs money to take them."

Bo nodded. "Good for you to follow the money. Better to earn it than to spend it."

"You got that right."

"Then maybe I'll have some work for you."

"Good. I don't like to lay low for too long. Makes me itchy."

"I always knew you'd be good for my business, Rick." Bo slapped him on the back. "Welcome home."

"Thanks." Now Rick was even more curious about what kind of *business* his cousin was involved in. But he couldn't push Bo or he'd get suspicious. He'd just have to ride, relax, and wait for Bo to come to him.

Which hopefully wouldn't be long. If his cousin really was heavily involved in the drug trade, there was always something going down. Especially at an event like bike week, where deals could be made by the hour.

Yeah, Rick expected to be useful before the end of the day today.

And that meant he might have to juggle undercover drug work with Bo, and handling Ava.

The assignment had just gotten a lot more interesting.

Riding on the back of a motorcycle gave Ava a lot of time to think. It was sweet mindlessness, the kind that required no concentration.

She enjoyed it, because she had a lot to think about, mainly having to do with Lacey. Okay, not so much about Lacey. More about the tall, leather-clad biker who rode the bike she was sitting on.

She sighed and felt just a little foolish and lovesick.

The kiss Rick had given her in the elevator this morning had shaken Ava to the core. But it had also relaxed her. While Rick hadn't exactly said how things were between them, the kiss was an unspoken bond, his way of saying there was definitely more between them than one-time phone sex.

Not that she'd been at all worried about it. After all, if that's all they'd shared, she would have just chalked it up to a new and unique experience and moved on.

Moved on to what, exactly, she didn't know, but she was here to spend time with Lacey. Though doing that was proving difficult since Lacey seemed to spend most of her time with Bo, either plastered right next to his side or on the back of his bike. Which gave Ava more free time than she'd expected.

Fortunately, Rick seemed to want to spend his free time with her. And she couldn't complain about that. The more time she spent with Rick, the more she could find out about the Hellraisers—and about his cousin, Bo. So being with Rick served a useful purpose.

Like making her breathless, hot, turned on, and quivery. She wondered if all bikers had this kind of effect on their women, or if it was just Rick and the fact she wasn't exactly the most experienced in the men department?

Surely it wasn't just her. After all, Lacey certainly seemed entranced by everything Bo. So maybe it was the whole biker mystique. She supposed at the end of this week she'd have it figured out.

Maybe.

Rick didn't seem to be the kind of guy any girl could figure out. He was chivalrous and kind and at the same time mysterious and aloof. And oh so sexy. Like the kind of guy every girl had a crush on in high school. The bad boy kind of guy, the one you wanted to redeem with your love.

But was he really bad? She didn't know the answer to that.

There were a lot of things she didn't know the answer to. Maybe she should start thinking with her head instead of the other parts of her anatomy that had seemed to take prevalence since she'd met Rick.

Or maybe she should have sex with Rick, get that out of the way, and then she could start thinking with her head.

She liked the latter idea a lot better.

They'd taken a long ride in the desert after breakfast, and the view in the daylight had been breathtaking, nothing at all like the blind ride in the dark last night.

She'd lived in Las Vegas her entire life, had ridden through the desert hundreds of times, but there was something about being exposed to it from a motorcycle point of view, where the air whipped in your face and you could see everything more clearly because you weren't bound by glass and metal on all four sides. This way made her *see* it for the very first time.

The desert was burnished copper and sage and golden sunlight, a cascade of color that painted the landscape of this place she called home—a place she'd taken for granted and had never appreciated for its awesome beauty until now. Maybe it was because on the bike she wasn't just seeing—all her other senses were in play, too—the smell of the earth rose up to meet her, the sound of a hundred motorcycles seeming to wake the desert's primal beauty and put on a spectacular show. Whenever they slowed down, Ava would spot lizards or other creatures hiding among the tall rocks. Soaring birds overhead seemingly kept pace with the Hellraisers.

They rode for over two hours, and it was exhilarating. She'd never enjoyed seeing the desert more.

They stopped at Joey's house again. This time Ava could see it in the light. It was a huge place, two stories with a wraparound porch on both the top and bottom floors. Behind the house was a barn and several sheds. And he had horses.

Ava climbed off the bike and immediately headed over to the fence to watch the horses that had gathered around the shaded areas. At least there were plenty of trees to shield the horses from the blistering desert heat.

"You like horses?"

She nodded at Rick. "I rode when I was younger. My dad used to take me to this place that would give rides. I even took lessons. I wanted to own a horse ranch."

"You did?"

She laid her arms on the top post and rested her chin on top of them. "Yes. A child's dream, of course."

"Why did it have to be a child's dream?"

"I don't know. Just not feasible, I suppose."

"Anything's doable, Ava. You just have to want it, then work for it."

She turned her head to the side. "Other dreams replaced that one."

"Like becoming a social worker."

"Yes."

"When was the last time you saddled up and rode?"

"Oh, I haven't ridden in years."

"Let's fix that." He walked away and Ava turned around, not sure what he meant by that.

Until he flagged down Joey. The two of them talked and Rick motioned to the horses, then to her. Joey nodded.

Oh, no. He hadn't.

But when he came toward her with a grin on his face, she was afraid he had.

"Let's saddle up."

"Are you serious?"

"Sure. You want to ride, don't you?"

"Uh, I guess so. But really, you didn't have to do that."

"Sure I did. Come on."

She followed him toward the barn. "Are you sure it's okay?"

"Joey said the horses need to be ridden. He said we'd be doing him a favor by taking a couple out."

There were already a couple horses near the barn, and they were very tame, came over willingly when Rick called them. Ava couldn't resist drawing closer to one, a chestnut mare with a white star-shaped mark above her eyes. She was simply gorgeous. Ava lifted her hand to the mare's muzzle and let her get a whiff of her scent so she'd get used to her.

"She likes you," Rick said as he came over with a saddle. "You want to ride that one?"

"Yes." She went to take the saddle from Rick. "Here, let me do it."

"Do you know how?"

She rolled her eyes. "Some things you never forget. Do *you* know how?"

He grinned. "Of course."

"And how is that? I thought you grew up in Las Vegas. And then spent time in Chicago. Sounds citified to me."

"You grew up here. How do you know how to saddle and ride?"

"Good point." And yet again he'd avoided revealing

anything about himself. He sure liked being a man of mystery.

After they'd saddled their horses, Ava mounted hers, realizing it had been a very long time since she'd ridden. But oh, it felt great to be seated again, to feel the strength of a horse underneath her. She was so ready to ride.

They took a slow walk out of the barn and down the road, taking it easy while the horses got used to them. Ava slanted an occasional glance over to Rick, who seated his horse like he'd been born on one.

"Where did you ride before?" she asked.

"I had a friend with horses when I was a kid," he said. "I helped him out as much as I could, mucking out stalls, brushing the horses. His folks liked me so they taught me to ride."

"That's nice. But you didn't have any of your own."

He snorted. "Uh, no. Barely had a roof over my head."

"No wonder you enjoyed spending time with your friend who had horses."

"Anything was better than being at home."

"That bad, huh?"

"That bad."

"Do you want to talk about it?"

He looked at her. "What do you think?"

"I think sometimes it's good to exorcise the pain of the past by getting it out in the open. Do you ever talk about it?"

"Nope."

"Then it still festers inside you."

He laughed. "Yeah, you can tell I hold a ton of anger."

Okay, so he did look relaxed, and he was almost always calm and in control. She'd never seen him angry, but then again she hadn't known him all that long. But he didn't project that kind of chip on his shoulder like some men did. The man was a mix of complexities and incongruity. She couldn't figure him out.

"I'm not a textbook case, Ava. Don't look for problems that don't exist."

"Everyone has problems, Rick. Some just bury them better than others."

He pulled up on the reins and slowed. She did, too.

"And some of us might be playing at being a social worker."

She lifted her chin. "I am not."

"Good." He clicked the reins and started his horse on a trot.

Ava kept up with him, giving her horse some leg, which she seemed to enjoy. It was exhilarating to bounce in the saddle, reminding her of what it was like when she was a kid. When Rick passed her, she urged her horse on, and soon they were galloping into the pasture. The horses seemed to love going at full tilt. Ava certainly did.

They finally pulled up under a group of trees near one of the small ponds. They climbed off and tied the horses up to give them some time to breathe and get a drink. Rick sat under one of the trees and Ava joined him.

"I'm not making you an experiment, you know."

He uncapped a bottle of water and handed it to her, but didn't say anything. She took a long drink and handed it back to him. "I don't like talking about my past."

"It's easier to put it behind you if you do."

"I've already talked plenty about it. I don't want to do it again."

She turned to face him, crossing her legs over each other. "So you had counseling?"

His lips curled. "You could say that."

"Did it help?"

He shrugged. "It forced me to face some things I didn't really want to examine again."

"Like?"

"There you go again . . . probing. Maybe you should have been a psychologist."

Funny he should mention that. "That was Lacey's major."

"Was?"

"Yes. She dropped out midway through her master's."

"Why?"

"Because she met Bo and joined the Hellraisers."

"You don't approve."

Her head shot up. "What makes you say that?" His smirk irritated her. He seemed to be able to read her so well. Was she that transparent?

"The tone of your voice."

"Oh. Well, it's not that I don't approve."

"Maybe she didn't want to be a psychologist after all."

"I guess not."

He tilted his head and studied her. "But you don't believe that."

She leaned against the trunk of the tree, wondering how the topic had drifted to Lacey, when what she really wanted was to talk about him. But she supposed having someone to talk to about her best friend wasn't a bad idea. "Honestly? I don't know what to believe. She had a complete personality transformation in the past year."

"Since she met Bo."

"Yes."

"Falling in love can change someone. Maybe meeting Bo switched her priorities."

"It shouldn't."

"Bo's lifestyle is a lot different than Lacey's. Maybe he introduced her to things she'd never known before, forced her to examine the life she had and she found it lacking. Maybe she prefers the life of the Hellraisers to one of academia."

Huh. She'd never thought of those things. Now it was her turn to study him. "You're very smart for—"

He laughed. "For what? For a biker?"

"I'm sorry. That didn't come out like I meant it to."

"If you think bikers are so dumb, what are you doing here, Ava?"

"It isn't what I meant at all. I guess I just have my own preconceived notions of who bikers are. I didn't expect . . ." She couldn't go on. There was nothing she could say to get her foot out of her mouth.

"Go ahead," he said, laughter still tingeing his voice. "It takes a lot to insult me. I really want to know what you think."

"I guess I don't expect you all to be college educated."

"We're not. I'm not. But some are. Bikers come from all walks of life, Ava. Open your eyes and take a look around. Talk to some of the people in biker groups. They're anything from day laborers to doctors, from fast-food employees to scientists, and everything in between. All you need is a love of motorcycles and riding."

"To be in a regular motorcycle club, you mean. Not necessarily the Hellraisers."

Rick grabbed a hunk of grass and pulled it, then let it sift through his fingers, piece by piece, to the ground. "The Hellraisers are different. They're more like a lifestyle."

"So there is a difference in the type of people who become Hellraisers?"

"Maybe."

She sighed. "You confuse me."

"Good. I'd hate to think I was predictable."

"You're definitely not predictable."

He leaned in, and once again she inhaled the scent of leather, of horses, and the outdoors. Of him. She mainly liked his scent and moved a little closer.

"Predictable is boring. It's safe. Knowing everything about someone is the kiss of death to a relationship."

He was coming closer, and she knew he was going to kiss her. "Knowing everything about someone means you can trust them."

He paused, his lips lifting. "I don't think you can ever trust someone completely. Or know everything there is about them. That's part of the fun. Peeling the layers back a bit at a time instead of all at once."

"Like what we're doing now?"

"Yes."

So close she felt his breath brush her cheek. He combed his fingers through her ponytail, letting the tendrils fall back onto her shoulder like a soft rain. Her lips parted on a sigh and he pressed his mouth to hers.

God, it was sweet. The day was warm but there was a cool breeze. She needed it to cool down her raging libido, which

had come to life in an instant as soon as Rick's lips touched
hers. She melted into him and he pulled her onto his lap. She
went willingly, his arms wrapping around her in a cocoon.
Oh, she liked the feel of him surrounding her. She laid her
hand on his chest where his jacket was open, felt his heart
beating—strong, steady, gradually increasing in rhythm as
his lips plundered hers. She imagined her heart doing the
same, pumping a mad rhythm as his tongue slid between her
parted lips. He dipped her head down in the crook of his
arm, cradling her as he kissed her with more depth, more
passion, until she was swimming in sensation and wholly
unable to catch a breath.

This was madness, this loss of control out here in the wil-
derness. Already her mind was pummeled by images of what
Rick could do to her out here, and all of them were naughty,
forbidden, and everything she wanted. Undressing her completely, until she was naked to the elements, then licking
every part of her body until he devoured her pussy, making
her come over and over until her screams echoed off the
canyon walls.

She shuddered in his arms and he pulled away, looking
down on her with eyes dark with passion.

"Do you want to peel some layers, Ava?"

Physical or psychological? She didn't know what he
meant. Should she ask? Did it matter?

Why did she find it so hard to breathe whenever he got
close to her? She wasn't a teenager anymore. She was an
adult. A woman experienced in sex and relationships. Yet her
pulse raced and all her intimate body parts swelled and
throbbed in anticipation, as if this was the first time, the
first man.

Getting involved in an intimate relationship with Rick
wasn't why she had come to the Hellraisers. She was supposed to be spending time with Lacey.

But finding out more about bikers might give her insight
into what the attraction was for Lacey. And that might help.

You're making excuses. You want him. So he wasn't part
of her overall plan for being here this week. So what? Why

couldn't she just jump into something without thinking about it, plotting it, charting it, or examining it a hundred different ways?

Rick smiled and gently lifted her off his lap, then stood, held his hand out. "Come on."

"Where are we going?"

"Back to Joey's. I think the horses have rested long enough."

What? Why? She took a quick glance at him before he turned away and headed toward the horses, saw the outline of his erection, knew what would have happened if she hadn't hesitated.

Dammit. She'd ruined another moment by having to think out every possibility. What the hell was wrong with her anyway?

She hurried to catch up with him. "We don't have to leave yet. I'm sorry. I didn't mean to—"

He dragged her into his arms and ravaged her mouth with a demanding, hard kiss, the kind that curled her toes, made her stop breathing—stop thinking—the kind of kiss that melted her right there and made her as hot as the desert sun. When he pulled away, she had no idea what to think, other than her legs were shaking. And she wanted more of his mouth on her.

"You didn't do anything wrong. We need to get out of here. I don't want to make love to you in the middle of the desert. It's getting late and the others will be leaving Joey's house soon. I need to get with Bo about something before everyone takes off."

"Oh."

"But I *am* going to make love to you, Ava. Count on it."

He untethered her horse and handed her the reins. She mounted up, the tenderness of her pussy making contact with the saddle reminding her of what was going to happen between them.

But when? And where?

Six

Timing was everything. Or in Rick and Ava's case, never a good thing. Why was it that every time things got hot and heavy between them, the timing wasn't right?

He supposed that meant that once the timing was finally right, it was going to be damn good.

He hoped it was going to be soon, because his balls were aching. Getting off with her by phone last night had just been a teaser, had left his mind filled with images of her naked and touching herself, her fingers buried in her pussy. He got hard just thinking about it. And this afternoon in the desert he'd edged toward stripping her and fucking her right there on the ground.

But something just wasn't right about that. When they got naked together he wanted some goddamned privacy—with nothing to interrupt them. So again he'd put the brakes on.

He wondered when he had developed scruples. Typically he didn't care where he pulled out his dick, as long as he and the lady got off. And he knew damn well he could get Ava off. From the way she wriggled in his lap, her heavy breath-ing, the way she clutched his jacket—she was primed for an orgasm or ten.

But no, not there. Not then.

Tonight, for sure. Other than the apocalypse, nothing was going to keep him from getting naked with Ava.

They'd ridden the horses back to Joey's, unsaddled and brushed them down, which gave them just enough time to make it back to Joey's house for one cold beer before every-one was ready to ride out of there. There was a bike event that Bo wanted to check out on the Strip, and then an outside band playing tonight where they were all going to gather.

It was dark by the time they reached Las Vegas, the lights of the city just beginning to show their sparkle. Rick had forgotten how much he liked being on the Strip. When he was a kid he used to imagine being rich and making it big in Vegas. He and Bo and their friends would play cards in one of the guys' garages and Rick would imagine himself as a high roller, welcomed at all the casinos as a hotshot who won big and spent big. He laughed at how naïve he'd once been.

Now he just enjoyed seeing the allure of Vegas—but knowing that he'd leave it as soon as this assignment was over. Las Vegas was part of his past, but would always be home to him.

He'd outgrown the desire to be rich and famous. He was content enough to have stayed out of trouble, to have the job he held, a few people he could call friends. He wondered how things would have been different if General Lee hadn't walked into his life all those years ago. Would he lead the Hellraisers by now, like Bo did, or would he be rotting in a jail cell somewhere? Or something even worse than that?

He'd gotten damn lucky. He wondered what choices Bo had made for his life, still didn't know the extent of what the Hellraisers were up to. Part of him hoped that Bo wasn't into anything bad. They might not be close anymore, but Bo was the only family Rick had. At least the only family Rick acknowledged having. Rick's parents had long ago given up on him. As far as he was concerned, they were dead. For all he knew, they really were dead by now. Given their lifestyles as cokeheads, they probably were. Or in jail. He didn't care. The only person he'd ever cared about was Bo.

But he also knew Bo was an adult, and as an adult you made your own choices, chose what road you traveled. If Bo was down and dirty there wouldn't be much Rick could do to help him.

But considering the hellholes they'd both been raised in, Rick hoped Bo knew better than to involve himself in the same kind of corruption, knowing where he might end up.

The last thing he'd want to do was arrest his cousin. But if he had to, he would. The Hellraisers would let their own kin rot in jail if they got caught by the cops. And Rick would take his own cousin down if he was dirty.

That's just the way it was. In some areas, you didn't protect family. You had to stand on your own and face the consequences.

They grabbed some dinner and then hit a bar to kick back and have some beers for a couple hours. Ava went off to chat at a table with Lacey. Bo was off somewhere, so Rick had some time to catch up with guys he hadn't seen in a while. It was good to hit some downtime, to see what he could find out about what the Hellrasiers were up to. Unfortunately, no one was going to tell him anything, despite his connection as Bo's cousin. Until Bo gave them the okay to bring Rick into the inner sanctum of the Hellraisers, all the talk was going to be surface at best.

After dinner, Ava and Lacey wanted to wander the exhibits so he and Bo fell in behind them while the girls shopped. Bo spent most of his time on the phone, so Rick contented himself with watching Ava as she walked ahead with her friend, stopping at a booth to admire jewelry or a painting. While Lacey oohed and aahed over trinkets, Ava seemed more reserved. She didn't spend money extravagantly. Lacey ran to Bo every time she saw a bauble that caught her eye.

Bo would just roll his eyes and fork over the money. And from what Rick could see, Bo had one hell of a wad of cash in his wallet.

Rick wanted to know where Bo got that kind of money, but knew better than to ask. Asking too many questions too soon would only cause suspicion. It was still time to lay low and wait for Bo to come to him. Rick knew how the game was played. Sooner or later Bo would come around, and then Rick would know what the Hellraisers were up to. Playing it cool was always the best bet. Getting too eager was the easiest way to blow a cover.

After a couple hours of shopping Bo had had enough and dragged Lacey away from the booths, saying it was time for some guy fun. They were burning rubber at an exhibition at the end of the Strip—where bikers could trash their tires by revving up their engines in one spot to see who could bring up the most smoke. That's what Bo had wanted to see. Some of the Hellraisers had gone off to do other things, while a group hung with Bo to watch the burnouts.

Rick glanced over at Ava, who seemed fascinated by all the smoke and noise of the screeching tires. She lifted up on her toes to see the wheels, so he pushed his way into the crowd, pulling her along with him to give her a closer view.

"This is awesome," she whispered when he drew her in front of him.

"Yeah, it can be."

"They're ruining their tires."

"Yes."

She tilted her head back, her hair brushing his chin. "Why?"

He laughed. "Because they want to win."

She shook her head and waved at the smoke wafting their way. "Men. Testosterone. Competition."

"Yeah, that's pretty much it."

The next bike pulled up to try his burnout, and Bo came up behind Rick. "Got a second?"

"Yeah." He leaned down to Ava. "Stay here. I'll be right back."

Ava nodded, her gaze fixated on the biker who revved the throttle and started spinning his wheels. Rick moved through the crowd with Bo and they rounded the corner, away from the smoke and noise.

"What's up?" Rick asked.

"I need you to make a delivery for me tonight."

"What kind of delivery?"

Bo's lips lifted. "I think you know." He pulled a small padded envelope out of his pocket.

Yeah, Rick knew exactly what that was. "Okay, what's in it?"

"You don't need to know that."

Rick frowned. "I don't make deliveries unless I know what I'm delivering. You tell me what's in there or I walk."

Bo studied him for a second and Rick read the anger in his eyes. Tough shit. Rick wasn't going to be played by anyone, including his cousin.

"Coke."

"Fine. Where's it going?"

Bo gave him the name and address of the delivery—some liquor store in the city, but not on the Strip.

"Ask for T-bone. Buy a bottle of Jack Daniel's. He'll meet you around back and hand you the money."

Bo was specific about the amount of money Rick was supposed to get.

"I want you in my hotel room with the cash right after that."

"What, you don't want me spending some of the profits at the Venetian?"

"Funny. Just bring it to me and you'll get paid."

Rick took the package and slid it inside his jacket. "Sounds easy enough. When do you want the drop made?"

"Before midnight when the store closes. Meet me back at my room at the hotel."

"You got it."

Rick pivoted around the corner and went back to find Ava. Along the way, he pulled out his cell phone and sent a quick text message to General Lee, letting him know he'd just been recruited by Bo to make a drug drop. He had to maintain cover, so it wasn't like he could tell Bo what he really did for a living, which meant he was going to have to break the law. But everything he did gathered evidence against the Hellraisers.

Not ideal, considering Bo was his cousin, but Bo had made his own bed. There wasn't much Rick could do about that. Just like the Hellraisers had cut ties with Rick after Rick disappeared, a bond only went so far.

And it wasn't like he could have turned down the job. To get back into the Hellraisers he had to be a Hellraiser, 100 percent. He felt a momentary shadow of guilt over what he was doing, but brushed it aside. Bo was dirty.

He dug into the crowd by the burnout demo to find Ava. She hadn't moved, but a couple bikers had muscled in and flanked her. She was talking to them—laughing as they pointed out what was happening.

Rick pushed back his irritation at seeing the guys trying to muscle in on his woman.

He stopped himself. Ava wasn't *his* woman. She didn't belong to him. He was on a case. She wasn't his girlfriend.

Jesus. He really needed to get a grip and remember his priorities.

Still, seeing one of the guys rub her back made him want to break the dude's arm. Which meant he was getting closer to Ava than he should.

But wasn't that the assignment? He just didn't want another guy stealing her away. Then he couldn't do his job. That was it, and that's all it was. Nothing more.

He nudged a few people aside and elbowed the back-rubber out of the way, moving to Ava's side. Her face brightened with a smile.

"Oh, hey, I thought I'd lost you."

He leaned in and pressed a long, soft kiss to her lips. "Not a chance. Sorry I was gone so long."

She licked her lips, her pink tongue darting out to sweep along her bottom lip. His dick noticed, quivering to attention.

"It's okay. Axe and Roger kept me company."

She seemed comfortable enough with the two guys. Did she know them? Had he been wrong about how naïve she was about the gang? Maybe she knew more than he thought. And maybe she didn't. That's what he was here to find out.

Either way, he didn't like the guys being so close to her. Rick slung his arm around Ava's shoulder and sent a very clear signal to the two men, who backed away instantly. "I'll just bet they did."

"No, really, they were very nice."

"Uh-huh. Let's go."

He'd been planning to leave her here to hang out while he ran the errand for Bo. But now that he saw two guys moving in on her? No fucking way was he leaving her alone.

He moved them out of the crowd and headed down the street where his bike was parked.

"Where are we going? And why are you so angry?"

"For a ride. And I'm not angry."

"Yes you are. You're all tensed up and your teeth are clenched."

He relaxed his muscles, turned to her, and gritted out a smile. "There. Better?"

She laughed. "Not really. But nice try."

She didn't seem upset, instead looped her arm through his while they walked, which helped to dissolve his anger. They climbed on the bike and took off.

The ride to the liquor store took almost thirty minutes. Traffic was getting heavier because of the influx of bikers, so the streets were crowded. But at this time of night and the fact that most of the events wouldn't start until tomorrow, it wasn't bad. Besides, he'd grown up here, so he knew all the side roads to take.

He pulled up in front of the liquor store and climbed off. Then turned to Ava, hating that he'd brought her along. This wasn't the place for her. Shitty neighborhood. But he couldn't very well drag her inside with him.

Fuck. He had to do this quick.

"I'll be right back. Just hang out here."

Ava looked around, probably not thrilled with the prospect of being left alone in this part of the city. He couldn't blame her but there wasn't much he could do about it. If for some reason this sale went bad and he got busted he didn't want her in there with him.

"I promise, I'll be right back."

She nodded and he strolled inside, the envelope tucked into the inside of his jacket.

The only person working was a guy sporting a red Mohawk and more tattoos than he could count.

"I need to see T-bone."

The dude lifted his head. "Yeah? Why?"

Rick shrugged. "I don't know. I guess Bo thought I could get a good deal on whiskey here."

T-bone eyed him up and down. "I'm T-bone. What kind of whiskey you like?"

"Jack Daniel's."

T-bone nodded. "That'll work."

T-bone rang up the small bottle of Jack. Rick put it in his jacket, then circled out the front door, raised his hand to Ava to tell her to stay put. He strolled around the corner and toward the back of the store. T-bone was waiting for him. Rick handed him the package. T-bone opened it, nodded, and handed Rick an envelope. Rick pulled it open and flipped through the bills. Satisfied it was the right amount of money, Rick slid the envelope into his inside coat pocket. Without a word he went back to the bike.

"Where did you go?" Ava asked as Rick put on his helmet and got back on the bike.

"I had to take a leak."

She laughed, which meant she'd bought his excuse. "Oh. How convenient to be a guy where the world is your urinal."

He shot her a grin over his shoulder. "Isn't it?" He started up the bike and headed out of there, hating that he'd just broken the law, even if he was undercover and therefore immune from prosecution. It still didn't sit right with him. But he had to do what was necessary to stay with the Hellraisers, and saying no to Bo wasn't an option.

"Where are we going now?" Ava asked over his shoulder.

"Back to the hotel."

"Oh. Okay."

They parked the bike and headed to the elevators. Ava frowned when Rick pushed the button.

"That's not our floor."

"No, it's not. I need to stop at Bo's room for a minute."

"Why?"

"I need to talk to him."

"Couldn't you just call him?"

"No."

"Why not?"

He rolled his eyes as they walked down the hallway. Intelligent women were really difficult sometimes. "Because I need to talk to him in person."

"Why?"

Fortunately, they got to the door just in time. He was running out of lame responses. He knocked. No answer. Knocked again, harder this time, hoping he'd be heard over the loud music and laughter coming from Bo's room. The door finally opened. Bo stood there, shirtless, a bottle of beer in his hands, his jeans unbuttoned.

"Oh, hey. Come on in. We're partying."

Yeah, partying was right. Rick smelled the pot as soon as Bo had opened the door. Lacey was on the bed, obviously drunk—or maybe stoned—laughing her ass off with some other girl. Another guy sat on the chair smoking a joint and drinking a beer.

Lacey wore only her jeans and her bra. She was barefoot. Her jeans button was undone. The other girl was in her underwear. The guy in the chair had his shirt off, too.

And the room wasn't so hot they needed to be stripping due to the room temperature, so there was some fun going on in here.

He should have taken Ava to her room first.

Then again, this was a good opportunity to gauge her reaction to hard-core partying.

She didn't seem uncomfortable, just went into the room and sat on the edge of the bed and started talking to Lacey and the other girl. Lacey introduced Ava to the girl and they engaged in conversation.

So far, so good.

"How about a beer?" Bo asked, motioning Rick into the bathroom where there was a cooler in the tub.

"Sure."

Rick followed, and Bo turned to him. "Did you make the drop?"

"Yeah." He pulled the envelope out and handed it to Bo, who pulled out the money, counted it, then handed some over to Rick.

"Any problems?"

"None."

"Good." Bo pocketed the cash and fished into the cooler for two beers, handed them to Rick. "I'll have more work for you, then."

"You can count on me. I need the cash."

Bo slapped him on the back. "That's what I like to hear, buddy."

They stepped into the room again and Rick handed Ava a beer as he walked by. She looked up at him and smiled. He took a seat on one of the chairs and propped his feet on the edge of the other bed to watch her, conscious of her watching Lacey interact with the other girl, whose name was Rachel.

Rachel was a hard-core biker chick, born and bred to the lifestyle with bleached blond hair that fell to her shoulders, well tattooed on various parts of her body, and a scar or two that said she'd had to fight for her life on several occasions. She looked tough, like she'd seen a lot and been a lot of places—places a nicely bred daughter of a senator had probably never been.

Ava seemed to be studying Rachel, too, and not saying

much to either Rachel or Lacey, just watching the way the two women interacted with each other. Ava was more of an observer, though Lacey seemed to be trying to get Ava involved in whatever game Lacey was trying to play.

Rick wondered just what kind of game that was—and how into it Ava would be.

Ava sat back and watched Lacey interact with Rachel, wondering if Lacey had undergone an entire personality transplant. Because Lacey had transformed into a complete stranger.

Gone was the shy, introverted best friend she'd always known. In her place was a wild party girl, obviously drunk, stoned, or possibly both. She was half naked and lying on the bed with a tattooed, gorgeous woman and about to do—well, who knew what had been going on between the two women and two men in this room when they had walked in? From the various states of undress, Ava could only guess at what had been going on.

She had to ask.

"Lace, what are you doing?"

Lacey turned glazed eyes in her direction. "Partying, honey. Come join us." Lacey raised a bottle of beer and saluted Ava, then guzzled the remnants of the bottle and put it on the nightstand. "Hey, Bo, I need another brew. And another buzz."

"Sure, babe." Bo rose from his seat, went into the bathroom, and came back with an open bottle of beer. In his mouth was a lit joint, its pungent smell filling the small suite. He took a toke and handed it to Lacey, who inhaled deeply, held it, and blew out the smoke with a satisfied smile before holding it out for Ava.

"You want some?"

Ava shook her head. "No, thanks."

Lacey shrugged, giggled, and handed the joint off to Rachel.

Ava was no prude. She'd seen her fair share of wild sex and partying at college, though she hadn't participated. She'd been exposed to plenty of drugs and alcohol at those parties, too. It was easy to just say no. And they both had. She and Lacey had been to a ton of parties, some of which had gotten pretty out of control. She'd admittedly stayed and watched a few that had gotten into full-on orgy mode, though she was mostly a sideline viewer. And Lacey hadn't wanted part of any of it, including drinking, doing any kind of drugs, or participating in the unbound sex romps that always seemed to be happening in the dorms or the frat houses.

Now, Ava sat on the edge of the bed watching Lacey, who didn't seem tentative or turned off at all. Rachel leaned back on her elbows while Lacey leaned over her and smoothed her hands over Rachel's hair. Ava had to swallow a gasp when Lacey kissed Rachel.

"That's hot, babe," Bo said from his spot on the other bed, his erection clearly visible against his tight jeans. "Keep doing that."

Ava swiveled and caught Rick's gaze. He, too, seemed riveted on the action between Lacey and Rachel. Ava rose from the bed and went over to Rick, who pulled her onto his lap and wrapped his arm around her.

"Do you want to leave?" he asked.

She looked over her shoulder at him. "Do you?"

He gave her a half smile. "I'm leaving it up to you. I'm good either way."

She slid into the chair next to him. "Far be it for me to deny you some voyeuristic action. Go for it. You can even participate if you'd like."

Rick pulled his gaze from the two women and leveled it on her. "But you're just here to watch. You find the whole thing distasteful and you're suppressing your puritan instincts for my benefit."

She laughed. "I never claimed to be a puritan."

"So maybe I just see you that way. Girl on girl and orgy just doesn't seem to be your scene."

"Really? And what does?"

He nuzzled her ear and whispered. "No clue, since I haven't fucked you yet. I don't know what you like . . . or don't like."

Her body heated at his blunt words, at the thought of Rick discovering in detail what she did like. "Wow, you just put it right out there, don't you?"

"Do you want me to hedge?"

"I guess not." She would rather know what he was thinking. She just wasn't used to a man like him. Maybe that's what made him so interesting, so sexy. He was a man who seemed to know exactly what he wanted and didn't want.

"Do you want to leave right now, or stick around to see what happens?"

Sitting next to him, her thigh pressed against his, her breast against his chest—made her want only one thing. But she was here for Lacey. She needed to find out what the hell was going on with her best friend. And frankly, she was curious about what was going to happen in this room between these four people.

"I'd like to stay for a while."

"Okay. But you might want to relax a little. Your elbow is poking my ribs."

"Oh. Sorry." She leaned back in the chair and Rick put his arm around her.

But relax? Not likely. Not watching what was going on in the bed.

Bo put his beer down, wiped his mouth, and crawled on the bed with the two women, got between them, framed Lacey's face between his large hands, and planted a long, hard kiss on her lips. Lacey rolled over and wrapped her legs around Bo.

Bo's friend—Nathan was his name, she thought—also got up and went over to the bed. Rachel straddled him and rocked her panty-clad pussy against his jeans while Nathan held her hips.

Bo shifted Lacey to the side so he could fondle her breasts

through her bra and watch what Nathan and Rachel were doing. With his other free hand, he pulled the zipper down on Lacey's jeans.

Ava felt like a dirty voyeur, like they should get up and leave. They shouldn't be watching this. Then again, if the couples had wanted privacy, they would have said so, wouldn't they? And they certainly wouldn't be doing what they were doing while the other couple watched.

Still, Lacey was her best friend, and she'd never seen her best friend be so—intimate—with a man. It felt wrong. Yet, she couldn't seem to muster up the willpower to tear her gaze away, or tell Rick they should leave. Instead, she gripped the arm of the chair with one hand, Rick's thigh with the other, and tried to ignore the pinging arousal of every nerve ending in her body. Which was damned difficult to do with Rick sitting next to her. She heard him breathing, felt his gaze on her. She didn't know who he was watching more— her or the foursome on the bed. She was afraid to glance over in his direction, not sure what she'd do if she made eye contact, if he was as aroused as she was.

Watching these couples shouldn't turn her on, but it did. It was like a movie come to life, four couples writhing together on the bed. Touching, kissing, undressing each other. And though she knew she shouldn't be there, nothing could tear her away.

If she was any friend at all, she'd drag Lacey out of there.

But Lacey was an adult and capable of making her own decisions. Gone were the teenaged days of having each other's backs. Lacey'd made her choices. And if her choice was to engage in group sex in a stoned, drunken stupor, so be it.

And now Ava was bearing witness to it all, which should make her feel squeamish as hell, not hot and bothered.

But Ava realized it had nothing to do with her best friend being star of the show, and everything to do with a hard-bodied sexy male crushed tightly in the chair next to her. The room was hot and his scent filled the space around them. Earthy, musky, like leather and the outdoors, Rick's scent obliterated the stale odor of pot and beer that permeated the room.

She found she'd much rather focus on him, smell him, look at him. He was way more appealing than the action on the bed. She shifted, tilting her hip into the chair so she partially faced him.

"You bored?" he asked, picking up a strand of her hair.

"Watching other people have sex isn't nearly as much fun as doing it."

He cupped her chin between his fingers and brushed his lips across hers. Feather light, the shock to her senses was electric, more powerful than if he'd bruised her with a demanding, hard kiss. It left her wanting more . . . much more, charging her nerve endings with tiny pinpricks of awareness. Her body felt alive, needy. And with each slow slide of his mouth across hers, she was the one who felt drugged, drunk, and all she'd had was two sips of beer. It wasn't alcohol driving her haywire. It was Rick, making her forget where she was, even who she was. All she could think about was grabbing on to his leather jacket and drawing him closer, throwing her leg over his so she could rub her pussy against his thigh.

She was wet, the denim of her jeans pressing her panties into her moist flesh, making her aware of how much she wanted him, wanted this. When he pulled away, Ava glanced over at the bed.

Lacey's jeans were off. So was her bra. Rachel was naked and Nathan's mouth was latched onto one of her nipples.

Bo had moved Lacey underneath him and ground his jean-clad body against her, his hands all over her breasts while he kissed her.

The sensory overload was too much, the decadence exciting her to boiling point. She couldn't take any more of this.

She turned to Rick. "Take me out of here now and fuck me."

He stood, offering his hand to pull her up.

In that split second she caught sight of his erection visible against his jeans. She shuddered and tilted her head, licked her lips.

Rick grabbed his jacket, hers, and walked them out of the room without a word. Really, there was nothing to be said. The others were too engrossed in their own passion to even care . . . or notice . . . that they were leaving.

And Ava was too intent on Rick to care about saying good-bye. There was only one thing she wanted now.

Rick.

Seven

Ava shivered in the elevator.

"You cold?"

She shook her head.

"Nervous?"

"No. Not nervous."

Rick moved in, palmed the wall on either side of her shoulders, his erection making contact with her aching pussy. She nearly died right there, shocks of pleasure centered at her clit, right where he touched her.

"Then what's wrong?"

"Just get me to my room, unless you're fond of elevator sex."

His lips curled, and oh, God, the heat in the elevator tripled when he smiled like that. It was a good thing she had the wall at her back for support, because her legs were useless.

"I'm okay with elevator sex if you don't think you can wait that long."

Thank God the doors opened right then because she was just about ready to take him up on his offer. He took her hand and dragged her down the hall.

"Your room or mine?" he asked.

She'd already fished her key out of her bag. "Mine's closer."

He grabbed the key from her hand, unlocked the door, and pushed it open. She was inside, the door shut, and Rick had her in his arms a split second later. Their jackets fell to the floor. It was pitch-black in the room and she felt blind as Rick walked her backward a few steps until she hit the wall.

That's as far as they got before his lips came crashing down on hers.

Ahh, contact. His body moved in, flush against hers so she could feel every muscle, every hard, throbbing part of him. His mouth was on hers, his tongue sliding inside to lick against hers. His hands roamed her shoulders, down her arms, stroking her hips and waist, traveling around to cup her buttocks and bring her even closer to the rock-hard heat of his cock.

His mouth did delicious things to her senses—what little senses she had left, anyway. All she could focus on was his touch, the way he tasted, the masterful way he held her—so firm and tight in his arms—and yet she sensed a strong desperation like maybe he, too, wanted this as badly as she did. Could that even be possible? Rick always seemed so laid-back, like nothing really mattered to him.

Did this matter?

When he pulled the bottom of her shirt out of her jeans and he laid his palm over the bare skin of her belly, she shuddered and tilted her head back, breaking the kiss. She needed air, some coherence, something to balance her. She felt out of control and she was never out of control. Sex had always been easy, a natural progression that arose out of dinner, a few drinks, being comfortable and relaxed with her partner.

This was anything but easy and relaxed. It was tense, agitated, crazy, a frenzy of passion and pent-up anxiety. Her entire body felt like it was ready to explode at the slightest touch—Rick's touch. She couldn't handle this.

"What's wrong?"

She panted through the words. "I can't . . ."

And then she felt Rick's tension. He took a step back.

Oh, no. That's not what she'd meant.

She didn't want to be anywhere else.

"No." She grabbed his arms. "Wait." She wasn't going to let this happen again. She wasn't going to let him slide on the brakes because she hesitated. Because she feared that loss of control.

Maybe it was good to experience out of control for once, to let someone else take charge and see what it felt like. So far, it was giddy and exhilarating, even if it did make her dizzy. Maybe it was all the secondhand pot she'd inhaled in Bo's room.

But she doubted it. Not when Rick's hands snaked up her bare belly, moving her shirt with them.

"You sure?"

The warmth of his breath caressed her cheek.

"Yes." She clasped onto his wrist, held him there. "Touch me."

Her heart skittered and raced as his fingertips hit the edge of her bra and skimmed over the satin.

"You have nice breasts, Ava. I want to suck your nipples."

His whispered words in the dark made her wet, made her clit tingle, made her want to slide her hands down her jeans and make herself come right now. But before she could do anything, he lifted her shirt, forcing her arms in the air so he could remove it.

He laid his hand on her cheek and slid his palm down her neck, along her collarbone, and to her shoulder, then walked his fingers to the swell of her breasts, caressing her with feather-light touches that made her gasp.

And then he lingered against her left breast, as if he were feeling her heartbeat. Just a slow slide of his fingers, back and forth. Maddening. And too damn slow. It was time to speed this along. She wanted him inside her right now.

She grabbed his wrists and pulled his hands down, then reached for the clasp of her bra.

But he was faster than her. He pushed her hand away.

"That's my job."

"You're too slow."

"You in a hurry?"

She blew out a sigh. "Kind of, yes."

"You have an appointment?"

He was laughing at her. Dammit. "No."

"Then why rush this? We have all night."

"Because. I want this. I want you. I want it now."

He slid his arms around her waist and jerked her against him. Her thighs pressed against his, her hip rubbed his erection. She reached between them and palmed his cock, measuring him, feeling the heat of him that permeated the denim. When he hissed, she knew his control came at a great cost. Somehow it made her feel better, like her frenzy wasn't as one-sided as she'd thought.

But he obviously had much greater control than she did at the moment. And she'd always prided herself on her control. But not tonight, and definitely not right now. She went for his belt buckle, and once again he stopped her.

"Uh-uh. Not time for that yet, honey. We need to relax you."

Relax? Out of the question.

But then he distracted her by kissing her. God, could he ever kiss. She couldn't remember any man spending so much time kissing her, and especially not so thoroughly. He pulled her ponytail holder out and threaded his fingers through her hair, held her head and plundered her lips with the intent of a pirate searching for treasure.

His kisses mesmerized her, made her tingle all over, but they didn't relax her. If that was his intent, then he failed miserably. She heard the sound of her own blood rushing in her ears, felt her heart beating erratically against his chest, and her legs trembled so much that if he hadn't been holding on to her she might have fallen. This—this was not relaxed. Did he have any idea what his kisses did to her?

And when he pulled his lips away from her mouth and kissed his way down her neck, using his tongue to lick her throat and nibble at that oh-so-tender spot on her shoulder, goose bumps broke out on her skin. And she was anything but cold. She was hot. On fire. Her nipples were hard, tight points of tingling pleasure, just waiting for his touch, his mouth, anything that would give them relief, because with every movement they brushed against his shirt—his chest—only torturing her more.

He stepped back and reached for the clasp on her bra, unlatching it and baring her breasts. Cool air slid over her nipples, but it was no relief from the heat blasting her body. She held her breath, needing his touch right there. And when he slid his hands over her breasts, his thumbs gliding over her distended nipples, she couldn't hold back the moan of exquisite pleasure that escaped her lips. The rough contact of his hard, calloused skin against her soft nipples sent shocks of sensation straight to her pussy. She arched her back for more.

"Like that?"

"Yes." Her response had come out as no more than a whisper, a soft plea in the darkness. It was all she could voice. Her throat was dry, raspy from panting.

He put an arm around her back and swept another under her legs, lifting her, carrying her toward the bed. The room was pitch-black, the drapes drawn so no moonlight or neon from the Strip showed through. She didn't know if she liked that they couldn't see each other, or if she'd prefer the soft light of the room so she could see his face.

But this way, they had to rely on their other senses—on sound, on feel, on scent to guide each other.

He set her down on her feet next to the bed. She reached for his shoulders, laid her palms over his chest—a solid wall of muscle. She flexed her fingers in, then curled them, grabbing his shirt to lift.

This time, he let her, raised his arms so she could take off his shirt. After she discarded it, she laid her palms flat against his chest again. It was smooth, bare, and she let her hands discover his chest, his shoulders. Boulders of muscle that she traversed with her hands and fingertips, learning his body like she was reading a road map. His body was warm, hard all over. She wondered what he did with his time besides ride around the country. No man built like this spent all his time on a bike. He either worked out or worked physically for a living.

And now she could see the benefit of slowing down, of not being in so much of a rush for sex. How else could she get to experience the thrill of discovering his body, of running her hands over every plane, every muscle, sliding her hands down his arms and back up again, feeling the goose bumps rise on his flesh? It was such a heady experience, and empowering to realize that her touch elicited a reaction in him, gave him chills.

She rose on her tiptoes and wound her arms around his neck, pressing her breasts against his chest. Her nipples scraped his flesh and she couldn't resist sliding them back and forth, even though the sensations aroused her to the point of madness.

Rick pulled her hips against him. His erection seemed harder than ever, if that was possible.

"You trying to tease me, woman?"

"You're teasing me. It seems only fair to return the favor."

"We'll see about that."

He pushed her then, and in the dark she had no balance. Good thing she felt the bed against the back of her knees because she fell against the mattress, waiting for Rick to fall on top of her.

He didn't. He was on the floor, pulling her boots off, pressing kisses to her feet as he gently removed each sock.

Her toes curled and she shuddered out a sigh. Okay, so maybe the tense frenzy she'd initially felt had dissolved into a puddle of delicious arousal now. Maybe Rick had been right about taking their time to enjoy the moment.

She hated being wrong.

He rose and undid the button on her jeans, and with a slow slide drew the zipper down. He tugged at the waistband and she lifted to help him as he drew her jeans down her legs.

That left only her panties. But he didn't take those next. He leaned in, and she felt his warm breath caressing her bare belly.

"You smell good. Like cookies and hot sex."

She smiled even though he couldn't see her. "That's an interesting combination."

"It makes you special. No one I've ever known smelled like cookies and sex." He pressed a kiss to her rib cage, and she shivered. When he went higher, just below her breasts, she stilled, not wanting to do anything to make him stop.

He didn't stop. He cupped her breast and his lips covered one aching, desperate-to-be-sucked peak. Her body nearly shot off the bed at the first lash of his tongue against the sensitive bud. He curled his tongue around it, flicked it, then sucked, gently at first, then harder, and she could have cried it was so damn good. And by the time he moved to the other breast and lavished equal attention on it, she arched her back to feed more of her starved nipples into his mouth.

And just as he'd done since they'd come into the room, he took his time, seeming in no hurry to move south, to fuck her, to do anything other than play with her breasts and nipples.

The man was inhuman, his obvious intent to drive her to the brink of insanity—and over.

"Rick. Please."

He lifted his head. She could only make out his silhouette in the darkness, but she knew he was looking at her.

"What do you need?"

How was she going to voice what she needed when she didn't even know? "More."

"More of this?" He captured her nipple in his mouth again and sucked and the rapturous pleasure settled heavy between her legs, teasing her, letting her know how damn good it was going to be between them.

"Yes. No. I don't know."

"Or this?" He took her other nipple between his fingers and rolled it. Heat shot to her pussy, making it quiver.

"Yes. No."

He laughed. "Maybe I know what you need."

He abandoned her breasts and kissed her rib cage again, moving down to her belly, and lower. When he settled himself on the floor, then dragged her butt to the edge of the bed, she raised her head, wishing now for the light so she could see what he was doing—what he might do.

But she could only imagine, could only feel his breath against her thigh, his fingers parting her thighs, his hair brushing her skin. He dragged her panties slowly down her quivering legs, his hands moving over her calves, her knees, her thighs as he drew out the agony even longer.

And then she felt it—a light touch along her inner thigh. Hot, wet, she thought she had imagined it, but there it was again, and she knew it was his tongue, creeping ever closer to her—

Oh, God. He laid his tongue on her, and then licked along her pussy. Then there was definitely no mistake. It was real, and she was drowning in sensation—the most pleasurable, soaking sensation she'd ever felt. He gripped her hips and buried his face in her pussy, licking her like he was dying of thirst.

And she absorbed every lash of his tongue like she had never been licked before. Though she had—but not like this—not by a man who knew exactly what he was doing, who did it for her pleasure and her pleasure alone. She had waited so long for this. They had danced around each other, teasing, tormenting, and now that he was exactly where she wanted him, the floodgates had opened. His mouth and his tongue did the devil's work on her clit and pussy—relentlessly stroking, licking, nibbling—giving her no time to think, to breathe, to process. She gripped the sheets in her hands and held on, but knew she had no hope of lasting. It was too good, too wet, and she was going to come.

"Rick."

That was all she could say before she lifted her hips and fed him her pussy. And shattered.

Her orgasm was like a runaway train. She had no control over her wild response that took her completely over the edge. Rick's fingers dug into her hips and held on while she bucked against him in a frenzy of pleasure. It had been so long . . . so long, and she rode this one out like holding on to a precious gift she might never receive again.

Even after it was over she still felt tiny quakes of sensation, pinpricks of pleasure that seemed to never stop. When Rick kissed her thighs and her belly, she smiled, certain she'd never been so content.

And they weren't even close to being finished. They had just started.

Rick moved away from her. The loss of his body contact against her made her feel chilled. She lifted up to a sitting position and wrapped her arms around her legs. She could make out his form in the darkness as he stood at the edge of the bed.

She heard his belt buckle, then a zipper.

"How about some light?" she asked.

He leaned over and flipped the switch on the nightstand.

Ava blinked, forcing her eyes to adjust to the sudden light.

Rick stood in front of her, bare-chested, his jeans unzipped all the way. She swallowed—or tried to—but found nothing to coat her throat.

Da-yum. The man before her was a god, pure and simple. Tall, well muscled, bronzed, and gorgeous, with the kind of wicked smile that could make a woman hope and pray that he was thinking about her. Her gaze traveled down his chest, the wall of muscle at his abdomen, to the dark line of hair that led down to the hidden place where his jeans lay open.

How did she get so lucky to land a guy like this? Rock hard and sex on two legs.

She wasn't about to question it.

Because for tonight, at least, he was all hers.

Rick looked down at Ava, at the way she stared at him with a mixture of satisfaction and need, her dark eyes saying a lot about what she wanted.

A man could develop a hell of an ego having a woman look at him like that.

Especially a woman as beautiful as Ava. With her clothes on she was distracting enough. Her face could stop traffic.

Naked, she was like a siren about to lure him to his death. Damn good thing the lights had been off earlier, or else he might have been afraid to touch her.

He and perfection? Yeah, they never occupied the same room—until tonight.

Ava was perfect, from her beautiful full breasts with dusky, tasty nipples right down to her luscious hips and thighs and the sweet pussy between them. She was all woman. And tonight, all his.

He'd just had a taste of her, the sweetest honey a man could ever drink. And now he wanted more.

She sat in the middle of the bed, her legs pulled up, her arms wrapped around them. He dropped his jeans to the floor and her eyes went smoky dark.

"Come here."

She shifted, scooted to the edge of the bed and let her legs dangle over the side.

Rick took a step forward, pulled her to her feet, and slid his arms around her. His erection wedged between them. God, it was tight, hot. He was ready to burst, especially after tasting her and having her come for him. He wanted her to come again—while he was inside her.

"I like having you naked against me."

She tilted her head back and offered up a smile, then slid her palms up over his shoulders. "It's about time."

He arched a brow. "Did I make you wait?"

"Seems that way."

"Then no more waiting." He took her mouth in a kiss—he really liked her mouth. Sweet, pliant, he could kiss her for hours. He turned, shifting them, and fell on the bed, bringing Ava down on top of him. She lifted her head and stared down at him, her hair like a raven waterfall across her cheeks. He swept it to the side, then rolled his hands down her back, grabbed her ass, and squeezed.

Her lips parted and her eyelids drifted partway closed.

Ah. So easy to tell what she liked. He'd have to remember

to do this with the lights on again, so he could see her reactions.

And there'd be an *again*. He already knew once wouldn't be enough. He'd already waited too damn long.

He rolled her over, pinning her by climbing on top of her. His cock slid between her parted thighs, rubbing against her moisture-coated pussy. Like wet silk.

He reached over to the nightstand for the condom he'd pulled out of his pocket, tore open the wrapper, and lifted only long enough to put it on. Then, bracing himself on his arms, he watched as his cock nudged against her pussy lips.

Ava parted her legs, held on to his wrists—tight—oh, man, he liked the way she gripped him.

He slid inside her pussy, slow and easy at first, gritting his teeth because it was just so goddamn good. She pulsed around him, sucking him into the vortex of her hot, tight pussy.

He lifted his gaze to hers. Her lips were clamped shut, her nostrils flaring. And when he rolled his hips she let out a soft moan.

Oh, yeah.

And still, she held tight to his wrists, dug her nails into him every time he pulled partway out, then drove in deep.

She liked it deep.

So did he.

He dropped down on top of her, careful to keep his weight off her slight frame, and slid one hand under her to cup her buttocks, tilting her up, giving him more access to her depths.

And then he thrust again.

She let out a gasp, a little louder this time, her pussy rippling in response.

"Rick. Oh, God. Oh, damn."

"Yeah, baby. I know. You feel good."

He kissed her again, enjoying the feel of her breasts against his chest, her nipples scraping against him as he rolled his hips from one side to the other. He liked the sounds she made when he fucked her. It made his balls tighten up, fill with the come he was going to shoot.

But first, he wanted to make her come. He intensified the friction, sliding against her clit every time he thrust. Again and again until she tilted her head back, closed her eyes, and lifted her hips to cry out for more.

He gave her more, grinding against her until he felt her walls closing in around his cock, squeezing him while she dragged her fingernails across his back and called out his name as she climaxed.

He wanted to hold on to this moment and watch her face, her lips parted as she cried out, her head tilted back, her eyes squeezed tighly shut as she felt it all course through her. He knew what that felt like because it took every ounce of strength he had to keep his own orgasm from bursting. But he couldn't hold back anymore because his orgasm ripped through him, tearing through his nerve endings like a flash of lightning, so hot and hard he shuddered, buried his face against Ava's neck, and let out a loud groan of pleasure that he felt from his head to his feet. He continued to rock against her, feeling her shudder as he emptied himself of everything he had.

It had never been this good, this intense, this involved.

Spent, he licked her neck, kissed her jaw, her lips, then rolled to the side and held her there, the two of them still connected.

Ava slung a leg over him and laid her head against his chest.

Rick inhaled, exhaled, stroked Ava's hair.

Yeah, really damn good.

Too damn good, in fact. He'd never been with a woman who matched him more perfectly.

And he still really didn't know a damn thing about her, or why she was with the Hellraisers.

Reality intruded and he had to start thinking clearly again. Sex had been fun, but it was time to start thinking with his head instead of his dick.

Ava moaned and shifted in his arms. Said dick noticed and began to spring to life again.

Ava smiled and tilted her head back.

"I thought guys needed recovery time."

"This guy doesn't."

"Hope you brought a lot of condoms, then."

He didn't think he'd brought nearly enough for what he'd need with Ava.

Eight

Ava stretched and rolled over, searching out Rick's warm body to help ward off the morning chill.

The other side of the bed was empty. She blinked her eyes open, sat up, and searched the room.

He wasn't there. Neither were his clothes. She got up and looked in the bathroom, and he wasn't in there, either.

Well, fine. She pulled on a pair of sweats and a T-shirt, then flopped onto the bed, forcing herself not to pout.

Maybe he had something important to do this morning. Her gaze slid over to the clock on the nightstand—seven-thirty. It was still early. They hadn't gotten more than four hours of sleep last night. What could he possibly have to do this early in the morning, besides hightail it out of her room so he could get away from her?

Guys did that. A lot didn't care for the "morning after." Sex was fine, but they didn't stay the night. Rick had at least stayed the night—or a few hours, anyway. They'd had sex again, and promptly passed out in each other's arms. Maybe he'd only needed a few hours to rest, then wanted to get out of there before he had to—gasp—talk to her.

Guys did that, too—left before they had to have the morning-after conversation. The few guys she'd had sex with hadn't been the "cuddle and talk after sex" type. Hell, they hadn't been the "stay in the room after sex" type. Which was probably why sex hadn't been high on her priority list the past few years. Being used wasn't fun.

But for some reason she'd thought Rick was different. How stupid of her. He was just like the others. Get off and get out of there before the woman wants to talk.

It wasn't like she was going to rehash the sex from the night before.

She stretched, raised her arms above her head and pointed her toes, smiling at the soreness in her muscles. No, she was pretty certain the sex spoke for itself and needed no further conversation.

But Rick didn't know that, and he was probably used to clingy women who thought one night of sex equaled a relationship.

She wasn't that kind of woman. She knew where they stood—nowhere. He was a biker who traveled all over, was part of a gang. She was a graduate student trying to decide which college to attend for her Ph.D. She was nowhere near looking for a relationship, and she doubted he was, either.

But if she was . . . oh, wow, it had been incredible last night. Rick knew his way around her body without instruction or a road map. He'd done it entirely by feel and by reading her responses.

He was really damn good at it.

Her body swelled with heat remembering his touch, his kisses, how he felt inside her. She slid her hand inside her sweatpants and cupped her sex, let her fingers dance around her clit, recalling how his mouth and tongue felt there last night. What an incredible orgasm he'd brought her to.

When she heard a click in the door lock, she removed her hands from her pants and slid her feet over the side of the bed. Rick pushed the door open. He had two cups of coffee in a cardboard container.

"Oh, hey, you're up."

Ava couldn't resist a wide smile. He hadn't left her. He'd gone for coffee.

"Good morning," she said, suddenly feeling giddy, and then felt stupid for feeling that way. It was just coffee.

But he hadn't run like hell to escape.

"I wasn't sure how long you'd sleep, but I hate in-room coffee, so thought you'd want the good stuff."

"You're right. Thank you."

He handed her a cup and cream and sugar. "I wasn't sure how you took it."

"With cream and sugar." She added both, then put the lid back on, slid back against the pillows, and took a sip of the hot brew. "Oh, this is really good."

Rick shrugged his jacket off and lifted the lid off his cup, took a swallow, and sat in the chair across from the bed. "Sleep well?"

"What little sleep I got was fine. You were gone when I got up. I thought maybe you wanted to avoid seeing me."

Why had she blurted that out? She sounded needy.

Way to be mature, Ava.

He quirked a brow and propped his feet up on the edge of the bed. "Why would I want to do that?"

She shrugged. "I don't know. Avoid the morning after?"

"The morning aft—oh." He laughed, then pinned her with a direct stare. "I'm not the type to fuck and run, Ava."

She liked hearing that. She didn't know why she cared, dammit, but she did.

"You must have dated some miserable assholes."

She lifted her gaze from her coffee to him. "Not really. Just none that were memorable enough to keep around."

"Yeah? Tell me about them."

She shifted and made herself more comfortable against the pillows. "My first was in college."

"Late bloomer, huh?"

"Yeah, you could say that. My parents overprotected me, kept me busy with school and social activities."

He grinned. "All to preserve the sanctity of your virginity, no doubt."

She sipped her coffee and nodded, remembering having to account for every second of her time back then. "No doubt. But once I hit college and wasn't under their thumb every minute of every day, I had more freedom to go wild."

"And did you?"

"Go wild?" She let out a soft laugh. "No."

"Why not?"

She shrugged. "I didn't know how. I was tentative. I'd been sheltered. Having all that freedom scared the hell out of me."

"And you had guys beating down the door to get at you, I'd bet."

She laughed. "Not really. I was painfully shy. Pretty much a wallflower."

"I can't see that."

"Thanks. But I was. Fortunately, I had my best friend, Lacey, as my roommate and we stuck close together and weathered the first couple awkward years of college. And boys. And then men."

"So your sexual awakening was in college, with the frat boys?"

"Yes."

"Did they treat you good?"

What an odd question. Why would he even care about that? "I suppose. I wasn't mistreated. I didn't end up on a website or in a *Girls Gone Wild* video. But then again I was never a big drinker, so I always knew what I was doing. And I was selective in who I went out with."

"Sounds practical."

He made it sound like she was boring. Maybe she had been. She certainly couldn't pinpoint anyone or anything remarkable from her undergrad days.

"So how many?"

"How many what?"

"How many guys?"

She lifted her chin. "That's a bit personal, don't you think?"

"Okay. You don't have to tell me."

"Four."

"That's it? Four? You've only been with four guys? How old are you?"

"Twenty-five."

Rick dragged his fingers through his hair. "Damn."

"How about you?"

"Uh . . ."

"That many, huh?" And why did it irritate her so much that he couldn't just pull a number out of his head right then? "Go ahead. Give it some thought. I'll wait."

And she did. Drank her coffee, twiddled her toes, glanced over at the clock, then back at him while he stared up at the ceiling and did mental math.

"Are you kidding me? It's that hard to count a few sex partners?"

"Uh . . ."

Oh, for God's sake. "Never mind."

"Thirty-three."

Her eyes widened. "What? Are you serious? Thirty-three?"

"Give or take."

"Jesus. Am I thirty-four or thirty-three?"

His lips curled. "I didn't count you."

"Why the hell not? Because you only counted the memorable ones?" Which meant she'd been utterly forgettable. Great. Just great.

"No, that's not what I meant at all."

And he was laughing. Asshole. She put down her coffee and stood. "Get out."

"What?"

"You heard me. Get out."

"You're serious."

She pointed to the door. "Get. Out."

"You are serious." He stood. "You're really going to toss me out of here because of the number of women I've had sex with."

Men were so clueless sometimes. "I need to take a shower. And I need some time alone."

"I could wash your back." He lifted his brows.

"Oh," she muttered a sound of disgust. "Just get out, Rick."

"Okay. Jesus. Sorry." He went to the door, turned, and looked at her. "Call me when you're over being grumpy."

She slammed the door in his face, double locked it, and flopped back on the bed to stare up at the ceiling.

Her heart was pounding and her face was hot, flushed with the heat of anger and embarrassment.

Thirty-three. What a man whore. Damn good thing he'd worn a condom, since his cock had been so well used before he'd been with her.

But as the minutes ticked by and she continued to gaze up at the monotonous white ceiling, she didn't know what she was more upset about—that Rick had had so much sex, or she'd had so little.

Maybe it was the combination of Rick's experience and what she'd seen with Lacey last night. It seemed like everyone was so adept at broadening their horizons—except her.

Though she'd certainly gotten a good start last night with Rick, as well as the night before. Phone sex, and a night of awesome in-person sex. She couldn't recall ever climaxing like she had with Rick. He brought out a wild, uninhibited side to her she never knew existed, and she had a feeling they'd only scratched the surface of what she was capable of—what they were capable of doing together.

So what the hell was she doing throwing a tantrum and tossing him out of her room, when instead she could be tapping into his wealth of experience while she had the chance?

Dumbass.

If she'd spent less time holed up with books and more time with men, she'd have known how to handle this—how to handle him. Instead, she'd acted like a fourteen-year-old with a bruised ego when, really, his prior sex partners had nothing to do with her—with them.

She jumped up and took a shower, dried her hair, and got dressed, then grabbed her jacket and bag and marched down to Rick's room, raised her hand, then paused before knocking, feeling every bit of two inches tall for her ridiculous outburst earlier.

She knocked, her pulse pounding, not sure what she was going to say when he opened the door.

If he was even still in there.

He pulled open the door and her breath caught.

He was wearing jeans, unbuttoned. No shirt. Bare feet. His hair was still wet like he'd just gotten out of the shower and pulled on the jeans to answer the door.

"Sorry," she said. "Did I catch you at a bad time?"

"No. I was just getting out of the shower. Come on in."

She did. He closed the door and she stepped into his room.

He was a typical guy—clothes tossed everywhere. She resisted the urge to straighten up.

"Sorry. I just toss shit around. Let me move that."

"It's fine." She moved his discarded shirt so she could sit in the chair.

"You want some coffee? I brewed the in-room stuff. It tastes rank, but it's better than nothing."

"No. Thank you."

"Okay." He turned around and reached into his bag to grab a white T-shirt and lifted his arms to put it on. While his back was turned, Ava had an unrestricted view of the way his muscles stretched across his back and shoulders.

So much she hadn't seen last night, hadn't touched. He had a few scars, too, white lines that stood out against his darkly tanned torso. She itched to run her fingers, her tongue, across those scars, and ask how and where he'd gotten them.

Too personal, too intimate. She didn't want to know. She'd already told him too much about herself and look where that conversation had led. It was best to keep things impersonal between them. What they had wasn't going anywhere beyond this week, anyway.

"I'm sorry about earlier. I behaved badly and I had no reason."

He turned around and smiled at her. "It's not your fault, darlin'. I was a dick."

"No you weren't."

He squatted down in front of her and laid his hands on her knees. "Yeah, I was. I was teasing you and you hated it."

"I didn't hate it. Much." She looked down.

He tipped her chin up with his fingers, forcing her to meet his gaze. "You hated it. I'm sorry."

He spread her knees apart and moved between her thighs, cradled her face in his hands and kissed her. It was soft, the touch of his lips so light she could barely feel it. And because of that, she held her breath, absorbed the utter sweetness of his apology. For a man who looked and acted so hard, the lightness of this kiss rocked her.

When he pulled back, she felt shaken, disoriented, like she was drugged.

"Thank you," she managed.

He swept his hand along her hair. "For what?"

"I don't know. I just like being with you. You do something to me, Rick. I can't explain it."

His hand stilled and she studied the expression on his face. She'd almost call it shock or surprise, but she certainly hadn't said anything shockworthy.

"You hungry?"

She nodded. "Starving."

He pushed off the arms of the chair and stood. "Me, too. Let's go get some breakfast."

Rick ate his breakfast, inhaled a few more cups of coffee, and pondered what Ava had said earlier.

She'd surprised him, and women generally didn't. That alone made her unique.

He'd felt bad for teasing her, because he could tell he'd hurt her feelings.

She was way more innocent than he'd originally thought, which only made this assignment more confusing.

What was a woman who had a total of four sex partners—and he figured he was probably included in those four—doing with a gang like the Hellraisers? It made no sense. She wasn't worldly or streetwise. She was sheltered. She'd said so herself. After being all but monitored 24/7 by her parents, she'd gone off to college and . . . studied. She hadn't partied her ass off and fucked one guy after another. She'd gone to college and gotten an education. And then a master's degree after that.

She had no history of drugs or violence or hanging out with gangs.

So what the fuck was she doing here with this gang?

He supposed he could just ask her. But what if for some reason she was embedded in the Hellraisers for a reason? Hell, for all he knew she'd been paired up with him to test him, since he'd asked Bo to get back in the gang.

Her whole innocent act could be just that—an act. She could be lying to him about everything—including the four guys she'd fucked.

Which meant he was going to have to keep doing what he was doing. He'd have to stay close to her to figure out her angle, without revealing his own.

Dammit, he hated being in the dark.

"You're quiet over there."

He lifted his head to look over at her. God, she was beautiful. He really couldn't get over her. Today she wore a burgundy turtleneck sweater that clung to those gorgeous breasts of hers, tight jeans that molded to her full hips and thighs and outlined her sweet ass just perfectly. He'd enjoyed walking behind her as they were led to the table. She'd left her hair loose, and it hung like a waterfall of raven silk over her breasts.

He could stare at her all day and not say a damn word. But that wasn't what he was supposed to do, so instead, he grinned. "Sorry. I really was hungry."

"I can see that. I was afraid you were going to lick your plate."

He looked down at his empty plate, then over at her partially finished one. "I thought about grabbing that last piece of bacon."

She picked it up and offered it to him. "Be my guest."

He took it from her. "Thanks."

She shook her head. "I don't know where you put it all. There isn't an ounce of fat on you. Do you work out or run or something?"

"I work out when I can."

"I thought you rode a lot."

"I do. But you can't ride twenty-four hours a day. And wherever I go I make sure there's a gym where I can go a few rounds in the ring."

"You box?"

He nodded and pushed his plate to the edge of the table. "It's great exercise."

"I'll bet."

"What about you? What do you do for fun?"

"Yoga."

"That figures. You look like the spiritual guru, get-into-the-head kind of person."

She laughed. "It's not at all like that. Well, it can be. But it's a great muscle workout, too. And it relaxes me."

"If you say so."

"You should try it with me sometime."

"Can we do it naked?"

She looked at him, then burst out laughing. "Only you would suggest that."

"That's why you like me."

She quirked her lips. "Probably."

"Hey, you two snuck out of our room last night and missed all the partying."

Ava looked up to find Lacey leaning over her shoulder. "You and Bo were kind of busy."

Lacey fell into the chair next to her and grinned. "Yeah, we were. We just got up. Oh my God, what a fun night." She grabbed Ava's hand. "You should have stayed. We could have had a . . . sixsome." Then she laughed so loud that the customers in the restaurant began to look their way.

Ava shifted and leaned over the table, whispering, "Probably not something you want broadcast to the entire place."

Lacey waved her hand and sniffed. "Oh, who cares. Bunch of prudes, anyway. So, did you and Rick get it on?"

Who was this person?

"I don't think Ava's interested in giving you the details of her sex life," Rick said, saving Ava from having to tell her best friend that she was being too intrusive.

"Why not? Oh, I know, because Ava rarely even has a sex life." Lacey snorted.

Ava's face flamed, and she fought hard to retain her concern for her friend. "Lace, have you eaten yet?"

Lacey's gaze flitted around the room, as if she'd just now discovered she was in a restaurant. "Oh. No. I'm not even hungry." She laughed again. "What time is it?"

"Ten."

"That early? What the hell am I doing up? I thought it was like . . . afternoon or something. I think I'll go back to bed." She pushed back from her chair and stood, then walked away without saying good-bye.

Ava watched her go, concerned more than ever about Lacey's increasingly bizarre behavior.

"She always that disjointed?" Rick asked.

"No."

Rick leaned back and leveled his gaze at her.

"What?"

"You're worried about her."

"Yes, I am."

"Why?"

"Because who you just saw is not the Lacey I've always known."

"Yeah. Who is she?"

Ava watched Lacey disappear, then blew out a breath of frustration.

"I wish I knew, Rick. I really wish I knew."

Because the way things looked now, it was much worse than Ava had originally thought. She had thought it was just love that had changed Lacey from studious to flighty.

Now she feared it was more than that.

And a lot worse.

Nine

Rick studied the concern on Ava's face, and wondered if her friend Lacey was the primary reason for Ava being with the Hellraisers.

Not to irritate her father, not because she was involved in drug distribution.

But because she was concerned about her friend.

He'd have to walk a fine line here, but he intended to find out. And he hoped that Ava was in the mood to talk.

"Let's head on out of here." He pushed his chair back and stood. Ava followed.

"So tell me, what's different about her?" he asked as they headed toward the elevator.

She stepped inside, waited while Rick pushed the button and the doors swooshed closed, then turned to him, seemingly eager to unload her concerns on someone. He was glad to be that person.

"She's frenetic. All over the place. Lacey used to be calm, organized. And shy. Oh so shy. Does she seem shy to you now?"

Rick laughed. "Uh, no. Not from what I saw in their room last night."

"Exactly. Everything about her changed after she . . ."

"After she what?"

She hesitated. "I don't want to make you mad."

He cocked his head to the side. "How could you make me mad?"

"It's about Bo."

"You can be blunt with me about whatever you want, Ava, including Bo. Say what's on your mind."

"Everything changed after she met your cousin."

The doors opened and they started down the hallway toward their rooms. "And you think it has something to do with Lacey hooking up with Bo."

"Yes. As soon as she started dating Bo, her entire life changed."

She handed her key to Rick and he opened her door. Ava slid into the chair near the window and Rick took the chair on the other side of the small table. Sunlight streamed into the room, highlighting her hair and face. She didn't turn away like she had something to hide; instead she leaned into the light like she was soaking up the warmth.

"Tell me how her life changed."

"She quit school. We were in the master's program together, and she dropped out with only one year to go."

"Was she struggling?"

Ava let out a short laugh. "Not at all. Lacey was an ace student with plans far into the future for both her academics and her career as a psychologist. But after she met Bo and started riding with the Hellraisers, everything changed."

Rick shrugged. "People grow up, Ava. Sometimes that happens. What they thought they wanted when they were younger is sometimes altered when they get a little age and experience in them."

"I realize that. But not Lacey. She knew what she wanted to do, what she wanted to be. She was focused, had short- and long-term goals. She knew on Monday what she was going to do on Friday."

"A little anal?"

Ava managed a slight smile. "A little. But I've known her all my life. I know how she thinks, how she acts. The woman you saw downstairs isn't anything like her."

"And you think that has something to do with her relationship with Bo?"

Ava worried her lip, hesitating.

"You can talk to me without worrying I'm going to go running to Bo. I don't tell him anything."

She nodded. "I think joining the Hellraisers had everything to do with her change in personality, but I don't think it's just Bo."

He didn't want to ask leading questions, so he just let the silence drift between them and gave her time to think it out.

"Her eyes were so glassy. And we knew they were smoking pot last night."

"Yes."

She waved her hand in the air. "But that wears off. And it wouldn't account for her frenetic behavior. She's been sniffling a lot. Her nose is irritated."

He knew where she was going, but he wanted her to say it.

"I think she's taking drugs."

"Really."

"Yeah." She looked down at her hands for a while, played with the cuticle on one of her fingernails, then swept her gaze back up to Rick. "She never even liked to take acetaminophen for a headache, Rick. So how could she make such a drastic change?"

Now he knew he'd have to say something. "Drugs alter people's perception of things."

"Do they? I don't know. I've never known anyone who took them."

"I've known plenty of people who have. It changes them."

She wrapped her arms around herself and stared out the window. "I don't know what to do for her." She looked at him. "I mean, I do, from a professional standpoint. But she's my friend."

He nodded. "It's different when it's someone you're close to. You lose your objectivity."

"So what do I do?"

"You can't make her stop taking drugs if that's what she's doing. All you can do is talk to her, see if she'll open up to you, then try to make her see the reality of it."

"I know all that. But I want her to stop. Right now. Selfishly, I want her to be the old Lacey—the one I grew up with, the one I've been friends with since we were kids."

"That person is gone, Ava. That's the first thing you're going to have to accept. Time and experience changes a person. You'll have to learn to live with Lacey as she is now, and move forward."

He saw the shimmer of tears in her eyes and wished he could wipe them away. But if Lacey was on drugs, then what he'd told Ava was the truth. Only Lacey could help herself. Ava could only be there to support her. Deep down, Ava knew that. It might take her a while to come to grips with it, though.

She sighed. "How did you get to be so wise? You're almost like a counselor yourself."

He laughed. "Me? Hardly. I've just been on the streets a long time. Seen a lot. Know when to get involved and know when to back away. Sometimes you can lend a hand, and sometimes just an ear. You learn to recognize the difference."

"Thank you."

"For what?"

She went over to him and sat on his lap. "For being willing to listen. We don't know each other all that well. And I don't have many—any—friends. Except Lacey. We used to confide in each other. There's been a void in the year she's been out of my life. I hadn't realized until now how much I've missed having someone to talk to."

"Maybe you need to broaden your circle of friends."

She wound her arms around his neck. "It's not that easy for me."

He slipped an arm around her waist, liking the feel of her

sitting on his lap. Comfortable. Too comfortable, actually. He'd fallen into an easy rhythm of talking to her, listening to her.

"You have another friend already and it wasn't so hard, was it?"

Her brows arched. "I do?"

"Yeah." He kissed her, a light brush of his lips across hers. He didn't want to take it further than that because he knew once he started he wouldn't stop. Not when he liked kissing her so much. "Me."

Her lips lifted. "Is that what we are, Rick? Friends?"

Warning bells clanged, loud and clear. Did she want more than that?

Did he?

No. He didn't. It wasn't in his nature. In his lifestyle. In his future.

"Yeah. We're friends."

He saw the light dim in her eyes, wished he hadn't been the one to put it there, but he wouldn't give her false hope.

"I can't be what you want me to be, Ava. All there can be between us is what there is right now."

"Which is what? Sex and friendship?"

He smiled. "What's wrong with that?"

She sighed. "Nothing at all. I'm hardly an incurable romantic looking for a happily ever after, so you don't have to worry about me."

It was sad that she wasn't. Weren't women supposed to be out there looking for the man of their dreams?

Or maybe those kinds of guys didn't exist. He just knew he wasn't one of them.

She leaned into him then, laid her head on his shoulder, and, goddamn, it felt good. There was something about holding Ava in his arms that was unlike holding any other woman. Maybe because she wasn't like the other women who'd passed in and out of his life before. She was solid, steady, knew exactly what she wanted out of life—and what she didn't want. And rather than being closed off to new experiences and things that might be a little scary, she opened herself up to them, took a chance on being hurt. She was an adventurer, even if she didn't know it.

For the right guy, she was perfect.

He just wasn't the right guy.

He wrapped his arms around her and held her, expecting nothing.

But he sure got a hell of a lot in return.

More than he'd ever expected. And maybe he could offer her something. Comfort. Take her mind off her friend.

He tilted her back and she lifted her dark lashes, looked at him with eyes that made his gut clench and his dick harden. She must have read his mind, because she reached up, caressed his cheek with her soft hand, and rubbed her thumb across his bottom lip.

He kissed her, and she sighed into his mouth. A sigh of surrender, of giving herself to him. She told him by leaning into him and sliding her tongue against his that this was the kind of comfort she wanted. No hesitation at all. The way she seemed to melt into him made him tighten his hold on her with a fierce possessiveness he'd never felt for a woman before.

He'd felt lots of firsts with Ava, and none of them were good for his long-term outlook. But he wasn't going to think about any of that right now. He was going to think about Ava's breasts pillowed against his chest, her full lips sliding across his, and those sweet sounds she made that made him rock hard in record time.

He dipped her over his arm and ran his hand over her breasts, absorbing the sound of her gasp as he scraped his palm back and forth on her nipples. Wanting more of that, he raised her shirt, released the clasp on her bra, and freed her breasts, then lifted her just enough to fit one soft peak into his mouth.

Ava fisted her hand in his hair and held on tight while he sucked her nipple. Her body writhed against him, lifting and rocking, and she made this sound that drove him crazy—a purring sound that came from deep in her throat, almost like a soft growl.

Every time he thought she was calm and soothing, she taught him something new about her.

Ava could get riled—sexually wound up like a wildcat. And, oh man, did that turn him on. His balls tightened feeling her squirming against him, knowing all he was giving her was his mouth on her nipple, and knowing she wanted a hell of a lot more than that right now.

He released her nipple and lifted her upright on his lap, then pulled her shirt off, followed by her bra.

"Stand up."

It wasn't a request, but he couldn't wait any longer. Fortunately she didn't seem to mind. She stood and watched while he unzipped her jeans and jerked them down to her ankles.

"Goddamn boots," he murmured, but didn't take the time to sit her back down to remove them. Not when he wanted her—just like this. He slid his hand between her legs, felt the wetness there. And her legs quivered.

He wanted her really ready for him. He pulled her by the hips and drew her against him, then leaned between her legs to take a nice long lick of her sweet pussy. This time she let out a soft moan and laid her hand on the back of his head, her fingers curling into his hair.

God, she was hot, tasted like butter, and he could lick her like this all day. The way she responded, arching her hips forward to feed him her pussy, gave his hard-on a punch that made him ache all over to be inside her.

"Yes," she whispered, her voice laced with a hard edge of need. "Right there."

He gave her exactly what she asked for, swirling his tongue around her clit. He tucked his finger inside her pussy—damn—so hot and wet. He finger fucked her, slow and easy, just like he licked her, listening to her gasp, moan, whimper, and, oh man, he really loved those sounds she made. They made his balls quiver. He lifted his head and used his thumb on her clit, taking a moment to gaze up at her face. Her expression was tight, pained, her lips parted as she panted hard and fast. Her hips were thrust forward, undulating against his hand as he worked her pussy and clit with his fingers. He leaned in and licked her again, took her clit between his lips and sucked.

She exploded, crying out, pushing her sex against his face as she came. Her pussy convulsed around his finger in tight contractions. He held on to her, licking her until her tremors subsided.

But she was still shaking all over.

He knew the feeling. So was he.

He lifted her then, his patience long gone, and laid her on the bed, taking only a few seconds to yank her boots and jeans off. He grabbed a condom, unzipped his pants, pulled out his cock, and crawled on top of her.

She was ready, her legs spread, her arms wide open and beckoning to him.

He dragged her hips to the edge of the bed and slid inside her, felt her close around him, her pussy gripping him tight. He gritted his teeth to keep from shooting off right then. She'd gotten him so hot so fast he was ready right now. But he wanted her to come again.

He held his arms rigid so he could watch his cock go in and out of her, could watch her pussy lips grip his shaft every time he thrust against her.

"Come on, ride with me," he said, pulling out and sliding inside her, forcing himself to take his time despite the need to fuck her hard.

She grabbed his arms and dug her nails in. The pain only ratcheted up his pleasure, made it even harder to maintain control. But he did, because with every thrust she tightened around him, the look on her face told him she was getting closer. He leaned down, pressing their bodies together. He swept his hand under her ass to lift her up, and ground against her.

"Rick. Damn. Yes. Just like that. I can feel it against my clit."

He loved when she talked to him, told him what she needed.

She bent her knees and gave him more access, and this time he couldn't hold back. He drove inside her hard, letting out a guttural cry when his orgasm ripped through his body like a rush, blinding him to anything and everything but the feel of Ava's body shaking underneath him, the sounds she made making him shudder against her as he lost control and gave everything up to her. He drank in her loud cries with a kiss, his tongue dueling with hers as they went over the edge together.

Spent, sweating, he could only take in deep gulps of air with every breath. They slid onto the floor and Rick pulled Ava on top of him, hoping like hell he hadn't hurt her. He'd had her in such a tight hold at the end he was afraid he'd crushed her.

She lifted her head and he swept her hair away from her face, hoping he wouldn't see anger or fear there.

Instead, her lips curled in a smile. "Well, that was fun."

He let out a short laugh. "You surprise me."

"Yeah? How?"

"Sometimes you seem so straitlaced, like I have no idea what you're doing hanging out with a bunch of bikers. Other times, like this, you're so wild and out of control."

"Really?" She grinned. "Hmm, maybe I'm a woman of mystery."

He cocked a brow. "Maybe you are."

"Good. I like that."

"In other words, you aren't going to tell me which one is the real Ava."

She sat up. "What fun would that be?"

What fun indeed? He had to admit he liked her just the way she was. He'd never known another woman like her. Maybe it was because she was wholly unpredictable.

Which didn't make his assignment any easier, because as soon as he thought he had a handle on why she was here and what she was doing, she surprised the hell out of him. She was innocent one minute, a wild vixen the next. And he still had no idea who she really was.

As soon as they cleaned up, there was a knock on the door. Rick went to look at the peephole. It was Bo and Lacey, so he opened the door.

"Oh, you're here, too. Hi," Lacey said as she brushed by Rick.

Bo nodded and walked in.

"What's going on?" Rick asked.

Bo yawned. "Nothing much. Late start today."

"Long night?"

Bo laughed. "Yeah. But oh so worth it. You two should have stayed. We'd have had some fun."

Rick didn't share women. Not his kind of fun. "Yeah, well, some other time, maybe."

Like never.

"What's going on over there?" Rick motioned with his head to the excited conversation between Lacey and Ava.

"Oh. I'm giving Lacey a trip to Mexico. She wants Ava to go with her."

"Yeah? When?"

"Today."

Those warning bells clanged so damn loud inside his head that Rick couldn't hear himself think. "In the middle of the rally? Why not wait 'til it's over?"

Bo shrugged. "It just hit me spur of the moment."

"What hit you?"

Bo looked over at the women. "Lace, you okay for a few? Rick and I are gonna go grab some coffee."

Lacey waved her hand. "Go on. We'll meet you down there."

They ordered two coffees in the small coffee shop downstairs, since the restaurant was full with the lunch crowd.

"So what's with the impromptu vacation?"

Bo shifted, leaning forward. "I have a seller just over the border, and Lacey's my mule. She's going to do the pickup for me."

Rick tensed, hid the shock that rocked him. "Yeah? Does she know that?"

Bo's lips lifted. "Hell no."

"Has she done this for you before?"

Bo let out a soft laugh. "Yeah. A few times, actually. She thinks I love her so much that I routinely send her on these spa trips while I have business to attend to. I tell her it's because I feel guilty and I don't want her to be lonely."

"Unaware she's transporting drugs across the border, of course."

"Of course."

What a fucking asshole. Rick hid his disgust with a smirk. "No wonder she's in love with you."

"Hey, man, I treat her like a princess. I buy her presents, feed her, clothe her, cater to her, and once a month she gets a free trip. What more could she want?"

Honesty? Integrity? A man who actually cared about her and wasn't putting her future on the chopping block for his own selfish gain?

"I can't imagine. So what's the deal? What are you running?"

"Cocaine. We've got a great supplier and he gives me plenty of product. I just sent the money over. It's a nice clean transaction, and so far no hassles with the Border Patrol."

"You've been lucky. How are they hiding it?"

"I had several hiding spots made in the new car I bought Lacey this year. And the scent is masked in case there are drug dogs. It's slick, I'm telling you." He leaned in closer. "We're running a ton of coke here in the city alone. I'm looking to branch out territory, take it statewide and then beyond. You came back at just the right time. I'd really like to tap into your Chicago connections."

His nonexistent Chicago connections. "You got it. Anything you need me to do, just let me know."

As if he finally relaxed, Bo leaned back in the chair. "I have some really good guys working for me, but none that I'm close to like you and I were. I'd like to have you as my second-in-command someday. If you're interested."

"You know I would be."

Bo nodded. "You'll need to prove yourself, of course. Not just to me, but to the higher-ups in the Hellraisers national organization. Once you do, then you'll progress fast and I'll have you positioned right where I want you."

"Okay. What do you need from me?"

"I need you to do a run for me into California tomorrow."

Rick just bet he did. What he wanted was to make sure Rick had no ties to Ava, so that he could ship Ava off with Lacey into Mexico. If Rick objected, then there'd be trouble.

This was make it or break it time.

The problem was, everything was now on the line—the assignment, Rick's cover, and Ava's safety. Rick would have to be very careful how he played the game moving forward.

"That sounds fine."

"Good." Bo paused, looked around, then back at him. "So tell me what's the deal with you and Ava."

Rick shrugged. "Ava's just a fuck. I don't even know her. I figured she was a Hellraiser babe."

"Nah. She's Lacey's friend. Pops in to see Lace every now and then, but otherwise she's nothing to the Hellraisers. I just wanted to know if she meant something to you."

Rick had to play it cool, had to know where Bo was going with this. "To me? She doesn't mean anything at all."

"So she's disposable."

"Hell yes, she's disposable. I don't keep women in my life. Never have, never will."

Bo's smirk sent a warning signal his way, especially when Bo lifted his gaze over Rick's shoulder.

Rick turned around.

Fuck.

Ava was standing right behind him. And the shocked expression on her face told him she'd heard what he'd just said.

Ava swallowed, but there was a lump in her throat the size of a baseball.

She was just a fuck. Disposable. He didn't even know her.

The things he'd said shouldn't hurt, because he was right. He was right about all of it.

But goddammit, it did hurt. It hurt bad. She didn't know which was worse—being stunned over hearing Rick tell Bo how he really felt about her, or finding out how she felt about him.

When had she started to care?

Rick pushed back from the table. "Ava."

She held up her hand. "Don't. Just . . ."

She pivoted and turned, pushing past an openmouthed Lacey. Hoping like hell that no one followed her, she punched the button for the elevator, grateful that the doors pulled open immediately and no one was in there. She hurried in and jammed the button for the second floor, her gaze fixated on the lobby in front of her, searching out Rick or Lacey.

The doors closed and she exhaled.

When she got to her room, she bolted the door and took a moment to lean against it.

You're waiting for him. You want him to come after you.

You are so stupid, Ava, because he isn't going to. Weren't you listening downstairs? You're disposable.

What was she so upset about anyway? She'd come here to see Lacey, to find out how she was doing and see if she could repair their friendship.

That part, at least, seemed to be going well. Lacey had asked her this morning to go to Mexico with her. A short, two-day trip, but Lacey said she often went, stayed overnight at a wonderful resort and got the full spa treatment, then headed back. A gift from Bo, Lacey had said, because Bo traveled a lot on business—what business that was Ava had no idea—and he felt guilty leaving Lacey alone so much.

Of course if Lacey was in school she wouldn't be lonely and bored, but that was a topic Ava intended to bring up once she got Lacey all to herself in Mexico. So she agreed to accompany her, in fact couldn't wait for some one-on-one time with her best friend.

Time to focus on Lacey, not on Rick. She'd already wasted too much time with Rick, and look where it had gotten her. She'd conjured up ridiculous notions that he cared for her, that she cared for him, as if they had some kind of relationship, when in fact all they'd had was sex.

She might have been nothing but a fuck to him, but guess what? That's exactly what he'd been to her. A hot guy she could stretch her sexual muscles with. He'd at least been fun for that.

Now that it was over, she'd concentrate on Lacey.

And forget all about Rick.

Easy, right?

Rick dragged his fingers through his hair and paced, trying to figure out how the hell he was going to make this right.

The first thing he did after Ava ran off was pretend it didn't matter. Lacey glared at him and called him an asshole, but he just shrugged and Bo laughed. He'd done his job, even if he felt like shit about it.

He'd hurt Ava. He hadn't meant to. If he'd known she had come into the coffee shop and was within earshot, he'd never have said those things to Bo about her.

Bo had set him up, had seen Ava and Lacey coming in and wanted to make sure Ava heard Rick say those things.

He had his cousin to thank for this mess.

But Rick wanted Bo to think that Ava meant nothing to him, to clear the way for his advancement in the Hellraisers, and to make sure nothing stood in the way of Rick being in the right position to find out what Bo was going to do. There was a major drug buy on the line, and Rick needed to make sure it didn't get cancelled.

The problem was, he did care about Ava. He did worry about her. The best thing that could come out of her eavesdropping would be her falling apart and deciding to run home to her father, thereby clearing the way for him to focus only on what Bo was up to. Ava would be safe then, and that part of his job would be over.

Unfortunately, no such luck. And despite the illegal drug distribution angle, Ava was his primary assignment. His job was to prevent any major connection between Ava and drugs. Bringing in cocaine across the border would be a massive clusterfuck, and probably cost him his job.

He really liked his job. And it was damn time he stopped

playing around with Ava and started doing his job. What the hell did it matter what she thought of him? When this assignment was over, he was off to the next one and Ava would be nothing but a distant memory.

After Bo and Lacey took off, Rick went back to his room, grabbed his cell phone and dialed Grange's number. The general picked up on the second ring, and Rick filled him in on what was going to happen.

"Well, shit," Grange said. "So your cousin is using his girlfriend as a mule, and has decided to drag the senator's daughter into his game."

"Looks that way."

"It's obvious Bo doesn't have any idea who Ava is, does he?"

"I don't think so. No way would he allow a high-profile person like Senator Vargas's daughter to carry drugs across the Mexican border. A bust could break the Hellraisers and lead directly to him."

"Okay. What do you want to do about it?"

Leave it to Grange to drop the ball right at Rick's feet. "I want to let Ava and Lacey go into Mexico. But I want to be there. I also want to get Bo into Mexico. This is an opportunity to break up a major drug import and distribution ring. I can't just walk away from this by pulling Ava out."

Grange went quiet for a few seconds. "Risky. The Feds aren't going to like this."

Rick smiled. "But you aren't going to tell them yet, are you?"

"Of course not. I'll wait until you're already in Mexico and I'll take the heat for the decision to let this play out."

Just like Grange to shoulder the burden.

"Thanks."

"You'd better have something figured out that clears Ava by the time you reach the U.S. border, though."

"You got it."

"And if things get sticky, get Ava out of there and let this drug business with your cousin go."

"I know. She's the number one priority. I'll keep you posted."

He hung up and paced again, trying to formulate a plan. Bo wanted him out of the state. Rick would have to change his mind.

Then again, maybe not. Maybe he could head on down into Mexico without Bo knowing. Or at least without Bo knowing just yet. Because Bo would find out eventually—after Rick got there.

And that's exactly the way Rick wanted this game to play out.

He grinned and went in search of Bo.

Ten

Ava inhaled and exhaled, sinking deep into the cushy table where she was being massaged. She could almost imagine she was floating somewhere in the deep sea, lost amidst the creatures that inhabited the vast ocean. Just drifting endlessly without a care in the world.

Lacey was right. Mexico was heaven. She was oiled, rubbed, pampered, the strains of some sweet classical music lulling her into a near coma of bliss.

All this lavish attention almost took her mind off the gnawing emptiness and pain of what Rick had done to her yesterday.

Almost.

Fortunately she had Lacey with her—at least some of the time—talking to her nonstop about everything and nothing.

Now that they didn't have school and their future careers to work on together any longer, Ava realized she and Lacey had very little common ground. Lacey liked to talk about Bo—a lot. Her entire world revolved around Bo. What she and Bo did together, where they went, what little presents he bought for her . . .

And sex. She talked nonstop about all the sex she was having with Bo.

Which would be fine if all the sexy talk didn't make Ava think about Rick. And she'd vowed she wasn't going to think about Rick anymore. After all, he wasn't thinking about her. He was probably off picking up a new girl, what with women being disposable and all.

"You're tensing up, ma'am. Try to relax."

"Sorry." Ava cleared her mind again and focused on the soft music and equally soft hands of Carla, her masseuse. She closed her eyes and imagined herself rich and pampered, getting massages like this every week, having an idle life where all she did was shop and live in the lap of luxury.

Ha. She'd be bored senseless. She was already bored senseless. She'd been here twenty-four hours and she was ready to go home. How Lacey did these trips by herself was beyond Ava's ability to comprehend.

It was certainly a nice experience. The town was lovely, the people were friendly, there was plenty of shopping, and the food was good. The spa and hotel were awesome, catering to her every need. The staff knew Lacey very well since she'd been coming here often. Still, Ava was bored.

And dammit, she couldn't stop thinking about Rick.

After her massage, she went to search for Lacey, who'd gotten a massage at the same time. They were going to meet up for a late lunch afterward. But she was nowhere to be found. The woman working the front desk at the spa said Lacey had left a message saying she was going up to her room to take a nap.

Figured. Lacey was always either talking Ava's ear off or sound asleep.

She decided to go take a shower, wash the oil off from the massage, and maybe relax and read.

She grabbed a sandwich on her way up to her room, and after her shower, grabbed it and took a spot out on the balcony. Such an amazing panorama of the town, and off to the right she caught a peek of the ocean and white sand.

While she ate, she enjoyed the warm air and beautiful view of the waving trees and the colorful town below. Such a mix of colors, and Ava had always enjoyed people watching. She always wondered what people were doing, where they were going.

Maybe because watching other people go about their lives was so much more interesting than her own. Because here she was, sitting up in her room when she could either be out shopping or at the beach on this beautiful day.

Hadn't she learned anything? They had one more day here and she was sitting on a hotel balcony when a once-in-a-lifetime experience was just a short walk away.

So what was it going to be? Shopping or some time on the beach?

She and Lacey had shopped yesterday. She'd even haggled with a few of the merchants—it was expected, as Lacey explained.

She should check out the beach.

It was time to dig her toes in the sand and live a little. She didn't need Lacey to hold her hand—or Rick. She could do it by herself.

She threw on her swimsuit and cover-up, slipped into her sandals, and made her way down the slope toward the water. Dusky-colored rock walls rose up on either side of her. There was no concrete path, just sand, worn from the people who'd come before her. She made her way through the maze of rocks until she found the clearing.

Breathtaking. Clear blue water, mountains on the other side, and no one was around. She stood and listened to the crashing sound of the waves, watched them ride their way to shore. She kicked off her sandals and moved in a few feet so the water trickled over her toes.

It was warm, inviting. She dropped to the sand and straightened her legs, clearing her mind.

This was so much better than sitting in her room.

She dragged the beach towel out of her bag, pulled off her cover-up, and lay down.

As soon as she closed her eyes, Rick's face swam before her. She sighed, giving up the thought of forgetting about him.

She wished he were here with her, lying on the beach with her, folding her into his arms and kissing her. She missed talking to him, hearing the sound of his voice, his laughter. He seemed to understand her in ways no other man ever had. What man had ever even bothered to listen to her before? And he didn't agree with everything she said just to get her in bed. He helped her reason things out about Lacey.

But it went beyond just talking. She missed making love to him, the way he'd awakened her body. Her senses throbbed every time she thought about his kisses, his touch, the way she felt when he was inside her.

How could a man affect her so deeply after only a few short days? What was so special about him that was different than any other guy she'd known?

He had seemed so perfect for her. They had seemed to fit so well together. How could she have been so wrong about him? What he'd said to Bo just didn't fit what she knew about him. Was she that bad a judge of character that she hadn't been able to see who he really was? Had he played her that well? She was a reasonably intelligent woman who knew how to spot a player. Or at least she thought she was.

Too much thinking. Thinking that was getting her nowhere. She and Rick were over. Why couldn't she just let it go?

"You could tempt a man to sin looking like that."

Ava shot up and grabbed her cover-up, shielding her face from the sun. A silhouette stood in the bright sunlight, a dark shadow she couldn't make out. She grabbed her bag, then scrambled to her feet, hoping to hell someone else was on this stretch of beach besides her and some stranger. What the hell was she thinking coming out here alone?

"Ava."

Her whole body went rigid. "Rick?" She fished into her

bag for her sunglasses, slid them on. He stood there, barefoot in jeans and a sleeveless muscle shirt, holding his boots in his hand. His dark sunglasses made him look reckless, sexy, like the bad boy she figured him to be. Her legs went weak. "What are you doing here?"

"I came here to find you, to talk to you." He pushed his sunglasses up on his head.

She should be angry with him—furious, in fact—not falling to his feet in a gush of female libido. "Why?"

"Because what I said back in Vegas . . . I didn't want you to hear that."

Her anger rushed to the surface. She preferred that to being so damn glad to see him. "Obviously."

"No, you don't understand." He grabbed her hands and pulled her down to sit in the sand with him. "It wasn't what I meant, what I felt."

"Why did you say it?"

"Because that's what I wanted Bo to think."

She cocked her head to the side. "I don't understand."

"In order to get back into the Hellraisers I have to prove my worthiness."

"And treating a woman like shit is the way to do it?"

He rubbed a spot above his brow with his fingertip. "No, but telling him that I cared about you puts me in a bad position."

She didn't know how to respond to that. Was he saying he cared about her? "Why?"

"I'm not sure I can explain this well."

"Try."

"I've been gone for ten years. I just came back. They want me to be free to work for them, to ride with them. You're not one of the Hellraisers."

"Oh. So if you hooked up with me, I'd be a hindrance to you doing that."

He nodded. "It's a shitty excuse, I know. I didn't expect him to ask me about you. So I shot off that you meant nothing to me, that you were just a fuck. They were just words said to placate him. I didn't expect you to be there to hear them."

"You didn't mean them."

"No. I didn't."

"But you still said them."

"Yes."

"They hurt me."

He looked down at the sand, then swept his gaze back to her. "I know. And I'm sorry. It was thoughtless. I was an asshole."

If she were smart, she wouldn't believe him. She'd tell him to turn around and head back to Las Vegas. That she wasn't interested in his explanations or excuses. That they were over. That they never had anything to start with.

But she did believe him. He'd come all the way to Mexico to explain to her, to apologize. What kind of man did that?

"If it would make you feel better you could throw sand at me."

She laughed. Damn him. "I can't believe you're here. You came all the way here just to see me? You could have called me."

"I could have. But this kind of needed to be handled face-to-face."

"You could have waited until I got back."

He shifted, rubbed his hands together to wipe the sand off. "I didn't want to wait. Besides, I missed you."

She looked away, stared out at the water. "Don't say that."

He tipped her chin, forced her gaze back to his. "Why not?"

Her eyes filled with tears and she hated herself—and him—because of it. She pulled her sunglasses off and looked at him. "I don't want to care about you, Rick."

He paused, then lifted a strand of her hair and sifted it through his fingers. "But you do."

She wouldn't admit it—refused to give him more ammunition to hurt her. Until he leaned in, and before she could object, fit his mouth over hers. The kiss was slow and easy—he wasn't demanding, it was more like he was testing the waters.

God, she'd missed his mouth on hers. She sighed and pressed into him, felt weak and ridiculous for giving in so easily. She should have walked away. This man was trouble, was only going to hurt her.

But he'd come all the way to Mexico to apologize. What man did that?

Rick.

So as his lips brushed over hers, seeking, searching, all her resolve melted and she kissed him back, her answer—a resounding *yes*—to everything.

She was so easy. She was going to hate herself later for this. But right now he was pulling her onto his lap, onto his strong thighs, and wrapping his arms around her, deepening the kiss until she was heated all over. And it felt so good—so right. She couldn't muster up any reasonable objections to why she shouldn't be with him.

As long as she guarded her heart.

He dragged his lips across her chin, spreading hot kisses along her throat. She felt the mad beat of her pulse against his lips and tilted her head back, not caring that they were on the beach where anyone could see them. No one knew her here—she was a stranger. Even if someone did see them, it wasn't like she was ever coming back to this place again. And she didn't want this moment to end.

She shifted, rocked against him, riding his cock through the denim of his jeans.

Rick grinned. "Out here?"

"Yes."

"I have a better idea."

He put his hands under her buttocks and stood, carrying her over to a secluded cove where the water met the rocks.

"Your jeans are getting wet," she said as he rested her back against the cool rock and set her on her feet.

"I don't care." He planted his lips on hers and she soon forgot all about his jeans, or anything else. All she knew was his hard cock against her sex, splintering her with pleasure that rocked her senses.

She wanted more of it. She wanted him inside her. Now.

"Rick, please."

He leaned back, his gaze questioning. "You want to do this upstairs in your room?"

She shook her head. "No. Here. Now."

His face was as filled with the dark, ravenous need that she felt inside as he dug a condom out of his pocket, then took a quick glance around, making sure they were alone.

He unzipped his pants and pulled out his cock, and she couldn't resist wrapping her fingers around it. So hot, thick, pulsing with life.

"Christ, Ava. You're going to make me explode."

She liked knowing she had that effect on him. She stroked him while he tore open the condom package. He brushed her hand away, then reached between them to pull the fabric of her bikini aside.

The first touch of his hand against her bare flesh made her gasp, lift up on her toes to drive against his palm. He rubbed her sex, used her own moisture to lubricate her clit.

She'd done nothing but think about him, think about how good the sex had been between them. That in itself had been foreplay. And out here in the heat, with the waves crashing against them, she was already so close to orgasm it was embarrassing.

Rick leaned into her, his gaze hard and direct as he watched her.

"Come on," he said, driving his palm against her clit as his finger slipped inside her pussy. "Let me feel you come, Ava."

The touch of his hand against her, the way he looked at her, coupled with their forbidden location, was all too much, ratcheting up her excitement to a frenzied level. She gripped his wrist, held him right where she needed. She moved against him and her climax rushed at her like an overpowering wave. She kept her focus on Rick, letting him see what his touch had done to her.

His smile was devastating, the darkness in his eyes making her throb inside.

He jerked her bikini bottom down and placed it on the rock ledge above her head, then lifted her legs, wrapping them around him. Ava held on to his shoulders while he guided her onto his cock.

Sweet heaven. She pulsed around him, gripped him in a tight vise that overwhelmed her senses. He rocked against her, thrusting slow and easy at first, then harder, dragging his cock over her sensitive tissues until all she could do was squeak out breathless pants.

But no words were necessary because they spoke to each other with their bodies, communicating in a way that said everything. She dug her nails into his shoulders and he grunted, driving deep until she cried out because it both hurt and felt so good. Her back scraped the rock as he fucked her, but she had no complaints. She wanted him deep inside her, fucking her fast, because she was going to come again.

"Oh yeah, just like that," he said, and she knew he felt her pussy contracting around him. She tilted her head back and watched with him where their bodies were joined, knew he enjoyed watching his cock slide in and out of her. She held back, wanting to suspend this moment, holding her breath as if that very act could hold back the rushing tide of her climax.

But then he lifted his gaze to hers.

"Ava," he said, his fingers digging into the flesh of her hips. "Come on my dick."

With a hard shudder, she let go, her orgasm catapulting her to a place where logic had no play—only mindless pleasure.

Rick went with her, thrusting hard against her once, twice, before letting out a guttural cry that was lost in the crash of the waves. He pulled her against him and she held tight to him, allowing herself to just feel every pulsing sensation of him rocking inside her, of her own body's response to being with him.

She'd never experienced anything so perfect.

When he let her down so her feet touched the ground, she realized how shaky she was. He kept his arm around her waist until she found her footing. She laughed, looking at the bottom of his jeans, soaked by the water rising up around them.

"I hope you brought swim trunks."

"I did."

"Maybe you should change."

"Maybe I should."

He did and they spent time playing in the water together. After, they spread towels out and lay on the beach, soaking up the sun.

This was so much better than reading a book in her room. Or, she had to admit, hanging out with Lacey, who'd turned out to be a dud.

Rick rolled over onto his stomach, his hair flicking water onto her breasts. She laughed and rubbed the water off.

"Keep playing around with those and we'll be back where we started."

She laughed. "Is that so bad?"

"No." He tipped his head toward the hotel. "Where's Lacey?"

Ava turned on her side to face him. "Passed out in her room again, I imagine."

"Again?"

She nodded "She's either going nonstop talking and running me ragged, or out cold."

"So you haven't been having a good time?"

She shrugged. "I thought Lacey and I would reconnect like we used to. I see now that's not going to happen."

"What do you mean?"

"I think it took this trip to make me realize she's not the same person she once was. She doesn't live the same lifestyle. She's different. And maybe so am I. We can't seem to communicate anymore . . . at least from my perspective."

"You've grown apart."

"I guess." She picked up a handful of sand and sifted it through her fingers. "I feel kind of stupid for doing this."

He frowned. "For doing what?"

"For coming to bike week and trying to immerse myself in her life, become what she is. For coming to Mexico with her. I realize now that she has her life and I have mine, and they don't mesh anymore."

Rick smoothed his hand over her hair. "You were worried about your friend. That's admirable."

She shrugged. "Not that it did much good. I thought I could make her into who she used to be. I can't do that."

"At least you found that out."

"You're right. I needed to know that."

"And now you can let her go and move on with your life."

"Sort of."

"What do you mean?"

She sat up. "I'm still worried."

He sat, too. "About Lacey?"

"Yes."

"Tell me what's bothering you."

"You'll think it's stupid. Plus, your cousin is involved."

"I'm not married to Bo, Ava. If something's bothering you about him, I'd like to know about it."

She studied him, the sincere look of concern on his face. He had come all the way down here to find her, to apologize to her. That meant he cared. Even if they didn't have a long-term relationship in the works, she felt he was someone she could trust.

And even if she and Lacey were no longer tight, she wasn't going to just walk away if she had concerns.

"Why does Bo keep sending Lacey down here?"

"To Mexico?"

"Yes. She told me he gifts her with a trip down here once a month at least. Don't you find that strange?"

He shrugged. "What's strange about it?"

"I'm not stupid, Rick. I know what goes on with the Hell-raisers."

"Do you? Then why don't you tell me?"

"I think they're running drugs. And I think Bo is using Lacey as a mule to carry drugs from Mexico into the U.S."

Whoa. Rick had to bite his tongue to keep from spitting out a response to Ava's accusation.

Because she was dead-on right. But how had she figured

it out? He'd have to play things pretty close. The less she was involved the better.

"That's a pretty big leap. Why would you think that?"

"Lacey seems high. Like all the time. And she was smoking pot in the room the other night. Drugs seem to be used freely among the Hellraisers. Plus a trip to Mexico once a month while Bo travels"—she held out quote marks with her fingers—"'on business'—I mean, come on. What kind of business does he have?"

"I have no idea. We haven't gotten into it yet."

She cocked her head to the side. "You aren't involved in all this with him, are you?"

"In all what?" Now he'd have to be really careful how he answered her, and make sure to play dumb.

"In whatever he's doing."

He held up his hands. "Hey, I just got back into town, remember? I have no idea what Bo's up to. He told me he was sending Lacey down here for R&R. That's it."

She laid her head on her knees. "Are you positive? You wouldn't lie to me, would you?"

He felt the gut punch of the lie he had to tell her. This was one of the times he hated his job. "I'm positive. That's all I know."

"Still, it doesn't make sense. This is a prime resort. Where's he getting the money?"

"Maybe he does have a legitimate business. Did you ask Lacey?"

"No, I haven't. I don't want to do anything to alienate her. Our friendship is tenuous enough as it is. Saying anything negative about Bo will only push her further away."

"Do you have any proof?"

She wrinkled her nose. "No."

"Then what do you want to do?"

She inhaled, sighed. "I have no idea. I don't trust Bo. I can't help but think his motives in sending Lacey down here aren't pure ones."

"Maybe you should talk to her. Find out what she knows. It's possible—and I'm just saying it's possible—that if Bo is running drugs from here, maybe Lacey already knows that."

Her eyes widened. "Oh, God. Do you think so?" She shook her head. "That's not possible. Even madly in love and blind to everything, Lacey wouldn't be that stupid. She wouldn't risk going to jail for any man."

He shrugged. "If you say so. You know her better than I do." It was about time that Bo's game reached an end. An enlightened Lacey was a start.

"You're right. She might get mad at me, but I have to say what's on my mind. I wouldn't be a good friend if I didn't."

He stood, wiped the sand off, and held out his hand. "Come on. I'll go with you."

Rick grabbed his stuff and took it up to Ava's room. They showered—together—which was always a fun experience. If it wasn't for Ava's distraction over wanting to talk to Lacey, Rick would have lingered with her in the shower, making her come again. Then he'd have liked to take her out on that nice secluded balcony and fuck her.

Maybe later.

They dressed and Ava called Lacey, told her they were coming over.

"She sounded groggy, like she'd spent the entire day asleep." Ava sighed, worry etching her features.

"Maybe she stays up all night partying. What did you two do last night?"

"We went out to dinner, then to the club downstairs to dance and have a couple of drinks. I was exhausted so I came up and went to bed about midnight. Lacey said she wanted to stay and party."

"With who?"

"Some random people who joined our table. She said she knows them from coming down here a lot."

"Locals?"

"Yes."

"Hmmm." Probably the ones who dumped the drugs on Lacey. He could be wrong about that, but he doubted it. Bo would have people in place to keep an eye on his mule.

They headed over to Lacey's room and knocked. Lacey's hair was a mess, makeup smeared on her face like she hadn't bothered to wash it the night before. She leaned against the doorjamb and yawned. "What time is it?"

"Four-thirty."

"Really?" She laughed. "I slept all day."

"Yes, you did." Ava walked in and Rick followed. They took a seat at the table near the sliding doors to the balcony.

Lacey came in and flounced onto the rumpled bed.

"Hey, Rick. What are you doing down here?"

"I missed Ava. I wanted to talk to her."

"Awww, how sweet. So you two are back together?"

"We're fine," Ava said. "But I'm worried about you."

Lacey lifted her chin. "Me? Why?"

"You party all night. Sleep all day. You're a mess, Lace."

She frowned. "Excuse me. I am not a mess. I'm just a little tired from dancing last night. Jose and Marco took me to this rocking club. I didn't get home until after dawn."

"That's exactly what I'm talking about. How do you manage to stay up so late?"

Lacey laughed. "I sleep all day."

"This isn't the kind of life you used to lead."

Lacey sighed and leaned against the headboard of the bed. "Ava, we've been over this. I know it isn't. But it's who I am now. Why can't you just let it go?"

Ava got up and sat on the edge of the bed next to Lacey, picked up Lacey's hand. "Lace, I've known you since kindergarten. We're like sisters. I love you like you're family. That's why I have to be honest and tell you . . ."

"Surprise!"

The door flew open and Bo walked in.

Rick stood. Lacey squealed in delight, leaped off the bed and into Bo's arms, planting kisses all over his face.

"Baby! What are you doing here?"

"My business was finished early so I thought I'd surprise you."

"Oh my God, you so did."

Ava shot a look over her shoulder at Rick, who held up his

hand, signaling now was not the time for a come-to-Jesus discussion with Lacey.

Because given the hard edge to Bo's gaze as he looked at Rick, he had a feeling the come-to-Jesus meeting was about to happen between the two of them.

Bo was not happy to find Rick here.

Which was okay, because now that Bo was here, Rick's plan was working out perfectly.

Eleven

Ava looked from Rick to Bo, watching the tense exchange between the two men.

Bo wasn't happy to see Rick. She wondered why.

"Bo."

"Rick. Weren't you supposed to be somewhere else, doing something else?"

Rick didn't seem at all concerned. "Already got it done. So I thought I'd pop down here and see Ava."

"Yeah?" Bo set Lacey on her feet and moved toward Rick. "Why?"

"I don't think that's any of your business."

Uh-oh. The tension grew thicker.

"I'm making it my business."

Ava stood and moved next to Bo. "We had a fight. He came down here to make up with me." She tilted her head back and shined a brilliant smile up at him. "And, oh, did we ever make up."

Rick slanted a grin down at her. "Yeah, we did."

"Can I see you on the balcony for a second?"

Rick nodded at Bo. Ava grabbed his hand.

"It'll be fine."

At least Rick hoped it would be fine. It was finesse time. Bo slid the door closed so Ava and Lacey couldn't hear what was being said.

"What the fuck are you doing here?"

"What are *you* doing here?" Rick figured turning the tables on Bo would give him some time to think.

"Following you. Did you make the drop?"

"On my way down here. Money's in my bag."

"This is messed up."

Rick leaned against the wall and let a smile slip out. "Why? I don't see what the problem is."

"You don't?"

"No."

"You know what's happening here, right?"

"Yeah."

"Then tell me again why you're here."

"To see Ava. I didn't like what happened between us in Vegas."

"So she means more to you than you told me earlier."

Rick turned away, hoping Bo would think he was embarrassed about revealing his emotions. "I guess she does. I didn't know that until she was gone. I missed her. Maybe I care about her more than I let on to you that day. I don't know. Anyway, after I made the drop I decided to head on down and talk things over with her."

Bo didn't say anything, just paced the balcony. Rick turned to face him again.

"Bo, this isn't going to change anything. I have my bike, Lacey and Ava have their car. I'm not traveling with them. The operation will still go as planned."

Bo dragged his fingers through his hair. "I guess you're right." He lifted his gaze to Rick's. "Next time let me know what you're doing so I don't think you're up to something."

Rick clapped Bo on the back. "The only thing I've got going on is getting back in the good graces of that woman in there."

Bo looked inside the room. "Can't say I blame you. She's prime."

"That's what I thought. Nice piece of pussy like that doesn't come around all that often. I figured she was worth the trip."

"Just stay away from the other part of the business that's going on down here."

"That's not why I'm here."

He just intended to stop it from happening. Or at least prevent it from happening the way Bo had it planned.

Because despite his cousin being family, Bo was a scum-sucking bastard for setting up his girlfriend this way. The man had no honor. And once you lacked honor, there was nothing left. Rick felt no loyalty to his cousin anymore.

Bo was going down. Which meant Rick was going to be his shadow until they left Mexico.

Fortunately, Rick was very good at that. It was his job.

"So, now what?" Rick asked, trying to act nonchalant.

Bo visibly relaxed. He threw his arm around Rick's shoulder and reached for the door. "Since we're both in Mexico with our ladies and it's not time to leave yet . . . we might as well party."

Bo knew how to put a party together in a hurry. After they'd gone back inside the room, Bo had grabbed Lacey and said he was going to get a suite, then invite some people in for a small get-together that night.

Apparently Rick's idea of a small get-together was different than Bo's. By nine that night there were over fifty people in Bo's suite, an ostentatious, oversized, top-of-the-hotel apartment that must have cost Bo a small fortune.

The drug business must be lucrative for his cousin.

And keeping Ava in the dark about everything was get-

ting more difficult. One look at this suite and she arched a
brow, wrinkled her nose, and turned to Rick.

"What does your cousin do for a living again?"

Rick shrugged. "No idea. I think he's in sales. That's why
he travels so much."

She cast him a dubious look. "Uh-huh. I think you know
more than you're telling me."

"No, I just don't make it my business to pry into what my
cousin does for a living. He's got his life and I've got mine.
I'd like to leave it that way for now."

She sighed. "You're right. I'm sorry."

Ava wasn't stupid—one of the things he admired so much
about her. She wasn't buying the *sales* angle at all. He couldn't
blame her. Anyone with half a brain knew this whole setup
smelled like someone in the drug business.

He turned her to face him. "You look beautiful."

She cocked a brow. "And you're trying to distract me."

Partly, yes. But she did look amazing in a red dress with
tiny straps over her shoulders. And the top kind of swooped
down with this extra material that covered her breasts. Every
time she bent over, he thought her breasts would spill out.
They didn't, but the cleavage was tempting. The dress hit her
right at the knee, and every time she moved, so did the bottom of the dress.

Swish, swish, swish.

She had great legs.

Hell, she had great everything. She'd make a stellar agent,
because she was damned distracting, which made it hard for
him to do his job.

This was going to require his best juggling—and undercover act—ever.

She'd pulled her hair up tonight, giving him access to her
throat. He pressed his lips against her neck, inhaled her
sweet scent. Damn, she smelled good. No perfume, just soap
and her shampoo and the sweet scent of her skin. He kissed
her, letting his tongue slip out to lick across the softness of
her skin, ending up at her ear.

"I like distracting you," he whispered.

He heard the catch of her breath. She clutched his arms. "When you do that, it makes my nipples hard."

He smiled. "Good, because it makes my dick hard." He pulled her close, and she tilted her head back.

Whether in jeans and a T-shirt, or dressed up like a socialite, Ava was a beautiful woman.

Why the hell she wanted anything to do with him he didn't understand. He was one lucky guy. And even though this was temporary, he intended to enjoy every second of it.

"You want a drink?"

"Sure."

They made their way to the bar. Rick ordered a beer for himself and a glass of wine for Ava.

"I don't see Lacey," she said, her gaze searching the room.

Rick spotted Bo off in a corner talking to a few guys. "There's Bo. Maybe he knows. Come on." He took Ava's hand and headed in that direction. His motive, of course, was to ease in and see if he could overhear something of what was being said. It might be nothing at all. Then again, it might be important.

Bo had his back turned to them, so when Rick moved close, he was surprised to discover them talking in Spanish.

Fortunately, Rick knew enough Spanish to understand what was being said. Something about taking care of things later tonight, when the party was in full swing. And Bo was counting on being able to slip away. Now that Rick was here, he'd be able to see firsthand how things were done.

Perfect.

But Ava was frowning and he'd bet she'd understood every word, too. Not good.

Rick nudged Bo with his elbow. "Hey."

Bo smiled and made room for Ava. "Evenin'. Don't you look pretty."

Ava gave Bo a return smile that didn't quite reach her eyes. "Thank you. Where's Lacey?"

Bo rolled his eyes. "Still in the bedroom getting dolled up.

That woman takes forever to get ready for a party. Why don't you go see if you can hurry her up? All the way at the end of the hall."

"I'll do that. Thanks."

Ava turned to slip away, but Rick grasped her wrist and planted a short kiss on her lips.

Her lips lifted, her cheeks darkening to a dusky pink.

Sometime tonight he was going to find time to make love to her. While she was wearing that sexy red dress.

"You look sad and pathetic whenever she leaves a room. You got it bad, man," Bo said with a laugh. "Be careful, or we'll be planning a Hellraiser wedding."

If only his cousin knew what was really going to happen. A wedding would be the least of his worries. Rick managed a wry smile. "She's sweet. Like nobody I've ever met before."

"Give her a few months with our gang. We'll squeeze the sweetness right out of her."

When hell froze over. Hopefully this assignment would be finished by the time they crossed the border. Then Ava could resume her life in Las Vegas—go back to school—back to the safety of academia, where she belonged. Not out here on the fringes of drugs and destruction.

Look at what it had done to Lacey. He wouldn't allow the same thing to happen to Ava.

Ava walked out with Lacey, and the truth was right there.

Lacey, though only with the Hellraisers for a year, had the look of a jaded biker chick about her. It started with the way she dressed—tight dress cut up to there—hell, she probably figured everyone had seen it all anyway. If she so much as bent over even a little, the mystery would be gone. And the look in Lacey's eyes as she scanned the room said she'd been there and had done just about everything. Lacey's lips lifted as if she'd just entered heaven. Innocence lost.

With Ava, the innocence was still there in the way she took in the party atmosphere with a wide-eyed look. Rick took a glance around the room and tried to see it through Ava's eyes—the free-flowing alcohol, the drugs moving about the room unhidden, the way people kissed and fondled as if they didn't care who saw—and this wasn't even a Hell-raisers party. But it was the lifestyle, and one Ava wasn't yet accustomed to.

If he had his way, Rick was going to get her away from this as soon as possible.

You sound like her father now.

Maybe her father was right. Maybe he understood why Senator Vargas wanted her out of a lifestyle Rick had always found acceptable.

For Ava, it wasn't acceptable.

She smiled when she saw him. Lacey made a beeline for Bo and Ava came his way.

Dammit, he liked that she only had eyes for him, liked seeing her walk, that skirt swishing around her fabulous legs. The look in her eyes was a punch to his gut—dark, smolder-ing, barely banked sensuality that with one kiss, one touch, he could stoke into an inferno.

When she reached him, he pulled her into his arms. De-spite his better judgment, he was unable to resist her.

"When you smile at me like that . . ."

She let the end of her sentence trail off.

"Yeah?"

"It makes me think all kinds of dirty thoughts."

He shook his head. "You? A proper young lady with a master's degree?"

She tilted her head back and laughed. "A proper young lady with a master's degree who really likes having sex with you."

"Consumed by it, are you?"

She laid her palm on his chest. "I wasn't before. I am now."

His cock twitched. "You're good for my ego."

"You're good for all of me."

Son of a bitch. Women did not give him warm feelings and an unfamiliar tightness in his chest. This wasn't happen-ing. Not to him. He didn't fall in love. He didn't even know what love was. Love wasn't for a guy like him who'd grown up in foster care, who'd never had the care of even one parent, let alone two, who'd spent all his time on the streets, who'd never had a woman tell him she loved him. He didn't know the meaning of the word *love*.

Did he?

No. He didn't. Ava was an assignment. A fun assignment, for sure, but just an assignment. And when it was over, he was walking away. He was always walking away first, before someone walked away from him.

What the fuck would he do with love? With a woman in his life? His kind of life wasn't suitable for a woman in it, and especially not a woman like Ava.

Even if he wanted to—try to make things work between them—he'd be no better than Bo if he tried to drag Ava into his lifestyle. She had a career ahead of her. More school. Her Ph.D., followed by a job in social work. Her future didn't include him any more than his included her.

But they could have fun fucking until it was over. Then he'd walk away, disappear, and she'd move on with her life, thinking he was some dickhead biker who'd found better things to do. Yeah, it would make him look like an asshole, but it was better for her this way. She'd forget about him soon enough. They always did.

But for now? Yeah, he'd enjoy the hell out of her for now.

"So I'm good for all of you, huh? I'll have to see 'all of you' to find out if I'm good for it."

She laughed. "I'm sure that can be arranged . . . uh, later."

"What? Not here in the middle of the party?"

"You have a wicked mind, Rick."

He bent her over his arm and kissed her, long and hard, then tilted her back up on her feet. "And that's why you like me."

She blew out a breath and smoothed her skirt, then leaned into him to whisper in his ear, "That's one of the reasons why I like you. But not the only one."

She pivoted and walked away, found Lacey, and the two of them took up a conversation.

Yeah, he was in deep shit with Ava. The woman rocked

him back on his heels. He usually found women pretty predictable. Easy to come by, easy to fuck, easy to drop and forget.

Ava? There was nothing easy about her.

For the next few hours, Ava divided her time between him and Lacey. He liked that she didn't cling to him, needing him for her entertainment. She even talked to some of the other people there, since there were women as well as men. She wasn't uncomfortable at all in her surroundings, though he kept an eye on her at all times. If any of the guys got too close, thinking she might be there on her own, he was right there by her side to let those guys know she was off-limits. From the scowl on his face they got the message loud and clear and backed off right away.

Which seemed to amuse Ava. She started referring to him as her Knight in Shining Armor.

If only she knew how little that applied to him.

Rick divided his time between keeping an eye on Ava and surreptitiously watching Bo. Though Bo made no moves other than drinking and partying with his guests and with Lacey, Rick knew tonight was the night, and he planned to be right on top of it when it happened.

The suite was packed a little after one in the morning. Lacey was either drunk or stoned, sitting on one of the plush white leather sofas near the open doors by the balcony, looking pale as death and like she might puke at any minute.

Which gave Bo the perfect opportunity to slip away. He motioned to the guys he'd been talking to earlier, and they walked out the front door.

"Lacey doesn't look like she feels well." Rick pointed to Lacey, and that's all it took.

"Oh, no. I'd better go take care of her," Ava said.

Ava was off seeing to Lacey, which left him free to follow Bo. He walked out the front door and down the stairs, taking three at a time so he'd be there before the elevator. He inched the main floor door open, watching as the elevator doors slid open.

Bo and his friends came out, made a left turn, and headed

in his direction. Rick closed the stair doors in a hurry and hoped like hell they weren't going to take the stairs. After counting a few seconds, he breathed a sigh of relief and cracked the door open again.

Bo and the others had headed through the back doors and toward the parking garage.

Rick followed, keeping a respectable distance so Bo wouldn't see him.

Lacey's car had been parked outside the garage, toward the back of the lot, far beyond where anyone usually parked.

Either Bo had her park there, or had moved her car to this remote location.

Rick moved around the back of the building where it wasn't lit so he could observe without being seen.

And watched another car pull up beside Lacey's. They cut the lights, the trunk popped open, and within a minute they'd opened Lacey's trunk and popped down a false inside top from the hood of her trunk. In the space there, Bo and his friends placed several packages. It was too dark to see shapes or sizes or even how many, but Rick knew it was the drugs Lacey was going to transport across the border tomorrow.

Asshole.

They finished up and climbed into the car that had dropped off the drugs, then sped out of there. Rick melted into the side of the building until they passed, then walked toward Lacey's car.

He waited a good fifteen minutes to be sure no one came around.

They didn't. It took a little maneuvering but Rick had been stealing cars since he was twelve years old. No amount of today's technology could get in his way. He popped the trunk and the false inside top, whistling low as he saw the booty there.

Cocaine. Nicely packaged up in tight, brown-wrapped bundles. Probably the same amount on the other side, too.

If Lacey were caught by the authorities smuggling this amount of dope, she'd do maximum time.

And Bo wouldn't give a shit. He'd just pick up some new, naïve chick and do the same thing to her.

That wasn't going to happen.

Not this trip.

Never again.

Twelve

Ava finished wiping up the bathroom in the suite, washed up, then switched off the light and went into the bedroom to check one more time on Lacey.

Her breathing was shallow, but she seemed to be resting now.

God, what a mess. Ava had barely gotten Lacey into the bathroom before she'd lost it. She didn't know what Lacey had eaten, drank, smoked, or snorted, but she'd heaved for nearly an hour straight, then nothing at all. Once she was empty, Ava had cleaned her up and poured her into bed. Light snores were all she heard now.

If that was the result of drugs, alcohol, and excess partying, Ava wanted no part of it. She was grateful all she'd managed was a few hors d'oeuvres and one glass of wine. Right now her stomach felt queasy after witnessing Lacey's gastronomical debacle. She turned off the light, closed the door, and went down the hall, making a beeline for the bar so she could grab a club soda with lime.

She searched for Bo, found him, and told him Lacey was sick and out cold.

He rolled his eyes. "She never could hold her stuff. Guess my party is over for the night."

How sweet of him to be so concerned about her. "She'll be fine. Thanks for asking."

She walked away before she could say anything more to him, like what she thought about his inability to watch over his own girlfriend, and went in search of Rick. He was just stepping back through the front door.

She quirked a brow as he approached. "Where did you go?"

"I had to make a phone call and it was too noisy in here."

"International?"

He laughed. "Well, it's not like I know anyone in Mexico. I have a line on a job."

She glanced down at her watch. "It's almost three in the morning."

"It wasn't an interview. Buddy of mine I've been trying to get hold of finally got back to me, and I didn't want to miss the call again since he's on the road a lot."

"Oh. So, what kind of job is it?"

"Construction. That's why he's hard to get hold of. He's leaving in a couple hours for Texas and wanted me to hop on this job with him."

Her stomach clenched. "Do you need to leave right now?"

"No. I'll meet him in a couple days."

"Oh. Well, that's great." She ignored the stab of disappointment. Of course he was leaving. So was she. They both had lives separate from each other. This . . . thing between them wasn't permanent. How many times did she have to keep reminding herself of that?

Many, apparently.

"How's Lacey? She didn't look good."

At least someone cared about her. "She's okay. She was pretty sick there for a while, but she's resting now."

He swept his hand down her back. "She's lucky she has a friend like you to look after her."

"Thank you, Rick. That's nice of you to say. I'm not sure how much help I am to her, but I was glad to be here."

"You help her more than you know. Not everyone has someone to care about them."

He led her to the table where the food was, his cryptic words ringing in her ears.

The party had started to break up, so they found Bo and said good night, made plans to meet tomorrow. Bo and Rick would follow on their bikes while Ava and Lacey drove the car back into the States.

But for now, all Ava could think about was getting back to her room and being alone with Rick. Their last night in Mexico, alone. Probably their last night together, period.

She felt the melancholy settle over her, but brushed it away, refusing to let it ruin what little time she had left with Rick.

The sound of the water crashing against the shore was a musical interlude as they stepped into the room. She was going to miss this tropical paradise.

"This has been a nice little vacation," she said, stepping out onto the balcony. "I'm afraid I'll be spoiled when it comes time to settle back into academia again."

Rick came up behind her and placed his hands on her shoulders. The smell of the ocean, salty and tangy, tantalized her almost as much as the man whose body heated her.

"You're way too practical to be swept away by vacations."

She turned in his arms. "Am I? I'm not so sure. You've swept me away."

"Yeah?"

She tangled her fingers in his hair, loving its softness, so incongruous to the hard body pressed against her. "Yeah. I think I like this."

"It's a fantasy. Not reality. Reality is you being a social worker, doing the right thing, helping kids."

Her brows rose. "Really? I thought you didn't believe in social workers."

"I didn't believe in the ones who'd been assigned to me. I believe in you. I believe you can help people."

The sting of tears pricked her eyes. He had such faith in her. She wasn't so sure she had that same faith in herself. But to know a guy from the streets, a man the system failed, still believed in that system, in her ability to effect change, made her heart leap.

"Thank you." The words tumbled out in a whisper, her heart filled with emotions she couldn't—wouldn't—think about. She sifted her fingers through his hair, then let her palm slide down his cheek, over the scruff of his unshaven jaw. "You do mystifying things to my heart and soul, Rick."

This time, he didn't smile. "I'm just a guy. A guy with a lot of flaws."

"No one is perfect. I'm not looking for perfect."

Just someone to love me.

She didn't say it, but the words were there, hanging suspended somewhere between thought and voice. She so wanted to say it, but was too afraid she wouldn't like the response—if there even was one.

And maybe she didn't want a response—not from Rick. Maybe she just wanted to make up his reply in her head. After all, wasn't all this a fantasy anyway?

And wasn't love the ultimate fantasy?

He kissed her, a perfect kiss that was no fantasy at all. His mouth against hers, coaxing a response that was oh so real. She held on to that reality, the feel of his body, so hot and hard against her. That's what she wanted, what she needed tonight.

And the way he touched her—the slow glide of his hands down the bare flesh of her back—was both perfect and frustrating. She wanted to make it last forever, but she wanted to hurry up, get naked, feel his skin against hers.

And yet out here on the balcony, the night was oh so right. Warm, a soft breeze ruffling the hem of her dress, and Rick's mouth intoxicating her senses.

He backed her against the wall, his body following, pressing against hers. All that hard male flesh she wanted access to was impeded by clothing. That wasn't going to do at all.

She pulled away from his kiss, pressed her hands to his chest, and he took a step back.

"What's wrong?"

She smiled. "Nothing at all." She swept her hands down the planes of his chest, pressed in with the tips of her fingers—nothing but a solid wall of muscle. She felt like such a . . . girl around him, soft where he was hard. She couldn't remember ever being with a man who'd made her feel so feminine before.

She let her hands wander farther south, reached for his belt buckle, sliding his zipper down, reveling in the way he sucked in a breath. She let her body slide down with her hands, her legs parting as she sat on her heels.

"Damn, Ava."

"I wish I could have you naked out here," she whispered, more to herself than him. She'd love to see the moonlight washing over his magnificent body.

But now she focused on one part of him. She tugged on his jeans, just enough to pull them over his hips, giving her the freedom to reach in and pull out his cock. He hissed when she wrapped her hand around it, which only heightened her pleasure, making her want to prolong his. There was something so intoxicating about being in control of a man.

She stroked him, slow and easy, loving the feel of him in her hand. She tilted her head back to watch his face, the tight strain reflected there, the barely leashed control.

That's what she always saw, what she always felt in Rick—control. Tonight, she wanted to shatter his control.

She leaned forward and licked the thick crest. It was warm, soft, and a salty pearl of fluid spilled onto her tongue. She curled her tongue around the head, then covered it with her lips.

Rick groaned, tangled his fingers in her hair.

"Sweet Jesus, Ava, that's so good."

Was that his control slipping just a bit?

He pumped his hips forward, feeding her his cock. She tilted her head back farther, giving him access to her mouth. He tightened his hold on her hair as she took him in. And then he pulled out, slid in again, developed a rhythm of back and forth, the same way he fucked her.

It made her wet, made her nipples and clit tingle as he fucked her mouth with slow, deliberate movements that drove her crazy.

This was supposed to be for Rick. How could this turn her on so much? How could she be the one losing control?

She removed her mouth, licked her lips, loved seeing the dark desire in his eyes. She reached under him and found the sac containing his balls, massaged them, and his lips parted. Now he was the one who tilted his head back and groaned, the sound harsh and filled with need. She grabbed the base of his cock and this time she did take control, compressing her lips over his shaft and letting her tongue slide along the underside as she rolled her mouth over his length.

"Ava. Stop. You're going to make me come."

There was no way she was going to stop, not with his balls tightening in her hand, his whole body tensing and jerking as she loved him with her mouth, her lips, and her tongue. She wanted him to come apart for her the way she had done for him. She took a deep breath and took him in deeper.

"Christ. Oh, fuck, Ava."

He jerked, thrust his cock against the roof of her mouth, and jettisoned all that sweet come into her mouth. Ava felt the spill of her own moisture against her panties, the quiver of desire at his climax. She held on to him until he was empty, his breath ragged, until he palmed the wall for support.

Rick held his hand out for her and she reached for it. He lifted her to a standing position and before she could utter a word his mouth covered hers, his tongue sweeping in to take the last of his own flavor from her.

Passion exploded inside her, and all the control she'd held was gone. He curved his hands along her hips, her thighs, then raised her dress and smoothed his fingers along the silk of her panties. He pulled them aside and palmed her sex— her ripe, throbbing pussy craving the touch of his hard, calloused hand. Oh, the way he rubbed her felt so good, sent sparks to her clit. She lifted on her toes to reach for more of that sensation, arching her pelvis toward his hand.

"That's it," he whispered, his voice the sensual darkness against her ear. "Come on, baby."

He inserted one, then two fingers inside her, driving his palm against the swollen nub while he fucked her with his fingers. The scent of him, his taste, all swirled around her, mixing with the heady pleasure of his masterful hand. Suddenly she was falling, unable to stop the rush of her climax. She thrust against him over and over while he fucked her with relentless strokes, her pussy spasming around him in waves of nearly unbearable pleasure.

Panting, she laid her head on his shoulder while he withdrew his fingers, moved around behind her and said, "We're not anywhere near finished yet. Fucking your pussy with my fingers got me hard again."

He led her inside, to the spacious living room. She thought they were going to the bedroom, but instead he took her to the edge of the sofa and stopped there.

"I need to fuck you while you're wearing this dress. It's been driving me crazy all night."

She heated at the visual of him doing just that. She leaned back against him, twining her arms up and around his neck. Rick reached around to her breasts, covered them with his hands, his thumbs scraping over her nipples. Even through the material of her dress she felt it, the tingles of pleasure shooting straight to her pussy.

"These have been driving me crazy all night, too." He held her breasts in his hands, drove against her buttocks with his cock.

Ava hissed out a breath. "You're driving me crazy. Fuck me now."

"What's the matter? Don't you like this?" He pulled the bodice of her dress down and filled his hands with her breasts, teasing her nipples with his fingers. The contact was electric, shot straight to her pussy.

"Yes. I like it. A lot. Fuck me."

His low laugh vibrated against her back. "You were a little more reserved when we first met. You're a hellion now."

"You made me that way. Now fuck me."

"I think I get the hint." She heard the laughter in his voice, but also heard the hard edge of desire, knew he was as aroused as she was.

He bent her over the sofa. She held on to the edge while he lifted her dress over her hips and pulled her panties down, blazing a trail of kisses along the way. By the time he made it back up to her hips, her legs were shaking.

"Rick."

"Yeah."

"Hurry up."

His laugh only made her hotter, quivering in anticipation while she waited for him to apply a condom. He hadn't even bothered to zip up his jeans after their episode out on the balcony, and he pressed against her now, his skin to hers, his cock searching between her folds until he thrust hard inside her.

She gasped, arched her back, her pussy clenching around him as waves of pleasure shot through her.

"That what you wanted?"

She let out a moan, tilted her head back. "Yes."

He held on to her hips and drove harder, deeper this time. "Like that?"

"Oh, yes. Give me more." Exactly what she wanted—to be connected to him in this most primal way. To not think about anything except this joining, the way he fucked her, the way he powered hard so he could get deeper inside her, like that was the only thing that mattered to him.

It was the only thing that mattered to her.

Until he reached around and strummed her clit with one hand while he continued to pound her with relentless strokes. The sensations were powerful, and with every touch her pussy gripped him tighter.

He leaned across her back, his hand never leaving her pussy.

"I like the way your pussy grips me. Do you know I can tell when you're getting ready to come?"

"Yes. I feel it, too."

"I want you to come on my dick, Ava. I want to feel every

muscle inside your pussy squeezing me when you go off. Come on, baby, make me come."

His voice made her wet, made her pussy tremble. She'd never had a man talk to her like this. She'd never felt so incredibly one with a man before.

It was heaven. No one had ever fucked her like this. No one. And she realized as Rick gripped her hips and thrust hard, pulled out, and powered inside her again, that she didn't want this to end.

She wanted more of this. More than just tonight.

He continued to murmur against her ear, moving to the back of her neck. And when he bit down lightly as he fucked her, that was it. She spiraled out of control, climaxing in giant waves that took her breath and forced her to grip the edge of the sofa for balance.

"Oh fuck," Rick said behind her, and held tight to her hips, his body glued to hers while he shuddered and groaned behind her.

She couldn't move, could barely form a coherent sentence. Fortunately, she didn't have to, because Rick picked her up and carried her to the bedroom. He helped her take off her dress, then pulled the covers back and, after he undressed, he climbed in bed behind her, pulling her against him before he wrapped his arms around her.

He kissed the back of her neck before his breathing evened out and she knew he'd fallen asleep.

She felt safe . . . loved.

Love? Was that what she felt?

Yes. It was. She'd never felt it before. It made her giddy and nauseous and scared shitless. And hopeful.

Maybe this could work after all.

She drifted off with a smile on her face.

Ava woke the next day alone in her bed, immediately squelching the feeling of disappointment.

Okay, so it was ten-thirty. They'd been up late. And she already knew Rick never slept in. Maybe he'd gone off to get coffee somewhere.

She showered and packed, a sense of reluctance settling

over her. Maybe Lacey had been right about this place having a magical lure. Though admittedly, Ava hadn't enjoyed her time here until Rick had showed up. He'd made this trip special. Which didn't say much at all about her friendship with Lacey.

Ava would always be friends with Lacey, but she had a feeling they were going off in opposite directions now. And that made her sad, but it was time to face reality. Ava wanted no part of the life Lacey led. And Lacey was a grown woman now. Ava couldn't mother her or force her to do what she wanted her to do. Lacey had to make her own choices, even if Ava thought they were bad choices. There was nothing Ava could do about it, except be there for her friend if and when the bottom dropped out of Lacey's life.

It was time to let go, time for Ava to concentrate on her own life, her own future. It was time to make some decisions about what she was going to do with that life.

And who was going to be in it.

The door opened and her heart did a little leap at the sight of Rick walking in with two coffees in hand. She smiled.

"Good morning."

"Wow, already showered and packing?"

"The bed gets cold and empty when you're not in it. It's like an automatic wake-up call."

He set the coffees down and came over to her, pulled her into his arms and kissed her. When he pulled away, her toes were curling and her nipples beaded against her bra.

"I like that," he said, rubbing his thumb over her bottom lip.

She liked it, too.

He handed her a cup of coffee and they went outside on the balcony to drink it.

"I'll miss this place." She looked out over the turquoise water, as calm and peaceful in the morning as the lazy town it blanketed. It was already warm, though at least there was a bank of clouds this morning instead of heavy, hot sun.

"Yeah, it is kind of nice."

"I might want to come back here someday."

He glanced over at her, his expression unfathomable. "Well, maybe you will. You can always come with Lacey."

Not with him. With Lacey.

She shrugged. "Maybe. Not sure Lacey and I will be hanging out much anymore."

"Yeah? Why's that?"

"I've come to the realization that we need to go our separate ways. We have nothing in common anymore."

He nodded. "It happens sometimes. You're probably making the right choice."

He said it so matter-of-factly, as if twenty years of friendship meant nothing. Her emotions were tied in knots, like her stomach.

"What?"

"You just made it sound so easy. As if walking away from someone close to you would mean nothing."

He shrugged. "I wouldn't know. I've never felt close to anyone."

She drew her knees up to her chest, pondered how that would feel. To be so isolated, so alone.

"Don't feel sorry for me, Ava."

"I don't feel sorry for you. Okay, maybe I do. You're too old to have gone that long without having someone . . . some attachments in your life."

He shrugged. "I'm fine with it."

"Are you? Are you really?"

He opened his mouth, no doubt to shoot off some smart-ass retort. This time, she wasn't going to let it happen.

"Rick. Tell me."

He stopped then. Looked at her. "I had shitty parents. So did Bo. Not everyone comes from a great family. So Bo and I bonded, and for a long time we had each others' backs."

"Did the courts take you away from your families?"

"Off and on. You know how it is."

"Yes, I do. Too often the removal isn't permanent, though many parents should never get their kids back."

He looked over the balcony. "Amen to that. There were times I was happier with my foster parents than I ever was at home. But I knew better than to get settled or to think I'd stay."

"Because they'd send you back home."

He nodded.

Ava ached for him, for the child who'd craved stability and someone to love him, but had none. "I'm sorry."

He half turned and gave her a smile, but she saw the sadness in his eyes. "Not your fault, darlin'."

She stood and went to him, wrapped her arms around him and laid her cheek against his back, wishing she could love him, that he'd let her. But she knew anything she said right now would only be taken as pity. And that's not at all what she felt for him.

"You can't fix me, Ava. I'm a grown man. I survived it."

She squeezed him a little tighter. "It doesn't make the past hurt any less, or the memories go away."

She was in love with him. She knew it now for certain. He'd been through so much, could have turned out so differently. He could have been a prick, treating people like dirt, like he'd been treated. Instead, he had a heart, emotions, warmth, and passion and he needed to give that to someone.

Only he didn't see it. He didn't see it and Ava didn't know how to make him see what he needed.

Rick didn't form attachments like she did. Maybe it was easy for him to walk away. Like it would be easy for him to walk away from her.

A man like him, with his background and the way he was raised . . . yeah, Ava could certainly see him leaving and not looking back.

He turned, smiled down at her, and kissed her. "The past is dead. Leave it there."

She blinked back the rush of tears that threatened to burst. "You're right. Everyone needs to look forward. Even me."

He tipped her nose with his finger. "That's right. Which means that you need to stop thinking about vacations in Mexico and get back to reality."

She laughed. "So true. It's time for me to start thinking about my doctorate degree. I have to find a school."

"Yeah. Time for me to get back to work, too."

"I guess this is the end of the fun, then."

"Fun never has to end if you don't want it to."

He winked and smiled, and dammit if her stupid heart didn't feel lighter at his words.

She didn't need him. Love between them would never work. When they got back to the States, it was over between them.

And that was that. She wasn't going to think about it anymore.

Much.

Fortunately, Bo must have dragged Lacey out of bed, because Rick's phone rang, signaling they were ready to go.

"Ready to exit the Garden of Eden?"

"I suppose so."

He grabbed their bags and they went downstairs. Bo had already brought Lacey's car around to the front, then went to fetch his bike. Rick packed Ava's bag in the trunk of Lacey's car.

"We'll follow behind you."

She nodded.

He put his hands on her hips, kissed her. Her stomach fluttered. Really, she wasn't a teenager, and they'd been intimate several times. His kiss shouldn't still affect her like this.

But it did.

"I'll see you back in the States," he said with a wink.

She smiled and felt giddy.

Lacey laughed at her as they climbed in the car.

"Girl, you got it bad for him."

That was an understatement.

Rick followed close behind Lacey's car all the way to the border, paying very little attention to Bo other than making sure Bo stayed with them.

He did. They stopped once for gas, and otherwise made good time all the way to the California border.

Now it was showtime. The border was crowded, the going slow, and for good reason.

DEA was stopping traffic to do random inspections.

Rick masked his smile.

Bo pulled up next to Rick and turned to him.

"Fuck. This isn't what we wanted today."

Rick shrugged. "You said it was hidden well, right?"

"Yeah. Still, I'd hate to lose all that inventory."

What an asshole. He'd throw Lacey and Ava under the bus to protect his assets—and his own ass.

They moved up the line and Rick slid his bike in front of Bo's. Lacey's car was up next. Rick looked over his shoulder at Bo, who licked his lips.

Nervous. Good. He should be.

The car was inspected thoroughly, and the drug dogs sniffed around the vehicle. Ava and Lacey appeared to be chatting amicably while they waited, unsuspecting of a setup.

After the longest five minutes ever, the guards waved the car through.

Even with the bike engines idling, Rick heard Bo's sigh of relief.

"We're home free now, pal," Bo said.

Rick smiled and goosed the throttle, taking his bike to the checkpoint. He cleared it easy, moved across the border, and pulled over at the roadside truck stop where Ava and Lacey were waiting.

"Wow, huge inspection going on today," Lacey said. "That's never happened before."

Rick climbed off his bike. "It's a random checkpoint. The DEA does this every now and then to sniff out possible drug mules."

Ava's brows rose. "Really? Fascinating."

Rick leaned against Lacey's car and crossed his arms. And waited.

Bo pulled his bike to the inspection station. The guards and dogs went over to the bike. It didn't take any time at all before the dogs started signaling with loud barks, lunging

toward Bo and the Harley. Bo took several steps back, guns
were drawn, and Bo was ordered to hit the ground.

"Oh my God. What's going on?" Lacey asked in horror.

"Just keep watching," Rick said.

Bo's saddlebags were opened and the brown paper–
wrapped drugs were lifted. There were no clothes or any of
the items Bo had brought with him to Mexico. Just drugs.
Everywhere on the bike.

"Holy shit," Ava said. "Are those drugs?"

"Yep."

Lacey shook her head. "That's not possible. Bo wouldn't
do that. He doesn't—"

"He does, and he did. In fact, he did it to you, Lacey. He's
been doing it to you."

Her eyes widened. "What? What are you talking about?"

"Those drugs you see them lifting off Bo's bike? I saw
him and a few of his buddies plant them in your car last
night."

Lacey shook her head. "No. You're wrong."

"Yeah. Bo was using you as a mule. This wasn't the first
time, either. These spa trips to Mexico you've been taking
once a month? Every single one has been so you could bring
drugs across the border for him."

Lacey's eyes filled with tears. She backed away from
Rick. "That's a lie. You're full of shit. Bo would never do that
to me. He loves me."

"He loves your car and loves that you were an easy mark."

"I don't believe you," she croaked.

But Rick could tell from the defeated slump of her shoulders that Lacey did believe him. Ava put her arms around
Lacey and Lacey crumpled against her and dissolved into
tears.

Lacey turned her tear-streaked face to him. "A mule? He
used me to transport drugs?"

"Yes."

"What would have happened if they'd found drugs in
my car?"

"You would of been arrested."

Lacey's hand flew to her mouth and she cried hard for a few minutes. Then anger took over as she glared at the border where they were handcuffing Bo. "That son of a bitch. He used me. I trusted him."

Ava held on to a sobbing Lacey as she raised her gaze to Rick. "How did you know?"

"I suspected based on a few things Bo said to me. I didn't know for sure until I saw them moving the drugs into a removable rear hood on Lacey's car last night."

"Why didn't you tell me?"

Rick shook his head. "It was better that you not know until I had you two in the clear."

"I understand. I think. But God, how could he do this to her? When I think of what could have happened . . ."

"I know."

"So what about Bo?"

Rick couldn't help his smile. "He's on his own now."

Lacey jerked her head up and spun around to look at the checkpoint where the agents were putting Bo in an unmarked car. "I hope the asshole rots in prison for the rest of his life."

Rick put his arm around her. "That's a pretty good estimate of what's going to happen to him."

Ava frowned. "Aren't you at all upset about this? He's your cousin."

"Yeah, he is. And he's dirty. And he used two women as drug mules. He has no honor. As far as I'm concerned he deserves everything he gets. So how about a cup of coffee?"

Lacey sniffed and raised tear-stained eyes and a tremulous smile to Rick. "I'd love one."

"Come on. Let's go inside this greasy joint and get a burger. And celebrate."

Ava shook her head and twined her arm with Rick's. "I can't believe you knew about this. That you did this. For us."

They ate, and Lacey washed her face and calmed down a bit. By the time they were ready to leave, she seemed to be okay enough to drive.

"So what are you going to do now, Lace?" Ava asked.

"I'm going home."

"Home where?"

"To my parents' house. I need some family time. Bo screwed with my head. I need time to think, to figure out how I could be so stupid."

"You weren't stupid, Lacey," Rick said. "You just picked the wrong guy."

She sighed. "I made a lot of really bad choices. I need some time to refocus. Some time alone to think about a lot of things." Lacey turned to Ava. "Can you get a ride back with Rick?"

"Are you sure?" Ava asked. "I can ride with you. We'll talk things out."

Lacey shook her head. "I'm not ready to talk just yet. I'm exhausted and pissed and confused. I need some time alone, Ava. Maybe in a few days we can talk."

Ava nodded. "I understand." She turned to Rick. "Can I hitch a ride?"

"No problem." Rick went over to Lacey and laid his hands on her shoulders. "Get clean. And I don't mean by yourself, even if you think you can, because that shit never works. Get into a program that can help you. Lay off the drugs and alcohol. Clear your head. Once you do, I think you'll find you'll get past this—past him—and it won't be as hard as you think."

She sniffed, nodded. "You saved my ass. I'm scared shitless, Rick." She glanced down the highway toward the border and wrapped her arms around herself. "I could be in jail now."

"Yeah, you could. But you got out in time and you got lucky this time. Use it wisely."

She sniffed, nodded, and raised her gaze to his. "I'm grateful. When I think about how blind I was—"

He stopped her. "Don't do that. You aren't the first woman it's happened to. You loved him and you let the real you go because of it. Go find that person and get her back."

She shook her head. "I don't think she exists anymore."

"Then make a clean slate and start over. You can be anyone you want to be."

Her eyes filled with fresh tears. "My best friend is one very lucky woman. I envy her."

He kissed her forehead. "And you were too good for my cousin."

"Thank you, Rick. I'll work on trying to believe that."

Rick waited while Ava hugged Lacey and they exchanged a few words. He carried Ava's bag over to the bike and stashed it on the back. Lacey got in her car and took off. Ava walked back to Rick and took the helmet he held out for her. "I heard what you said to her. Thank you for that."

He shrugged. "She'll be fine. She just needs some time to realize what an asshole he was. It shouldn't take long for the hurt to be replaced by some righteous anger."

Ava nodded. "I just hope he burns for a long time."

Rick put on his helmet and smiled as he climbed on the bike. "Oh, he will. Trust me."

It was late by the time they made it back to Las Vegas. Rick drove Ava to her apartment and carried her bag upstairs.

She'd never brought him here. For some reason it felt . . . strange. She was nervous. What would he think?

She opened the door and he went in, set the bag down on the floor, and waited while she stepped in and flipped on the light.

"This is nice."

Nice. Wasn't he just oh so polite? She scanned the room, trying to see what he saw. Two sofas positioned perfectly in front of the fireplace. Nothing on the tabletops. Not a speck of dust. No knickknacks, no art on the white walls.

Nothing at all to indicate anyone with a personality lived here.

It was boring. Sterile. Devoid of life. She thought of Rick, of the color of his life. He might have no walls and no furniture, but his life was full.

"I'm usually at school. I haven't really . . . uh . . . given much thought to decorating."

"How long have you lived here?"

"Two years."

He cocked his head. "There's nothing of you here, Ava."

She twisted her fingers together. "Force of habit, I'm afraid."

"Which means what, exactly?"

"Decorating equals clutter, unless it's done precisely right and only my mother has that magic touch. I was never allowed much in the way of . . . things as a child."

"Things?"

"Leaving things out. Toys, books . . . anything really. Everything had to be put away. God forbid your life and your interests should be put on display so others could get a glimpse into who you were."

Had she just said that out loud? Dear God.

"Sorry. I don't usually vomit out such personal information about my life and my family."

Rick laughed and took her hand. "I like who you are. I think you should show yourself off. This isn't your parents' place. It's yours. Isn't it time you be yourself?"

"Yes. It is." And she could already envision splashes of color—pillows and fabric and art on the walls and place mats and plants and . . . clutter. How she had changed during the short period she'd hung out with Rick.

He'd been good for her, had drawn her out of her shell, out of her fears of living life and just existing on the fringes.

"Would you like something to drink? I have soda and bottled water. No beer or anything. Sorry."

"Bottled water would be fine." He shrugged out of his jacket and laid it on the top of the sofa. "Did you want me to hang this up?"

She laughed. "No."

And wasn't that a first? She didn't even twitch when she said it. Maybe there was hope for her after all.

She went into the kitchen and grabbed a couple bottles of water, then came back and sat on the sofa. He sat next to her and she handed him a bottle. As they drank, she pondered.

What was going to happen now? To them? She didn't want this to be over. Not after realizing how much life he'd brought to her, how he'd changed everything about her. She was more relaxed now, less tense, less worried about what other people thought.

She wanted more of that. She wanted more of him.

She shifted to face him. "What's going to happen to Bo now?"

Rick shrugged. "I imagine he'll be brought up on federal charges and do time."

"And you aren't concerned for him."

"No. He has to face the consequences of his actions."

"Like you did when you went to prison."

"Uh, yeah."

"I feel bad for Lacey, though."

"Lacey has to grow up, too, and face the consequences of her actions."

Harsh words. But Rick was right. Lacey had made the choice to be with Bo, to do drugs, to let that lifestyle overtake her. Lacey had been blind to who he really was. Surely there had been signs . . .

"Do you think she knew?"

Rick shifted, put his arm over the top of the sofa. "About what?"

"About Bo using her to run drugs."

"I doubt it. Or maybe she suspected something and was too blinded by love to face the truth about him. Or too afraid. I don't know. I don't know much about love and how people behave when they love someone."

"You've never been in love?"

He smiled. "No. Have you?"

"No. Well . . ."

"What?"

It occurred to her as soon as he asked her that she wanted to tell him how she felt. But the thought of putting herself out there, making herself vulnerable like that, made her stomach twinge. Should she tell him about these feelings? They were so new, even to her, she hadn't wrapped her head around them yet.

She had to. Because otherwise he was going to walk out

of her life without ever knowing how she felt. That might be how she was raised—to keep her emotions to herself—but she wasn't going to continue to live that way. Besides, he'd come all the way to Mexico to see her. Surely there was something between them.

She took a long drink of water and set it down on the table—without grabbing for a coaster. A monumental start. She took a deep breath, and let it out.

"I'm in love with you, Rick."

His eyes widened. "What?"

"I'm in love with you. I want to be with you, to continue this—whatever it is that we have together—after today. I want to ride with you for a while and see where it goes. I don't want to lose you."

Oh, shit. Rick was simultaneously filled with a stab of incredible joy and utter panic.

No woman had ever told him that she loved him. Hell, he couldn't even remember his parents telling him they loved him, or if they did he'd never believed it. Love had to be expressed in action, otherwise it was just empty words.

That Ava did was something he hadn't expected. He had no idea what she saw in him, but he was damn glad she did. She was beautiful, smart, and adventurous. The thought of having a woman like her by his side filled him with a warmth he'd never felt before.

Was that love? Maybe it was. But he had no room for love in his life. And he sure as hell couldn't be in love with Ava Vargas. She was his assignment, not his girlfriend. And he couldn't even tell her who he really was or what he did for a living.

Fuck. This was bad. Really bad.

And maybe she really didn't love him. She was just leaning on him because of everything that had gone down with Lacey. Her best friend had just been shit on by the man she loved. Wouldn't it be natural for Ava to see—to want—a different outcome for herself?

That was probably it. She didn't want to be screwed over by a guy like Lacey had. She wasn't really in love with him. She just didn't want to get dumped.

Ava laughed and grabbed his hand. "Say something, Rick. I just put my heart in your hands."

Son of a bitch. His gut twisted because he knew exactly what he had to do.

He pulled his hand away and stood, dragging his fingers through his hair. His heart pounded and his palms began to sweat. Hell, he'd walked away from plenty of women in his lifetime. It had always been easy. Why wasn't this easy?

"Ava, we had a great time together, no doubt about it. But my life is solitary and I like it that way. I don't do relationships."

Her smile died instantly. And a part of him died with it. The hurt in her eyes was palpable. He felt like someone had just stabbed him in the heart with a knife.

"Oh."

"Look, darlin'. I think you're beautiful, intelligent, sexy, and I had a great time with you. Let's just leave it at that."

She nodded and stood. "Sure. You're right." She grabbed his coat from the other sofa and handed it to him, refusing to meet his gaze. "You should probably go. It's getting late and I have a lot to do tomorrow."

He felt like an asshole. He *was* an asshole. But if he lingered any longer, he'd pull her into his arms and kiss those tears away that trickled down her cheek. He'd tell her that he was in love with her. He'd tell her who he was. He'd fuck everything up.

He needed to get out of there and fast.

She opened the door and he stepped outside, turned to look at her. "I'll see you later."

She raised her gaze to his, her eyes glittering with tears and her lips lifting in a tortured smile that wrecked him. "No, you won't. Good-bye, Rick."

Thirteen

t took Ava two days before she could leave the house. Two days of crying, of feeling empty inside. Two days of feeling stupid, of feeling just like Lacey must have felt.

She'd fallen in love with Rick, and had been blinded to the reality that he'd felt nothing for her. She'd been fun for sex, and that was all. And when it was time for him to walk away, he'd done it so easily.

Oh sure, he'd appeared to be having a difficult time, his expression pained, his tone one of regret. But he'd still walked and done so without thought of hurting her. And right after she'd declared that she loved him.

How naïve could she be?

Obviously she and her best friend still had more in common than she thought.

She'd called Lacey, who'd gone home to her parents. She said she was resting and trying to get over what Bo had done to her. She was already involved in a drug and alcohol rehabilitation program. Other than that, she had no plans beyond avoiding drugs and alcohol and clearing her head. Ava promised to go see her as soon as Lacey was up to visitors.

And as soon as Ava was up to it, too.

Right now her only intent was to head to campus and start redirecting her focus back on school. It was time to get back to work. Burying herself in her search for a school for her Ph.D. would take her mind off Rick, off ridiculous notions of love and bike riders and living the wild life, which wasn't her at all.

Her life was clean tabletops, bare walls, and buried emotions. She should have known better.

After showering and packing her laptop, she straightened up her apartment and was just about to grab her purse and head out the door when the doorbell rang. She opened it, shocked to her toes to see her father standing there.

"Dad?"

Her father was still as imposing as ever, filling her doorway with his frowning persona. Even at sixty, with his full, thick head of salt-and-pepper hair, he was still robust as ever. And still as intimidating as he'd always been.

"Ava. May I come in?"

"Of course." She stepped aside and he moved in, scanning her apartment as if he were looking for something. Or someone.

"Would you like some coffee? I don't have any made, but it would only take—"

He waved his hand. "No. Not necessary. I just wanted to check on you, to see if you were all right."

She cocked a brow. "Of course I'm all right. Why?"

"I got the report about your activities with the Hellraisers. Have you finished cavorting with this biker gang now?"

Ava inhaled and sighed, then moved away to sit on the sofa. Her father had always known every move she made, especially since he took public office. It irritated her, but she tried to remain oblivious to his interference. He mostly just kept tabs on her without getting involved. Then again, she usually never did anything for him to get involved with. "And how did you know about that?"

"I've known about it for some time now, ever since you started hanging out with Lacey and that undesirable boyfriend of hers. Do you have any idea how that would look for me if you were involved in illegal activities with the Hellraisers?"

How nice of him to look after her welfare. Then again, he was more on the mark than Ava cared to admit. "Well, I'm fine. And I won't be hanging out with them again."

"I'm glad to hear that, especially since you barely escaped federal drug charges at the Mexican border. Good God, Ava, what were you thinking?"

The blood in her face drained, leaving her cold. "What did you say?"

"You heard me."

"How did you know about that? Did Lacey tell you?"

"I don't speak to Lacey and you know that. I've never thought that girl was an appropriate friend for you."

Ava's stomach knotted. No one was good enough for Ava according to her father. After all, Lacey's parents were blue collar. Not the right connections for the great Senator Vargas's daughter. She tried to love her parents, but their narrow-minded view of the world made it so damn hard.

"So if you didn't hear it from Lacey, how did you know?"

"Because I've had you under surveillance. The Feds put someone undercover to watch you."

"What? Are you kidding me? When?"

"As soon as you hooked up with the Hellraisers for bike week."

No. That couldn't be. She would have noticed. She always noticed. Her father had security personnel tailing her all the time. She'd become an expert at dodging security detail when she wanted to be alone with a date, or go out with her friends. Security personnel were always so obvious. And if there'd been a federal officer . . .

Undercover.

Undercover in the Hellraisers? Who? And why?

Her curiosity turned to anger. "You had me watched? I want to know why."

Her father took a seat on the sofa across from hers. She noted the crisp, perfectly starched line in his trousers, thought of her mother. Everything so perfect . . . nothing out of place.

"As you can imagine, there was some concern about my daughter being involved with a gang suspected of heavy involvement in drug distribution. You know I head the committee drafting major antidrug legislation. I told you that when you made contact with Lacey after she joined that gang."

Ava rolled her eyes. "I wasn't joining the gang, Dad. I was trying to reach Lacey."

"Nevertheless, imagine how it would look if you somehow got tangled up with this gang, with drugs, and me heading this committee. It could seriously undermine this important legislation."

Yes, God forbid the *legislation* be harmed.

"And you were so worried about the harm I'd do that you put someone undercover to keep an eye on me."

"To protect you from harm."

Bullshit. More likely to preserve his reputation.

"And it turns out my fears weren't unwarranted. Look at the mess you got yourself into. It's a good thing we had a federal agent on hand to save the day."

Instantly it clicked. Rick. Oh, God, it was Rick. He was the federal agent.

That's why he'd "dumped" her. That's why he'd nearly run out of her apartment that night. He couldn't tell her who he really was. Then again, maybe she was just his assignment and nothing more. Maybe he didn't care about her.

Or maybe he did, and he wasn't supposed to.

God, she had to know, had to talk to him and find out.

"I want to talk to this federal agent."

Her father shook his head. "Not possible."

"It's possible and you know it. I want to see Rick and now."

Her father raised his brows. "You do not speak to me that way, Ava."

Ava stood, so angry she could barely breathe. "Look. You're the one who set me up. Do you think I'm such a child that you couldn't have just come to me and talked to me rationally about your concerns? I'm an adult, Father. I understand legalities and your job and your reputation and PR. But no, you continue to worry more about the shit I might step in and how it might affect you, and worry less about how I feel. So now I don't care how you feel. I need to talk to Rick."

Her father looked stunned. Good. It felt damn good to finally unload her frustrations on him.

"I have no idea what you're talking about. You have always been treated well."

"Yes, like a caged pet."

Her father stood. "I don't need to listen to this."

"Find Rick for me."

He shook his head. "Getting involved with an undercover federal agent is unacceptable."

She rolled her eyes, frustration knotting her stomach. "Oh please. He's a federal agent. How much more aboveboard can it get?"

"No. I won't have it."

Then she realized her father's refusal had nothing to do with Rick, or even her. It was about him, his political career. He didn't care how she felt, never cared about what was important to her or what she wanted. Somewhere down the road he'd probably find some lawyer or politician that he thought would be a good match for her. Love didn't matter with him. It never had. There was no love between her parents, so that shouldn't surprise her. He'd expect her to be dutiful and find a man who would cement his political career.

Hell could freeze over before she allowed that to happen.

She marched to the front door and opened it. "Good-bye, Father."

"We'll speak again soon."

Not likely.

She closed the door behind him, blinking back the tears that pricked her eyes.

Now she had no idea how to find Rick, no clue which branch of the government he even worked for.

And without her father's connections, she was afraid Rick was lost to her.

Fourteen

"He's moping."

"It's pathetic, really."

"He might need an antidepressant."

"Or, I could beat the shit out of him."

"I'm *in* the fucking room, assholes." Rick refused to turn around and acknowledge the other Wild Riders, who'd decided to give a verbal report to their superior officer, General Grange Lee, on the state of Rick's emotional health.

General Lee rounded the corner of the main living area, where Rick was trying to lose himself in a video game.

"Is that true? You moping?"

"No, sir. I'm playing video games."

"Yeah, he's playing video games," Diaz said, coming around to stand next to Grange. Diaz crossed his arms and stared down at Rick. "And he's sucking at all of them."

Grange arched a brow. "Rick, sucking at video games? You're the house champ."

"I'm a little off my game."

AJ leaped over the sofa and grabbed one of the controllers. "Seriously off his game. Even Jessie can beat him."

"Hey, dickhead, I heard that." Jessie sauntered into the room, stuck out her tongue at AJ, and linked her arm with Diaz's. "But seriously, Rick, you do look kind of sad."

"I'm not sad. I'm not depressed. I'm not moping. Why don't you all leave me the hell alone?"

"Now what fun would that be?" Mac asked as he came in, an apple in his hand. "You know none of us get to have secrets."

"I don't have any secrets."

"He's hung up on his last assignment," Spence said, leaning his beefy frame against the doorway.

Rick had just about enough. He tossed the controller on the table and stood. "My last assignment is over."

"Yeah," Spence said with a laugh. "And that's your problem. You fell in love with her."

"Spoken by someone who knows all too well what it's like to fall in love while on assignment," Jessie teased.

Spence nodded. "You got me pegged, darlin'. In fact, my lady is waiting for me at home. My paperwork is done, Grange. I'm outta here." Spence pivoted, but stopped and half turned. "Rick, trust me. If you love her, go tell her. The ache doesn't go away."

"I don't love her." But he couldn't look at any of them when he said it, because that was his problem. He couldn't stop thinking about Ava, couldn't get her face out of his mind. He didn't like the way he'd left her, the things he'd said to her. He'd hurt her. It was wrong.

"All of you, go find something to do. You, come with me." Grange motioned to Rick. And when Grange commanded, you went.

The rest of the team scattered, and Rick followed Grange into his office. The general shut the door and they took seats in front of the general's desk.

"Okay, so this Ava Vargas. You love her?"

Leave it to Grange to be direct. "I don't know."

"Then go find out."

"She was an assignment. She doesn't even know who I really am."

"Then go tell her."

"Her lifestyle isn't conducive to—"

"Boy, quit drumming up excuses. You guys had shit for upbringings, and very little love in your lives when you were younger. If it comes to you now, don't spit in its face. Now get on your bike, go back to Las Vegas, and see if you can find a way to make it work with this woman."

And just like that, it all fell together. Grange was right. "Yes, sir."

The fresh air of campus had done a lot to clear her head. Seeing the colorful trees lining the sidewalks, stopping at a bench to eat lunch and soak up the fall weather all helped keep her mind off Rick. Spending time at the library and working with the counseling office to investigate different schools' Ph.D. programs kept her busy enough that Rick didn't creep into her mind until she crawled into bed at night. Only then did his face appear before her, only then did her mind dredge up memories of his hands on her, his mouth on her. Only then did her heart ache from missing him.

So she spent as much time as possible on campus, and she went to the gym for a couple hours every day, hoping by the time she fell into bed at night she'd be physically and mentally exhausted.

Her backpack filled with brochures and laden down with her laptop, she took a brisk walk from the library on her way to the administration building, breathing in the crisp air.

She paused when she heard the revving sounds of a motorcycle approaching behind her, sucked her bottom lip between her teeth, and shook off the moment of melancholy.

The bike would pass her shortly, and so would the feeling of loss.

The bike slowed as it approached behind her. She waited for it to turn at the nearby corner.

Go away. I don't want to hear you. I don't want to think about him.

She heard the bike's throttle revving as it drew closer,

closer. Unable to help herself, she turned, her heart leaping as Rick pulled up alongside her.

He parked just ahead of her, climbed off his bike, and removed his helmet, shaking out his dark hair.

He looked so damn good dressed in black leather chaps and matching jacket she wanted to melt right there on the cement walkway. She licked her lips, parched for a taste of him, for his touch.

"What are you doing here?" she asked as he stepped up to her.

He didn't say a word, just pulled her into his arms and kissed her, a kiss filled with longing, with passion, that spoke volumes without him needing to say a word. He wrapped his arms around her, pulled her backpack off her shoulders so he could hold her closer. She moaned, felt like she was home again as she moved into his embrace, as his tongue swept in and found hers. And when he finally broke the kiss, she was out of breath, panting from shock and excitement and wonder.

"My name is Rick Benetti and I work undercover for the United States government. We're called the Wild Riders, a special group of operatives. Not many people know who we are, because we work special projects for the government. I was assigned to keep an eye on you because of who your father is. My assignment didn't include kissing you, touching you, making love to you, or falling in love with you, but I did all of those."

Stunned speechless, Ava could only look at him, and listen, her heart rejoicing at what he said.

"I can't tell you how bad I feel about what I said to you that night at the apartment. Part of it was needing to retain my cover. The other part was fear. No one has ever loved me before, Ava. I didn't know how to handle it and I didn't handle it well at all. I'm sorry. I hurt you and I know it and I feel like an asshole. If it makes you feel any better, I haven't slept since I left you."

She smiled. "That does make me feel a little better."

"There's a hole inside me without you. I hurt when I'm not

with you. And I think that's what love is all about. It means you hurt when you're not with the person you love."

She let the tears fall down her cheeks. She laid her hand on his chest, felt the strong beat of his heart. "Love is a scary thing. It's risky."

"I know. I'm afraid. I've never told anyone that before in my life."

"I'm afraid, too, Rick. But you're worth the risk."

"So are you."

He pulled her against him again, kissed her breathless again, and when she no longer felt the chill in the air, when she began to sweat under her jacket, she pulled away, licked her lips, and swallowed hard.

He swept his knuckles against her cheek. "God, I missed you. Can we go to your place, because if I can't get my dick inside you within the next ten minutes I might push you up against the tree here and fuck you."

She laughed, and her body swelled with arousal at the thought of him taking her right here in front of the administration building. "I might like that."

His eyes flashed heat. "Don't tempt me."

She'd like to tempt him, but her need for him was as great as his for her. She grabbed his hand. "Come on."

Fortunately, she lived right down the street from the campus. They hopped on his bike and were there a couple minutes later. Ava fumbled with the keys to the front door, but managed to open it with shaky hands. Rick pushed her inside, shut the door, dropped her backpack, and turned her around, his mouth on hers before she could draw her next breath.

He pushed her against the wall and pulled her jacket off, lifted her sweater over her head, then reached for her jeans. She did the same, her fingers fumbling as they hurried to strip clothes off. She kicked off her shoes while Rick jerked her jeans down. It would have been comical, this rush to undress, if Rick wasn't looking at her with a heated gaze of lust and need in his eyes, a look that made her wet, that made her throb.

In the end, they only ended up half undressed. She still

wore her bra, and her socks, and he still had his jeans on, but she managed to unzip him enough to reach for his cock, wrap her fingers around his hot, pulsing heat. He grabbed a condom and sheathed it around his shaft, then dragged her onto the floor, right there on her pristine, perfect rug.

She couldn't have thought of a better spot to make love. He pulled her legs apart and plunged inside her, and she gasped at the perfection of it, at the way her body welcomed him.

"I've missed you inside me. This is where you belong." She swept her hand across his face.

"I love you, Ava."

She came almost as soon as he started moving against her, and he lifted his head and smiled at her in such a devastating, purely male way that it moved her to tears.

"Does coming always make you cry?"

"Only when you fuck me. Do it again."

He shifted, rolled his hips over her, sliding against her clit as he thrust inside her, and then there were no more words as they had at each other with a primal passion. His fingers dug into her hips, hurt so good. She raked her nails over his arms, his back, needing him with a fierce possessiveness, as if she were marking him as hers forever.

Perhaps she was—in her own way. He reached underneath her, grabbed her butt to tilt her toward him so he could drive in deeper, then slid his finger down farther, teasing her anus. She gasped, raising her gaze to his, uttering a hoarse "yes" to him as he slid the tip of his finger inside her puckered hole and continued to fuck her.

"Like that?" he asked, his voice rough with need.

"Yes. God. Yes."

"You're mine, Ava. All of you."

"Yes. And you're mine." She scored her nails down his back and he rewarded her by thrusting harder.

The sensation was incredible. He powered inside her again, his shaft rubbing her clit, his cock inside her pussy, and his finger teasing her anus, and she went off again, this time with such intense spasms she cried out, holding tight to him. He thrust hard, then fell on top of her, shuddering as he came.

Ava held on to Rick, unable to believe this had really happened. He was here, he'd made love to her—he loved her. She stroked his sweat-soaked back, his hair, touching him in wonder.

He pulled her up and they finally undressed all the way, took a shower together, and got dressed. Ava fixed them something to eat and, as Rick sat there at her kitchen table drinking coffee, she realized her life was in utter disorder.

There were towels on the floor in her bathroom, her backpack had spilled all over the living room. God only knows what had happened to the rug there.

Chaos.

And she had never been more content in her life.

Yet there were so many gaps to fill. She grabbed her coffee cup and pulled up a chair next to him at the table.

"Where do you live?" she asked.

"Nowhere, really. I work out of Dallas and stay at headquarters there most of the time. But I don't have a permanent place because I'm on the road a lot."

They were silent for a while as they both drank their coffee.

"Do you need to stay in Las Vegas to do your doctorate?" he asked.

Ava realized then that Rick was wondering about her life, her future, and the two of them, the same way she was.

"Actually, I've spent the past few days researching doctorate programs nationwide. There's a program at one of the schools in Texas that looks very good."

He lifted his head. "Really?"

She smiled at the light in his eyes. "Yes. Would you mind if I went to school there?"

He leaned forward and kissed her. "I wouldn't mind that at all. I figured it was time I moved out of General Lee's— that's my superior officer—house. Time to get a place of my own."

"Is that right?"

"Yeah. Might be nice to have someone to share it with. But you know, I don't know much about furniture and decorating and all that, so I'd need someone who did."

Ava looked around at all her sparse furnishings. "Well, I have to say I don't know much about that, either. But I think it's high time I add some—stuff—into my life. Some color and flair and excitement. I can't think of anyone I'd like to share that with more than you."

There was a warmth in his gaze—was that love?—that she'd never seen before. It made her heart melt.

"Could you do that? Could you leave Las Vegas, your family and friends?"

Without hesitation, she nodded. "I think it's time I made my own life."

"There are some great programs in Dallas that I think you might like. Programs for social workers. And lots of kids that need help."

"Oh, so now you think social workers might have some value."

"I told you, babe, I think you have something to offer. Look what you did for me. I never believed in love until I met you."

Tears filled her eyes. "I think you underestimate yourself. You're not the only one who never believed in love, who never felt loved. For the first time in my life, I want to fill a house with warmth and love and I have you to thank for that."

Rick took her hands and pulled her onto his lap. "I guess we can teach each other."

A new life. New opportunities. Scary, but oh so exciting. She wrapped her arms around him. "I'm looking forward to that."

He raised his lips to hers, and at the first brush of his mouth against hers Ava knew it would all work out. All she would ever need was his touch.